SILENCE
IN THE
SHADOWS

DARCY COATES

Poisoned Pen
PRESS

Published by Poisoned Pen Press, an imprint of Sourcebooks
P.O. Box 4410, Naperville, Illinois 60567–4410
(630) 961-3900
sourcebooks.com

Library of Congress Cataloging-in-Publication Data

Names: Coates, Darcy, author.
Title: Silence in the shadows / Darcy Coates.
Description: Naperville, Illinois : Poisoned Pen Press, [2020] | Series:
  Black winter ; 4
Identifiers: LCCN 2020023582 | (trade paperback)
Subjects: GSAFD: Horror fiction. | Dystopias.
Classification: LCC PR9619.4.C628 S55 2020 | DDC 823/.92--dc23
LC record available at https://lccn.loc.gov/2020023582

Printed and bound in the United States of America.
VP 10 9 8 7 6 5 4 3 2 1

CHAPTER 1

"YOUR TIME TO SHINE, map reader. Where to?"

The bus's engine rumbled underneath Clare's feet. Dorran sat in the driver's seat next to her, his dark eyes warm as he smiled. Behind them, the Evandale Research Institute's metal fence rattled in the chill morning air, and ahead, hundreds of kilometers of road separated them from Winterbourne Hall.

Clare held the map tightly, tracing the edges of the worn pages. "We're about three days from Winterbourne, barring any unforeseen delays."

"Will we be following the path we arrived on?"

"Only for a few minutes. After that, we'll be on new terrain." Clare could visualize the path in her mind. "It will mean going through the mountains, but it will save us at least two days of driving."

The narrow dirt road ahead of them was cloaked by forest. Mist coiled along the ground, weaving through the exposed roots and playing tricks on Clare's eyes. She knew there were likely hollow ones in the trees, watching, waiting. As Dorran put the bus into gear and eased them forward, doubts crowded Clare's mind.

Maybe we really should have stayed in Evandale. Maybe we could have made it work.

She swallowed and refocused on the road ahead. They had a purpose: save Winterbourne, if that was possible. Behind them, the Evandale researchers were doing everything they could to reverse the effects of the thanites and destroy the hollow ones; if that turned out to be impossible, humanity would need safe locations to consolidate and survive. And Clare didn't know of a location more defensible than Winterbourne.

They just had to get there. And that meant going through the mountains—something Clare wasn't looking forward to.

The last time I saw Beth, she was traveling toward the mountains.

Clare blinked furiously to clear her mind. The last time she'd seen her sister had been traumatic. Beth, corrupted and ravenous, had nearly killed Dorran—would have if Clare hadn't intervened. She still had scratches on her throat from that final encounter.

She glanced at Dorran. Like her, he was developing a map of scars across his body. The latest set ran across his arms and his shoulders. He'd earned them while saving Niall, Evandale's doctor, from a swarm of the monsters, and the following hours had been so tense that he'd never bothered to bandage them. They had already scabbed over. Soon, even those red marks would begin to fade: a gift from the thanites, almost as though

2

they were apologizing for the destruction they had wrought on humanity.

Clare was surprised to realize Dorran seemed happy. The emotion stayed reserved, but something bright sparkled in his eyes and the corners of his mouth had lifted a fraction. Clare found the good mood infectious and couldn't suppress a smile of her own. "What are you thinking about?"

"Oh." He chuckled, his dark eyes crinkling as he met her gaze. "I can't hide anything from you, can I?"

"No better than I can hide things from you."

Dorran turned the wheel, carrying them out of the forest and through the small town of Evandale. "It isn't much, just that they didn't think I was strange."

"The Evandale research team?"

"Yes." Twisted figures moved through open doorways and broken windows, but Dorran didn't seem to be bothered by them as he deftly drove through the town. "I never told them about my family or my upbringing, and they didn't guess. They…didn't guess."

He repeated that last phrase as though he was still coming to terms with it. Clare's heart ached. *After all this time, he still thought he wouldn't belong in the regular world.*

She reached over to take his hand. He let it drop from the wheel so he could hold hers, their arms resting in the space between their seats as they passed beyond Evandale's bounds and returned to the empty rural roads.

"I thought that they would," Dorran said. "They would hear

it in my voice or realize that I didn't know how to use their television or talk about something I had never heard of before. And I certainly gave them enough opportunities to notice something was wrong. But they didn't."

"They couldn't notice something was *wrong*," Clare said. "Because there's nothing *wrong* with you."

A hint of laughter slipped into his voice. "Then you are overlooking many, many flaws."

"I'm serious. Everyone in that bunker was weird in their own way. Probably everyone left in the world has some oddness about them, including me. Your brand of weirdness is no worse than theirs."

He made a noise in the back of his throat, and although he stayed quiet, his thumb traced over the back of her hand in small, sweet patterns.

Clare didn't try to press the point. He was happy. He'd spent most of a week in the bunker without its occupants suspecting his upbringing hadn't matched theirs. And even though Clare didn't think that was surprising—or that it would have mattered if they had known—she kept that to herself. It was a victory to Dorran, and she wanted him to enjoy it.

The drive through the rural roads was easy. Clare and Dorran talked occasionally, and the pale sunlight began to look beautiful as it shimmered off lifeless trees and sparse farmhouses. Clare mixed bowls of dried fruit and instant porridge for their lunch.

As the sun passed its zenith and began to descend, the landscape around them changed. Gentle hills and scrubby patches of trees transitioned into rocky forest. The road narrowed and became harder to navigate. Dorran leaned forward, fingers light on the wheel but eyes keen as he watched the road.

The abandoned cars became fewer and then vanished entirely when the road climbed into the mountains. Clare wouldn't need to use it for another hour, but she maintained her hold on the map, rubbing her thumb across its corner until her skin was raw.

There are no cars because almost no one lived here. With no one living here, there weren't enough thanites to transform anyone travel-ing through the area. They would have kept driving, oblivious, until they reached the nearest town.

Much like Clare herself had been oblivious. If she hadn't crashed inside the forest that surrounded Winterbourne, she very likely wouldn't be alive at that moment.

She couldn't stop her mind from crafting a picture of her probable fate: she would have seen the thanites' effects once she left the forest, but with nowhere to take shelter, she wouldn't have been able to stop. She likely would have continued on her path, trying to reach Beth's house, only to become trapped on the freeway as so many other unfortunate souls had. She won-dered how long she would have stayed inside her car while the transformed creatures scrambled over it, whether she would have succumbed to dehydration or whether desperation would have forced her to open her door.

She had turned clammy. The trees surrounding them grew tall and dense, their branches overlapping the road and plunging them into shade. With the sun smothered by the perpetual smog, it felt more like twilight than afternoon.

Just because there had been no humans in the mountains to be transformed into hollows didn't mean the roads were safe. The creatures traveled, sometimes huge distances, in search of food. They liked dark, cool areas—just like the thick trees provided. Clare's attention flicked toward every trace of motion—a bobbing branch, a falling leaf, a shadow that might have held eyes. Dorran no longer drove with leisurely patience but kept a steady pace. Hollows would be attracted to the noise of their engine. The faster they passed through the region, the safer they would be.

"Can you tell me what the road up ahead looks like?" Dorran's voice was just as gentle as ever, but Clare still scrambled for the map.

"The road stays bendy for a while, then straightens as it travels over the mountain for about forty kilometers. After that, we're back into easier terrain." She had worked out their path earlier that day. Their journey from Winterbourne to the research institute had been a deep curve; first the trip to Beth's house, then to the city had more than tripled the distance to be traveled.

She hated the way the mountain felt, though—as if she didn't belong there, as if she were a guest in a foreign land.

It won't last long. One hour, two tops, then we'll be out the other side and heading toward Winterbourne.

Dorran's eyes darted to her before reaffixing on the road. "The path is straight?"

"Yeah." Clare caught herself. She hadn't considered it before, but now that she looked again, the straight path seemed odd among the squiggles climbing the slope. *It makes no logistical sense to have a straight trail through unsteady terrain. Unless... Oh.*

"It's a tunnel," she said, her mouth suddenly dry.

"Hmm." Dorran chewed on that for a moment without slowing the bus. "Are there any other routes around?"

Clare flipped through the map, scanning page after page. Her heart quickened, pumping a nauseating dread through her veins. "Uh...we would have to drive around the range."

"How far is that?"

"Far." She tried to picture the distance. "Ten, fifteen hours, maybe. Or more, if we can't take the main roads."

"We'd better continue along this path," Dorran said.

"Are you sure? I don't mind the extra drive."

Dorran's voice was soft, even comforting. "No, I think this is the best route."

Clare frowned. It wasn't like Dorran to be so comfortable about choosing a more dangerous path. The thought of what the straight line represented—miles upon miles of enclosed, pitch-dark road with no escape on any side—left her cold.

Then she tilted her head back to see into her side mirror. Strange, gangly shapes followed the path behind them. She tried to count the creatures, but there were too many glinting eyes weaving over and across each other to keep track of.

It's not a choice. We can't go back. There's not even the room to turn around before they catch up.

Dorran had seen them too. He took her hand and squeezed it before returning to the wheel. "Don't be afraid. We will be fine."

She needed Dorran to be right. Because they had no option except to find out.

Warning signs lined the road, cautioning about tight bends with no guardrails and turns only wide enough for a single vehicle. The path wove wildly, and Dorran's lips set in a thin line of concentration as he fought to keep enough speed to move up the slope and handle the narrow bends as well.

Something chattered near the back of the bus. The vehicle stuttered as an unseen force pulled on them.

"Don't be afraid," Dorran said, and applied more pressure to the gas pedal. The bus surged forward and the weight disappeared. Clare forced herself to breathe through her nose—deep, slow breaths that wouldn't let her hyperventilate.

Perspiration dotted Dorran's forehead. He didn't try to wipe it away, not even when it trickled toward his eyes. His attention was wholly absorbed by the path ahead.

Then, suddenly, the road turned toward the mountainside. A gaping hole had been carved into the massive, gray rocks. More warning signs flashed past too quickly for Clare to read them. Dorran turned the headlights on as their bus lurched into the tunnel's opening.

CHAPTER 2

CLARE'S KNUCKLES WERE WHITE where she clutched the map. She didn't need it—wouldn't need it for more than an hour, until the road deposited them back into the fields on the other side of the mountain—but she held on to it like a lifeline.

Glass light casings glittered across the ceiling, but the tunnel's power was gone and the arched passageway was desperately black. The sunlight flowing through the entrance faded within seconds, until their only illumination came from the headlights forming two shimmering circles ahead of them.

Clare didn't like it. The high beams didn't reach as far as she thought they should have. They revealed patches of the road, perfectly straight and seemingly endless. The light's diffusion brushed across the ceiling, enough to flash off anything reflective and tease the shadows in between. But at the speed Dorran was driving, the lights weren't reaching far enough to show any obstacles and still leave enough time to brake.

Please, please, let the tunnel be empty.

Clare knew hope was thin. The tunnel's perfect darkness and moist chill would make it an ideal home for the hollows—even more so than the forest. But the lights skimmed across foot after foot of ground, and still, they were undisturbed.

The bus began to slow. Clare finally tore her eyes off the road to glance at Dorran. His brows were low, casting heavy shadows across his eyes.

"What's wrong?" Clare whispered, even though there was no risk her voice would attract attention when the engine would accomplish the job first.

"They are not following us any longer."

Clare twisted to see the side mirror. When Dorran tapped the breaks, red light flowed across the tunnel behind them. It was empty.

Clare's stomach turned. She faced the path ahead again, trying to ignore the prickles growing across her arms. "You weren't driving fast enough to lose them, were you?"

"No. They could keep up." He flexed his fingers on the wheel. "They followed us into the tunnel for a while. Then they stopped, almost as though they had been spooked and turned away."

What could spook a hollow?

She could see the same anxiety reflected in Dorran's face. The car continued to coast forward at less than half its previous speed, and he kept his attention fastened on the road. "What do you think? Drive cautiously or as quickly as we can?"

Not knowing what might be in the tunnel made the question

impossible. Driving slowly would allow them to be followed, to be anticipated, or to be ambushed. But driving quickly could come to a sudden and unpleasant end if they encountered a blockage.

"Faster than this," Clare finally decided. "But…not too fast."

Dorran gave a short nod and the bus sped up. Their headlights flashed over rock walls, the old, unmaintained white lines painted across the road, and the dead lights set into the ceiling. Clare craned her neck as they passed an unusual shape. It looked as though one of the lights had been torn out of its socket and was allowed to dangle from two cables. They passed the shape so quickly that she couldn't get a good look at it.

Something had left score marks on the walls, she thought. The stone was rough to begin with, which disguised the marring. But the tunnel was old—at least forty years based on the style of the lights—and very rarely maintained. The old rock on the walls had been blackened by the soot left from thousands of vehicles. Long gashes cut through the decades of grime, leaving marks of lighter gray decorating the walls.

Then something small appeared on the ground ahead. At first glance, Clare thought it was a stray rock. It was only when it crunched under their wheels that Clare realized she'd been looking at half of a skull.

"Slow down," she whispered.

The vehicle's speed reduced, and Clare saw they were surrounded by bone fragments.

The off-white shapes littered the floor, sometimes gathering at the tunnel's edges like leaves. None of the bones were intact. They had all been broken into fragments, the marrow inside sucked out. She didn't think the bones belonged to humans. Or, at least, they hadn't been human when they died.

Inside, the bus was so quiet that Clare could hear her own heartbeat. Dorran leaned across the wheel, his breathing shallow as he tried to protect them against a threat they didn't yet understand.

Then a pole-like shape loomed in the shadows ahead. Impossibly tall and thin, it stretched from the ground toward the ceiling. Clare looked for any semblance of life—eyes, a mouth, limbs, anything—but couldn't find it. The shape was gray and curved gradually, segmented in two places. It looked more like a streetlamp than a hollow.

Dorran hit the brakes, pulling the bus to a shuddering halt.

The shape's base lifted off the floor, seeming to hover as it drifted toward them, then stabbed back down to land on the road. Its base was pointed and looked sharp.

It's a leg. Clare's heart skipped. She followed the shape up to where its top nearly vanished among the shadows of the ceiling—to where it merged with a body.

Five more legs descended from the malformed creature. Two of them glided forward, stabbing into the road, bringing the whole being into terrible relief. Legs bent as the body descended. Two heads gaped at them out of the distorted torso: one near where the shoulder should be, the other in the center of its chest. The eyes were witless, but the jaws stretched as it moved more of its impossibly long, sticklike legs to pace toward them. It was immense. The tunnel was wide enough for two lanes and high enough to carry trucks, and the hollow filled the entire space.

Dorran barked an involuntary noise, something between revulsion and fear. Color had drained from his face as his wide eyes stared up at the creature.

It raised one of its six legs. The tip looked horribly sharp. Clare had a sudden image of it piercing through the roof of their bus, stabbing into them, impaling them. The metal structure was sturdy enough that the regular hollows couldn't break inside, but something told her the enormous creature could cut through the metal like a can opener. She screamed, "Drive!"

Clare only wanted to be away from the many-legged behemoth, and as far as her brain was concerned, driving faster would *get* them away from it. She had no time to reconsider the instruction or think about the fact that the creature blocked the road because Dorran obeyed as soon as the word left her. The engine roared and the bus surged forward, plowing them toward the legs with reckless abandon.

He really shouldn't trust me so much.

The inane thought came out of nowhere, and through the haze of panic, Clare had the impulse to laugh. Instead, she reached her arms forward and planted them into the dash in an effort to brace herself.

The legs blocked the road, as thick as young trees. Clare knew they had to be made of bone, though. And bone could be fragile if you hit it hard enough.

The raised leg aimed toward them and began to descend. The bus lurched as Dorran threw the wheel. Rubber screeched as they spun, and the limb stabbed into the place they would have been. A small crater appeared in the concrete as the sharpened tip impacted it.

Dorran swiveled the wheel back in the other direction, checking the bus before it could tip over. They were heading straight for one of the legs. There was no time to correct. Clare put her head down and squeezed her eyes closed. The seat belt snapped hard into her chest as the impact threw her forward. A horrible cracking sound rattled around them. She saw the leg bend across the bus's front, the bones splintering like a snapped branch, their shards poking through a thin layer of gray skin.

Then the leg lifted away, and they were charging forward, past the monster. Clare twisted to see behind them. In the faint, red glow of their brake lights, she watched the creature topple. It seemed to move in slow motion, each of the six legs scraping off the floor as its center of gravity dragged it down. Screams, wrenched out of two inhuman mouths, echoed through the tunnel as the body hit the ground. Clare's last glimpse was of the sharpened leg tips twitching as they tried to right the body again.

Dorran didn't make any sound. He sat back in his seat, eyes wide and unblinking, perspiration shining on his face as the speedometer rose dangerously high. The bus rattled around them. Part of Clare wanted him to slow down. Another part wanted him to go even faster. Neither thought could be expressed. She had no breath left for anything except feeding oxygen into her racing heart.

Then light appeared ahead of them. The arch-like glow was one of the sweetest things Clare had ever seen.

"Slow," Clare choked out, grabbing Dorran's arm. He tapped the brake, and the dangerous trajectory eased off as they neared the tunnel's end. They were just in time. The road outside the tunnel curved sharply to the right, and Dorran had to slow to a crawl to handle the bend.

Then they were descending the mountain, once again surrounded by trees and light. The tunnel felt like a feverish nightmare, as though Clare had lost consciousness for twenty minutes before opening her eyes again. As though it couldn't possibly have been real.

But the bus's front held a new, deep dent. Their memento from the creature's spiderlike leg.

Dorran and Clare didn't speak as they descended the mountain. Dorran's pulse jumped in his throat, and Clare let him focus on navigating the twisting roads. There was no chance to stop. Hollows had heard them coming and appeared through the trees. Soon, they had a new collection of monsters darting through the shadows behind them, trying to catch up to the bus. Dorran kept the pace aggressive. Within another fifteen minutes, the paths eased out into the foothills and the trees cleared. Most of the hollows gave up as they lost their cover. The few persistent ones were soon lost as the open road allowed more speed. Dorran drove until they reached a gentle hill with views of the land around them, then he pulled onto the side of the road and parked the bus.

He turned to her and ran a hand over her neck. "Are you all right?"

"Yeah, I'm good." Her voice shook despite her best efforts.

Dorran exhaled, his shoulders dropping. "Stay here and keep warm. I'll check there isn't any damage to the engine."

He brushed past her, opening the door, and a gust of cold air coiled over Clare. She shivered, then watched through the cracked front window as Dorran wrenched the hood up. He wasn't dressed for the cold; he only wore a shirt and light coat.

Clare retreated deeper into the bus, looking through the clothing stored in the baskets above the seats. She found two jackets and two scarves and swaddled one set around herself before opening the door and leaping out.

Dorran lifted his head as Clare approached, and smiled at the sight of the jacket. "Ah. Thank you."

She helped him pull the coat on, then tugged on the collar until he bent and let her wrap the scarf around his neck. "How's it looking?"

"Not too bad, considering. It's a hardy beast."

Clare hung to his side as she watched him feel around the engine. The minibus had hit trees, been through water, and now, survived impact with the creature in the tunnel. The metal front had been twisted so badly that the hood didn't shut properly. She silently thanked the bus for holding on for so long.

Dorran's long fingers felt across the metal, searching for leaks or damage. He was moving slowly and his eyes seemed distant.

"Are *you* all right?" Clare asked.

"Yes. Of course." He shot her a quick smile.

Clare knew him too well to think it was genuine. "You listened to me when I told you to drive," she said.

His glance seemed surprised. "Of course I did. I trust you."

"You shouldn't have. It was terrible advice. We got lucky, and that's the only reason we're still alive." The laughter that had threatened her in the tunnel suddenly poured out, gasping and thin. Clare clamped her lips shut to cut it off early.

Dorran bent forward as he searched her face. "I will always trust your advice. It has saved us more often than I can remember. You have good instincts."

"Next time my instincts tell us to drive toward a living nightmare, feel free to ignore me."

He laughed, and after a second, Clare joined in. The ache in her chest lessened. Icy wind whistled across them, pulling on their coats and tangling Clare's hair, as Dorran continued working on the engine.

Then Dorran voiced the question they were both thinking. "What *was* that?"

"It was a hollow," Clare said. "It had to be. But…the others all looked at least vaguely human. You could see traces of what they used to be. But that…"

She pictured the malformed torso growing two heads, the six enormous legs that held it suspended in the air.

"The others were afraid of it," Dorran said. "That was why they wouldn't follow us into the tunnel."

"There were bones everywhere. Mostly hollow bones, I think. It was eating them. That's something other hollows don't do either." Clare shook her head. "I mean, they *will*, sometimes, if they're trapped in an enclosed place like a room or a car. In the wild, though, they mostly just ignore each other. But that thing…"

"It almost seemed to be waiting for prey."

Clare nodded. She could picture it, lurking in the dark, suspended on those impossibly long legs as it waited for hollows to enter its domain. The bones had all been picked over dozens of times before the fragments were finally discarded.

In a world that felt miles from rational, Clare hadn't realized how much she relied on rationality to cope. She knew the hollows' rules. She knew what they looked like and what they were capable of. Now, they had encountered something that ignored all established principles, and Clare was back to feeling as helpless and vulnerable as she had been on the day she had discovered the world had ended.

"This is okay," Dorran said, shutting the hood as securely as the twisted metal would allow. He took Clare's hand, infusing some confidence into his voice. "We'll be fine."

CHAPTER 3

CLARE TOOK OVER DRIVING in the afternoon to give Dorran a break. He made an excellent assistant, keeping her cup full and bringing her snacks at regular intervals. They didn't talk about the spiderlike hollow again, but it stayed in Clare's mind, and she guessed it was still in Dorran's too.

They held to the most rural roads, which lengthened their trip but kept them away from large towns. Twice, Clare had to backtrack when fallen trees or broken bridges interrupted their route.

The sun dipped toward the horizon. They discussed stopping, but Dorran thought they could safely continue through the night, and Clare agreed. Stopping created its own risks. They paused for a final break before sundown, stretching their legs and refueling the bus. Then Clare filled thermoses full of coffee, while Dorran served dinner, and they prepared to drive through the night.

Vivid colors splashed across the hazy horizon, then faded. Stars appeared. They passed a sedan moving in the opposite direction and exchanged a wave with the driver. Clare was glad to see it. After a day with the roads to themselves, the car reminded her that they weren't alone in the world.

Dorran noticed Clare was tired before she realized it. He rested a hand on her shoulder. "Time to switch over. Do you think you can sleep while I drive?"

"Sure." She coasted the bus to a halt, its lights splashing across the long, weedy grass that flourished in that region. Dorran took over her seat. He waited until Clare settled into the makeshift bed at the back of the bus, then began moving again, keeping the speed steady and gentle.

Clare lay awake, staring at the boarded-over window beside her bed. The bus's rocking motions were exhausting, and the motor's purr lulled her toward sleep. When she turned her head to the left, she could see Dorran, the edges of his features pulled out of the blackness by the glow from the dashboard. The light almost seemed to be flickering over him as though it came from a fire. He must have felt her eyes because he turned his head slightly to look at her.

"Go back to sleep, Clare." A languid smile spread across his face. She loved seeing him smile, would never get enough of it. Clare smiled back, then the muscles in her face seized up. Something loomed out of the darkness ahead of them. Enormous legs, long and narrow like needles, punctured the road. The headlights washed over the gray skin stretched over brittle bones.

Dorran hadn't seen. He was still looking back at Clare, smiling at her.

Clare tried to yell. The word became trapped in her throat. Dorran didn't stop smiling. There was no time to brake, no time to brace herself, no time to even breathe. The bus hit the creature's limbs. Clare's vision blurred as the impact wrenched her from the bed. Metal screamed as it twisted around her. She was tumbling, falling, unable to tell where she was or which direction was up. Then, suddenly, she came to a halt.

She didn't feel any pain. It would come eventually, she knew, but her mind was mercifully clear at that moment. She opened her eyes. The bus was upside down, the rows of seats suspended from the ceiling. Flames crackled where fuel had spilled across the metal. The bus's structure, which had seemed so solid before, was nothing but a contorted wreck. She couldn't see the driver's seat. Couldn't see Dorran.

Clare pulled herself toward the bus's front. Her legs didn't want to move. She used her hands instead, resting her weight on her forearms to drag herself among the twisted metal and spot fires. Tears ran down her face. She had to be in pain, but she couldn't feel it. She could only focus on the dark console at the bus's front. It had collapsed in, a pure wreck. The driver's seat had come free from two of the bolts holding it to the floor and swung loosely.

Then she heard Dorran's voice. It was full of fear and pain. "Clare…Clare…"

"Where are you?" She dragged herself closer, not noticing or caring as her chest scraped over loose bolts. Every limb shook. Smoke was filling the space, obscuring her vision and sticking in her throat.

"Clare…"

Then she saw him, lying behind the space where the driver's seat had been. He was on his side, blood running across his forehead and dripping past wide, terrified eyes. His mouth opened, but it was the only part of him that moved.

"Clare!"

Something dark rose from behind him. Beth's lips pulled back from her teeth, a tangle of gore and blood running down her chin.

"Clare!"

She jolted awake, a scream choking in her throat. She was back in the bed. Light washed over her, and it took her a second to realize it didn't come from a fire but from the bus's internal lights. The vehicle was intact, parked in the middle of the road.

And Dorran was there. He was crouched at her side, his brows heavy, his hands strong as he held her shoulders.

"You're all right," he said, his eyes tight with worry. "You're safe."

She keeled forward, gasping, shaking, and sticky with sweat. Dorran caught her against his chest and held her tightly. She could hear his heart racing almost as fast as hers was.

"Sorry," she mumbled into his shoulder. "Bad dream."

"You're safe. You're okay." He tilted his head to nestle it on top of hers.

It felt so real. Her eyes burned. Her heart hurt. Her nerves felt as though they were on fire, sharp and raw with fear. *I can't let him be hurt like that. I can't let him be hurt. I can't...*

"You're all right." Dorran eased her back and found a handkerchief in his pocket. He used it to wipe the moisture off Clare's cheeks and chin, then kissed her in every place the fabric had touched. He ended with his forehead resting against hers, their noses brushing, their eyelashes close to tangling.

"You're safe," he murmured. "There's nothing to be afraid of now."

I can't let him be hurt. But I already did. She realized she was still clinging to his shirt, her fists scrunching up the fabric. "I'm so sorry."

"Shh, don't be. It was just a dream."

He didn't understand. Clare shook her head, forcing the words through a too-tight throat. "I'm sorry for leading you into the tunnel. It was really stupid and dangerous."

"You didn't know it was a tunnel."

"I should have, though. I should have realized. And I'm sorry for bringing you out here, away from your home. And I'm sorry for letting Beth stay with us for so long after we knew she was a hollow. I'm sorry for letting you get hurt. I'm so sorry."

A smile pulled at his lips, sweet, confused, and sad all at once. "This is what is upsetting you?"

"You deserve better than this. Every single one of my choices makes things worse for you."

"That's not true." He leaned back so he could look at her properly. "Why would you think that?"

She shook her head. Her throat hurt, every word feeling as though it were slicing through swollen flesh.

Dorran cupped her head in his hands, thumbs brushing over her burning skin. "What would my life have been without you? That is a serious question. I would be back at Winterbourne, alone, and slowly going mad in those empty halls. Or worse, I would be back under my mother's control."

She shook her head again.

Dorran smiled. "The time I have spent with you has been challenging, frightening in some places, and even occasionally horrible. But it has also been exhilarating and full of hope and joy. I cannot remember ever feeling as alive as I feel with you. So, believe me, I will take a thousand misadventures with you over a month alone."

An admission tumbled out of her, leaving her vulnerable, raw, and frightened. "I don't want to lose you."

"And you won't." He bent forward to steal a kiss. "I am going to repeat something you told me some time ago: you are stuck with me now."

Strangled laughter escaped her. Dorran's hands roved over her chin and neck, then down her arms, rubbing warmth and feeling back into her. "Come sit up in the front with me. I can watch you better there and wake you sooner if your dreams turn bad."

"You shouldn't have to."

"I want to."

He kept hold of her hands as he coaxed her out of the bed. He'd left the bus's engine running. Bright golden lights washed over the road ahead. She remembered the sight of the monster's legs puncturing the asphalt, and shuddered. Dorran responded by pulling blankets down from the upper compartments and wrapping them around Clare's shoulder.

She let him fuss over her, just enjoying his proximity. Her nerves were still raw, and when he pressed a water bottle into her hands, she had to clench it to stop her fingers from shaking. Every time she blinked, she saw him again, limp on the ground, blood draining out of him.

"I want you to teach me things." The words came out too loud, and Dorran, hunting through the overhead baskets for snacks, blinked at her.

"Things?"

Clare swallowed and brought her voice back to a comfortable level. "You know first aid. And how to repair the bus when it breaks. I want to know how too."

I need to know what to do if you're hurt again. If we're stranded. If you need me, like you did before.

Dorran, looking thoughtful, placed a packet of toasted nuts in Clare's lap. "That might be a good idea. I don't have comprehensive knowledge on any topic, but…"

But it will be enough. "Teach me everything you know."

He chuckled as he returned to the driver's seat and put the bus into gear. "I'm not sure you'd want to learn *everything*. I have exhaustive knowledge of formal dining conventions, which, thankfully, I don't think I'll ever need to use again."

Clare matched his grin. "Okay, maybe we can skip that."

"Where would you like to start?"

"First aid."

Dorran's warm eyes were caught in the headlight's backwash as he smiled. "Good. Let's begin with puncture wounds."

CHAPTER 4

NIGHT GRADUALLY MORPHED INTO morning while Dorran talked. He told her about compressions, about sunstroke symptoms, and about emergency surgery. Clare did her best to absorb it all. She didn't realize how quickly time was passing until dawn lit up the edges of distant trees.

Dorran had driven through the night, and he looked it. His eyes were heavy lidded and his slightly too-long hair ruffled as he tilted his head to flex his neck.

"Ready for me to swap over so you can get some rest?"

"I'll keep going for a while longer."

"No, you won't," Clare said, and Dorran laughed as he pulled over to the side of the road.

"All right. I don't have a good record of winning arguments against you. I'll cut my losses this time." He yawned as he rose and stretched both arms above his head.

They had parked in a marshy field that looked like it was only a few feet above the water table. The ground was clear and flat for miles around. Clare liked that; it saved her the worry that something might be able to creep up on them.

Dorran refueled the bus while she prepared a light breakfast, then she took over the driver's seat as Dorran adopted the passenger's. He folded a blanket, propped it between his head and the window, and relaxed. He was asleep within minutes.

Clare held the bus at a steady speed where the bumps and jolts would be minimized for Dorran. She couldn't help smiling to herself as she watched him; his long legs were askew, and one arm crossed his chest, which rose with deep, steady breaths.

The drive was hypnotic. Trees rushed past them, thicker and lusher than those in other parts of the country. Mist wove between the trunks in mesmerizing coils, light and ethereal. Occasionally, Clare saw eyes flashing from between the trunks, but nothing tried to interrupt the bus's passage through the forest.

Above, the sky was dull but not quite as smoggy as it had been around Evandale. A dark, hazy line ran across the horizon. Clare slowed the bus, squinting through the windshield. Dorran stirred beside her, blinking first at her expression, then at the sky. "What's that?"

"Smoke." She flexed her hands around the wheel. It wasn't dense enough to be from a forest fire. *It has to be coming from a campfire or a chimney. And that means humans.*

They hadn't spoken to anyone since leaving Evandale, and Clare had been prepared to continue in solitude until they reached

Winterbourne. The possibility of a chat with other humans, even for just five or ten minutes, was tempting.

Dorran was looking to her. He'd only had a few hours of sleep and seemed to be struggling to rouse himself. "Should we stop?"

Beth wouldn't have. She believed other humans were dangerous. And she had good cause to think that way. But they aren't all bad. And we might regret it if we don't at least try to make contact.

She chewed on her thumbnail as she weighed up the risks. "Do we need any supplies?"

"We are low on fuel," Dorran said. "We should have enough to get us to Winterbourne, but not much extra. And it seems prudent to gather more while it is still possible."

"Mm. If fuel is growing as scarce as Beth said it would be, they might be reluctant to trade. We don't have much of value except for food, and we can't really spare that."

"True. But maybe they could give us advice on the best places to search. And we can share what we know too."

"Good call." Clare saw motion out of the corner of her eye and pushed their bus back up to speed. "No one except us and the Evandale team know about the thanites yet. They might have information to help us too. It could even be a safe haven."

"Will we take a chance, then?" Dorran asked.

"I'm game if you are."

"All right. Let's see if we can find our way there."

The road curved gently, weaving between shallow hills. There were no crossroads, but every few kilometers, they passed a gate edging a dirt road or a fenced-in patch of cleared land. There were no houses in sight. Clare guessed the area had to be remote enough that anyone living there would have escaped the thanites' mutations.

Will it be a house? A campsite? They must know that anyone traveling through would see the smoke, so hopefully they won't mind visitors.

The smoke came from the road's right and didn't seem too far away. She slowed their pace as she hunted for a way to reach it. As it turned out, the side path advertised itself.

An old metal gate had been left open, lashes of rope tying it to a tree so the wind couldn't blow it shut. A wooden sign had been attached, with a pond-blue title hand painted on it: *Mother Gum's Nest*. And then, in smaller text that seemed to have been added hastily: *Weary travelers welcome*.

"Mother Gum?" Clare smiled despite herself. "Odd name."

"At least she's not hostile to guests." Dorran tucked the blanket underneath his seat, then ran his fingers through his hair in an effort to make it more presentable. He ended up looking even more disheveled. Clare loved it.

The road became narrow and bumpy, and Clare gripped the wheel more tightly to brace against being shaken. Trees and shrubs grew on either side of the road, so close that their branches scraped across the bus's sides. The sun felt muted. It was only allowed through the canopy in scraps and flecks, like confetti caught in the mist. Clare tried to see where they were headed, but the road kept moving in erratic curves, hiding the trail ahead. The path seemed well used if a little neglected, but she managed to avoid the worst of the potholes.

All of a sudden, the road straightened, and Clare found herself facing a wall made of wood.

Mother Gum's Nest had been such a charming name that the blockade gave Clare a sense of cognitive dissonance. It wasn't a simple fence. Built at least twelve feet high, its surface was covered with poles pointing outward. They were angled downward, and their ends had been sharpened into spikes. They glistened, almost as though they were wet.

They've been waxed, Clare realized. *If a hollow tries to climb them, they'll slide back down.*

It must have been a herculean effort to construct. The wall wound away to either side, curving gradually before the ends disappeared from sight, sheltering the unseen home. Clare could see no way to get inside.

Dorran made a faint noise of unease. He leaned forward in the seat, expression dark as he surveyed the structure. Clare took his hand, a silent confirmation that she was feeling the same misgivings as he was.

"Perhaps we should keep driving," Dorran said.

Clare was about to agree when motion ahead silenced her. A section of the wall slid to the side, creating a gap in the structure. Through it, Clare caught a glimpse of a clearing.

She rested her hand over the gear stick, ready to shift into reverse at the first sign of danger. The gate shuddered away from them until the opening was wide enough for their bus to fit through. Then a figure stepped into the opening.

Tall and thin, he brought up instant memories of the stretched

31

hollows Clare had seen. But the man was very much human. His face was pink from the effort of opening the gate, and he stood with human uneasiness. He looked young. Early twenties at most, Clare thought. Baggy, dirty clothes hung loose on him, sweat stains marking the tank top's sides and grease on the jeans. His limp hair needed both a cut and a wash.

It was not the sort of welcome Clare had expected from Mother Gum's Nest. She looked at Dorran again, waiting for his reaction. His uneasiness was evident; he worked his jaw, his eyes narrowed, but he didn't make a noise.

The impassive man lifted an arm, the hand flapping as he beckoned them forward. Then he stepped aside, granting them passage inside.

Dorran's inhale sounded uncomfortably tight. "Should we?"

Clare hated the idea of the gate shutting behind them, blocking a possible escape. But they were being welcomed into what she assumed had to be a safe haven. *And isn't it worth the risk if these strangers can help us?*

The man stepped back into view, eyebrows squeezing together to crease his forehead. He waved again, more urgently this time. He didn't like leaving the gate open. Clare couldn't blame him. Dorran made a soft noise in the back of his throat, and he gave her a stiff nod.

They coasted through the opening. Almost as soon as they were inside, the man was back at the gate, pushing furiously to roll it across mud-clotted tracks and close it.

The space inside the fence was big enough to hold what

could have been a small village. Three buildings stood about, all made of wood and seemingly constructed by hand. One looked as though it might have been a small meeting hall. Plain fabric curtains had been pulled over the windows. Another of the buildings looked a lot like a worn-down, broken version of the sheds behind Winterbourne. And the third building was unmistakably a house, a column of thick smoke rising from its oversize chimney. The house looked like a jigsaw puzzle put together incorrectly. Three and a half stories, it had rooms and verandas jutting out at odd angles, and in some places, age-bowed support beams held up expansions that looked as though they shouldn't have been possible.

More than a dozen cars and vans were scattered about the field in various states of road worthiness. Some looked like they might have been there for a decade and were little more than rusted shells. Others were more recent, and some even had modifications for the stillness, like Dorran and Clare's own minibus.

Clare drove slowly, creeping along the dirt path toward the main house. Figures were appearing between the buildings. More young men and several young women, all with the same tall, thin appearance, all wearing old, grimy clothes. Clare couldn't tell if they looked similar because of the clothing and identically long, straight hair, or whether they were actually related. She was leaning toward the latter. Adam's apples stood out on their throats, and their eyes were almost universally deep in their skulls, leaving thick lids hanging over them.

We shouldn't have come here. It was too late to turn around now;

the gate had shut behind them. But Clare's instincts were screaming. Her mind leaped to their choices for defense. They still had
their axes, their knives, their implements for bludgeoning.

She had killed plenty of hollows. But murdering another
human was a different matter. She tasted fear in the back of her
throat—a thick, bitter ooze. Dorran's breathing was quick and
shallow.

The door to the main house groaned open. The hinges were
audible, even inside the bus. Clare squinted to see the figure in
the doorway's gloom.

CHAPTER 5

AN OLD, WIZENED WOMAN stood there. She would have only come up to Clare's shoulders, even though Clare herself wasn't especially tall. Long, pure-white hair had been braided tidily, the thick plait running over her shoulder and down to her waist. The skin around her eyes crinkled up as she smiled, and she lifted a hand in a cheerful wave.

She looks nice. Some of the fear ebbed. Clare relaxed her grip on the wheel and pulled the bus to a halt near the house. Dorran kept his attention moving between the elderly woman and the young adults who sullenly watched from the buildings surrounding them. "Stay alert. Be prepared to run if things turn sour."

She gave a short nod, taking a small blade from where they stored it beside the driver's seat and tucking it into her pocket as insurance. Then she pressed the button to open the bus's door.

The scents of mud, of decaying hay, and of the crisp freshness of pine trees and the sharp chill of mist all swirled together. A bird set up a chattering call from somewhere outside the walls, and dripping sounds came from many directions.

"Welcome, friends." The woman's voice sounded like a cooing bird. It warbled, shaky and dainty, filled with cracks from age. "I'm Mother Gum. Why don't you come in for a cup of tea?"

When she spoke, Clare saw she was missing her front teeth. Her lips stuck to the gums, faintly concave, adding to the creases around her mouth. She had warm eyes, though, and the layers of shawls and cardigans she wore looked hand-knitted.

Mother Gum turned and shuffled back into the cottage. The door wasn't entirely straight and began to glide closed. Clare hurried to catch it and hold it open.

Inside, the house was cozier than she would have thought. Bunches of drying herbs hung across the walls. An odd assortment of china and crockery, at least a dozen different patterns, was stacked on hand-carved shelves. A large fur rug covered most of the floor ahead of a rough wooden table, where Mother Gum was setting out three mismatched cups.

"Have you driven far, lovelies?" she asked.

Clare squinted as she stepped inside. A fire kept the room warm, though the chimney must have been choked. A thin haze of smoke tickled her throat. "A ways, yeah."

"You look it." Mother Gum winked. Her eyes were a watery green, the same shade as the herbs she tipped into the teapot. A cast iron kettle was already boiling by the fire, and she crossed to it. "I can tell when people come from a long way. They have a look about them. A look that says they're missing home."

Clare exchanged a glance with Dorran. His smile was thin. Even after Evandale, he was still uncomfortable talking to strangers.

"Find yourselves a seat. Move the cat if he's in the way." Mother Gum shuffled back toward the table, the teapot sloshing with each step. She poured the liquid into the cups she'd laid out. "I make this from my own garden. It's good for the body and good for the soul."

"Thank you." Clare gently sat in one of the wooden chairs. It had a thick, quilted cushion on the seat, and the legs were so short that she had to stretch her feet out to one side to get comfortable. Dorran sank down beside her. Lounging on the chair to his other side was a massive ginger cat. It was so still that Clare would have thought it was a toy, except for the way one eye lazily drifted open to fix on them.

Dorran made a soft noise as he held one hand out for the cat to smell. The black of its eye narrowed into a slit, but it didn't try to greet the offered fingers.

"Don't hope to be too friendly with him," Mother Gum chuckled. "He's a sourpuss. He'll shred your fingers before he lets you pet him."

Dorran withdrew his hand.

Clare took one of the cups Mother Gum pushed toward her. Steam rose off the swirling, green liquid, carrying the faint scent of herbs and flowers. She wrapped her fingers around it to keep them warm. "I hope it's okay to stop. We saw the sign—"

"Of course, my lovely." Mother Gum took her own seat, her

lips puckering as she smiled. "I welcome all visitors. It's the only way we'll make it out of this dark time."

"That's very kind. It's nice to talk to another person." Clare glanced at Dorran. He remained quiet and let her take the lead in the conversation. "I noticed some other people outside. Are they family?"

"Oh yes. Not all are my flesh and blood, but they're all my children, regardless." She bobbed her head in a happy nod. "My daughter says I have a compulsion to take in strays. Both the animal and human kinds. People who weren't well liked by the rest of the world but who just need some love."

"They're lucky."

"We all are. There's nothing better than family. And my family is very good."

Clare glanced at the teacup. Beth would have cautioned her about accepting food from strangers. But as she watched, Mother Gum lifted her own cup to her lips.

She's nice. And I can't survive by being as hostile as Beth was. Clare sipped the tea. It made her throat tingle and had an unpleasantly earthy taste. She tried not to cough. "How many live with you?"

"Nearly twenty now. It is such a blessing."

Clare tried to hide her surprise. *Twenty is a lot. They must have found a way to get enough food for everyone. I didn't see any farms inside the compound.*

Mother Gum blinked, then laughed. "Silly me, you'd probably like some biscuits with your tea. Luckily for you, I baked some just this morning."

Dorran tried his drink. His expression remained perfectly passive, but as Mother Gum turned to look at the cabinet behind them, he grimaced. He carefully leaned over the ginger cat to empty his teacup into the potted plants on the windowsill, then sat back, lips pressed tightly together.

Clare bit down on her laughter as Mother Gum turned back to them, carrying a metal tin. "Here, my special biscuits. Take some."

"Thank you, I'm fine," Dorran murmured as Mother Gum shook the tin under his face. Evidently, the tea had been more than enough for him.

Clare took one to be polite, but they smelled like grass. She placed hers on her saucer and hoped it wouldn't be too rude if she left without sampling it.

Mother Gum pulled her shawl higher around her shoulders as she reclined back in her seat, a cookie perched on the edge of her own saucer. "Where did you come from, darlings?"

"Evandale. And that's actually part of the reason why we stopped here…" Briefly, Clare told Mother Gum about the thanites, the medical nanobot invention that had been designed to treat disease but had gone rogue. How it had lived in the air and, on activation, had infected human hosts and indiscriminately grew stem cells that caused drastic mutations.

She finished by saying, "There are scientists who think they can treat it. They think that destroying the thanites will kill the hollows. If you have a radio, I can give you the frequency to listen for updates."

"I'd like that." Mother Gum had listened patiently to the story, though Clare wasn't sure how much she had understood. The gentle, unchanging smile reminded Clare of the way her aunt Marnie had smiled when Clare talked about technology. She liked being part of the conversation, but the intricacies were beyond her.

Clare cleared her throat. Even though the house held an intimate atmosphere with just her, Dorran, Mother Gum, and the cat, she couldn't shake the memory of the surly children outside and how they appeared almost too tall and thin. "I hope it's okay to ask, but…has anyone here…*changed* at all? Started to grow things, I mean?"

She recalled the blank stares that seemed to hold echoes of the hollows' incomprehension. Their arms held limply at their sides. Their sullen features.

The infection might not have been severe enough to strip their humanity immediately, but Beth was proof that it would continue to degrade a person with each passing day. She didn't want to imagine the sweet Mother Gum being torn apart by the brood she loved.

Mother Gum only chuckled, though. "Oh, don't you worry, my pretty. My children aren't like those monsters outside. They don't like strangers, and they don't like letting new people into our home, but they're all good souls deep down."

"But…" Clare took a gulp of the tea to buy herself seconds. "But if they're changing at all…"

"You worry so much." Mother Gum reached across the table

and patted Clare's hand. "You're a sweet girl. But my children are all right. I only had eight to begin with. They were all away, working in the farms or hunting in the forest, on the day it happened. Some were more than an hour away. When they returned late that night, they told me about the things they had seen. And I said, we need to close the gate, and we won't be going back out for a while. The others—the ones I didn't bring into the world myself—they came later. Visitors who were trying to run from the outside, who were lost and scared, and who just needed a place to stay. It is so hard to turn anyone away."

"Oh." Clare let herself relax again. The thanites' density had been controlled by how many people lived in an area. Cities had been swarmed with them; rural areas, not so much. Eight people, spread across kilometers, would still have gotten a dose of the thanites, but probably not much more than Clare herself had.

"Our fence keeps us safe," Mother Gum continued. "And my children know how to kill the strange ones before they grow close. They only really come at night. It is secure here, a good home."

"Are you doing okay for food?" Clare asked.

"Oh, yes, yes. We have a garden behind the shed. We eat well."

"Good."

"What about you, my lovely? Where are you heading?"

"Home." She and Dorran had made a point of keeping Winterbourne's location a secret. Even though they wanted to open it up to outsiders once it was stabilized, they couldn't risk raids or hungry visitors before the garden was established and the defenses were in place. "Another couple of days from here."

"Do you need any bits and bobs for the trip?" The watery eyes blinked dozily.

"Oh…" They had come with the hope of finding fuel, but seeing how basic Mother Gum's home was, Clare didn't feel comfortable asking. She swallowed. "We're all right. I mean, if you know anywhere nearby that might have gasoline, that would be a big help—"

"Don't worry about that, my sweet. We have gas here. Take a few cans."

"Are you sure?" She looked between Dorran and Mother Gum. "You probably need it yourself—"

"Not since we can't travel to the farms." Mother Gum flapped a hand to wave away her concerns. "There's nothing we need fuel for except the tractors. You'll be able to use it, and this way, it won't go bad."

"Oh. Thank you so much. It would really be a huge help." Clare felt strangely giddy. She grinned at Dorran, but his returning smile was brief.

"Henry will take you." Mother Gum twisted in her seat to face the door. "Henry?"

One of the sullen young adults appeared in the doorway. His hair hung to his shoulders, greasy and limp, and he didn't return any of their smiles.

"He's a sweet boy," Mother Gum said to Clare. "Henry, take our new friends to the shed and fetch them some fuel. You know where it is."

He turned and disappeared outside without waiting for them.

"Thank you so much," Clare repeated, standing. The chair's awkward height had cut off part of the circulation to her legs, and she had to catch herself on the table's edge. Dorran gave the orange cat a wide berth as he accompanied Clare to the door.

"I'll pack you some biscuits for the rest of your drive," Mother Gum said. She folded her hands in front of herself, beaming. "Make sure you pick them up before you leave."

CHAPTER 6

THE MAN, HENRY, HAD nearly disappeared around the building's corner. Clare hurried to catch up with him. She was grateful she had Dorran with her. More faces watched her from the weed-choked yard around them.

What an odd family. How did so many people end up living here?

She supposed, in the silent world, any kind of safe home would be highly sought after. And Mother Gum was very sweet. The idea of joining the family could be tempting for someone who didn't have one of their own.

Henry led them toward the third building in the compound: the roughly built wooden barn. He shoved on the door, forcing it open, and stepped back for Clare and Dorran to enter.

"Clare," Dorran said.

She'd already stepped over the threshold and turned to face

him. He looked conflicted. Henry waited, frowning slightly, and after a second, Dorran also stepped inside.

"Is something wrong?" Clare whispered.

He shook his head.

Clare had enjoyed talking with Mother Gum, but now, all of the earlier anxiety returned. Something was bothering Dorran, and she knew better than to doubt his instincts. She kept close to his side as Henry stepped around them, moving toward the back wall.

The shed had a thick, unpleasant scent. A mix of spilled oil, decaying hay, and rotting food, Clare thought. She pressed her sleeve over her nose and tried to breathe through her mouth. It was strong enough to make her dizzy. There was no light in the shed. She relied on the hazy glow from the open door to see the contents. Beams and benches, sack cloths, barrels, machines— nests of shadow and dust.

Henry didn't seem bothered at least. He stopped at the back wall and pointed toward metal cans stacked on a shelf.

We shouldn't take them all. No matter what Mother Gum says, she might need some. But…one or two. That would buy us the time we need.

The hay-coated floor was uneven, and Clare stumbled as she moved toward the cases. She caught herself against the wall and chuckled. "Bit dark in here, huh?"

Henry's lips twitched, in a smile or a grimace, Clare couldn't tell. She took another step toward the shelf, then hesitated. From her angle by the wall, she could see around a stack of crates. The wooden boxes, filled with what looked like rusted machinery, created a simple wall around the shed's back corner. A gap had been left, wide enough for a person to walk through, and inside it Clare could see more hay, sackcloths, and an odd shape.

It looked strangely like a human hand.

She tilted her head to the side. It *was* a human hand. The fingernails were starting to peel off as decay split the skin.

A hollow. Dead at least. One must have made it over the wall.

She took another step forward, then stopped again. The fingernails were short. They had been cut no more than two weeks before. The hollows had all either grown long fingernails or lost them since their transformation.

This is wrong. This is very, very wrong.

Clare turned toward Henry. She barely had the chance to open her mouth.

Dorran hit her side. Clare's world spun as he pulled her down and pinned her to the floor. Her nostrils were filled with the scent of hay and dust and rotting flesh. She heard the smack of an ax hitting the wood above them, but it took a beat to recognize what it was. Dorran was already up. He grappled with Henry, gripping the ax's handle, the weapon suspended over their heads.

Clare rolled onto her side. She felt dazed, as though the fall had knocked something loose in her mind. Everything seemed to be happening too fast. She couldn't make sense of it.

Two more men were running toward them, crude weapons in their hands, their thin hair haloed by the light coming from the open shed door. Bloodless lips were pulled back from teeth as their earlier apathy vanished.

Dorran disengaged from Henry to dodge a pickax aimed for his knees. He leaped back, putting himself between the men and Clare.

Get up. Fight! Dorran needs you!

Clare searched for a weapon. She couldn't see any. That part of the floor was bare except for hay, and the three men stood between her and the farming implements. Her brain was slow to give her an answer, but then she remembered the knife she had tucked into her jacket pocket.

One of the men was almost on top of them, a length of chain clenched in his fists, aiming for Dorran's throat. Clare was close to his legs. She pulled the knife out and flicked the blade open, then stabbed it into the only place she could reach: his thigh. A spray of hot blood burst across her fingers.

Sickening horror latched on to Clare. In the moment, she had forgotten they were fighting real, living humans. The blood slicked her palm, and she lost her grip on the knife as the man staggered back, the blade still embedded. He released a choked, gurgling scream as he hit the blockade of crates, knocking them over and exposing the shed's back corner.

Bodies had been heaped there. Men and woman of all ages and in different stages of decomposition. The temperatures had been cold enough to slow the rot, leaving gray skin to fester.

Limbs were tangled in unnatural angles. One head faced the ceiling, lips open in a sigh of surprise, eyes turned hazy as they gazed at the rafters. Her throat had been cut, and the ragged line of flesh ran from under one ear to the other. Beside her, half-draped across her, was a man's body. His mouth was also open and held in place. A screwdriver protruded from between his teeth, stabbing up toward his brain.

These were never hollows. They were people. People who saw the sign for Mother Gum's Nest and took a chance on visiting.

Clare's balance was gone. A rushing noise filled her ears. She turned to look for Dorran. He was forced back, pinned against a barrel. He lifted his leg and slammed the foot into his attacker's chest. A bone cracked. The man fell back, face contorted in pain. He coughed and a dribble of blood ran over his lip.

"Clare." Dorran was back at her side in a heartbeat, grabbing her shoulders. He pulled her up. She struggled to get her legs under herself and clung to his jacket for balance. Henry dislodged his ax from where it had become embedded in the wall. The second man, the one with the knife in his thigh, staggered closer.

Dorran pulled her toward the door. She ran with him, desperate to be out of the killing shed, away from the collection of bodies. A spit of rain hit her cheek as they made it outside. Dorran swung sharply, slamming the shed's door behind them before catching Clare's hand and leading her forward. Ahead was Mother Gum's house, and just beyond that would be their bus.

All of the cars scattered about the compound...I think we just met their owners.

Tears burned Clare's eyes as she dragged in ragged breaths. They skidded in the cold mud as they ran for their escape. As they came out near the house's front, Clare saw Mother Gum waiting for them on the porch.

Her hair was gone. Instead of the soft, downy white, her head was covered with gray stubble, roughly cut. She held her old hair in one hand, the plait bundled up so that it wouldn't drag on the ground. A wig. Without the softening hair, it was starkly obvious that the rosy cheeks were rouge, and the watery, green eyes held a spark of severity.

She faced their bus, watching as her children unloaded the supplies. A routine she had undoubtedly watched many times before, Clare realized.

A rumble grew in Dorran's chest, escaping him as a furious snarl. Mother Gum swung toward them, her mouth puckering with anger and shock. She leaped back with unexpected agility, away from Dorran's path. He wasn't aiming for her, though. He was moving toward the four men and women carrying boxes out of the bus.

This time, the element of surprise was on their side. The two women scattered. One man dropped his burden and lifted his fists. The other hesitated, torn between running and fighting.

Dorran's fist snapped past the first man's defenses, connecting with his jaw and dropping him to the ground. That made the second man's choice for him. He turned and fled toward the hall.

"Drive," Dorran barked. He forced metal into Clare's hand. Then he ran past her, disappearing around the bus.

CHAPTER 7

CLARE STARED DOWN AT her hand. Dorran had given her the bus's keys. She was still caught in a fugue of shock, and it took a second to pair the keys with the word *drive*. Then she aimed for the bus's open door and leaped aboard.

Mother Gum was yelling. The grandmotherly, warbling tone disappeared in a slew of profanity. She was giving instructions to her children. *Don't let them leave. Slash the tires.*

Clare struggled to get the key into the ignition. Adrenaline roared through her, but it felt muted, as though all of the noises and sensations were coming through a veil. She didn't know where Dorran had gone, and it frightened her that he was no longer with her.

The engine clicked over and came to life. She put the bus into gear and leaned onto the accelerator, her motions coming more from muscle memory than conscious thought. Tires dug through the mud as the bus rocked forward. Dorran was nowhere to be seen.

Where is he? I can't go without him. I can't leave him behind, not here.

She leaned over the wheel, searching through the field of broken-down cars for signs of movement. People were coming toward her. The lanky, too-thin men and women of the compound, carrying machetes, their loose, brown clothes billowing in the wind and spitting rain.

Can't stay here. Can't leave without Dorran. Where is he? Why did he go?

Then, she saw him. He'd run ahead of her, along the dirt track leading to the impossible fence. He leaned against the gate, his muscles straining as it ground open.

Others were running toward him, though. They had weapons. They would be upon him in a moment, but Clare wasn't even sure he had seen them. His head was down as he forced the gate open with painstaking effort.

She pushed onto the accelerator, dragging energy out of the sluggish bus. One of the men leaped out of the way.

What do I do? Her reflexes felt blunted, her mind full of cotton. She didn't know if she should slow down or go faster. She needed to get Dorran onto the bus—she was sure of that much. But if she slowed down, the others would catch up to her.

The gate was just barely wide enough for the vehicle to fit through. But Dorran continued to strain against it, and he was in her path. In a burst of blind panic, Clare hit the brakes. The momentum was immense. The bus wouldn't slow in time. She was aimed right for Dorran's back.

He moved at the last second, darting to the side with lithe agility. The bus rocketed through the open gate. She felt something snag on its side and bit her lip as she leaned forward to see into the mirrors.

Dorran had grabbed onto the plywood nailed to the windows. He had his feet pressed against the bus's side, shoulders hunched as he held on to the vehicle. Clare hit the button to open the doors. They were slowing, the brakes finally stopping their mad rush downhill, and Dorran leaned into the momentum as he slipped forward, neatly stepping through the open door. He was breathing heavily, his eyes full of fire as he looked behind them.

"Faster," he said.

She put pressure on the accelerator. The open door nearly clipped a tree as they picked up speed. Dorran wrenched it closed, then stood beside her, legs braced to balance against the rocking motion.

The road ahead was blurry. Clare tried to navigate, but she wasn't reacting with enough dexterity. The bus's other side scraped a tree, wrenching a branch loose in an explosion of splinters.

"I can't—" Even her words felt faltering.

Dorran came up beside her, a gentle hand on her arm. "I can drive."

The changeover was faster than Clare had thought possible. She slid out of the seat while Dorran held the wheel, and in a second, he had taken her place. The engine rumbled as he pushed it to move faster. Clare caught herself on the passenger seat and dropped into it, then looked in the side mirror.

Three of the gaunt youths were running in their wake, but they were already disappearing into the distance. As she watched, they slowed to a staggering halt, lips peeled back in angry, fearful grimaces.

Dorran braked suddenly as they burst out of the forested area and back onto the main road. He wrenched the wheel, coaxing the minibus around to face the setting sun. But before they had traveled more than a dozen meters, he braked again.

Clare opened her mouth to ask what he was doing, but the sudden direction changes left her dizzy and sick. She clung to her seat, one hand braced on the window, as Dorran put the bus into reverse. He adjusted their angle using the side mirrors and backed into the hand-painted, wooden sign. *Mother Gum's Nest, Weary travelers welcome* bowed under the pressure from their bus's rear, then cracked and collapsed into the mud.

"I know they'll just put it back up," he grumbled. "But at least this way I feel better."

Clare cracked a smile. Dorran ran the bus's rear wheels over the sign before turning back to the road. The path was mostly straight, and he allowed the bus to creep up to an aggressive pace as they sped away from the compound. For a moment, Clare's head was full of the roar of motion and Dorran's ragged breaths. They seemed too loud. Deafening. The palm she pressed to the window was slick with sweat.

Then Dorran spoke. "I should have known better than to stop. I am sorry for putting you in so much danger."

She wanted to tell him it was all right, that she'd been lured in just as much as he had, but the words wouldn't come. She shook her head instead. The air was too hot; it choked in her throat before it could reach her lungs.

Dorran glanced at her, and his expression drew tight. "Clare? Are you hurt?"

"No. Uh…no…I…"

The bus began to slow. Real alarm was growing in Dorran's eyes. "You're white. What happened? Did one of those people hurt you?"

"I can't breathe." Her stomach was burning. Her lungs ached. She shook her head as a drip of perspiration ran down her cheek. "Pull over… Need air…"

The bus was already coasting to a halt on the road's shoulder. Dorran put it in park but didn't turn the engine off as he opened the door for her.

Clare rose and tried to climb out. The cold air felt good on her face. She leaned into it, and realized a second too late that she was falling.

Dorran barked her name as he caught her before she could hit the ground. His voice sounded as though it echoed from a long tunnel. He carefully lowered her to sit on the bus's step, then his hand moved across her forehead, then her neck. He took a sharp breath. "The tea. She drugged it."

Oh, she is such a monster. Clare tilted her head back, begging the swimming nausea to subside. *Thank goodness Dorran didn't drink it. He still had his wits and his reflexes when they attacked us.*

"What was it?" Dorran muttered the words not at her, but a question to the universe. "A sedative? Poison?"

"I'm fine," Clare mumbled, vaguely aware that the words were slurred. "Just got to catch my breath."

Dorran darted away from her, disappearing into the bus, and returned a second later with the water bottle he kept near the driver's seat. He unscrewed the lid and held it to her lips. "Drink."

She shook her head. "Feel sick…"

"*Please.*" Desperation bled into his voice. "You have to drink."

Reluctantly, she swallowed the water. It tasted off, and her body wanted to reject the liquid. She managed to swallow three mouthfuls before she keeled over, violently sick.

"Good. Good." Dorran held her with one arm across her chest, the other rubbing her back. "Get it out."

Clare hung off him, gasping, sweat sticking her clothes to her skin. She tried to straighten, but her stomach muscles contracted again, forcing her back down.

The sickness didn't stop until bile burned her throat and her body had no more energy to move. Dorran gave her the last few spoonfuls of water from the bottle to help wash her mouth out, then half guided, half carried her back into the bus.

"Bed or seat?" he asked. His voice was beautifully soft compared to the roaring noise in Clare's ears. She squinted, trying to think. The back of the bus was dark, almost unpleasantly so. Lights danced across her eyes. To her disoriented mind, they looked like ghosts. "Seat."

Her throat burned, her stomach muscles ached, and her

legs were uncoordinated. Dorran lowered her into the seat and adjusted its back so that Clare was half reclined in it. He bucked her seat belt, then fetched a blanket from the bed and draped it over her.

Her mouth still tasted foul. But her nausea had finally passed, and a deep thirst had risen. "Water?"

Dorran's hand ran over her shoulders, a comforting caress. He didn't move to fetch her a drink, though. He only stood beside her, facing the bus's insides, a horrible grimness haunting his features.

Clare tilted her head back. Her vision swam, and it took her a moment to see the racks above the seats. The bundles of clothes and blankets were still in their place. But the jugs of water and food were gone, leaving row upon row of empty shelf space.

Oh. She closed her eyes and dropped her head back. *That woman. This is why she invites people into her compound. With hollows in the fields, her family can no longer farm...so they lure people to them with the smoke and the sign, drug them until they can't resist, kill them, and take their stores.*

The hand on her shoulder squeezed, then Dorran spoke, his voice hoarse. "I will find you water. Just rest, my darling."

CHAPTER 8

CLARE DRIFTED IN AND out of a surreal series of dreams. She felt cold, even with the blanket and the bus's heater, and a chilled sweat coated her. A thick, pounding headache began at the base of her skull and spread across her head. Every bump in the road or tap of the brakes intensified it, until she couldn't even escape it in her dreams.

When she woke, she looked to Dorran. His back was straight and his expression was kept carefully blank, but his knuckles were white as they gripped the wheel. He had the map book open on the dashboard. Clare let her eyes drift closed again. She knew the maps well. There were no rivers in that part of the country. And there wouldn't be any for a long while.

She was desperately thirsty. Her tongue stuck to the roof of her mouth, a sick, tacky flavor across it. The sweat had dried, and she could feel the fever continuing to burn at the end of her nerves. She needed something to drink. Even just a teaspoon… an ice cube to suck…*anything*. The request hung on her tongue, wanting to be asked, but she wouldn't let it out. Dorran was doing as much as possible, and hounding him wouldn't change their situation.

The dreams began to encroach on wakefulness. When she looked into the rearview mirror, she thought she could see Beth walking along the length of the bus, blood dripping over her jaw. Clare blinked, and the aisle was empty again. A knuckle rapped on the window, and Clare turned to see Mother Gum standing at the door, her white-haired wig askew and her smile wide as she knocked to be let in.

"Go away," Clare mumbled.

Dorran stroked her hair back from her forehead. "Shh."

She lost track of time. They could have been driving for twenty minutes, or for days. The headache was so much worse. Every small jostle and movement sent it beating behind her eyes like a war drum. She thought she might be sick again, except there was nothing left to bring up.

The bus slowed. Clare cracked her eyes open, but her vision was blurred. They were passing something incredibly bright. It made her head worse, and she wished it would go away. After a moment, it did. The bus sped up again. She could sense Dorran fidgeting, fingers picking at the wheel as his anxiety broke through the carefully cultivated poise.

The next time she woke, they had parked. The bus was dark and quiet, the door closed, the engine off. Dorran was gone.

Clare tried to sit up. Her arm slipped out from under the blankets, but she had no energy for anything else. The need for water was excruciating. She thought she could still hear Mother Gum tapping on the window, this time a long way away, whispering, "They're all my children, they're all my children."

She tried to speak Dorran's name, but only a dry rush of air made it past her lips.

Don't leave me. I don't want to be alone.

It was night. Through the front window, she could see trees in the distance, cutting across the haze-blurred stars. They didn't seem to be forested trees, though. They were spaced too far apart. The word *landscaping* ran through her mind without making much sense.

He didn't leave me. He wouldn't.

But she was alone. And she didn't know how long she had been lying there, in a dead bus, surrounded by the stillness of night.

She was more afraid than she had felt in a very long time. The sensation felt different, though; the hollows inspired a sharp, angry fear that beat at her heart. But this was something else. It was sluggish and cold, drawing over her like a damp blanket.

The fear of being forgotten. The fear of dying alone.

She counted her heartbeats. They were easy to keep track of, each one pounding at her skull, little stabs of pain that ran into her eyes and jaw. She got to fifty before she lost the number and had to begin again.

Then she heard a noise. At first it might have been the rustle of wind through branches, but as it grew louder, she heard the steady rhythm, almost matching her pulse. Footsteps, crunching through something that might have been gravel or might have been dead leaves. Too regular and steady to be a hollow.

Dorran.

The door's lock clicked as he unsealed it. Then he stepped into the bus, quietly shutting the door behind himself. It was too dark to make out much of his expression, but the familiar silhouette seemed to hold incredible tension.

He looked toward her but glanced away quickly. She tried to reach toward him. He didn't respond; he wouldn't even meet her eyes. Instead, he turned away and paced the bus's length in eight long, quick steps.

Doesn't he want to be near me? He had never been short in his affection before. The rejection burned in tandem with the lingering fever.

Dorran stopped at the other end of the bus, where Clare couldn't see him. She could still hear him, though. His breaths came quickly. They were too rough and uneven to have come from exertion. He was on the edge of hyperventilating.

Dorran took a stuttered inhale and held it. In eight more quick steps, he was back at the bus's front. He still wouldn't look at Clare as he took the driver's seat. This new angle let her see his features better, though. They were tight—his eyebrows heavy, his lips pressed together, a muscle leaping in his jaw. The creases around his eyes were painful to see.

Guilt. He wouldn't look at her because he was ashamed. Clare tried to lift her hand but couldn't move it. She wanted to tell him it was all right, that she didn't blame him. His eyes were fixed resolutely ahead, though. The key turned in the ignition. The bus's lights flicked on. He was bathed in the backwash of the headlamps.

Blood ran from his shoulder and arm, soaking into his shirt, saturating the fabric. He hadn't tried to bandage them. Instead, he used the injured arm to put the bus into drive and pulled back onto the road.

"Dorran?" she tried. Again, it came out as a rasping breath.

His eyes met hers, then were averted again in a flash. "I am sorry, my darling."

They had to be driving along a well-maintained road; it was too smooth to be anything rural. Through the windshield, Clare saw more of the trees she'd glimpsed before, as well as infrequent peaked roofs.

Houses, Clare realized. *He was trying to find bottled water in houses.*

She ran her eyes across the bloody marks again. He'd tried to go in alone and with no light besides what the moon could provide. It had not gone well.

I'm so sorry.

He needed her badly. She was supposed to help him, care for him, love him. That was what she'd promised. Now, her very presence was crushing him into desperation.

If she'd just been more wary, if she'd just asked to pass by Mother Gum's Nest, if she'd just tipped the tea out like he had…

His fingers shook, clenched around the wheel. He glanced at the dashboard, toward the fuel gauge. Some awful resolution seemed to form inside of him. His eyebrows flinched down further, then he turned the wheel sharply, the bus's tires scraping as he made a U-turn. Then their speed picked up, a racing, rattling pace that couldn't have been safe.

Dorran had a plan, and he didn't seem to like it.

Breathing hurt. Movement hurt. Clare couldn't even make it stop. The thumping in her head was worse, breaking her ability to think, consuming her consciousness into its agonizing rhythm.

Then, lights appeared ahead. The same intense glow they had passed earlier, Clare thought. They were too bright; even with her eyes closed, they hurt.

The bus was slowing, though. They weren't going to pass it like they had last time. In the harsh white, Clare could see the blood more clearly on Dorran's skin and shirt. A vivid, angry red, made starker by the lack of color in his face. He looked toward the lights with the quiet dread of someone on the edge of a cliff.

The bus went over a bump, bouncing Clare. She grit her teeth as the pain flared. Her vision flashed to black and came back slowly, a dizzying, sickening array of blurs and colors. She heard metal scraping. A gate, she thought. Then, the bus slowed to a halt.

Dorran stood. He moved toward the bus's door, grim lines ringing his mouth. Fingers brushed across Clare's cheek. A caress to comfort, or to say goodbye, she wasn't sure.

Then the door opened and Dorran stepped out. Through the

light and pain, Clare was aware of approaching footsteps. The click of something that sounded like a gun being cocked. Then a man's voice, thick with a country accent, gruff and cracked from age. "What's your purpose here?"

"I need water." Dorran's voice was steady and moderated, but Clare could still hear how desperately tight it was. "I have clothes and blankets to trade."

The other man broke into a crackling laugh. "We're a *shopping mall*. Clothes are the last thing we need."

"I…I don't have anything else. Please. You can take as much of it as you want. I just…I need water. Whatever it takes."

The man sighed. "Calm down, son. We're not in the business of sending people away to die, no matter how little they have. Here."

The bus rocked as weight moved into it. Then cold plastic touched Clare's lips, and Dorran was whispering, "Drink, Clare."

She opened her mouth. After craving water so badly, the fulfilment was shockingly unpleasant. The water stung the cracks in her throat and increased the taste of tacky saliva. Swallowing hurt. Water overflowed her lips, dripping down her cheek and into her hair. Dorran murmured apologies and used his sleeve to dab her dry. When he returned the water bottle, he kept the flow slower, so she could manage it.

Feet crunched outside the bus. Clare forced sore eyes open. She had the impression of gray hair framing a pink face, surrounded by the overwhelming glow of industrial lights. The stranger held a rifle over the crook of his arm.

"She's in a bad way, eh?" He made a clicking noise with his tongue. "How long have you been driving?"

"A while." Dorran's voice was subdued. He stayed focused on Clare, supplying water in small mouthfuls as quickly as she could handle. His back was to the strange man, and Clare could feel the uneasiness in his posture.

"Well." The man took a breath and exhaled it in a gust. "You'd better come in for the night. You'll probably be needing some food as well, I'm guessing, since you didn't offer that to trade."

Dorran was silent for long enough that the man behind them started shifting his weight. Then he said, "I would be grateful. But I don't know what I could give you in return, if you don't need clothes."

"We'll figure that out later. Like I said, we're not much into the business of turning people away to die. At least this way, you can get some sleep where it's safe. I find people are better problem solvers when they're not dead on their feet."

CHAPTER 9

THE HEADACHE PERSISTED, BUT it had faded from an all-consuming tsunami to lapping waves at the back of her head. Everything was sore. But her mouth had some moisture in it, and her eyes no longer burned when she opened them.

She was in a small, dark room. An oil lamp sat nearby, turned to its lowest setting to conserve fuel, the glow so soft that Clare could only make out the edges of furniture. Some kind of bookcase, she thought. A table. What might have been an empty clothing rack. The floor was concrete, but a plush rug had been laid out in the room's center, its fibers ruffled from foot traffic. She was in the room's corner, propped up on something soft.

Where am I? Where's Dorran?

Panic pulsed through her veins. She couldn't see him. Memories from the last time she'd been conscious began to drip back to her in confusing, disconnected scraps. They had arrived somewhere with bright lights. She remembered trying to swallow water and how painful it had been. And Dorran had been afraid. He was almost never that frightened. She could remember the conflict in his eyes, the desperation that came from being backed into a corner, the uncertainty. She needed to find him. She needed to make sure he was safe.

Clare tried to sit up and gasped as her muscles burned. Then the shape underneath her—what she had thought was some kind of chair—shifted, and Clare swallowed a yelp.

"Shh, shh, it's all right, my darling. You're safe."

"Dorran?"

She tilted her head back. Dorran sat with his back propped in the room's corner, a blanket draped around his shoulders. He held her snugly, one arm cradling her head and back, the other around her legs, holding her in his lap. The blanket had been tucked around her, cocooning her until she barely felt the cold.

He looked gaunt, the way he had been when he was sick. But he smiled at her. Clare's panic began to recede. "Are you okay?"

"Yes. And you will be too." He slipped the arm out from under her legs and reached for a bottle of water that had been left next to them. They were on a mattress, Clare saw. A set of pillows was stacked beside them, along with a folded set of sheets.

Dorran held the bottle up for her. The thirst was no longer all-consuming, but Clare still drank. This time, her throat handled it better. She took as much as she thought she could without becoming sick. Dorran exhaled as he put the half-empty bottle aside.

"Where are we?" Clare asked.

"At one of the safe havens. We will be all right. For now, just rest."

She was comfortable in Dorran's arms. She'd noticed that before; no matter how he arranged her, they always seemed to fit together like two perfectly matched puzzle pieces. She was tempted to close her eyes and fall back to sleep, but instead she stretched her legs to shake some life into herself. She didn't know how long she'd been out, but Dorran looked exhausted.

"You can put me down, if you're tired."

He pretended to consider that for a moment. "I can. But I will not."

"All right." She chuckled and rested her hand against a patch of bare skin at his shirt's collar. The blanket slipped from around his shoulders, and she caught a glimpse of red underneath.

Clare frowned, memories falling back into place. He'd tried to find water in a house, but one of the monsters had been inside. She didn't know how bad the injuries might be. "You're hurt."

"It is all right, my darling. Just rest."

She pulled herself out of his arms so she could sit at his side. When she tugged at the blanket, Dorran grimaced as the shirt peeled away from the raw skin. Clare felt her heart plummet. "Hasn't this been dressed? Do we still have the first aid kit? Or… or any cloths, or—"

"Shh, you need not worry. They are not bleeding any longer. I will dress them in due course, but not now."

He's using formal language. He's stressed.

Clare's head was fuzzy. Focusing was nearly impossible, but she made herself pay attention. Dorran had said they were in a safe haven. She remembered a slow, drawling voice coming from outside the bus and blinding lights and the glint of a rifle.

"Dorran, have you talked to the people who run this place?"

"Not much." He tucked the blanket around her a little more tightly. "Just to ask for water, and then they brought us to this room. They have left us alone since then."

"How long ago was that?"

"A few hours."

He spoke as though it was nothing, but the shadows around his eyes belied tiredness. He wouldn't have slept since the night before they stopped at Mother Gum's Nest. *How long ago was that? A day? More?* "Can you ask them to look at your arm?"

"They offered, but I declined."

"Huh? Why?"

He gave his head a brief shake. "I will look at it later. Right now, I'm more concerned about you. Your fever broke after you had water, but I do not know what was in the tea and whether it might still be in your system. Do you feel nauseous at all?"

"Don't try to change the subject." She gave his chest a light poke. "Why didn't you let them look at your arm?"

He ran his tongue over his lips as he glanced at the door. It was simple and narrow and made of metal. She thought they must be in some kind of storage room. The shelves and clothing rack were empty, but once, it would have held new shipments before they were put out for sale. The mattress was probably a new addition, though.

"That woman and her children took everything of value," Dorran said after a very long pause. "Food, water, fuel. I do not want to commit to a debt that I have no way of repaying."

Oh. She suddenly understood everything. His reluctance to fall asleep, the fear in his expression the previous night, that he had only stopped at the safe haven when he was forced to.

He had adopted Beth's mentality on humanity: that they were a roll of the dice at best. And he had every reason to feel that way.

Before Clare had arrived at his ancestral home, Winterbourne, he had been trapped with an abusive, hypercontrolling family. His worldview had been shaped by them, his defenses honed, and it had left him with a fear of vulnerability that Clare was still working to break through.

He was trying, though. He trusted Clare. He was pushing himself to escape the shadows his childhood had left hanging over him.

After leaving Winterbourne, they had encountered four groups of survivors. Out of them, only the Evandale Research Institute had kept their trust.

Ezra had tried to kill them. Beth had attacked him. And then Mother Gum…

After Evandale, Dorran must have been pushing himself to be more open. That was why he had agreed to stopping when they saw smoke. He had made an effort to trust, despite what his instincts wanted and despite his natural caution.

The betrayal had been cold-blooded. It was a special kind of cruelty to lure someone in with love and kindness before leading them into a killing barn.

And now, he had been forced to seek out humans again. Strangers, not too different from Mother Gum: a community that opened its gates to travelers, welcomed them in with the promise of food and shelter. *And then what?*

She watched Dorran as he watched the door. He hadn't let himself sleep because sleep could mean death for both of them.

"Dorran."

His eyes flicked to her, filled with fear, filled with love, saturated with the quiet need to protect. She didn't know what to say. She wanted to tell him it was okay, that he could rest, that they wouldn't be in any danger. She couldn't promise any of that.

For all she knew, he was right to fear the safe haven. The Evandale institute had been an exception. Secluded underground, they hadn't lived among the hollows, and they hadn't had to fight for limited resources. They were essentially a bubble of old-world morals.

Maybe the rest of the world had gone bad. The surviving humans could be a mixture of recluses and extremists, a map of spiderwebs built by predators waiting for naïve or desperate insects to alight on them.

"I'm here," she said at last. It was the only thing she could promise him. "Whatever happens, we'll be in this together."

He kissed her forehead, one arm moving around her back to hold her tightly.

The door creaked and clicked as its handle turned from the

other side. Dorran stiffened. His hand moved to his thigh, where he still had his knife strapped, half-concealed by the blanket.

The old metal door shuddered as it pushed inward. Their lamp was too weak to reveal anything except the edges of movement, so Clare reached for it and fumbled for the dial on its side. The flame grew as she fed it more fuel, and finally, she had a proper look at their hosts.

CHAPTER 10

THE MAN ENTERED FIRST. He was old in a wiry, tough kind of way. Creases ran around heavy-lidded eyes, and his face was framed by a shaggy beard and long, loose gray hair. Clare's first impression was of a lion's mane. He continued to hold his shotgun over one flannel-clad arm, its barrels pointed toward the floor.

"Heard you talking," the man said, the country drawl thick and slow like a stagnated river. "Figured you'd be ready for some food."

As Clare and Dorran stood, a woman entered from behind the man, carrying a tray with two bowls of stew and cups of tea balanced on it. She could have been the man's twin except she was a little smaller and a little thinner—and lacked the beard. Creases ran over her features, and they bunched up when she smiled. Steel-gray hair cascaded down to the middle of her back, and her outfit was so similar to her companion's that it could have been planned.

They were old, but in a completely different way from Mother Gum. That woman's facade had been sweetness and softness, cotton-candy hair and rosy cheeks. This couple had been weathered. There was no softness, just muscles from a lifetime of physical work. With their hair and flowing clothes, Clare was struck by the impression that they might have emerged from the sixties with ideologies that followed them for the remainder of their lives.

"It has beef in it," the woman said, and a hint of motherliness slipped into her voice. "I figure you could do with some."

"Thanks," Clare said, as the bowls were unloaded onto a table near them. As she moved, Clare caught sight of scars running across the woman's collarbone and up her throat like lightning. They were only a few weeks old.

The woman tucked the tray under her arm and left, one hand running over the man's forearm as she passed him. She left the door open.

The man cocked his head. For a moment, he simply stared at them, letting the silence hang, then he said, "You feeling any better?"

"Yes." Clare glanced at Dorran. The wariness hadn't left his expression. "Um, thank you."

"Take your jacket off," he said.

Dorran's expression flashed vicious, all hard lines and blazing eyes. He shifted his pose, lowering his center of gravity, energy coiling inside of him as he prepared to fight. The word came out as a snarl. "*No.*"

The shotgun rose and his fingers moved to hover over the trigger.

Dorran didn't back down. Clare touched his arm and felt the tautness running through him. In that moment, she realized with shocking clarity that he was prepared to fight to the death for her.

"It's okay," she whispered, squeezing Dorran's arm. "He just wants to make sure I'm human."

Dorran's expression didn't relax. He kept his eyes focused on the stranger, a hard challenge, a threat about what would happen if he moved any closer.

Clare's jacket was thick and puffy enough to hide her figure. She pulled the zipper down and shucked out of it. Underneath, she wore a tank top that clung to her. She turned in a slow circle, showing her sides and her back.

"All right," the man said, and the gun dropped down to his side. "Just wanted to be sure. You two eat your food, then come out to the meeting area when you're ready. Bathroom's in the hallway if you need it."

The man stepped out of the room, and Clare pulled the jacket back on. Dorran didn't relax until the door clicked closed, then he slumped back against the wall, swallowing thickly.

"It's okay," Clare said again. An awful idea had been forming, and it hurt her to voice it. "He was just being careful. I think…I think this might be the safe haven Beth stopped at."

When the woman had passed them their food, she'd exposed the scars on her throat and chest. It had called back the story Beth had told Clare about stopping at one of the few safe havens in the region and how they had welcomed her until they discovered she was part hollow. About how she'd been attacked by the kindly older woman who had brought her food. Beth had escaped the encounter with a patchwork of scars, but it seemed she had left some as well.

"They're probably hypervigilant about who they let in now," Clare said. "You're not wearing a jacket, so they could see you're fine. But my clothes were thick enough that I could have been hiding something."

Just like Beth hid her spines. Thick jackets, loose scarves. She tricked us for long enough.

The memory was too painful. Clare blinked quickly and took up the bowls of soup to distract herself. She passed one to Dorran and stirred the spoon through hers, acutely aware of how ravenous she was.

"I am sorry." Dorran sounded uncomfortable. "I overreacted."

Clare grinned and tucked herself against his side. "I like knowing you have my back. Just like I'll have yours."

"I always will. That is a promise." His smile was brief but genuine. Then he glanced at the bowls of stew and his expression darkened. Accepting food from strangers was how they had ended up in their situation.

"These people have guns," Clare said. "If they wanted to kill us, they wouldn't need to drug us first."

"Very comforting."

She chuckled at the dry tone, then sobered. "I guess it's still a risk. *Everything* is a risk. But I'm hungry enough to take a chance. Especially since we don't have food of our own."

"Or enough fuel to find more supplies."

She looked up at him, shocked. "We're out?"

"The bus still drives. But the fuel light is on." He sighed and ran a hand over her hair. "We will figure it out. For now, you need what energy you can get, so we will take a chance and trust you are right about the gun."

She chuckled and tasted a spoonful of the stew. It was good and, as far as she could detect, had no concerning flavors. She ate quickly, relishing the chunks of meat floating in the mixture. The bus worried her, though. Gas would be hard to come by, especially with nothing to trade.

Dorran relaxed, but he continued to watch the door. Clare wanted to let him sleep for a few hours, but she suspected he wouldn't agree to it, no matter how tired he looked.

"Did you want to go out to talk to them straightaway or stay here awhile longer?"

He opened his mouth, then closed it again. Clare thought she could guess his mental process. He wanted to stay where they were, in the dim room with the locking door. They were safe there. But he also knew it was nothing more than putting off the inevitable. If they sat in the dark, they would only soak in their fears.

Please, let these people be nice. I need to know that some good souls survived the stillness. I need to have a future in this world.

"Let's go now," Clare said.

Dorran took a slow breath, then nodded. He helped lift her up, and even though Clare didn't need the assistance, she was grateful for his closeness.

Clare reached the door first and nudged it open, squinting to make out the area beyond. It was nothing but blackness, and her immediate thought was that the safe haven had been a lie and that they had been abandoned in some desolate warehouse.

Then Dorran lifted the lamp, and she began to make out the nearby clusters of clothing racks and a sales counter.

Like she'd guessed, they had been left in a storage room at the back of a shop. Denim jeans and T-shirts covered with slogans hung from every surface. Someone had created a path through the clutter, pushing racks aside to clear a straight path to the door.

A figure loomed out of the darkness. Clare flinched away from it, and Dorran swung the lantern forward. It was only a mannequin, poised on top of a pedestal, one arm reaching out toward them. Clare pressed her lips together as they passed it.

The shuttered main gate was half-closed, so Dorran had to duck as he moved under it. Broad white tiles echoed under their feet. The shopping center had two stories. Above, Clare could see the balconies of the second floor and, beyond that, a glass ceiling that let in minimal light thanks to heavy rain.

All around her were shop windows and brightly colored signs. *Get cozy this winter*, a home goods store suggested. A gaming shop wanted her to preorder a title with a now-passed release date. A sultry woman posed in a bathing suit, sprawled on a pristine beach. It was a shock to remember she had once been a real woman. Wherever she was now, she would not be looking so glamorous.

It's large. Larger than the mall we stopped at with Beth. Clare turned in a semicircle, examining the shining metal and glossy tiles. The walkway stretched in both directions, moving through a nest of stores and eateries. Their lights were all out, their windows dark, some of them with closed shutters. A shopping center this large had to be in a well-established neighborhood. The stillness had probably hit it early, before all of the shops had opened.

Already, the first hints of neglect were creeping in. A spiderweb hung from one of the imitation-marble pillars. Dust collected on the thick cloth draped over a jewelry stand.

Light and noise came out of an open entryway to their left. Clare looked up at Dorran to confirm he was ready, then led the way forward.

The safe haven's owners had co-opted a large department store for their meeting base. Stock had been pushed out of the way, clustered into the corners and stacked toward the ceiling, to leave a patch of carpeted ground free in the center. A range of display tables and what looked like food court chairs had been dragged in to create a makeshift meeting room. The tables were covered with papers, maps, and a thermos and cups, as well as multiple lanterns identical to the one Dorran held.

The two closest chairs were occupied by the man and his wife. He kept his gun at his side, leaned against the table's edge within easy reach, but his pose was languid as he beckoned them forward.

"Here you are. Come grab a seat. The other two members of my team will be here soon."

Clare cautiously took the chair beside the woman, and Dorran settled next to her. The woman leaned forward to fill two new cups from the thermos. As she did, the man fixed them with a stare and said, "John. And that's my wife, Patience."

"Patty," she said in a softer and more melodic voice than her husband's. "Welcome to West Hope."

CHAPTER 11

THE LAMPLIGHT FLICKERED OVER the paper-strewn table. In the distance, something echoed. Noise seemed to travel strangely in the empty shopping center.

Clare tried not to let her uneasiness show. She was struggling to get a read on either of their hosts. They had been generous in their actions: the bed, the food, the drinks. But the way John kept his gun beside him and the way Patty never turned her back to them kept Clare on edge.

Dorran was still and quiet, watching her cues, the way he did whenever they met strangers. She was faintly aware that one of his hands was poised over the knife strapped to his side, though. She hoped it wouldn't come down to having to fight their way out of the safe haven. She had no idea how she would even find the exit—or how many other people might be living in the unlit halls.

We have to at least try to make this work. Show some goodwill.

"I'm Clare, and this is Dorran," Clare said. "It's nice to meet you. Thank you for letting us into your home."

"Hmm." John shrugged. "Couldn't have turned you away. You looked half-dead. How're you doing, anyway?"

"Better. Thanks." She still felt shaky, and a headache lingered at the back of her skull, but both sensations were ebbing.

"Probably got a dehydration hangover. That'll pass. And anyway, I'm not sure we could call this place a house, let alone a home."

"We used to live on a farmstead," Patty said, placing a cup each at Dorran's and Clare's sides.

A note of fondness grew in John's voice. "We built that beauty ourselves. Twelve acres. Trees on every horizon. We had goats that kept the lawn trimmed for us." He puffed out a breath that ruffled his beard, and the fondness evaporated. "Had to leave it behind. Indefensible. This place is all corporate coldness, but at least it's kept the hollows out."

Clare wrapped her fingers around the mug. Dorran didn't lift his hand from his knife.

"This is a safe haven, right?" Clare asked. "Are you in charge?"

"Yes, and yes, I suppose. West Hope. Patty and I founded it with a couple other souls who are no longer with us. People come and go, but we're always here, keeping it running for anyone who needs it. People like Hex and Alden. Come on in, you two."

Clare twitched as she suddenly realized two figures had appeared in the doorway: a young woman with short, shockingly blue hair, and a middle-aged man who was tall despite his hunched posture. The woman, Hex, moved forward first, narrowed eyes on Clare. "You checked her?"

"E-yup."

Her eyebrows twitched downward. "Are you *sure*?"

"I'm sure enough," John drawled, tapping the table. "She's as human as you and me. Come get your seat. Clare, and, huh, Dorran, was it? These two are on the committee with me. Between the four of us, we figure out how to keep this place running."

Clare nodded. Hex's frown stayed fixed in place as she dropped into her chair. She looked like she might be even younger than Clare herself. Although the roots were starting to show, they weren't long. She must have raided the shopping mall for hair dye. It felt bizarre that there were still people with enough security and free time to spend hours on cosmetics, but in a strange way, it was also comforting.

The man was even more of an enigma. He struck Clare as the sort of person who would become embedded in middle management: competent enough to be promoted, but without the charisma or ruthlessness that would get him to the upper levels. His whole face seemed heavy, his eyes drooping at their edges like a basset hound's, and he looked displaced in his navy sweater with a tie tucked under its collar.

"Is Dorran your real name?" His voice was missing the inflection it needed to sound truly alive.

Clare answered on Dorran's behalf, feeling oddly defensive. "Yes. It's a family name."

"Okay." It quickly became clear he wasn't trying to needle Dorran, as he turned to the woman at his side. "Guess you're still alone on this movement to adopt new-world names, Eugenia."

Hex's cheeks lost their color. Her gaze fixed on him, filled with unspeakable threats.

John raised one weathered hand, eyes closed as he seemingly fought to hold on to his patience. "Let's give that topic a rest for today. Especially in front of our guests."

"Who *shouldn't even be here*." Hex spat the words at him.

Patty moved around the table, dropping off two new mugs for Hex and Alden, her voice sweet. "We don't turn people away. You voted for that, too, remember?"

"I voted on mandatory body checks," Hex snapped. "*Before entry.*"

John sighed. "She was half-dead. I wasn't about to make her jump through hoops. And anyway, we kept the door locked until she could wake up."

Clare shuffled, feeling awkward. "I can take my jacket off again…?"

Patty rested a hand on her shoulder as she sank back into her seat at Clare's side. "Don't you worry. You've already been checked. Keep the jacket on so you don't freeze."

As Patty turned toward her husband, Clare again glimpsed the scars around her neck. She felt a cold pit in her stomach: grief, or guilt, or something in between. She wanted to apologize but swallowed the words before they could emerge. If she was right about her theory, bringing up her relation to Beth wouldn't just be a bad political move; it could be deadly.

Hex looked like she wanted to push the topic, but John raised his eyebrows at her, a silent challenge, and she backed down. She folded her arms as she leaned back in her chair. Four mismatched bracelets circled her wrist, jingling with each movement.

"I'd be interested to hear your story." John sipped his drink, and Clare, who had seen the cups all come from the same thermos, finally felt comfortable enough to try hers. "Where you've been. Where you're going. How you ended up with no food, water, or fuel."

The first two questions were difficult to answer. Clare and Dorran had promised Unathi they wouldn't disclose the institute's location, to protect it from being overrun by refugees. They wanted to keep their destination a secret for the same reason; the greenhouse was only large enough to support the two of them at the moment. She looked to Dorran for his approval and then answered the third question.

"We were doing okay for supplies until yesterday. We saw smoke from a fireplace and stopped. It was a really bad decision. They stole almost everything we had."

Hex leaned forward in her seat, suddenly interested. "Where was this?"

"I don't remember much after it happened. Dorran?"

"Six hours to the south," he murmured.

Clare nodded. "It was called Mother Gum's Nest."

"We know about them." The lines around John's mouth tightened. "Old woman and a group of youths she calls her children. Holed up inside a wooden fortress. People go in there, but not many come out."

Clare's heart sank. "Yeah. That was her."

"Did you go inside the fortress? What did you see?" Hex asked.

"There were three buildings. The woman, Mother Gum, gave us some tea in her home. She…she seemed sweet. She was being generous, too—said she had fuel we could take. She sent us to get it from the barn with one of her children."

"Was there anyone trapped there?" Hex asked. "Anyone alive?"

The memory of the decaying bodies in the barn resurfaced. Clare swallowed and shook her head. "I'm sorry. When you go to the barn, they kill you. There was something in the tea—some kind of poison that made it hard to think or react."

"A sedative, I believe." Dorran frowned at the table, reluctant to make eye contact as he forced himself to speak. "I avoided having any. But it hit Clare badly, and then I had no water left to give her."

Patty ran a hand over her face. "Those poor souls."

Hex turned to John, her eyes blazing. "We *have* to do something."

"My answer stays the same. There's nothing to be done, 'cept to warn people."

"How many's she gotten already? How many more?" Hex turned back to Clare. "She keeps changing her name once she realizes we're warning people. Always something familial that preys on emotions. It's Mother Gum now. A Cottage for Lost Children last week. Grandmother Goose before that. She's like one of those mantises that pretends to be a flower to lure its prey in."

Clare's mouth twisted. "She's sick."

"She's a witch, that's what she is." Hex switched back to John. "We've gotta purge that place."

He sighed. "It's a fortress. I'm not sending my people on a suicide mission."

"I'll go myself. A couple of Molotov cocktails would do the trick."

"You'd be shot before you even got close enough to throw one," John said.

Hex heaved back in her chair, its metal legs scraping over the floor. Blotches of color had appeared on her pale cheeks as she refolded her arms. For a moment, the meeting room was quiet. Alden scratched some pale stubble on his chin, then said blandly, "It's a bad situation."

"Understatement," Hex scoffed.

Patty rocked her mug on the table, swirling the contents. She seemed almost apologetic. "We knew about her before the stillness. Her fortress was a few hours' drive from our homestead. She was called just Annabelle back then. She said she ran a camp for wayward teens, but it was widely known that it was closer to a cult. Back then, she would have her...*followers* work the fields around her property. Since it is no longer safe, she seems to have turned to luring and attacking anyone who passes by."

"Oh." Clare thought back to the high wooden walls. They had been greased to keep hollows out. She hadn't actually considered that the walls had been constructed before the stillness, but looking back, that seemed obvious. They had been too high and stretched too far to be built in a day or two.

"Those people she calls her children?" Hex lifted her eyebrows. "Half of 'em don't even want to be there. But they know what happens if they try to dissent. And they think they don't have any choice, y'know? They can't talk anymore."

Clare frowned. "What do you mean?"

"She cuts their tongues out. Stops them talking to each other… and now, I guess, it stops them from warning any visitors. The witch took a very literal approach to stopping gossip."

Clare shook her head. She remembered the youth who had led them to the shed, Henry. How sullen and unhappy he had appeared. She felt painfully grateful to have escaped. But her mind and heart ached as she thought of everyone else who had not been so lucky.

Hex's mouth twisted into a snarl. "If we don't do anything to stop her, we're just as bad as her."

John scratched the side of his nose with a chipped fingernail. "We've been over this so many times it's exhausting. We have a job here. An *important* job. People need safe havens to stop, to heal, to learn about the road ahead. How many lives have we saved by being here?"

Hex mumbled something that Clare couldn't quite catch.

"We fight the witch, chances are we die trying to bring her down. Then *no one* can be helped."

"It's not right," Hex said, but there was a note of defeat in her voice.

John drained his cup, then passed it to Patty, who rose to refill it. "We have a job here," he repeated. "You want to help people?

You help me keep the lights on and the shelves full of food. And maybe don't throw a fit if I occasionally bring people in without checking them."

Hex lifted her middle finger toward him.

"If you're accepting feedback, you could tone down the edginess," Alden said. "Blue hair doesn't make you cool."

The finger swiveled in his direction.

He shrugged sloped shoulders, unconcerned, as he sipped his coffee.

"As much as I would enjoy it, this meeting isn't about Eugenia's real name or her fashion choices," John said, mildly ignoring the finger as it turned on him again.

"Or the fact that she was a small-town checkout girl before the stillness," Alden added.

There were now two fingers, one waving in each direction.

"No. We have guests." John sighed, stretching, before turning to sit sideways on the chair and draping one arm over its back. "Here's the situation. They need supplies. They don't have much of anything to trade. And we should figure out what we're going to do about that."

Clare swallowed. She'd begun to relax, lulled by the banter between Hex and her companions. They seemed to know each other well, like a family that exchanged barbs every evening over dinner but never with any real malice behind them. She'd almost forgotten about her own situation.

She looked at Dorran and was surprised. He rested both arms on the table ahead of himself, away from the knife, attentive to the conversation but no longer wary of it.

He doesn't think we're in danger any longer.

Clare had learned to trust Dorran's instincts. He always deferred to Clare when they had to speak to strangers, but Clare knew, between the two of them, he was more skilled at picking up on subtle cues. His mother's treatment of him had ensured that. Clare did her best to trust him again then. "We're low on… everything. They took our water, food, and fuel. We still have clothes and blankets, though."

Hex pulled a face. "We've got more than we'll ever need of that. There are a hundred and twelve stores in this shopping center. Out of them, sixty-two are either clothing or homewares."

She recited the numbers so easily. This isn't the first time she's had this conversation.

"West Hope is a sanctuary," John drawled. "We don't turn away anyone who is in need. If you're starving, we feed you. If you're hurt, we'll give you medical treatment. And when you move on, we advise on the road ahead and do what we can to give you a solid shot out there. But we also have to look out for our own survival, you understand? More than sixty souls live here full-time, and we can't give away our food if it means our own will starve."

"I understand," Clare said.

Patty spoke, her voice soft and a little sad. "That's especially true for the fuel. It's getting harder and harder to find, and fewer people want to trade it. But it keeps the parking lot lights on, and those lights are the only things stopping the hollows from swallowing us."

"West Hope can't last forever," Alden said. "We all know that."

John nodded. "But it's about extending our time as long as possible. Giving as many people a chance as we can before we run out."

Clare bit her lip. "Actually, with some luck, you might be able to outlast the stillness."

John tilted his head. "People who travel through like to tell us that the end is coming. They have all types of reasons. Raptures, the hollows dying under their own weight, some secret government military bases hidden under the arctic—which theory is yours?"

"None of them. And it isn't a theory." She took Dorran's hand. "We know how the stillness began. And we've met people who are working to make it end."

"All right, I'll admit, I'm intrigued." John chuckled. "Anytime a new soul comes through, we like to hear their story. It's how we know what's out there, who's surviving, what tricks and tactics are working. And it sounds like you have a hell of a story. Let's hear it."

"Okay," Clare said. "But first, you said you give medical treatment. And Dorran's hurt."

CHAPTER 12

PATTY BROUGHT A FIRST aid kit out of the room's corner while Alden boiled a kettle. Clare tugged the blanket off from around Dorran's shoulders and began unbuttoning his shirt.

"It's fine." He spoke quietly, looking uncomfortable. "Just leave it. I can take care of it later."

She narrowed her eyes at him as she undid more buttons. He just sighed.

Patty returned with the first aid kit and shook her head as she saw the shirt. "They've torn through it. May as well cut it off; it's not like it can be salvaged at this point."

She passed Clare a pair of scissors, then pushed stacks of paper aside and laid out instruments on the table.

"I treated most of our animals on the homestead," she said, setting out two pain tablets beside Dorran's mug. "It's not quite the same as working on humans, but it's enough."

Clare cut through the shirt with painstaking care. She felt guilty for letting Dorran sit like that for so long; shreds of cloth had become tangled in with dry blood, a matted mess that ran across his shoulder and upper arm, near the old wound where Beth had bitten him. She should have asked for someone to look at it as soon as they entered the meeting room. It must have been hurting him, no matter how well he hid it.

He flinched as she pulled the fabric out. Fresh blood began to ooze. Clare swallowed, feeling sick.

"It's really fine." Dorran spoke calmly, even as perspiration shone on his forehead. "They're not deep enough to require stitches."

"They are," Patty said. "You'll also need some antibiotics. Hollow bites don't seem especially prone to infection, thankfully, but you would still be courting sepsis if you don't take it."

Dorran shook his head. "They would be a waste now. Save them. Clare, would you like to explain?"

"Yeah." She shuffled back to make room for Patty, who drew her seat up to Dorran's side, dampened a cloth in the boiling water, and began to wash the dried blood away from the bite marks. Clare licked her lips, trying to center her thoughts.

It was the second time she'd told the story. Like when she'd shared it with Mother Gum, she avoided revealing that she and Dorran had experienced Ezra's experiments firsthand and omitted any trace of Beth.

Unlike with Mother Gum, she had her companions' undivided curiosity. Hex leaned forward, chewing on her thumbnail, eyes bright and keen. Alden was unreadable with his drooping features and lackluster expression, but his eyes remained on her as she talked. John occasionally interrupted with questions.

Clare finished her story with, "So we left the USB with the people at the research institute, who will be activating the code as soon as they can make sure it's safe. It might be a few weeks, or it might be longer. But they know how precious time is. I don't think they'll leave it too long. If you can keep the safe haven open until then, you won't have to risk moving the survivors here to a more remote area."

"Huh." John continued to watch her as he mulled over the story.

Hex's rapt attention had morphed into disappointment, and now her eyebrows were pulled low under her blue bangs. "She's making it up."

John held up a hand. "Well now, hold on, Hex."

"No, there's no way she's telling the truth. Nanobots and underground bunkers… it's about on par with that guy who said the Aztec god of death was punishing the world. I mean…" She shrugged at Clare. "It's a nice story full of hope, but *come on*."

John shrugged. "Possibly. Possibly not. Extraordinary situations can require extraordinary explanations."

Hex switched her attention between Clare and John. "What? You actually believe them?"

"Sure," he said. "I'm more inclined to than not."

Alden lifted a finger to catch attention. "I can't see much of a reason for them to lie. If it's a delusion, it's affected both of them equally. And if it's a lie, what do they get out of it?"

John shrugged. "Either way, it doesn't change our plans. We keep West Hope running as long as possible. If this code is real, and if it works, we'll know about it when it happens. But we don't bank on it."

"What do we do now?" Clare asked. She couldn't stop fidgeting but kept her hands in her lap, where they wouldn't be as visible. "Our bus is low on fuel. Probably not enough to get us somewhere with more."

"No," Alden said, agreeing. "The cars and houses around here have been pretty well emptied of their stores."

"We don't do loans, either," Hex added. "Too much of a risk you won't ever come back."

"Does that mean we just have to...stay here?"

"'Fraid that isn't doable, either, dove." John sighed. "We have a rule at West Hope. If you're capable of surviving out there, you have to move on. Only the people who are physically unable to fight can stay; otherwise, we'd be out of food in a week. No. Now that you're up and alive again, we'll be looking to move you on within the day."

"We're not going to send you out to starve," Patty said, seeming to sense Clare's growing stress. "There are options. You can try to trade with other people who stop here. Though, if the witch took everything of value, that will be difficult. Or you can hitch a ride with another traveler who'll take you somewhere with more supplies."

"Do you need any work done?" Clare asked. "I can do repairs, or cook, or..."

John shook his head. "We've got too many volunteers for that already. No, I think the best option would be to ask a traveler to take you with them. Someone with two extra seats in their car who won't mind you tagging along for a while in exchange for whatever's left in your tank and any fittings from your bus that they fancy to take."

Clare tried not to feel crushed. She'd grown fond of the bus; the idea of some stranger breaking it apart to scavenge for spare parts hurt her deep inside.

Don't be picky. You're alive, Dorran's alive, and you're together. That's all you need.

"Of course," John continued, "you won't have any say in where they take you. But they'll usually try to drop you off somewhere relatively safe. There are some walled communes up north that're still looking for able-bodied souls to work in the fields. It's hard work but honest, and you'll be fed and safe there."

Clare watched Dorran out of the corner of her eye. His lips twitched, but he stayed silent. Like her, he must have been thinking about Winterbourne. It was their own refuge, their home, and a destination that was feeling increasingly out of reach.

John swallowed the last of his coffee and set the mug aside. "The only question left is finding someone who'll take you. You both seem respectable sorts, so it shouldn't be too hard. Most people are decent about this sort of thing, and we usually have a couple of cars pass through each day. Sometimes they don't stop long. I'd recommend taking anything you want to keep out of your bus and storing it with you. You can stay in the room we put you in, and we'll come get you when we've found your ride. All right?"

Clare licked her lips. She didn't want to say it out loud, but the idea of throwing herself at a stranger's mercy terrified her. It sounded like they wouldn't even have a choice of who they left with. Once they were away from the safe haven, the strangers could ditch them on the side of the road with no repercussions.

John says most people are decent. Most, not all. It was a dice roll.

And they would have no choice about where they ended up either. Clare tried to picture the communes John was talking about. She liked nature, and she liked gardening, but the phrase *working in the fields* conjured up a very different emotion. It would be long hours of repetitive, laborious work. They would most likely have to share a bunk with other individuals, working only for food and shelter, nothing more.

Dorran reached out and touched her hand. In a reversal of their usual roles, he spoke when she couldn't. "We are grateful for all that you have done, and continue to do, for us. Pardon me for asking, but is there any other alternative? A way in which we could keep our bus? We had a destination in mind before we arrived here. Somewhere with sentimental value. It would be difficult to give up on it."

"I feel for you kids, I do." John scratched a hand through his mane of hair. "If I had a way to give you some of our fuel without hurting our own, I would. But fact is, you're not the first to ask, and you won't be the last. This council voted on a set of rules to keep us from bleeding ourselves dry. You get food and water while you're here, and medical attention and anything else that's necessary to keep you alive. But as long as you're capable of surviving in the stillness, you have to move on to make room for someone else."

"Understood. Thank you." Dorran met Clare's eyes. His were full of a quiet sadness, a wordless apology. He regretted ever being lured in by the trail of chimney smoke. She did too.

"Hang on." Hex leaned forward, tapping her fingertip on the table. She fixed Dorran with a hard stare. "There might be another way. Have you fought many hollows?"

"Yes."

"Successfully?"

His lips twitched up. "I wouldn't be here otherwise."

"Right, that was a stupid question. What I mean is, can you *fight* them, not just react to them? Can you face a nest of the beasts and charge in?"

"I can do that."

"And you're not squeamish about gore? You don't faint at the sight of blood or anything?"

Dorran wordlessly tilted his head toward his arm, where Patty was tying off the bandages.

"Yeah, okay, another stupid question." Hex kicked back in her chair. "Right. Here's the deal. A group of us are going out to a location where, we've been told, there might be more fuel. It's at a shipping yard. Someone who used to work for the company says there will be containers full of two-hundred-liter drums. As long as no one else has raided it and as long as we can get the fuel out, it will be enough to set up West Hope for at least another few weeks."

Dorran tilted his head to show he was listening.

"It's a dangerous job." Hex flipped her bangs away from her eyes. "We'll have two teams going in: one to fight the hollows that will inevitably be swarming there like the darkness-loving plague they are, and one to retrieve the fuel. We have enough hands to carry the fuel, but we could do with another body to fight off the creatures. Someone with muscles."

"I can do that," Dorran said.

"I won't sugar-coat it," Hex continued. "Based on previous recon jobs, there's a one-in-three chance of significant injury and a one-in-eight chance of death. And that's with a week of training, too, which you don't have."

Clare grit her teeth, trying not to interrupt. The idea of venturing into somewhere as cluttered as a shipping yard left her feeling queasy. And Dorran was handicapped: one arm swaddled in bandages, low on blood, tired from stress and lack of sleep. There was no waver in his expression, though.

"If you pull your weight, you'll be paid a portion of whatever we bring out," Hex said. "The goal is fuel, and if there's food, we'll grab some of that as well. But like I said, we don't know if it's still there. We might come out with nothing, in which case, you get nothing. Or you might die. That's a very real possibility too."

"I understand."

CHAPTER 13

CLARE, UNABLE TO STAY silent any longer, cleared her throat. "Hey, Dorran, mind if we have a word in private before you make any promises?"

He sent her an apologetic smile. "Of course."

John waved a hand, indicating it was fine, and Clare scraped her chair away from the table. Dorran followed as they moved deeper into the store, until they were half-hidden among the shadowed mannequins and dusty clothing racks. Clare folded her arms across her chest. "You're certain you want to do this?"

He glanced back toward the meeting table, and the lamplight played across his sharp features. "I feel as though I *have* to. As dangerous as it is, it seems to have better odds of success than striking out on our own and hoping to find a replacement vehicle and fuel."

"Yeah. And I don't want to be part of a compound." Clare took a slow breath. "We'll both go."

He chuckled as he tilted his head in the way she loved. "You knew I was going to suggest you stay here, didn't you?"

"It's only an argument we've had, what? A dozen times before?"

His smile faltered. "In this case, I hope you will let me win for once. I cannot risk losing you again. You don't understand how desperately I need to keep you safe right now."

"That's the thing. I *do* understand." Clare stepped closer until she was nearly standing on Dorran's toes. "It's why we're having this argument. What gives you the right to assume *I'm* okay with being left behind?"

He closed his eyes and dropped his head until he was exhaling into her hair. Clare waited, knowing he needed a moment to process his thoughts. His fingers traced across her shoulders, then he raised his head again.

"You're right. And I should apologize. I have this…overwhelming belief that it is my responsibility to keep you safe."

Clare pressed her lips together. Dorran's mother, Madeline, had controlled him with a mixture of violence and threats toward his younger cousins. He'd been cut off from the world, his entertainment restricted, and his only friends being staff who had an unwavering loyalty to the matriarch. Since leaving Winterbourne, he'd grown remarkably, but he still struggled with relics from his adolescence. A cloak of irrational guilt clung to him, he had blind spots about most of popular culture, and when he was stressed he still slipped back into the more archaic language he'd been raised with. But he was growing. Clare didn't know if she could have adapted to such a different world as readily as he had.

Dorran drew a ragged breath. "That impulse to protect you… that it is my job, my duty…it is not an easy mindset to change. Especially when changing it involves placing the one thing I value above all else in danger."

"But that's not always going to be a choice."

"No. And you are capable. Unexpectedly so." The hand moved from her fingers to her wrist, tenderly tracing up her arm, exploring, almost wonderingly. "I don't think you see yourself the way I see you. My darling, so much of you is soft. And I don't mean that as a criticism."

"I'll try not to take it that way." Clare was chuckling, but something about Dorran was so sincere that the laughter faded. He was making himself vulnerable, exposing his innermost thoughts, and Clare knew how hard that was for him.

"Your skin is soft. When you look at me as you're falling asleep, your eyes are so soft that it hurts. And you have so much empathy. In this brutal, unforgiving world, you never lost your ability to care. The stillness has sharpened everything into edges, and you, alone, are soft."

"Dorran…"

He blinked, and a shaky smile grew. "And I suspect that is why I am continually surprised by how fierce you are. You do not wither in the face of danger; instead, you blaze like wildfire. You remain soft, but you are just as capable as I am, perhaps even more so. And you have proven that to me again and again. At Winterbourne. On the road. In Evandale."

Clare reached her hand around the back on his neck and

pulled him down gently, until his forehead touched hers. His black lashes framed flickering eyes. She searched them and saw trust. She smiled. "Will we go together?"

"Yes. Let us go together."

Clare tilted her chin up to taste his lips. He sighed, then shivered as he wrapped his arms around her. She rested against his chest and felt his heart under her ear.

"But, please…I must beg a concession."

Clare looked up, surprised by the raw note in his voice.

"I know you are capable, but I fear I am not. If you are in danger, at least half of my focus will be on watching you. Would you be a part of the team that does not fight?"

"Ah." Clare chewed on that. Hex had said there was a second team that would be focused on retrieving the supplies, while the first team guarded them. It might not be a bad idea, she realized. Dorran said his attention would be divided if she was on the guard team, and she could say the same in return. Being a part of the retrieval team would make it easier to watch Dorran's back. "Yeah. Okay. I can do that."

He released a breath. "Thank you."

Dorran held her hand as they returned to the gathering. Hex looked impatient, rocking her chair so far onto its back feet that it was a wonder she didn't fall. Patty was packing away the last of the medical equipment.

Clare spoke first. "We'd like to take you up on your offer as long as I can come as part of the retrieval team."

Hex glanced across her, then shrugged. "A'ight. But we don't need any more volunteers for retrieval. I'll let you come, but if you're not a part of the guard segment, you'll still only getting one portion of the loot."

"That's fair."

"We'll be leaving once the sun rises, in about five hours." John stood. "Get some food and rest before then. We'll brief you on the drive there. And, Dorran, Hex is running the defensive group. You'll follow her instructions to the letter."

Dorran nodded, first to John, then to Hex. Clare tried not to let her surprise show. The girl looked young, and although she talked with confidence, it had struck her as false bravado. John and Patience made sense as council members, and even Alden looked as though he had enough experience to make calculated choices. Hex, still a teen, seemed to be the odd person out, but she was clearly more than a token member.

"Come with me," John said, dusting his jeans. He took one of the lanterns from the table and held it high as he led them through the shop and into the mall's main hallway. "I'll show you where the kitchens are."

"I hadn't realized it was night," Clare said, tilting her head back to see the glass ceiling two floors above them. "I thought it was just storm clouds."

"They can be hard to tell apart sometimes," John replied. "Especially since West Hope never sleeps. We need guards to watch the perimeter, especially at night. And those guards need food and water and backups to replace worn-out equipment, so those parts of the haven have to run constantly. We work on twelve-hour rotations."

Their feet made empty, ringing noises with each step. Clare spoke, just to break the awful noise. "Even so, I hope the others on the council didn't have to wake up just for our sake."

"Oh, nah. The four of us are constantly on, just grabbing a few hours of sleep when we can. Hex and Alden have been up for a few hours already, preparing for the raid."

Clare tried to poke around the source of her curiosity without sounding rude. "Did you know them before the stillness?"

"Nope." A lopsided grin developed, showing rows of molars with stains around their roots. "They're not what you'd expect on a council, are they?"

"No," Clare admitted.

"Patience and I founded West Hope, which meant we made the choices about how it ran. And we've always been of the mindset that power has to be earned. Lots of people know how to say the right thing and play the political game, and that might have been fine in an office, but the new world isn't so forgiving. We picked our council members because they *truly* deserved it."

Clare wanted to ask more, but they had arrived at thick sheets of black plastic draped from the ceiling like a curtain to form a temporary wall. At first glance, Clare had assumed it was a dead end, but now that they were closer, she could hear noises coming from the other side. John moved forward first, sweeping an arm out to force a gap through the sheets of plastic, and all of Clare's previous questions died on her tongue.

They had reached the food court. The atrium formed a circle of fast food stores, their lights all dead, ringing around chairs, tables, and live palm trees in planter boxes. Above, a massive domed roof looked into the night sky.

The shopping center had felt near empty up until then. But as she stared across the scene, she realized West Hope was more alive than she could have ever imagined.

CHAPTER 14

"FIGURED THE CENTER COURT made the most sense for a food hall, since it has all the implements already," John said mildly. "By the time Patty and I arrived here, the meat had mostly gone rotten, but there were still boxes and boxes of long-life food in the cold rooms."

Clare couldn't take her eyes off the occupants. Despite it being the middle of the night, they were loud, almost raucous, and moving with seemingly endless energy.

The food court was full of children.

A boy who couldn't have been more than four ran past her, chased by an older girl with an action figure. Two preteens sat nearby, chattering over each other while simultaneously biting chunks out of fresh bread slices. Another group of children had pushed chairs and tables out of the way to play a game of duck, duck, goose in the middle of the floor.

There were animals too. No less than eight dogs romped among the children or sat patiently at their sides or dozed nearby. She saw a couple of cats sitting on unused counters at the other side of the hall. There was even a duck eating beans out of a girl's hand.

Clare's heart felt as though it was overflowing. The room was full of life. More than that—it was full of *hope*. Children, so many of them, alive and safe. She squeezed Dorran's hand. He pressed back, fingers trembling.

John tilted his head toward her, his voice soft. "You see why we can't take in every traveler who stops here, why we have to keep West Hope open as long as possible."

Clare nodded, unable to find her voice.

The children weren't alone at West Hope. In among them, watching over their play and holding young babies, were a mix of elderly men and women. John's words came back to her. *If you're capable of surviving out there, you have to move on.* Those who weren't strong enough or fast enough to fight stayed behind—and cared for the children.

John indicated a sandwich shop counter. Two older women stood behind it, crushing canned tomatoes and scooping them into pots. They smiled when John approached.

"We're after some food for our visitors," John said. "Something with meat in it. They have a long day ahead of themselves."

The shorter one, with tightly cropped, gray hair and moles dotting her face, ladled three generous portions of the stew into ceramic bowls and passed them over the counter. Clare and

Dorran took theirs with muted thanks, then followed John to one of the tables.

Clare couldn't keep her eyes off the activity around her. As they sat in the hard plastic chairs, she asked, "Do these children… have family?"

"Some do. Not all." John stirred his stew, nudging around portions of canned carrots and beef. "Here is safer than being on the road, so some parents will leave their children with us. They come back every few days or weeks, bringing scavenged food and gasoline to help out, and to visit their kids. Sometimes they don't come back at all. That's always hard."

Clare pictured how it must be for a child, waiting for their parents to return, counting off the days. Clinging to hope even when it ran thin.

"Others lost their family before they came to us. Some parents would barricade them in closets, hide them in basements, just do anything they could to keep them safe. And strangers would find them while looking for supplies in the home. They know we take in children, so they bring them to us."

The sounds around her were still happy, but now, Clare could detect an undercurrent. There was so much loss and grief and confusion contained in the room. She put her spoon back into the bowl, her appetite vanishing as her stomach turned to ice.

John's smile was thin lipped. "There are a lot of remarkable stories that pass through this safe haven. And a lot of sad ones, as well. If this world recovers, it will be a very different one from what existed before. We do our best for these kids. The ones without families are looked after by our caretakers." He nodded to the elderly men and women who watched over the children. "We give them love. And food and shelter and safety. It's the best we can do."

That's all any of us can manage: the best we can do.

"Go on," John said. "Eat. You'll feel better for it."

Clare tasted her stew. It was lukewarm, but the center court was heated, so Clare didn't mind. It still hurt to swallow, so she spoke to distract herself. "It must be a challenge to manage this place."

"Oh, it sure is. That's why we have the council. It's a constant balance of compromise. The council votes on what's worth it and what isn't." He pointed to the lights above. "The center court stays lit. There are too many children here who are afraid of the dark, so we keep the lights on for them. But the lights in the hallways and stores have been disconnected to save power."

"Because you have to keep the outside lights on," Clare said.

"Exactly. Giant glass doors, glass windows… If too many hollows cross the parking lot, they could break through, no question. The lights keep most of them away, though. The stragglers who are hungry enough to approach are dealt with by the snipers before they can build up."

"You have the heating on too."

John sighed. "Yeah, that was a tough one. Heating uses up more juice than the lights, can you believe? And this thing is two floors, and warmth escapes through the ceiling faster than I'd like. But when the snows set in, it becomes too cold to do anything.

Too cold to stand guard, too cold to prepare food—the kids start crying, we start worrying about spreading infections—so the heat stays on constantly, keeping us a few degrees below comfortable, but warm enough that we can function."

A girl bumped Clare's chair as she ran past, chasing one of the dogs, her giggles infectious. Clare managed a smile. "I guess the animals are another compromise."

"Yep. A lot of food goes to those pets. But they're worth it. No matter what a child's been through, they can find comfort in an animal. And some of those dogs have proved their mettle on the field. Several kids came to us after their pets defended them from dozens of hollows. They'll be the last line of protection if our haven is ever breached."

A sense of dread moved through Clare. Her mind flashed back to Evandale, and the panic that had set in as the hollows poured through the open shutter door. She licked her lips. "Is that likely?"

"It's a risk we're prepared for. We have a plan, we've done drills, all the kids know what to do. If the haven is breached—if the sirens go off—everyone moves into the biggest store, the one down there." He pointed to the hallway Clare and Dorran had come from. "It has solid shutter doors and food and water stores. If we can't fight off the breach, we'll be protected in there while we put out a call for help through the radio network."

Clever. They would have made allies with the people who stopped here. A call for help would summon more than a few reinforcements.

Dorran spoke. "You said West Hope won't be able to stand

forever. What are you planning to do when you run out of supplies?"

"The fuel is likely to go first. When it does, West Hope won't stand a chance against the hoard—not unless we figure out some kind of new defense or the hollows are killed, like you say. When that happens, we have buses and cars on standby to move our population somewhere else. Another safe haven. One of the communes. Perhaps another location where the resources surrounding it have been less aggressively scavenged. We won't know until the days before our departure, when we'll finally have to make a choice."

"At least you have a plan," Clare said.

"Yes. Though I'll be sad when we leave this place." John turned his eyes to the glass panels lining the domed roof. "It's the only safe haven in this region, and without it, traversing the area will become much riskier. Still. We can only do as much as we can do and hope for the best."

The conversation lapsed, and for a moment, Clare was surrounded by the sounds of their scraping spoons and the chattering children nearby. A girl screamed as she was caught in a game of tag. A dog, overexcited, released a gruff, booming bark.

Then Clare returned to a question that had been hanging over her, the mystery of the council. "You said Hex and Alden were promoted because of what they'd done."

"That's right." John leaned back, bowl held in one hand. "We met Alden the day after the stillness happened, when things were still chaos. Patience and I were trying to find somewhere safe to go, but the roads were blocked and we'd been funneled onto a major freeway. Not a great place to be, as I'm sure you've figured out. It was a mix of cars that had been there when the stillness occurred and survivors who were trying to get into the city to look for lost family—or simply just trying to get somewhere safe, like us. Something had gone down ahead of us on the road. Cars were piled up; most were on fire. The people—the ones who were human—were all just trying to get past, even if it meant shoving cars out of the way. There were still hollows lurking about, most of them disoriented and staying away from the fire but still dangerous enough if you became stuck. And in among it all, there was one man who was trying to get into a car."

"Alden?"

"Yep. The car's roof was crushed. The driver was dead, I could see that straightaway, blood sprayed all over the windshield. But there were two children in the back seat. And Alden was reaching through the open window to pull them out. He was the only one who was even trying. But the fires were out of control. The fuel tank of the car next to him exploded, and this ball of flames just engulfed him. It was bad; I think I might have screamed. And he staggered away from the car carrying this little boy in his arms."

John lifted his own hands, mimicking the motion.

"You saw how his face droops. It was so much worse at the time. His skin—it was melting off of him. I don't think he could even see properly. But he saw us. We were the only ones who had stopped, who were even paying attention to him. He staggered to us, and when Patience opened the door, he passed the boy to her.

Then he turned around and walked straight back into the fire. Back to get the second child."

"Oh," Clare moaned.

"I thought, 'This is the caliber of man I want with us.' When he came back, we pulled him into the car with us. Bandaged him as best we could. He didn't speak for two full days. We thought he was going to die, but he pulled through. Even got his vision back—most of it, anyway. And when he came back, the first thing he asked about were the children."

John lifted a hand and pointed to a boy and a girl sitting in the duck, duck, goose circle. Old, faded burn marks ran along the boy's neck.

"And that's why he's on the council. Because he'll put other people ahead of himself every time."

"Wow." Clare thought of the man who had appeared so mild mannered, almost sleepy. She had a new respect for him. "And what about Hex?"

John chuckled toothily. "Hex is a whole other kettle of fish. You'll be working with her at the shipping yard, and I suspect you'll find out her deal for yourselves. Speaking of—if you've eaten your fill, I'd recommend you get some sleep. It's a long trip there, and the more energy you have, the better your chances."

CHAPTER 15

MORNING CAME FASTER THAN Clare would have liked. Early light filtered through the glass ceiling. The thousands of tiles and store windows glittered in a sedated kind of way, as though the shopping center itself was only just beginning to wake. Voices and laughter came from the food court. Heavy cardboard boxes slammed into the floor as supplies were ferried about. Clare passed a greasy, dust-covered man speaking to Patience and caught a fragment of the conversation: "Been driving since Tuesday. Will twelve packs of batteries be enough for a night here?"

She and Dorran pushed through the thick plastic drapes to the center court. They were running on just four hours of sleep, but it was hard not to feel the electric trepidation thrumming through the safe haven.

The sudden barrage of motion and noises was overwhelming. A toddler screamed, hands clasped over a bruised knee as an older couple hurried to help him. Two of the guards, older men wearing rifles slung across their backs, yelled over the commotion while they waited in line for food. A thermos boiled in the background, punctuated by shrieks, clattering crockery, laughter, and scraping chairs.

Tables had been lined up to support three pots of rich soup, and servers doled out portions into Styrofoam cups and distributed thickly buttered bread to the recon teams. It was hearty food, designed to give them energy through the day. Hex flitted among them, easily identifiable by her blue hair, her lips moving as she counted heads.

"It's busier than I expected," Clare said. There was too much movement to get an accurate number, but she thought there must have been at least thirty people gathered there.

Dorran nodded as he accepted a cup of soup. He still looked tired, and his hair was rumpled and damp from a shower. Clare moved closer to put her arm against his, and he leaned into her.

"Oy, recon teams. Sun's up. That means we're moving out," Hex yelled. "Eat on the road."

Hex had been borderline abrasive the night before, but her demeanor had changed that morning. She wasn't short-tempered or snappy, but her movements and voice were infused with intense purpose. *Focused*, Clare thought. She'd smeared lines of gray war paint on her cheeks, an effect that would have been comedic in any other situation.

They moved toward what would have been an entrance to the shopping center before the stillness. Massive glass doors, ones which would have once been motion-activated, had been boarded over with thick pieces of wood and reinforced with heavy furniture. They aimed for the fire door at the side, the only part of the entryway that hadn't been blockaded.

Hex shoved it open and led the way outside. Mist clung to the scene. Rings of bright lights worked to cut through the haze, illuminating the parking lot surrounding the safe haven. As Clare followed the group along a pedestrian crossing, she tried to get a proper look at the area. More than sixty vehicles were parked in a cluster, grouped in a way to avoid providing shelter to any hollows that wanted to pass through the lights. Near the back of the cluster, she thought she saw the bus she and Dorran had arrived in. It stood above the others like a hulking monster.

Straight ahead, two vehicles waited: a school bus, and a moving truck. The truck already had a driver hunched over its wheel. Hex waited outside while the crew boarded the bus. Clare and Dorran were some of the last to enter, and it was impossible not to feel self-conscious as they faced the rows of occupants.

The bus was nearly full. Most of the passengers—a mix of men and women, most young and fit—were engaged in quiet discussions. Clare, clutching her cup of soup, moved along the aisle until she found two empty seats, thankfully together. She gave Dorran the window seat, then tucked herself in beside him.

Hex stood at the front of the bus, counting the occupants. A frown descended, and she leaned back out of the bus's doors, hollering, "Marc!"

A moment later, a thin man stepped onto the bus. His skin was tanned until it was almost bronze, but his hair and eyebrows were so starkly blond that, in the glow from the overhead lights, they almost looked white. He slipped into the nearest empty seat, holding his own Styrofoam cup in one hand, and the bus's doors clattered closed.

"That's everyone. Let's go." Hex remained standing at the head of the bus, holding on to one of the ceiling straps as the vehicle lurched into motion. A rumbling noise started behind them as the truck came to life. The bus's occupants, who had been murmuring to each other before the trip began, fell into silence.

Clare leaned across Dorran to see outside. Mist swirled around them as the bus coasted through the parking lot. The illumination strengthened and waned as they passed under each lamp, then they rocked over a speed bump and cruised out of the shopping center's boundary.

The bus's headlights turned on as the mall's lights faded behind them. Something hit the bus's side not far from where Clare and Dorran sat. Then the vehicle rocked as another two impacts collided with the opposite side. Clare, throat tight, found Dorran's hand. He squeezed it. A hollow one screamed. Another impact, and then another, then the bus picked up speed and the hissing, chattering noises faded into the distance.

The bus turned onto a main road. Debris and cars had been shoveled out of the path, piled up in gutters and sidewalks. The mall was surrounded by smaller businesses: accountants, takeout places, hairdressers. Within a few minutes, they gave way to residential lots. The road curved gently, and the driver navigated it faster than Clare felt comfortable with. Evidently, he knew the route well.

"All right," Hex said, swaying lightly with each bump the bus traversed. "We have a five-hour drive ahead of us. So…get comfortable. I'll go over the location and plan in a moment. But first, we have some new faces with us. Dorran and Kent are new additions to our defensive team. Clare will be joining the movers. Keep an eye on them; make sure they're not getting overwhelmed. You all remember what your first times were like. And Marc"—she indicated the pale-haired man near the bus's front—"is our guide. He gave us the tip about the shipping yard and knows it pretty well, since he used to work there. He won't be joining us for the raid, but he'll give us directions on where to go."

Marc drained the last of the soup from his cup, sullen eyes scanning the crowd. He didn't look too enthused about going back to his old place of business. Clare wondered if he dreaded what he might find there. His old coworkers, maybe some of them friends, horrifically transformed…

"We know the shipping container we're after," Hex continued. "It's dark blue and fairly old, so the paint might be discolored. Its identification number ends in 4148, and there's a logo on the side that looks like this."

She held up a sheet of paper. It had a hand-drawn image of a wavelike design inside a circle. She kept the paper still, waiting until every person on the bus had examined it, then refolded the sheet and fitted it back inside her pocket.

"Marc says this was a bimonthly delivery. It should have been unloaded from the ship the day before the stillness hit, and it usually spent a couple of days in the loading dock before a truck picked it up. We know the area it's likely to be in, but not its exact location. So there might be a bit of hunting involved."

Clare lifted her Styrofoam cup and swallowed some of the stew, trying to be discreet while all eyes were fixed on Hex. The bus's wheels shuddered as it took a corner a little too fast, but Hex seemed to be expecting it and held her composure as the bus rocked around her. Clare wondered how often she had been on missions like this before. She was so young that she looked like a child playing at war, but she spoke with conviction.

"We have our two snipers, Bill and Charlene. As soon as we arrive, our first action is to get them into some kind of high position that the hollows will struggle to reach. Maybe on top of a shipping container. Hopefully we won't need them, but if we do, they'll provide coverage from the sky. Bill was in the army and Charlene hunted deer for a living, so they're pretty damn good at what they do. But as you know, when you make a noise, every hollow that can hear it will come to check it out. The louder the noise, the greater the area you draw them from. A gunshot will bring in everyone in a two-kilometer radius. Which, obviously, is not what we want to happen. They'll be a last resort *only*."

Tires screeched as the bus slowed to navigate an obstacle. Two more heavy thuds came from the left-hand side as hollows threw themselves at the vehicle. Clare flinched, but Hex barely paid attention to them as the bus picked up speed again.

"We have our two teams: the movers and the guards. You might be tempted to help out someone on the other team if you think they're having a tough time, but trust me, everything goes more smoothly if you focus on your own job. Movers: stick in a tight group. You'll be following me. We'll go through the shipping yard in some kind of logical pattern as we look for our container. Once we find it, we'll break it open, check it has what we need, then your job is to move as much back to the truck as quickly as you can. The fuel should be stored in barrels, and they'll be heavy, so you might want to roll them. Hold your formation at all costs. If someone falls behind, we wait for them to catch up. Don't rush ahead, no matter how bold you're feeling. Remember: anyone on the fringe is going to be picked off first."

Tightly packed town houses had given way to single-story residential homes. Speckled sunbeams flitted through the old trees, painting stripes across the asphalt and bricks. Resentful eyes watched them from the shadows, but the hollows weren't willing to attack. The bus began to slow to a more moderate speed.

Hex continued, "Guards, you'll do whatever it takes to keep the movers safe. They'll have weapons, but remember, most of them aren't fighters. You'll form a circle around the movers. Keep an even gap between yourselves, avoid the temptation to cluster, go at the movers' pace no matter how slow it is, and don't ever let your guard down."

Dorran sat still, gripping his empty cup, intent as he listened to his instructions.

"If you notice a mover having trouble with their load, don't try to help them. Hollows will see an exposed back and jump you, and then *no one* has a good day. Let the movers do their thing while you focus on yours: keeping them safe. Hollows can come from above, not just the sides, so stay alert."

Hex took a deep breath and let it out slowly. "We're very likely to be swarmed at some point. That's when the hollows just pour out of every nook like cockroaches in a feeding frenzy. When that happens, I'll yell *defend*. That's your cue to drop everything and clump together. Movers, bundle in close to each other. Guards, tighten your circle around them. You should be standing shoulder-to-shoulder. Face outward, hold your position, and slash at anything that comes near. It's going to be hell. You'll feel like you're being smothered, like the hollows will never end and you'll be crushed under the weight of them. But you *must* hold your position because it won't last forever. Eventually, they'll run out, and you won't have anything left to stab at, and you can pick yourselves up and keep moving."

Clare felt nauseated. She glanced at Dorran. If he was afraid, he hid it well.

"Once we have the first load of supplies on the truck, we'll take a second to regroup. If anyone is seriously hurt, they'll be sent to stay in the bus. Then we head out again. We keep making trips until the supply is either gone, or the truck is full, or I call it quits."

Hex fell silent. The rumble of wheels on rough road suddenly changed pitch, becoming smoother and quieter, and Clare glanced through the window. They were passing over a massive bridge. Below, a series of highways wove perpendicular to them, all choked. Clare caught a flash of a bone-thin arm that must have been at least two meters long, reaching out of a window and grasping futilely up toward them. Then the overpass coasted down again, back to ground level, and the grinding noise resumed. Clare glanced behind them to check that the truck was still following and saw its headlights bobbing through the rear window.

"You all know how to fight hollows by now, so I'm not going to teach you to suck eggs. Just remember, no two are made the same. Some have multiple spines. Some can have their heads turned into a pulp without dying. Don't take anything for granted. I find decapitation pretty effective, but you do whatever works for you." Hex pointed at the blond man sitting at the front. "Part of Marc's deal was that he would stay on the bus. If you're injured during the recon, you'll be joining him. Don't open the doors under any circumstances. If you're quiet, there's a good chance you won't be bothered. But if you are, just avoid the windows and try not to make any noise. We'll be back soon enough. Just sit tight."

Marc raised a finger, wiggling it slightly to catch attention. Hex broke off, eyebrows quirked. "Something wrong?"

"Just wondering what we do if the driver gets eaten." He paused to drink the last of his stew. "Do we just get stranded at the shipping yard because the keys are down some hollow's gut?"

Hex sighed. "Well, we're going to be trying to stop *anyone* from dying. But, yeah, this is a risk we've dealt with before. The keys stay in the vehicles' ignitions. Hollows aren't smart enough to try to steal them, and it helps with a quick getaway."

Marc nodded, evidently satisfied.

Hex shifted her weight as she turned her attention back to the crew. "The most effective defense against hollows is not being noticed, so we'll try to do that for as long as possible. That means keeping quiet. Even if we're attacked, keep the noise levels down. No war cries, please and thank you. The snipers are instructed not to fire unless they absolutely have to. If we're very, very lucky, we might get through this without drawing much notice.

"If you forget everything else I've said, I want you to remember these three key rules." Hex held up a finger. "One, follow my instructions immediately and without argument. I will be doing what's best for you and everyone else involved. If you think you know better, tough luck, do what I say." A second finger went up. "Two, do not break formation. I cannot drill this in deeply enough. *Do not break your damn formation.*" Another finger. "Three, nobody is being left behind. We don't do any of that sacrificing crap that you might hear about at other safe havens. We're not leaving until everyone is on the bus or confirmed dead. So don't go ballistic if you're separated from the group. Just hold your position as best you can. We'll come find you."

She lifted her chin, meeting every set of eyes, her expression full of hard lines and unspoken challenges. "Everyone understand?"

"Yes," they chorused.

"No one's going to argue?"

Another chorus: "No."

"Good. I'll give you a warning half an hour before we arrive. We've a while to go yet, so try to relax. Save your adrenaline for when you need it."

CHAPTER 16

CLARE TOOK DORRAN'S EMPTY cup and stacked it in hers, then tucked them under her seat. He slipped his arm around her, pulling her close, and kissed the top of her head. Clare took a stuttering breath, her insides a mess of hope and anxiety.

Ahead, Hex slid into the seat beside the driver, legs propped up and arms folded as she watched the road.

Gradually, the silence was broken as muffled discussions resumed. People were wiling away the time by talking about anything: work that needed to be done at West Hope, who needed a haircut the most, and theories about a popular book series that would now never be finished. The only thing not discussed was their destination.

A drawling voice came from behind Clare. "How're you two feeling this morning?"

Clare jolted and turned. John sat in the row behind her, one leg crossed over the other knee, his long gray hair hanging like curtains around his face. Beside him was Alden, head down, engrossed in a thick paperback novel. Clare had been so preoccupied with her own awkwardness on entering the bus that she hadn't noticed them.

"Hey." Clare looped her arm over the seat's back. "I didn't know you were coming."

"They need the help. The guard team is the most important part of this but almost always understaffed." John shrugged. "Not everyone can deal with it. Physically or emotionally."

John wasn't young. Clare suspected he was on the verge of being too old for the guard team. But then, many people on the bus were; some were as old as John, and a couple looked to be teenagers. West Hope couldn't afford to be picky.

"And Patience is back at the haven?"

"She sure is. We agreed that at least one person from the council needs to stay behind."

Clare caught the unspoken implication at the end of that statement: *just in case the retrieval goes wrong.* She thought Patience was a braver woman than she was to sit back while her husband walked into a nest of hollows.

John nodded toward Hex and lowered his voice. "You just listen to her instructions and you can't go too wrong."

Dorran nodded toward her too. "Earlier, you said we'd understand why Hex was on the council during the raid. I think I'm starting to understand what you meant."

"Ha." He scratched his beard. "You probably are. The silent

world is a war. But not all of us are good at fighting. Patty and I, we're pacifists by nature. We moved onto our homestead because of how petty and cruel the world could be. We didn't have to deal with much unpleasantness when it was just us and our farm, and I thought it was the smart way to live. But now, I see that avoiding confrontation may have made those forty-odd years comfortably peaceful, but it's done very little to prepare me for an actual battlefield."

Clare thought she could see where he was going. "You're not good at strategizing or fighting. But Hex is."

"You got it in one. A checkout girl named Eugenia from a small town doesn't seem like a likely war hero, but she has more guts and grit than many of the adult men I've met. Out of the four of us on the council, she's the only one who's any good at being aggressive."

"She's big into the psychology side of fighting, too," Alden said. His eyes hadn't moved from the novel, but he apparently wasn't as absorbed in it as Clare had thought. "It seems stupid, all these theatrics she puts on. Dying her hair. Changing her name. That guerrilla face paint…but it's what she needs to get into the right frame of mind, so I can't argue. Too much."

His lips twitched up, and Clare had the sense that teasing Hex was one of his favorite sources of entertainment.

As the hours passed, the shadows shortened. Clare had become used to spending days in her own vehicle, but the school bus was a very different experience. The seats weren't quite as comfortable as she would have liked, and the constant chatter around her left her on edge. An hour out from the shipping docks, they parked in the center of what had once been a community park. The two snipers, Bill and Charlene, sat on the bus roof and kept a lookout while people relieved themselves behind bushes. As they filed back onto the bus, they were handed granola bars and bottles of water. Hex set up the speakers to play music.

"Another psychology tactic," Alden murmured under his breath. "To psych us up, I suppose."

Clare knew he was right. The music wasn't for distraction; the songs had all been chosen carefully. The first few were about standing up for noble causes, songs of justice and hope. The energy began to build with the following songs, growing louder and wilder as they drew closer to the shipping yard. For the last part of the journey, when the bus had to slow to a crawl and use the metal plow on its front to shovel abandoned cars out of its path, the songs were full-on war anthems.

The music worked. Clare could feel adrenaline running through her, the desire to fight, to be brave. Dorran was practiced at keeping still, but she could feel restlessness simmering under the surface.

Hex turned off the music, then stood, feet braced against the bus's rocks and jolts. "Ten minutes out. Get your weapons. Heavy defense for the guards, light defense for the movers."

Dorran turned to Clare, alarm flashing through his eyes. "I didn't bring any."

"Weapons are stored overhead," John said. He took a hair tie out of his pocket and used his fingers to scrape his locks into a ponytail. "If people have a favorite, they can bring their own; otherwise, we supply them."

Sure enough, the bus became a hive of energy and movement as people stood and sorted through the racks above their heads. Down came machetes, hatchets, pikes, meat cleavers, even a pair of garden shears.

"Best to get something long range for your main weapon and a smaller knife for backup," John suggested.

Clare moved out of the way as Dorran picked out his own weapon. He chose a hatchet, something he had experience using, and tucked a kitchen knife into his jacket pocket. Clare picked out a hunting knife and fastened it around her waist. One of the passengers moved along the bus, passing out handmade helmets of leather padding and wire mesh, forearm and shin guards, gloves, and thick scarves to the guard team. Dorran took his, and Clare helped him strap the forearm guards on.

"Do you feel ready?" she asked.

"I do." He took her hand, but the grip was shaky.

Clare lifted it and kissed it, one finger at a time, then held it against her cheek. "Be safe."

"I will." Warm breath ghosted over her neck as he leaned close. "You do the same. Don't take risks. I'll watch your back."

"Two minutes," Hex called. Beneath the war paint, her cheeks looked pale. "Remember the golden rules. *Listen* to me. Don't break formation. No one gets left behind."

The movers didn't have anywhere near as much protection. Clare had been given a thick scarf and gloves. She guessed the lighter burden was to help mobility and visibility, since she wasn't supposed to have to fight. It still seemed painfully risky to leave so much of herself exposed.

The bus rocked as it struggled over a fallen branch. Through the windshield, Clare glimpsed a distant concrete building surrounded by blocky, irregular towers. The view was cloaked in mist, further dampening the haze-choked sun and turning the scene into something closer to twilight.

Then the headlights went out, and the scene disappeared from sight. Hex lowered her voice. "Keep the volume down. Remember, the longer we can go without drawing attention, the faster we can complete this job."

Dorran pulled his gloves on. They were thick and leather, and Clare prayed they would be enough to keep him safe from the endless teeth.

The bus moved into an empty patch of concrete, and the engine cut out.

"Stay safe," Dorran whispered, and kissed her a final time before pulling his helmet on. "I love you."

CHAPTER 17

THE GUARDS STEPPED OUT of the bus first, easy to identify by their bulky armor and long weapons. The movers followed, most of them with a knife or a crowbar strapped to their backs, but otherwise dressed lightly. Clare tied her scarf around her throat as she followed her team.

Marc, the only soul left on the bus, watched them with mild eyes as they filed past him. "Good luck." A few murmured responses; most were too tense to answer.

Clare took a deep breath as she stepped outside. Chilled mist flooded her lungs. The group gathered close to the vehicles, the movers clustering tightly together, the guards forming a circle around them, all alert, necks craned as they scanned their surroundings. Even under the mask, Clare could pick out Dorran easily by his height and broad shoulders. He'd chosen a position near the front of the group, close to her.

Hex stood at the head of the guards, fist raised to keep them in place. Then her hand flattened out and beckoned forward, and as one, they began moving into the shipping yard.

The air was thick and moist, and tasted of salt and seaweed. Within a few steps, the moisture began to stick to Clare's exposed skin. She was grateful the movers didn't have to wear anything bulkier. The humidity would make heavy lifting a struggle as it was.

They stopped near a stack of shipping containers. The first of the snipers, Charlene, threw her rifle over her shoulder and used the metal bars to climb the structure. It was a good vantage point. It had a view of the bus and the truck, and a large part of the shipping area. They waited until she had positioned herself at the top, lying on her stomach, rifle muzzle poking over the lip, before they moved on.

They stopped at another stack of containers, and this time Bill scaled them. He was opposite Charlene, but facing a different angle. It was a clever tactic. Clare knew, if they stayed quiet, the hollows would likely never find them in their nests, but the high ground gave them the perfect angle to take action if anything went seriously wrong.

They set out again. Clare had trouble making out her environment through the mist. The towers she'd seen from the bus were shipping containers, piled high and deep. The concrete building seemed to be some kind of office area. She couldn't see the harbor, but she knew it couldn't be far away. The briny air was too intense and deep in the echoing silence, and she thought she could make out the faint melody of lapping waves.

The movers kept in a tight group, their shoulders bumping. They didn't quite run, but their pace was as fast as they could go without losing formation. Shoes scraped across grimy concrete. Breaths, exhaled through open mouths, rasped around Clare. Her own heart was a thundering tempo that refused to abate.

A hollow one screamed. The wail, distorted by the humid air, echoed between stacks of shipping containers so that Clare couldn't even guess which direction it had come from. She kept her head up and her eyes moving, scanning through the billowing mist, hunting among the black shapes rising out of it. Trucks waiting for their loads, their cabs drooping as though forlorn, lingered around them. A forklift was butted against a concrete wall where it had crashed after its driver had fallen to the stillness.

Immense cranes broke through the mist like long brushstrokes piercing the sky. The concrete was stained with oil and long-hosed-away organic matter and occasional patches of something more recent: blood, left from unwilling victims, vast pools of it that had then been lapped up by the voracious.

Something skittered between shipping containers. Clare barely caught a glimpse of it before it was gone, leaving eddies of mist in its wake.

Hex led, her blue hair fluttering like a flag with each step. Dorran, two places to her right, glanced over his shoulder to check on Clare. He looked otherworldly in the distorted light and thick mist. Beautiful, even.

Something moved in the distance. Clare squinted, her pulse

skipping. One of the cranes had come to life. The long bars moved, cutting across the sky.

Impossible. Not a crane. A...

A hollow. Immense, tall enough to tower over the highest container stacks, its limbs elongated into stilts. A cousin of the creature from the tunnel. Its outline blurred by the mist, it had posed among the cranes, almost indistinguishable from them until it rocked into motion.

Clare opened her mouth to whisper a warning, but she wasn't the only one to see. A man to her right cried out, his voice choked. "Look!"

Murmurs ran through the others. Some of the movers stopped, and the guards backed up to maintain their circle around them.

"*Quiet.*" Hex's voice was subdued but cutting enough to break up the shocked voices. She raised her fist, holding them still, and stared at the shape.

The monstrous, elongated creature drifted away from them. Each step seemed to be in slow motion, the limbs rising, then plunging back down. It was too far away for the sounds to reach them. The silence was disconcerting.

Hex held them there for only a few seconds, then her raised hand, beckoned forward, and they began moving again.

Clare could barely breathe. The tension was echoed around her. She guessed most of the people at her side wanted to retreat to the bus, but Hex continued driving them forward.

The shipping yard became more cluttered the deeper they moved through it. They passed a stack of containers, and Clare tried not to shiver as the sound of dripping water reached her. Something crawled alongside their group, near invisible among the mist and shadows, its long limbs letting it glide effortlessly at their pace. It watched them, but it didn't try to approach.

They were moving closer to the concrete building. Scraps of paper fluttered in the wind, their edges caught in cracks and under rubble. A truck rested nearby. It carried a container but had never left the shipping yard. They skirted around its front, and Clare bit down on a cry as an open hand slapped against the windshield. The driver was trapped inside, half of his head gone from repeatedly beating it against the glass. What was left seemed to be rotting slowly in the moist air, gray flesh turning into a slimy, swollen pulp. His throat was gone, but he continued to beat his hand against the window, asking to be let out, inviting them to come in.

Hex barely spared him a glance. She moved them on, giving the truck less of a berth than Clare wanted. Then they were back on a patch of open ground, facing a covered area filled with more containers.

A figure darted out of the shelter, sprinting across the concrete, its teeth overgrown so that its canines pierced through its lips. It was on the group in less than a second. The two closest guards stepped forward, and with a pair of muffled *whick*s, the hollow fell dead to the ground.

Hex showed no reaction. Her focus was on the covered area. Screams rang from the dock, some close, some distant, bouncing from a dozen directions. Hex motioned, and the three foremost guards turned on their flashlights. Cool yellow beams cut into the mist and highlighted circles across the containers.

They were a mosaic of colors: iron reds, dull grays, faded greens, and every shade of blue. Hex wove them between the stacks, focused on the dark-blue specimens, until the flashlights could pick up the logo on the side or the identification number painted on the corner. Two more streaks of motion came from behind them. Clare felt it before she heard it. She turned, hand moving toward the knife in her belt, but the guards reacted first. The closest hollow dropped, its head cleaved in two. The second one shied back, jaws working, a hissing, angry chatter bubbling out of it.

One of the guards switched her pose, moving her weapon-bearing arm behind herself and extending her nondominant hand. She pulled her sleeve back to expose a strip of skin. The hollow responded to the offer, lunging forward again. It made it to within a foot of her before being cleaved down beside its companion.

Clare released a held breath and pulled the scarf a little tighter around her throat. The group resumed moving. Hex held her weapon in one hand—a wickedly sharp cleaver—and a flashlight in the other. Each step saw the light swept across the floor, across the ceiling, and across the shipping containers in a smooth arc. It caught on dozens of round, glinting eyes. The hollows perched all around them, clinging to the walls and the metal bars supporting the roof.

They turned a corner, moving even deeper into the maze. The

containers were endless. They found one with the right logo but the wrong numbers. They moved onward. A hollow pushed his way out from a crevice, trying to slink toward the group without being seen. It was quickly dispatched. They moved on.

The claustrophobia was grinding on Clare. The damp air made her feel as though she were drowning. The narrow passageways, the muffled chattering that had haunted her nightmares, the grinding tension. She felt like she was ready to snap.

Then Hex pulled them to a halt. They had found another shipping container with the same logo. The lights danced over the number sequence. Clare sucked in a sharp breath. It ended in *4148*.

Hex waved two of the movers forward. The massive metal doors groaned painfully as they swung open. A gust of cold, stale air washed over them. The three flashlight beams intersected as they bobbed over the crate's contents. Drums, painted bright red and with silver lids, were stacked inside.

Hex turned back to them. She didn't speak, but her grin was all Clare needed to see. They had what they'd come for.

CHAPTER 18

THE GUARDS ADJUSTED THEMSELVES into a semicircle, allowing the movers inside the shipping container. Clare stepped forward with the others, hyperaware of Dorran's eyes on her as she passed inside. The metal drums came up to Clare's waist and were heavier than she was. She joined another woman in trying to pull one out. The barrel scraped against the metal floor. Clare grimaced at the noise. Some of the other movers were debating in quiet voices, trying to find the best way to shift the barrels.

Hex leaped inside the container, beckoning them together. "There's no way to do it silently. Just tip them over and roll them out."

Clare nodded, and with her companion, they pulled their barrel onto its side. Even with both of them trying to brace it, it created a horrific ringing noise as it hit the metal. More bangs came from around her as more barrels were tipped. The container shuddered with each one, jangling Clare's teeth and making her palms sweat. She tried to push the barrel on her own. It was too heavy. The woman who had helped her tip it bent at her side, shoving, and between the two of them, they rolled the barrel out of the container.

Hex lit a flare. Bright red, hissing sparks exploded out of its end as she tossed it onto the ground to mark the location. They moved back toward the outdoors area, through the maze of containers. The passageway was so narrow that they had to travel in pairs, each set bearing a barrel with a guard flanking them. Clare could no longer watch for threats. All of her attention had to be split between the barrel under her hands and the hunched shoulders of the movers ahead of her.

The barrels were hard to get moving, but once they began to roll, the challenge became keeping them under control. If the pair ahead of Clare began to slow down, she had to slap her hands on top of the barrel, simply trying to stop its momentum before it bowled into them. Direction changes were even worse. They had to grind to a halt and painstakingly twist the container to face the direction they wanted before beginning to push again.

Hex seemed to understand the challenges. There was no pressure to move faster. All she cared about was keeping them grouped together, which meant frequent stops to let the teams at the rear catch up.

The guards lashed out on either side with growing frequency. The muffled *whick* noise of a cleaved head or the *thwack* of a pierced skull floated through the fog like the beats of a deranged song. The increased noise was calling creatures out of every corner of the shipping yard, but Clare barely saw what they were fighting. All she had the focus for were the barrels and sporadic glances toward Dorran to make sure he was safe. Occasionally, she saw him strike at the creatures, efficient and steady, and pride bloomed through her.

Hex dropped flares at intervals to ward off the shier monsters. When Clare had to slow to a halt to allow teams behind to catch up, she threw a glance over her shoulder. A line of red and green lights marked the way back to the shipping container like a trail of Christmas bread crumbs.

The effort, not only of keeping the fuel containers rolling but also of slowing and adjusting their direction, left Clare panting. The briny air stuck to her face and painted strands of hair against her forehead. Then, up ahead, a blocky shape appeared through the fog. The truck.

A flash of metal pulled Clare's eye up. She could just barely make out Charlene, in position on top of her stack of containers, rifle ready in case it was needed. In the mist, she looked more shadow than human.

The truck's lights turned on as one of the guards opened the back shutter. A ramp hit the concrete, wide enough to accommodate the barrels. The first team tried to push theirs up the slope, but even with momentum, couldn't get it more than halfway up. The barrel surged back down, and voices muttered warnings as multiple hands came in to grind it back to a halt.

Hex beckoned them in. Her instructions were stage whispers.

"Movers, huddle close to the truck. Guards, perimeter. Jake, Dorran, Stephan, get these barrels up."

She had called on the three largest men. They clustered around the container and, together, worked it up the ramp in agonizing inches. Hex didn't seem bothered that it was slow to load. She simply faced the outside world, cleaver swinging in arcs at her side, eyes narrowed as she scanned the mist.

More hollows came for them. The guards moved quickly, cutting them down in one or two sharp blows before stepping back. The grind of barrels climbing the ramp rang on, and by the time the last one was thudded upright inside the truck, a pattern of dead hollows had been left in a semicircle around them.

The men jumped down from the truck, and Dorran moved to Clare's side. Perspiration and condensation mingled on his face, dripping off his nose and chin and washing away flecks of dark hollow blood.

"You okay?" Clare kept her voice to a whisper. "How's your arm?"

"Fine." He flexed it. "Took some painkillers earlier. They're helping."

Hex, still breathing heavily from the first trip, the face paint running off her cheeks, moved through the guards, asking each one individually, "Are you hurt?"

A series of *no*s and shaken heads answered her, and then she did the same with the movers, asking each of them if they were still fit to go on a second retrieval. They all were. Hex moved back to the front of the group. "All right. Let's go."

They formed the same pattern as the first trip. Clare clumped with the other movers, with Alden beside her. Dorran had arranged himself so he was the nearest guard to her right. Hex led, using hand signals instead of words. They followed the flare trail that had been left on the first journey.

Clare's clothes stuck to her back, heavy with sweat and condensation. Every exhale put out a cloud that blended into the mist. The flares highlighted her companions' faces in cycling colors: a glaze of red would pass across their features, then shadows returned, to be relieved by a wash of sickly green.

The attacks were more frequent. The noise and lights had attracted hollows from throughout the shipping yard. Most chose to bide their time, lurking in narrow crevices and looming over them from perches on the concrete building and container stacks. Their jaws would open as the group passed, hisses and barely audible chatters rising and dropping in waves. One or two would lunge forward at a time, overeager, quickly knocked down.

Then they were back in the sheltered area, the claustrophobic hallways painted in harsh, glowing shades. A hollow howled. Tapping fingers and scabbed feet pounded across the containers and metal walls. They turned the corner, faced their container. Hex held them back from entering, one hand raised as the flashlights turned to focus inside the container. Two hollows had crept inside while they were gone. The creatures, hairless, their jaws open in silent screams, scuttled out of the light. Four members of the guard team moved in first to dispatch them, then stepped back out to allow the movers in.

Clare held her breath as she approached one of the fuel drums. The dead hollows had been left where they fell, one of them with its skull cracked in half like an egg. Its fingers still twitched. She tried not to look at it as she helped a man overturn a barrel and roll it outside.

They made it back to the open concrete area, but this time, Clare had trouble keeping her focus on the barrel. Faces peered out from every shadowed area. Their eyes glittered, soulless, mindless, in the flares. There were hundreds, crammed into every area, climbing each other in their eagerness to watch the humans.

The guards were becoming twitchy. They had been in the shipping yard for nearly an hour. The constant alertness and energy required had to be wearing on them, like it was with Clare. A sense of nausea grew as she worked with her teammate to maneuver their barrel. The chattering swelled, almost chant-like, coming from every direction, near deafening.

Hex held her fist up. Clare struggled to drag her barrel to a halt, then lifted her head, breathing heavily. She thought they had to be midway between the shipping container and the truck.

They were encircled. Bony, twisted bodies blocked their path ahead. The nearest one reared its head back, a glob of saliva dripping onto the concrete, its body lit by the flares.

"*Defend*," Hex barked.

It was the loudest noise she'd made since arriving at the shipping yard. Clare blinked, her mind still fogged by the exertion and the stress.

Then her companion grabbed her arm and yanked her toward

Hex. She reached out for their barrel. It felt wrong to leave it behind, but then she saw that everyone else was abandoning their posts as well.

Defend. That's the command. We're about to be swarmed.

She stumbled forward, tripping over her own feet, but hands were on her back—Dorran's, she thought—pushing her into the group of movers clustered behind Hex.

The guards turned, backing up, creating a tight circle around them. Body heat radiated over her and damp breaths filled her ears as the guards stood shoulder-to-shoulder. Dorran was positioned immediately ahead of her, his back to her, his too-long hair framed by the flare's light.

They made their formation just in time. Hollows lurched forward. Not just one or two at a time now, but in the dozens. Long arms extended grasping hands toward them. Clare flinched as a spray of blood speckled her cheek. A limb dropped near her feet, still spasming.

The noise was horrific: screams, wails, noises of hunger and anger and boiling frustration. Wet hacking sounds split through the cries.

Clare felt for the knife at her side and drew it. Most of the other movers had their own weapons at the ready.

She couldn't see much of the fray, just the backs surrounding her. Flexing muscles, arms rising and falling as the hollows bobbed around them. Dorran had to be tired, but he fought with harsh precision. Efficient. Unyielding.

Blood began to run across the ground, seeping toward Clare's feet. She was too tightly packed to avoid it. Someone behind her seemed to be hyperventilating. The screams and howls grew louder. The claustrophobia was worse. An impulse to run hit Clare hard. She turned her head, looking for a way out, and her stomach lurched as she realized just how surrounded they were.

They were an island in a sea of hollows. Elongated limbs, skeletal heads, flashing eyes—they spread as far as Clare could see. There was nowhere to escape to. No way out.

"Hold your formation!" Hex yelled. She could barely be heard above the cacophony. Clare swallowed, damp hands clutching the knife.

She said it will pass. She said we just have to hold out long enough.

It felt like a lie. There were too many creatures surrounding them. Too many teeth. Not enough guards.

Something large moved through the crowd. At least ten feet tall, it loomed above the other hollows. Limbs swiveled in the low light. So many limbs. A human head perched on top of an expanded torso. Every few inches, a new pair of arms sprouted. Like some kind of deformed insect, each limb bearing three or four joints, snapping forward like a crab's claws, growing closer.

One of the guards near Clare fell. The many-armed thing had caught his ankle and dragged him down. He screamed as the hollows descended on him, teeth fastening over him.

"Reform the line!" Hex shouted. She stepped backward, out of her space among the guards, to join the movers. Clare felt a stab of something between anger and panic. Hex was retreating. She had lied. There was no way out.

But Hex didn't stay among the movers. She pushed around them, moving along the narrow gap between the movers and the guards to reach the place the man had fallen from. Then she lunged out, back into the fray.

Clare couldn't see what was happening. She could only hear it: Hex, gasping, the cleaver stabbing out again and again and again. The guards on either side shuffled forward, joining her, and a moment later, Hex was retreating into the protected circle. She bent double, dragging the fallen guard's body.

Hex dropped him among the movers, where he lay curled on the ground. He held his arms in a cross in front of his face, shaking, blood and fluids dripping over him. The armor on his arms and legs were in tatters.

Alden dragged his scarf off as he knelt at the man's side, examining him, and then pressed the fabric to a wound on his throat.

Clare wanted to help, but there was no room for her to reach him. The guard's circle had contracted with one of their number missing. She was being jostled in front and from behind.

"Watch out for the big one," Hex called. "He goes for your ankles."

The many-armed hollow had retreated a few paces. It moved through the swarm, its swollen jaw working, arms twitching erratically. Two of them had been turned into bleeding stumps. There were many more to replace them. It let its smaller brethren swarm forward while it waited, watching, looking for a weak spot along the line.

They can't keep this up.

The breathing around her had devolved to ragged gasps.

Dorran was starting to lose focus, his movements still sharp but his reactions growing delayed.

"Hold your positions!" Hex yelled.

The many-limbed one moved forward again. Arms shot out, aiming for the man to Dorran's left. He countered, only to have his wrist caught by another hand.

Dorran swiped out to cut his neighbor free. He severed through the hollow's arm, but three more hands had snaked out where he couldn't see them. They fastened on his scarf, his shoulder, and his head, dragging him forward, pulling him into the horde.

No. Clare moved before her mind could catch up. She darted into the gap Dorran had left, knife held at the ready, hunting for human skin among the thrashing sea of gray.

"Hold!" Hex's scream contained panic. The many-limbed creature hadn't stopped with Dorran. It had created a gap in the wall of guards and grabbed at individuals indiscriminately. Men and woman screamed as they were pulled to the ground, the circle picked apart, the movers exposed.

Clare didn't stop to watch. She was focused on the man ahead of her. Dorran struggled to right himself, thrashing under the weight of bodies and arms pinning him to the ground. He was exhausted. Disoriented.

Clare's knife sunk into clammy flesh. A smaller hollow had been scrabbling to get through Dorran's leg guard and turned to hiss at Clare. She pulled the knife out of its back and sliced through its eye. It twitched, then fell, sliding off Clare's blade as she turned the weapon on the next hollow.

They were at her back, clawing at her. She pressed forward to free Dorran, stabbing and slashing at every angle.

Cracking noises pierced the air. Hollows dropped as the snipers fired on them. Hex was yelling, trying to regain order, but the screams and frantic interjections drowned her out.

Clare cut into a hollow's head, stabbing through its temple, and struggled to get her knife free. Dorran grabbed her arm, his breath hot on her cheek. "Back. Back to the group."

She found his hand and pulled, dragging him with her. She couldn't see through the ocean of limbs. The chattering was at a deafening pitch, pierced by the pop of gunfire and the human screams.

A hand grabbed her leg. Clare kicked to free it, but it didn't let her go. Her whole world lurched as she was pulled off her feet. Her shoulder hit the ground, jarring her, clashing her teeth together, sparks of black running over her vision. The knife ricocheted out of her hand. She was being pulled up. Pain sparked along her leg as she was suspended from it, dangled upside down.

The many-armed hollow had her. She was held fifteen feet in the air, suspended over its head. The jaw made crackling noises as it dislocated, opening wide, and it began to lower Clare into its maw.

A popping noise. Clare didn't see the bullet enter the hollow's head, but she saw the aftermath. A spray of blood burst out from the side of its skull. The eyes swiveled, then turned glassy. The hand holding her became boneless, and suddenly she—and the many-limbed hollow—were plunging toward the concrete.

She had just enough time to lift her arms over her head in a futile attempt to shield herself. She waited for the impact, the burst of pain across her skull, the sensation of her head breaking open and her spine shattering. Instead, the impact came from her side. A blow that knocked her sideways, tumbling her, grabbing her all in the same motion.

A familiar smell. Large hands wrapping around her back and her head to shield her. *Dorran.*

They hit the ground hard, tumbling and rolling, the concrete scraping across Clare's shoulder. The pain was all superficial, though. No broken bones. She held on to Dorran as they came to a halt. He laid her back onto the ground, eyes wild as he pulled back far enough to see her. A shaking hand ran over her face, then her chest, checking her, searching for injuries. Then he looked up, and his lips pulled back from his teeth in a snarl. He pulled Clare back to his chest and lifted her. The motion shook her as he ran, pushing past the snatching, scratching hollow limbs. The guns continued to pop, harsh snapping noises cutting down the bodies surrounding them. Then they were at the circle. Guards parted to allow Dorran through. He knelt, placing Clare on the ground with the other movers.

The circle now held a half dozen casualties. They were being tended to, cloths tied around wounds, jackets draped over their torsos. Alden was among the injured, his cheeks white as a woman staunched a gash on his forearm.

"All right?" Dorran's voice was breathless and ragged. Clare wanted to ask him the same, but her own tongue refused to work. She just nodded. Dorran said, "I need a weapon."

Three of the movers held out their blades. He took the largest one, and before Clare could catch the breath to object, he'd turned back toward the hollows and rejoined the circle of guards.

Clare pressed a hand to her throat, willing herself not to be sick. Aches and stinging pains dotted her body from a myriad of scrapes. The adrenaline hit of following Dorran had been brutal, and as it faded, it left her shaking and clammy.

But the onslaught still continued.

Somehow, Hex had managed to reform the circle after the many-limbed creature had broken it. With members missing, they no longer stood shoulder to shoulder—but they continued to fight. And the horde was growing thinner, Clare thought. The snipers were working, cutting down bodies before they could even reach the guards. It no longer felt like they were being pressed in at all sides.

Then, the hollows began to balk. It was like watching a wave wash out. One hollow shied away, then the creatures surrounding it picked up on its reluctance and hesitated as well. They backed up. They screamed toward the sky, angry and hungry. And then they began to scatter. In the span of just fifteen seconds, the field was clear.

The guards were slow to lower their weapons. It felt almost too good to be true, as though it was some kind of trick. The overwhelming noise dropped to silence. The sniper rifles became quiet.

Hex moved first, tucking her machete into her belt. She was painted red, the liquid matting her hair and saturating her clothes. She didn't seem to notice the dark blood dripping across her teeth as she smiled. "That's it. We're out of the woods."

CHAPTER 19

THE GUARDS RELAXED. SOME collapsed to the ground, shaking. Others went to their friends who had been injured. Dorran dropped to his knees beside Clare.

"You're all right?" he asked again.

"I'm good." She stroked her fingers through his wet hair, pushing it back from his face. "Were you hurt?"

"No." He sighed, shoulders slumping. His dark eyes continued to search hers, as though he was afraid that she would disappear if he looked away. "Thank heaven. You should have stayed at the safe haven."

She chuckled. Then she pictured what might have been if she hadn't joined the movers. Dorran, dragged into the swarm. No one to follow him. No one to get him out. Nausea reared again, and she lurched to the side.

"Oh, shh, shh, you're okay." Dorran caught her, bracing her

against his side as he rubbed her back. His shirt was sticky with gore. The smell was thick, overpowering, but there was no getting away from it. It surrounded them, the pool of blood stretching out from the scene for meters. What looked like a barricade of bodies had built up around the outside of the circle. It had formed as wave after wave of hollows piled on top of each other as they died.

"Time to go," Hex said. Her voice had returned to barely more than a whisper. She paced through the group, examining each party in turn. "If you can't walk, someone will help you. Movers, return to your barrels. Guards, look for an injured party to assist, or an unattended barrel to push."

Clare stared at her. *After all of that, we're expected to pick up right where we left off?*

"Yep," Hex said, speaking as though she'd heard Clare's thoughts. The response was directed at half of the group, though, who all stared at her incredulously. "We went through that to *get* this fuel. And the hollows spent all of their energy on that swarm. We'll have a few moments of peace, and we should take advantage of it."

She paused, and when the people crouched on the ground looked reluctant to move, she glared at them. "Don't forget who this is for. Most of you have kids back at West Hope—either your own, or ones you take care of. They *need* this fuel. Each barrel we bring back buys them another few days of safety. Don't try to tell me it's not worth it."

People started moving. Clare nodded to Dorran, telling him it was okay to let her go, then pulled herself to her feet alongside them. Aches ran across her body from a dozen origins, and her ankle, twisted, stung every time she put pressure on it. But she returned to her barrel, a forlorn shape that had been left outside the circle and was now splattered with hollow blood. She put her hands on it and began pushing.

Her partner was among the injured. Clare could see him ahead, one arm looped around a guard's shoulders as he limped toward the bus. Dorran carried another injured guard. That left her alone to push, so she put her head down and dug for any energy reserves she had left. The barrel stuck to the gore as it rolled, near-black liquid dripping off of it as it trundled between the bodies. Clare passed the many-limbed creature, collapsed into a pile, its jaw still stretched open as though waiting for Clare to climb into it.

There was one easier part about the second stretch of the trip, though. The formation had been loosened. Guards still flanked the movers, but they were spaced wide apart, and no attacks came. That meant Clare no longer had to stop her barrel's momentum to let others catch up. Once it started rolling, she just had to give it extra shoves to keep it moving.

They reached the bus in straggled groups. Hex unbolted the shutter and lowered the ramp. This time, she didn't delegate the job of shifting barrels into the truck, but four individuals stepped forward regardless. Clare sat on the ground, forearms resting on knees pulled up ahead of herself as she watched. All in the group were filthy. Through the haze of stress and shock, she still had space to think about how badly the bus's upholstery would be ruined.

The final barrel slammed into the truck, then the loaders stepped out, breathing hard. Hex gave them a tight smile, then turned to survey the team.

"We have a choice. And for once, I'm letting you guys make the decision. We can either get into the bus and go home right now, or head back out there for a final raid."

A few scoffing laughs echoed from the group, and Hex raised her hand.

"Hear me out on this. Any hollows that wanted a bite of us made their move during the swarm, and they're pretty much all dead now. If we make a final trip, our path will be largely clear. Just a few stragglers, if that." She patted the bus's side. "And one more trip would be enough to get the last of the barrels. That buys us extra time before we have to make another raid."

The participants glanced among each other. No one laughed anymore.

"But." Hex took a deep breath, and let it out. "That was brutal. So if you guys just want to go home, yeah, we can go home. It's your call. Raise of hands for people who are ready to leave."

A few hands twitched, but none were lifted.

Hex nodded. "And a raise of hands for anyone who is ready to go get the final batch."

This time, most of the group responded. Clare looked to Dorran, and he met her eyes, and she saw her own question reflected back at her. She gave a shaky smile, and they both raised their hands.

A faint glow of pride lit up Hex's face. She nodded. "All right, then that's what we'll do. Anyone who's injured is staying in the bus. And anyone who doesn't feel physically capable can sit with them. Let's get them inside first."

Out of the six injured parties, four of them were deemed too far gone to participate in the final raid. They were helped onto the bus, arranged into seats near the back with blankets and cushions to keep them comfortable, and given strong painkillers and bottles of water. Alden was among them, a scarf wrapped tightly around a gash on his forearm. He gave Clare a thin smile as she passed him.

As she tried to step out of the bus, Hex held out a finger to stop her. "You're staying."

"Huh?" Dorran had been following her, and Clare looked up at him for support. "I'm not hurt. I'm good for a final trip."

"No, no you're not." Hex raised her eyebrows, an expression that didn't welcome argument. "You're limping. Don't think I didn't notice. That makes you a liability."

"It's not bad," she lied. It ached, but at least she could still walk.

"On top of that, you disobeyed the golden rule. You broke formation."

"Yeah, because that freakish armed thing broke our formation first."

Hex looked as though she was trying not to laugh. "And if it were on our team, it would have been put on time-out as well. I laid out my terms before this started: break any of the three golden rules, you're out of the raid. No exceptions. Now sit down and chill. We'll be back soon enough."

Clare looked back at Dorran, begging him to take her side. He bit his lip, half-apologetic, half-relieved. "I'll be back soon."

"Traitor," Clare grumbled.

He kissed her cheek as he stepped past her. "Be good. Drink water. Try to sleep if you can."

Clare sighed as he stepped back out onto the concrete lot. Mist swirled around the group as it shifted back into its formation, guards ringing the movers. The shape was a little more wonky than it had been on the first journey. Exhaustion weighed them all down.

Hex had promised this final trip would be safer. That the seemingly endless hollows had been conquered. But Clare still felt the squeeze of anxiety at seeing Dorran go. Nothing was guaranteed in the silent world, especially not safety.

I called him a traitor. A sudden rush of fear squeezed itself through Clare's insides, turning her mouth dry. *What kind of goodbye is that? What if that's the last thing he ever hears me say?*

She pushed the bus door open, leaning through the gap into the mist-choked air, and called in a stage whisper, "Dorran! I love you!"

A smile lit his face as he turned. He pressed his hand to his heart, then extended it out toward her. She had his love in return.

"Aww," a voice drawled. "How sweet."

Clare jolted. She'd almost forgotten about Marc. The bronze-tanned, blond-haired man lounged in a seat near the front of the bus. Unlike the rest of them, he was unsullied by that day's journey. Clare was coated in drying sweat, hollow blood, and grime. Every time she moved she felt how gritty her skin was. By comparison, Marc was pristine, a leather jacket casually draped over his back, his high cheekbones and too-blond hair almost glowing.

She closed the door a little more sharply than she intended and cleared her throat. "It's been a rough couple of hours."

"It looks like it." One eyebrow quirked as he glanced her up and down. "Not so cute anymore, are you?"

Jerk. Clare turned away, intending to join her four teammates at the back of the bus.

"Hey, hey," Marc called, laughter in his voice. "Come back. I was just joking."

"I'm not in the mood."

Marc turned himself around to rest one elbow over the back of the seat. His grin was lopsided. "I just want to know how the raid went. Did you guys get enough fuel?"

"Yeah." She paused partway down the bus, one hand resting on the back of a seat. "They're making one last trip."

"Ah, I was wondering. So they'll be done soon."

How can he be so impatient when he's got the cushiest position out of all of us? Clare sank into the seat opposite Alden. The man's drooping face twitched into a thin smile. He looked dazed, probably a mix of shock and medication, Clare thought. He held the injured arm close to his chest and leaned at an angle, back toward the window, head propped up on a cushion. Clare didn't expect him to stay awake for long.

Marc stared out of the window for a moment, then stood and

stretched. Clare narrowed her eyes at him as he approached the bus's door. "What are you doing?"

"I need a bathroom break." He waved her away. "Don't worry your head about it."

"We're not supposed to open the door. Hex said—"

"Are you really listening to *her*?" Marc chuckled again. "She's a kid. Chill. I know how to handle hollows if any pop up."

The door clattered as it opened, and a moment later, Marc had disappeared into the fog, slamming the door behind himself.

Clare sighed and reclined back in her seat. Her companions were all quiet, sinking into the painless sleep that the drugs afforded them. The atmosphere in the bus had improved vastly with Marc leaving, but she still felt frustrated at his disregard for all of their safety. Even if the hollows had been weeded out by the swarm, having a human meandering around alone was still likely to draw them in. Clare had earned herself a time-out for a less idiotic infraction.

She closed her eyes and tried to relax. Her thoughts turned to Dorran. She hoped he was keeping safe. That he wasn't too hampered by tiredness and scrapes.

All of this for fuel. Who would have thought it would end up being valuable enough to trade lives for?

Clare's eyes popped open. Something hadn't been sitting easily with her, and now, the anxiety coalesced like a slime on her tongue. Marc had come as a guide, even though the convoy had no trouble finding or accessing the shipping grounds. He had specifically asked where the keys were kept during the raids. And his only questions to Clare had been whether the team was on their final trip and whether they had retrieved much fuel.

They had—enough to make a man very wealthy in the new world.

Clare bolted out of her seat as an engine rumbled. She threw the door open and stared into the fog. The truck's headlights cut through the shadows. A silhouetted figure poised in the driver's seat, leaning forward, focused.

No. He can't. He can't!

Clare's mouth was dry, her fingers turning numb. Her companions on the bus were all drugged. Even if she could call the rest of the team back, Marc would be gone before they could reach the bus. She could run to the truck, but he would have locked the doors. She turned, looking along the route he would need to follow. A narrow gate allowed exit from the yard. *If I can block it, I can trap him…*

She could run in front of the truck, arms outstretched, and block him with her body…and risk being run over. Marc did not strike her as a compassionate person.

But the machinery and debris scattered around the shipping yard would be too heavy to move. The truck's engine changed as it was put into gear. Clare's eyes landed on the bus's driver seat.

Yes. Yes, that would work.

She leaped for the padded chair. The keys were in the ignition, as Hex had said they would be. She wrenched them, throwing the bus into drive and hitting the accelerator. Wheels screeched. The bus lurched forward, and one of the injured in the rear seats grunted.

Marc had a head start, but Clare was closer to the gates. She barreled forward, reckless, turning the wheel to plant the bus in front of the exit. The truck's brakes screamed. Headlights flashed in her face, and Clare raised her hand to shield her eyes.

The impact jarred her. She doubled over, preparing for the stab of metal and glass, but none came.

She looked around her fingers. The truck had hit the bus hard enough to scrape it sideways and crack the driver's side window, but its brakes had saved Clare from any more serious damage.

Just outside the driver's side window, feet away from her, Marc sat stiffly in the truck's cab, white-knuckled hands clutching the wheel. A refracted glow from his headlights pulled out unnatural contours on his face. His teeth peeled back into a grimace, then he switched the bus into reverse.

Is there another exit? Clare couldn't see one, but the fog swallowed her view. The truck reversed far enough to detangle the two vehicles, then Marc threw open his door and leaped out. Feet crunched on the grimy asphalt. He was coming toward her.

Locks. Locks!

Clare felt across the dashboard, heart hammering. The controls were unfamiliar, and the truck's headlights bathed her, blinding her. The bus's door was wrenched open. Marc pulled himself on board.

"What the *hell* do you think you're doing?" A fleck of spittle hit his lower jaw.

The weapons were in the baskets above the seats, out of reach. Marc was blocking the door. The injured in the back of the bus stirred, disoriented and sluggish.

Clare did the only thing she could think of. She pressed the horn, leaning on it, the noise blaring across the frosty shipping yard.

Pain spiked across her head. Marc's fingers caught a fistful of her hair, dragging her out of her seat. She gasped as she hit the bus floor. Her legs scrambled for purchase as she tried to right herself. A fist hit her stomach, starving her of air and making her curl over.

Marc didn't stop. He dragged her by her hair to the door and hauled her out, her thighs hitting the steps, then he threw her onto the concrete.

Clare rolled over. She couldn't breathe, could barely think, but she knew she couldn't let him get back onto the bus. She threw out a hand and snagged Marc's pant leg, pulling him back. He stumbled, then kicked her, leaving a vicious red boot imprint on her forearm. Then he leaped up the step. The door slammed. A second later, the engine roared.

Clare struggled to breathe. Footsteps pounded in the distance. The bus reversed, pulling away to clear the gate. The tires ground close to Clare, and she scrambled back to avoid them. Hex's voice called, unintelligible. They were still too far away.

Marc had heard them, though. Clare could see him leaning over the dashboard, peering through the windshield. Perspiration sparkled in his frosty hair. His teeth ground as he glanced from the truck to the road ahead.

He didn't have enough time to exit the bus and climb back into the truck. But the road ahead was clear. He could take the bus and escape with his life.

The engine roared and the wheels screeched as he turned toward freedom. Then the bus jolted and ground to a halt. Clare staggered to her feet and, through the window, saw Alden grappling with Marc. He'd engaged the emergency brake. One arm was looped around Marc's throat, trying to drag him out of the driver's seat.

But Alden was drugged. Injured. Tired. And Marc's fist connected with his stomach and ribs again and again, until Alden crumpled to the floor.

"What in the hell?" Hex called, no longer trying to keep it to a stage whisper.

A crack pierced the cold air. Clare flinched. The engine's revs fell to silent. A hole had appeared in the windshield, tiny spiderweb cracks spiraling out from it. Marc sat stiffly in the driver's seat, eyes wide as they stared in shock at the wheel. The driver's side window had been painted red, and a thin line of blood ran down from a tiny, discreet hole in his temple.

Hex stumbled to a halt beside Clare, panting. She repeated her question, this time in tones of stunned resignation. "Oh, what in the *hell*."

CHAPTER 20

CLARE LAY ON ONE of the bus seats with a jacket draped over her body, her head in Dorran's lap. He stroked her hair tenderly, seemingly unbothered by the grime. His other hand rested on her shoulder, just firm enough that Clare knew he still hadn't fully relaxed. She'd been offered painkillers. She'd refused them; she still didn't feel safe enough to fall into a daze.

They were waiting for the last few barrels of fuel to be loaded on the truck. Dorran hadn't volunteered to help, and no one had asked him to. They understood that he needed to be close to Clare.

Alden had been laid in the aisle, with a blanket draped over him as he breathed in raspy gulps of air. To Clare's right, Charlene, one of the snipers, had curled herself toward the window, facing away from the rest of them. Her counterpart, Bill, sat with one hand simply resting on her shoulder. She'd seemed to be in shock at first, repeating the same phrase: "I shot him. I shot him." A pause, and then again, unbelieving, "I didn't know what else to do. I shot him."

Now, she faced away from them as she cried. Clare wondered if Marc was the first human she had killed. She'd felt the same effect in Mother Gum's slaughter shed, when she'd sunk her blade into one of the youths' thighs. Real blood running, real muscle tearing, a human's screams—it was so different from fighting hollows. A new level of barbaric.

Hex had told Charlene that she did the right thing. That she had saved Alden and the other injured in the back of the bus. Charlene had simply shaken her head, repeating with dull grief, "I *shot* him."

The movers had been told to wait in the bus while the remaining guards loaded the barrels. Cushions, jackets, and spare blankets had been brought in to make them comfortable. The driver's side window and dashboard had been wiped off with a scarf, though the smell still lingered. Clare did not envy the bus's driver, tasked with sitting in a seat still warm from a dead man.

Marc's body had been wrapped in a blanket and moved into the back of the truck, where he was tucked between the barrels of fuel he'd lost his life for. Hex had insisted on bringing his body back. *We bury people. We don't leave them to get eaten by hollows. It doesn't matter what they did in life. Someday in the future, a mother or a nephew or a grandchild might want to visit his grave. So we bury him.*

They couldn't do the same for the three other souls who had

been lost during the swarm. During the last trip to retrieve fuel, Hex had looked for any remaining traces of them, but there was no life in among the piles of dead creatures. The hollows were beginning to creep back in, emboldened by the noise.

There were injuries—almost none of the guards had gotten away without tears in their armor, and many of the movers were scraped, bitten, and bruised as well. But the circular defensive formation had worked. Even when it broke, when the many-armed creature had torn one side out, it had done enough to hold them together until they could regroup.

And, in return, they had the fuel. A lot of it. The barrels made thumping noises as they were piled into the truck. The shutter rattled as it was closed, and Clare raised her head to watch the remaining men and women climb onto the bus.

Hex boarded last, shutting the door behind her. Instead of walking around Alden, like the others had, she sat beside his head and tossed the hatchet aside. She settled, cross-legged, then gazed across the rows of volunteers. "I'm proud of you all."

Her voice was weary, and her face was still streaked with drying blood. Very little light made its way through the cloud cover, but Clare could still see the dragging tiredness on all of their expressions.

"That was a tough raid," Hex continued. "Maybe the worst I've seen so far. But we got through it. I know everyone back at West Hope will want to thank you, but I'm going to extend my own thanks now. You guys did great. All of you."

Murmured words echoed back through the truck. Clare

smiled. Dorran's fingers felt nice on her sore scalp. She didn't need to be fussed over, but he refused to let her up, and Clare wasn't going to argue. She felt safe there, close to Dorran, her tension being brushed away with careful, steady caresses, her bruises and cuts temporarily forgotten.

"Let's go home, yeah?" Hex nodded to the driver. The engine came to life, and the headlights washed over the foggy shipping yard. Hex looked down at Alden, then gave his shiny forehead a pat. "You nearly got yourself killed back there, idiot."

He managed a broken chuckle. "No…you…you're the idiot. Ugh. I can do better than that."

"Yeah, not really at the peak of your game, are you? I'll give you a deferment. You can insult me properly when we're back home."

Brakes screamed. The bus, barely outside the shipping yard's gate, shuddered to a halt, and Hex's head snapped up. "Talk to me."

"It's back." The driver's face had turned pale. His eyes, wide and glazed, stared into the distance. Clare pulled herself up to get a clearer view of the windshield, and her heart missed a beat.

Enormous, towering legs drifted through the mist. The creature, its body suspended so high that it vanished into the gloom, traveled toward them with ponderous intensity, each step moving it closer, faster than they could drive, faster than they could outrun.

"Lights!" Hex hissed. The driver turned the engine off and the bus's insides descended into shadows. Dorran's hands ached as he held Clare's shoulder. She could scarcely breathe. Every face inside the bus was turned toward the monster, taller than the cranes in the shipping yard, as it paced closer, bearing down on them.

We can't run. We can't stay here. A drop of gritty sweat ran into Clare's eyes, but she didn't dare blink. Hex remained crouched on the bus floor, her tense expression only just visible in the gloom, one hand poised in the air as a signal for silence. She was hoping they could go unnoticed if they held still. Clare wished she could believe that would work. The monster was upon them.

One of its immense legs stabbed into the concrete less than ten meters ahead of them. Cracks ran through the ground as the sharpened tip pierced it. The leg traveled up, disappearing into the fog and the gloom. Another limb drifted forward, swooping toward them, its tip just barely traveling over the bus's roof. Clare turned. Through the back window she saw the limb stab down behind them, just inside the shipping yard's bounds.

The monster's body had to be suspended directly above them. Not a soul in the bus moved. Dorran's hold on Clare was tighter, crushing.

The leg ahead of them quivered, then rose, skimming over the bus's top, inches away from clipping them. The monster was continuing on, pacing into the shipping yard.

Why? It must have seen us. It could have easily broken into the bus. Why did it spare us?

An awful noise rose from the fog behind them. Crunching, chewing noises. The sounds were muffled but unmistakable. Clare closed her eyes.

That's why. We're nothing compared to the feast we created.

The piles of dead hollows, stacked high and drenched in blood, was almost like an offering to the towering monster.

Clare could barely make out shapes through the briny fog. Long, pole-like limbs were spread wide as the malformed, many-mouthed body dipped down to eat.

"Go," Hex whispered. "No lights. Keep the engine quiet. But *go.*"

The bus's engine purred to life. The distant creature's body rose into the air, and Clare thought she saw shapes drop from its mouths—arms and legs, tumbling back to the concrete below. It stared at them for a beat, then the head descended again, intent on the easier meal.

They crept forward, slowly at first, navigating with painstaking care through the gloom. As they gained distance from the shipping yard, the bus gradually picked up speed, until they were back on the winding rural roads and Hex deemed it safe enough to turn the headlights back on.

CHAPTER 21

CLARE WAS HALF-ASLEEP BY the time they arrived back at West Hope. Her first clue that they were home was the horizon growing lighter, even though they were slipping into night.

Bodies hit the bus's sides as they neared their home. Hungry creatures, desperate creatures, frustrated into a futile attempt to reach their food. It was over within a moment. The lights surrounded them, and the bus began creeping over speed bumps as they approached the safe haven's entry.

"There'll be hot showers tonight," Hex said. "You deserve them. But the regular cold ones are available for anyone who can't wait for the water to boil. If you're hurt, join us in the meeting room to get patched up. Then get some rest. I'll recruit some fresh blood to unload the fuel."

Clare was one of the bodies who couldn't wait for the warm water. She showered in the cold downpour, scrubbing and scrubbing to cleanse herself. Dorran had her sit in the center court, near one of the foot heaters that had been set up, while he brushed the tangles out of her hair. He took painstaking care not to pull, but her scalp still ached from where Marc had dragged her out of the bus.

Night had fallen by the time they were both washed, dressed in clean clothes, and full of that night's stew. They returned to the meeting room. This time, only John and Patty were present. As John indicated for them to take a seat, he explained that Alden was in the medical bay sleeping off the medication, and Hex was trying to tie off the last details of the raid before she let herself rest.

"You did good out there," John said, leaning back in his chair with a weary sigh. Patty hovered around them, bringing Clare and Dorran mugs of coffee and patting John's shoulder each time she went by. Clare knew how she must feel. It couldn't have been easy to spend a day wondering if her husband was coming home.

"Yesterday, you wondered why Hex was on the council." John paused to sip his coffee. "I bet you have a pretty solid idea why now. We found Hex during an early raid for supplies. She was trapped inside the store she had once worked at. She'd defended it. Spikes in the windows, barricades over the doors. She'd made Molotov cocktails and attached broken bottles to broom handles to make spears. And when the hollows began to come through the roof, she had fought them off, nearly constantly, for two days straight. Backed into a corner and with no way out, the streets around her teeming with the creatures, she had stood her ground and just kept striking them down whenever they got close. I have never seen such grit before. And I figured, if someone can survive that, they must be able to survive almost anything."

"She helped fortify West Hope," Patty added. "She found all of the nooks and ventilation systems that the hollows might be able to get in through. Plus, the raids she runs have the highest survival rates out of any of the nearby safe havens."

"I talked to Hex, and she agreed," John continued. "We're giving you both an equal payment of what the other volunteers receive. Higher rates for guards, since they shoulder most of the risks. You'll get it in credits, which is what we're using now that money is worthless. You can spend that however you want. We have official guidelines for what everything costs according to supply and demand. I know you're keen to get some fuel, but we can sell you other things, including weapons, batteries, spare parts for your vehicle, or an extra night of accommodation if you want to wait until morning to leave."

Dorran glanced at Clare. "How much is the extra night?"

"It's two credits each, and includes food and showers. Here." John pushed a sheet toward them. On it, a list of items had been painstakingly printed, with the prices scribbled out and rewritten multiple times. "Between the two of you, you have eighty-five credits."

Clare and Dorran sat with shoulders bumping as they pored over the list and attempted to divide their credits carefully. It wasn't a simple task; the family at Mother Gum's Nest had taken most of their necessities.

"We're only a day from home, so we won't need a huge amount of fuel," Dorran said. "We should stock up on food, though. We'll have at least three weeks before anything in the garden will be ready for harvesting."

"We could scavenge for food on the road," Clare noted.

"True, but it would be safer to buy it here."

"Mm. But at least we have practice getting food out of houses. Finding fuel will be much harder; any obvious sources will have already been raided. Plus, we need fuel to keep the garden's lights running. We can't do without it."

Dorran chewed that over. "True. We'll focus on fuel, then."

The liquid was expensive. Purchasing enough to fuel the minibus and keep their garden's lights running used up nearly all of their credits. They spent the rest on shelf-stable food, with a focus on items they couldn't grow themselves, like meats and grains.

John was patient as they worked and reworked their budget, and when they were done, he double-checked their numbers and shook their hands. "I'll have someone help load your vehicle."

Clare stretched, yawning, as she tried to work some stiffness out of the muscles in her back.

"You look tired," Dorran murmured.

"Honestly, I think I'm just lazy. I've had more sleep than you, so I'll take the first shift driving tonight."

"Or…" He looked back at their list of purchases, thoughtful. "Let's stay here for the night. It's only four credits."

The idea was dearly tempting. Clare bit her lip. "I feel like those four credits are better spent on other things."

"If breakfast is included, we're scarcely worse off." Dorran smiled at her, warm and gentle. "We have already taken too many risks in the last few days. It would be nice to begin the last stretch of our journey in the morning, when it's safest."

"I can't argue with that." Clare grinned. "And it beats loading the bus in the middle of the night."

Clare slept more heavily than she had in a long while. No dreams troubled her. She and Dorran were surprisingly comfortable in the storeroom bed, an excess of loaned blankets keeping them warm, and when Clare finally stirred, she knew she'd overslept. Dorran was already awake, lying at her side, watching her sleepily. Clare rolled over to face him. "Hey."

"Hmm." His fingertips traced across her arm.

"Have you been up for long?"

"Not long."

Clare narrowed her eyes at him. She was starting to get good at telling when he was lying. Dorran grinned in return, and within a moment, they were both chuckling. Clare wasn't even sure why. It was like some euphoria had been released after the tension from the previous day, and once she started laughing, she couldn't stop.

"What time is it?" she asked, finally subsiding.

"If I trust the clock on that wall, eleven."

"*Eleven?*" She sat up and brushed her fingers through her hair to get it back in some kind of order. "I've gone and wasted half the day."

"You needed to rest. If it makes you feel any better, West Hope runs on a flexible time schedule. Some people would consider this very early morning."

Clare snorted. Dorran still lay in bed, one arm behind his head, his beautiful eyes full of contentment and his smile freely shared. Clare thought she could spend the rest of the day there, just soaking in his happiness and enjoying his company. But the road wouldn't get any shorter. She patted his chest and rolled out of bed. "We'd better get some breakfast before we leave. And…"

"Hmm?" Dorran caught her hesitation.

Clare cleared her throat. "It's just something I've been thinking. We're expecting the Evandale institute will activate the code and end the stillness. But we don't know when that will happen or if the code will even work. The fuel we got yesterday will keep West Hope's lights on for a few more weeks, but then they'll need to look for more. And it's getting harder to find. And eventually there won't be enough, and the lights will have to be shut off, and West Hope will be forced to find a new location."

Dorran rose gracefully and encircled one arm around Clare's waist. "I think I know what you're thinking."

They discussed it while brushing their teeth, approaching the issue from every angle and making sure they weren't about to do something they might regret. By the time they found John in the meeting room, Dorran held a small slip of paper in his hand. He passed it to John.

"If West Hope needs a new base to settle in, this is an option." Dorran cleared his throat while John examined the directions to Winterbourne. "The building is large enough for everyone currently staying here. It has a garden that will need to be expanded to handle a larger load, but if you bring food with you, that will buy us time to increase production. It is largely fortified against hollows and has an internal heating system. It is a day's travel away. Currently, only Clare and I will be staying there, but if you become desperate, it is an option."

John's gray mane of hair rustled as he shook his head. His lower lip poked out, a thoughtful expression, and he sounded touched as he said, "I appreciate this. I really do."

Dorran dipped his head. "And, please, one final thing. Keep that private. Don't give the directions to anyone else. It is only for you and the people at West Hope if your situation becomes dire."

"Understood." John tucked the paper into his breast pocket. "You take care out there, both of you. Safe driving."

They had their last meal at West Hope before stepping outside. The ubiquitous fog was still present, but the day was warmer and brighter than normal, and several of the parking lot lights had been shut off, as they were no longer needed. The air tasted crisp and fresh, and Clare stretched her back, appreciating the touch of sun on her skin.

Their supplies had been set aside for them in a loading bay. Two men helped Dorran and Clare cart it to their bus: canisters of fuel, boxes of food, a new first aid kit, and a radio. Clare refueled the bus while their supplies were stacked inside, and by the time she stepped back and realized there was nothing else to be done, she'd already started to miss West Hope. It was rougher than Evandale had been, with fewer comforts—a frontier settlement that welcomed strangers with a healthy dose of caution. But even that was something special in the silent world. There weren't many survivors that would take strangers into their midst at all, let alone share their food and safety with anyone who passed by. In the silent world, that translated to an awful lot of kindness.

"Ready?" Dorran asked. He stood on the bus's front step, one hand braced on the door, watching Clare as she watched West Hope. She nodded. As she moved to climb into the vehicle, a call halted her.

"Hey!" Hex's voice was unmistakable. Her boots pounded over the asphalt, her blue hair flashing in the light. She looked oddly different without the face paint, but she'd ringed her eyes in black liner to compensate. She slowed to a trot as she neared them. "Don't think you're leaving without saying goodbye."

Clare laughed. "Sorry. I asked John, but you were busy with the aftermath of the raid and probably exhausted as well—"

"Damn straight. But I wanted to thank you." She lifted her chin to fix them both with a piercing stare. "I chewed you out, Clare, for breaking formation—which I'm not forgiving, by the way—but then you did us a real solid by stopping Marc."

Clare shrugged, feeling awkward. "Anyone else would have done the same."

"Nah. Not everyone." Hex tilted her head. "There's one other reason I wanted to catch you before you left. You've been inside the witch's compound. Not many people can say the same. I put it to the council again, and as expected, they rejected my proposal to take down the cult. But, well, I earned some fuel with last night's raid, and me and a few friends were talking about going for a drive. And I wanted to make sure we knew exactly what the compound looked like, so that we can avoid it if we run into it on accident."

"Oh," Clare said, as realization drew over her. She bit her lip. "Do you have a pen and paper?"

The three of them huddled around the bus, a piece of paper held against the plywood covering as Clare and Dorran drew Mother Gum's compound from memory.

"As far as I can tell, she lives in this house," Clare said, tapping on a box shape. "But the rest of her followers seem to gather in a larger hall here. They kept the stolen cars in a cluster here."

Hex worked her jaw. "Were there any other ways in or out of the compound?"

"There might be, but we only saw the main gate."

"Huh. Hypothetically, if someone mistakenly threw some flaming bottles of fuel over the wall, what do you think their chances would be of catching those buildings on fire?"

Clare and Dorran raised their eyebrows at each other. "Pretty high," Clare said. "The buildings are made of wood, and there is a lot of flammable debris around."

"Well, let's hope that doesn't happen." Hex took the paper, folded it, and tucked it into her pocket. "It would be a shame to make those nice folks run out of their establishment, especially if there was someone waiting outside to jam their gate open. There'd be no way to protect against the hollows then."

"Be careful," Dorran said. "She has a lot of followers."

Hex waved him away. "I'm not actually planning to *go* there. This is all hypothetical, remember? Now, you two better scram, unless you want to pay for an extra night."

"All right." Clare chuckled. "Good luck, Hex."

Hex raised a hand in goodbye as she turned back to West Hope's reinforced glass doors. "Have a safe trip, you two. And hit me up if you're in the mood for another raid. I can always do with more guards."

Clare climbed into the bus. The door slid closed behind her, a gentle mechanical noise that blocked out the distant sounds emanating from the shopping center. Dorran fit the key into the ignition and waited for her nod before starting the engine.

Loose gravel crunched under the wheels. *Their* wheels. They had fought hard for the right to keep their bus and their agency, and despite the bruises forming across Clare's body, she didn't regret it.

They slipped through a gap in West Hope's temporary fence. The hollows outside the boundary attacked them just like they had attacked the convoy the day before, slamming fists onto the doors and scrabbling at the walls, but Dorran just increased their speed until they were weaving through the streets that led out of the town. West Hope's lights took a long time to disappear, fading gradually until the buildings blocked them from sight. Clare turned her eyes forward. Toward Winterbourne.

CHAPTER 22

CLARE HELD THE MAP in her lap as she pored over the pages. "As long as there are no obstacles, we should reach home just before sundown."

"That's good news." Dorran adjusted the visor to keep the sun out of his eyes. "Home isn't quite *safe*, but it still feels more secure than the road."

"Exactly. Though, it's been so long since we left Winterbourne that I've started to forget what it looks like."

"Imagine something between a vampire's palace and a dungeon," Dorran said, pulling laughter from Clare.

"It will be nice to build toward something, though." Securing the hallways, reviving the garden, and turning Winterbourne into their own personal fortress—it would take work, probably more than Clare felt prepared for, but she knew it would be rewarding. She'd spent the previous weeks relying on others' protection: Beth's bus, Evandale's bunker, West Hope's fortifications. It would feel good to have something of her own.

"We should try to find some food before we arrive at Winterbourne." Dorran's eyes flicked to the rearview mirror, which was angled to see the bus's insides. They had stacked their purchased food in the overhead baskets. It seemed horribly scant compared to the stores Beth had accumulated, but it would be enough for at least a few days. Clare knew what he meant, though. Once they were at Winterbourne, they would need long-life food to last them until they could get the garden producing again.

"I know the area," Clare said. "The towns around here are all small. They shouldn't be overrun like the cities were, but they still won't be empty."

"Do you have any ideas?"

Clare chewed on the corner of her thumbnail. Her house was only a few hours away. There were several small shopping malls nearby, but those would have been cleared out by scavengers already. Their best chance probably lay in raiding houses, as she and Beth had. "Maybe...maybe...Holgate? It has wide streets."

"That sounds good," Dorran said. "Tell me where to go."

"Follow this road for a while." Clare pulled one leg up underneath herself as the bus rattled over a pothole. "Holgate is one of the poshest suburbs around here. It's funny; I used to be grateful I didn't live there. All of those big houses with their manicured gardens, every one trying their hardest to conform, to be as expensive as possible without being *garishly* expensive."

Dorran chuckled. "I can't imagine you living somewhere like that."

"No. I lived in a cheap area, where none of the buildings matched and people grew gardens in their front yards." She grinned. "And I loved it. There was such a sense of community. Twice a year, the family a few houses down from me would have a street party. They would bring their barbecue out and cook sausages for everyone who stopped by. The people across the road brought their home-brewed ginger ale. I loved it."

Her smile fell. It made her uncomfortable to realize that she would never attend another one of those street parties…and to think about what had likely happened to her neighbors.

Dorran reached across the aisle and squeezed her hand. "Community will be important in the new world. They will need people like you, who value it."

Her throat didn't want to work, so she squeezed back to show her gratitude.

They were leaving the bare, rural roads, and nearing the suburbs. Houses became more common. Abandoned cars littered the area, though most blockages had been shoved out of the way by previous travelers. Large oaks flanked the roads as the small farmhouses were replaced with millionaires' estates. Once, the fields around them would have held thoroughbred horses, though the stillness had emptied them and let them become choked with weeds.

Clare didn't suggest stopping at any of the rural buildings. Being on the outskirts of suburbs meant they were more likely to have been looted, and every stop increased their risk. They would have more luck if they traveled to where the houses were built more closely together. She had one very specific street in mind. One of its sides held a row of houses. The other let on to a field belonging to a private school. She hoped the stretch of clear land would be safer than stopping somewhere wholly surrounded by houses.

"Did you have a plan for how we should get our supplies?" Clare was growing fidgety as they approached Holgate. Unlike the time when Beth had stopped to search for a map, there was no quiet space for them to leave their bus while they walked to town. The hollows would hear their engine. "Should we go slow and cautious or fast?"

"Fast, I think." Dorran's eyes had darkened as he scanned the cross streets they passed. "The hollows tend to be wary around anything they don't understand. Plus, the sun is out, which will make them reclusive. I say we pick a house, take what we can in the span of a minute, and leave before the creatures grow bold enough to approach."

"Okay." The anxiety was churning her insides. "We don't have the masks this time."

"No. That will be a risk. That's why I want you in the bus, watching the street. Hit the horn if you see anything approaching the house."

She narrowed her eyes. "Why do all of your plans involve me staying behind?"

"Because they're good plans." His smile was wolfish.

"All right, counterargument. We stay together—*like we promised*—and we clear out the cupboards in half the time."

"Tempting, but I'll have to insist on the original plan. It won't take me more than sixty seconds to fill a backpack and get out. I need you in the bus, keeping watch, and ready to drive if anything sneaks up on us."

"What if there are hollows inside the house?"

"Then I'll behead them and keep moving."

Clare bit her lip, trying to keep her frustration in check. "What if that doesn't work? What if they disarm you and you're stuck in there?"

"If I'm not back in two minutes, you can come after me."

She didn't like it, but Dorran was right. They would both be safer with someone standing guard. And between the two of them, Dorran possessed the bulk of the muscles, which meant he could break in more easily and carry more out.

"One minute," Clare conceded. "And you'll be careful."

"Excessively." Dorran turned the wheel, carrying them onto the sprawling street edged by the school grounds on one side.

It was a good location to attempt a raid. Only a few vehicles lined the road and the trees were sparse. The houses were clustered a little too close together for Clare's liking, but the wide road left plenty of room for a quick escape.

Clare grabbed the backpack from under her seat and held it out for Dorran. "Be safe. I love you."

"One minute," he promised. He swung the wheel sharply, pointing the bus's front toward the house he intended to break into, and turned on the high beams. Circles of harsh light splashed over the wooden door. When it was open, the light would flood the entryway, discouraging any denizens that lurked inside.

He left the motor running, slung the backpack over one shoulder, and bounded out of the bus's door. Clare slid into the driver's seat and rested one hand on the wheel, ready to press on the horn if she saw anything approaching them. Dorran was already at the front door. He smashed it open and disappeared inside.

Clare directed her attention from the houses to the banks of cars lining the street. One in the distance still held a hollow inside of it. The woman's skull had been broken like a ripe melon that had been dropped. She faced Clare, beating her smashed face against the gore-smudged windows. Clare swallowed thickly and kept her eyes moving.

A sedan was parked not far down the road. It had stopped at an angle, the front facing the curb, the rear jutting into the street.

I know that car.

Her mouth dried. She'd seen it twice. Once, they'd passed it on the road. But the second, more vivid memory came from when the driver pulled up beside their bus and risked his safety to help Clare.

His name had been Owen. He'd had stubble coating his face and two young daughters in the back of the sedan. The car was unforgettable. A fresh, curved mark scarred the hood.

Clare's heart felt ready to burst. From her angle, she couldn't see inside the tinted windows, but the vehicle was uncomfortably still.

You have a job to do. Focus!

She forced her eyes away from the sedan. Figures crept through the gaps between nearby houses, not yet bold enough to step into the light, but closer than Clare would have liked. She couldn't tell how many seconds had passed. It felt like an eternity. More than a minute, at least, and Dorran still hadn't returned. Bitter fear coated her tongue. She felt for the tire iron stored above the driver's seat, still not moving her eyes from the open door illuminated by the bus's beams.

He's been gone for too long. Something happened. He's hurt. He needs me—

She was out of the bus, her breathing strained and her paces long as she raced for the house. There was no time to scope out the situation when seconds could mean the difference between life and death. She ran through the open door.

Dorran gasped as she slammed into him. He reflexively grabbed for her arm, but they were both off balance and staggered into the closest wall.

Clare, breathless, stared at him. "You're okay?"

"Perfectly. This house is empty." He raised his hand, where an overladen backpack was suspended. "And I found supplies."

"Don't scare me like that. You promised you'd only be a minute."

An unsteady smile broke through his shock. "I am only five seconds late."

Is that all? Clare dropped her head, relief making her legs weak.

Dorran put his spare arm around her shoulders as he led her back outside. Eyes flashed in the low light. They were growing closer, but the path to the bus was clear. Clare broke into a jog to match Dorran's pace but stopped several steps from the open bus door.

"Clare?"

Her eyes were fixed on the sedan. It was hard to tell through the gloom, but she thought she saw a shiver of motion inside.

Dorran hesitated, one foot on the bus's step, eyebrows low with concern. "Clare, what's wrong?"

"Wait in the bus. I'll only be a second." She had to see. She had to be sure.

The car seemed painfully quiet. Its lights were dead and its engine silent, just as void and lonely as the rest of the vehicles lining the street.

She moved toward it, her breath shallow and her heart fast. The back tire had been wrecked, the rubber halfway torn off. Something white was still embedded in the material. A tooth, Clare thought. The car had been driven off the road. Or perhaps it had been at a stop when the occupants were attacked, Owen risking the houses just like Dorran had, searching for supplies.

A scattering of small leaves lay across the car's roof. They twitched in the wind, threatening to tumble off. Heavier twigs lay between them. The car had been dormant for at least a day or two.

Clare's mouth was dry. She was nearly at the driver's window. One of the doors was bent. It had been pulled closed, but the metal around the window was twisted by unforgiving hands, leaving a gap.

A small, black fly crawled out, then spiraled into the air.

No. No, please, no.

Specks of blood painted the inside of the window, obscuring the shapes beyond. Flies hummed, reveling in their feast.

No. Not them.

She reached for the door's handle. Her pulse rushed in her ears, drowning out every other sound. The handle was cool under her fingertips. Another fly crawled out of the broken door. Clare pulled and felt the subtle click as the door's latch disengaged. Her mind screamed at her to leave, to walk away, but her heart had to know. She had to be certain. She pulled, and the door rocked open.

An ashen, decaying limb flopped out. A head rocked backward, mouth gaping open. Empty eye sockets, their contents liquefied by bacteria and consumed by flies, stared toward Clare. The corpse had died against the door, scrambling to get out.

Clare pressed the back of her hand against her mouth. The rushing in her ears was louder. *It's a hollow.*

She sucked in a breath, and the air whistled painfully in her throat. The body had decayed far enough that, at first glance, it had passed as a human corpse. But it still bore the unmistakable signs: the skull had almost no hair, the body was naked, and the fingers that had scrabbled at the door before death had cracked, too-long nails.

A kitchen knife was embedded under its chin, cutting deep enough into the throat to expose the spine. The hollow had died before the thanites could repair the damage.

Clare pressed a hand against the car's roof to keep herself steady. Several cans had been left on the car's floor, but they had been opened and emptied and flies now feasted on the remnants. Clare saw a small white box: the painkillers she had given Owen. The box's lid hung open and a strip of metal poked out, the little alcoves that held the pills all empty.

She held her breath to lean over the hollow and look into the back seats. They were empty. The ring that had hung from the rearview mirror was gone.

Clare stepped back and closed her eyes as relief ran through her. They had left the car voluntarily. There had been enough time to gather their most valuable supplies. Most likely, the hollow they had killed had torn the tire and pulled them off the road, and they had been forced to move to a different vehicle. She hoped they were still out there, still safe, in their search for a permanent residence.

"Clare."

She barely had time to jolt at the booming voice. Then Dorran's hands were on her, pulling her away from the car. The rushing in her ears was subsiding. Another noise was encroaching. The low, hissing chatter of air pushed through a damaged throat.

Oh.

Clare was lifted off her feet. She yelped, clutching at Dorran's jacket. He held her tightly as he carried her away from the sedan. She glanced back at it and saw a twisted creature dragging itself across the street toward it. The hollow had lost both of its legs and used its hands to scrape its naked torso across the asphalt.

The jaw shivered as it hissed at them, already at the door Clare had just been standing in.

Dorran bounded up the bus's step and dropped Clare into the passenger seat. Then he reached back outside. The backpack—the one he had brought into the house in their search for supplies—had been left near the front wheel. He pulled it in, then slammed the door behind them.

"Sorry," Clare managed. "Sorry, I should've been watching more closely."

"We're okay." In the muted light of the bus's interior, shadows cut hard lines across his features. He seemed paler than normal. "It didn't get you, so we're okay. Was that—"

"Owen's car." Clare had already told Dorran about the man who had repaired their bus while he was unconscious, and he nodded, recognizing the name. "He wasn't there."

"Thank heaven." Dorran sank into the driver's seat and turned the key. Broken fingers began digging at the bus's walls, but he pulled away from the curb before the creatures could get a proper grip. "Wherever he is, we'll hope he's still safe."

CHAPTER 23

WITH A SOFT POWDERING of snow capping its shingles and window casings, Winterbourne looked beautiful.

Clare leaned forward in her seat to better see as their bus rolled out from the cover of the pine forest. Insipid sunlight glinted off a hundred dark windows. The field around the mansion was empty except for the lines of decorative shrubs spaced across the front court.

As they passed the groundskeeper's cottage, Clare glanced at her companion. Dorran's expression was unreadable. She knew he had to be feeling a lot at the sight of his home. He'd wanted to return, but she was also aware that the bad memories outweighed the good. She opened her mouth, but Dorran spoke first.

"We didn't have enough time to block off all of the concealed passageways before we left, so we will need to be cautious. We don't know how many of the creatures are still inside the house."

"We'll start by protecting the most important rooms," Clare replied. "The garden and the bedroom."

The bus neared the shallow steps leading up to the courtyard, and Dorran turned it around before parking. There were no hollows in sight, but that didn't mean they weren't watching. She squinted as she tried to see through the dark windows. It was impossible to know what might be on the other side, looking back out.

Four weeks since we left Winterbourne. The realization came as a shock. The trip, which Clare had first hoped would only take a day, had spread out in increments. At the same time, she had seen and experienced so much in that intervening month that it could have been a lifetime.

Dorran parked. As the engine's rumble died, a perfect silence filled the bus. Neither of them moved, but simply stared up at the building. It was vast, once home to dozens of family members and hundreds of staff. Three floors housed countless rooms and twisting passageways that Clare was still unfamiliar with. She struggled to understand the emotions running through her. There was dread, but there was also the faintly warm sensation of seeing an old friend again—and on top of it, the sense that this had been inevitable. That, no matter what, they were destined to end up at the old house again, staring up at its stony, unforgiving features.

Dorran's voice was only a little shaky. "Are you ready?"

"Yes." *I think. I hope.*

He found her hand and squeezed it. Then they both rose, picked up their weapons, and pressed the bus's door open.

The air was brutally cold. Fresh snow glittered around them, shining like a million diamonds, its glimmer promising heat without delivering any. Clare shivered. She patted the bus's door as she left, a final thank-you for carrying them as far as it had.

Dorran's boots crunched into the snow covering the entryway's lowest step. Clare kept close to his side, the crowbar clutched tightly in her fist, as they ascended to the front door. To their right was the pond that clung to the building's side. A thin layer of ice coated it, and through that, Clare thought she could see a head, its eyes bulging as they stared up toward the sky, mouth opened in a voiceless scream. One of the hollows Dorran had lured into the lake. She swallowed and turned away.

The doors were closed, like she and Dorran had left them. They weren't locked, though. Old, tired hinges complained as they turned the knob. As the door swung inward, a beam of light entered through the opening and spread across the tile foyer, up the dark wood paneling, and over the staircase leading to the upper floors.

The stench came quick and overwhelming. Clare squinted against the musty, sickly rotting scent of hollows.

"Ah," Dorran said. His grip on Clare's hand tightened.

Ahead of them, in the foyer's center, an effigy had been built out of bones. Femurs, skulls, ribs, and pelvic bones had been stacked over each other, tied together with strings of human hair, to create a statue nearly ten feet high. Three skulls had been bound together for the head. Angular limbs ran out from the waist, not unlike a smaller version of the spider monster they had passed in the tunnel. Something—blood, probably—had been used to paint the effigy in messy, irregular strokes of brown.

Clare moved herself closer to Dorran, so he could feel her warmth at his side. It wasn't hard to guess what the hideous construction was supposed to represent.

Did they create it as a tribute to her? Was their loyalty really so strong that they wanted to memorialize her, even though she was no longer controlling them?

Clare didn't like to think about the alternative, that Dorran's mother, Madeline Morthorne, had survived. That she had commissioned the statue herself to preside over the house's foyer. Because that couldn't be possible. Clare had forced the fire poker through Madeline's skull herself. The woman was dead. She couldn't hurt them any longer.

Except she can. Even if she's gone, her memory is still here. Not just in the statue, but in the house, in every pore of this building.

The awful blankness had fallen over Dorran's features. She remembered the expression all too well from her first days at Winterbourne, when he had been withdrawn so deeply into himself that Clare had struggled to get any kind of reading on him.

"She's dead," Clare said.

Dorran's eyes flicked down to meet hers before returning to the statue. He nodded, but the bleak panic in his eyes made her heart ache for him. His hand was clammy. Clare tugged on it, pulling him away.

"Let's go to the garden first. I want to see what we're working with."

Finally, he turned away from the bones. The garden had always been a sanctuary for him, and now, it would be a way to focus them both. The food in their bus wouldn't last forever. They needed to know whether the hastily constructed watering and heating system had survived their absence, or whether they would need to venture back into the town for food.

Clare kept watch over Dorran as they moved through the back rooms and into the gloomy, stone-walled servants' areas. Some presence returned to him as the effigy vanished behind them. He glanced over the rooms they passed, quick looks that took in the familiar shapes. Clare startled when he spoke.

"They have made use of our home in our absence."

As she looked around herself, Clare saw he was right. Furniture was overturned. Broken crockery and fresh scratches marred the kitchen. In some areas, blood spatter was over walls and floors.

They've been eating each other. That's where the bones came from.

They stepped into the massive stone chamber behind the kitchens and paused at the table to light one of the candles stored there. To Clare's left was the archway leading down to the wine cellar. She couldn't repress the twist of anxiety and quickly looked away. To their right was another set of stairs leading to the furnace room. And straight ahead waited the garden.

The lights were still on. Clare felt her eyebrows rise. Dorran had constructed a heating and watering system designed to maintain the garden for two or three days while they traveled to Beth. It had never been intended to last four weeks. It should have run out of fuel long ago.

She tried to look through the blurred window as Dorran unlocked the door. The metal groaned as it opened outward, and Dorran lowered his candle and weapon.

"How…?" Dorran stepped through the doorway with Clare close in his wake. They both stopped just inside the threshold, staring in wonder at the maze of green ahead of them.

The garden had flourished. All of the plants, which had only been seedlings on Clare and Dorran's departure, had grown and overflowed their beds. Trails of ripening cherry tomatoes hung nearly to the floor. Salad leaves burst up like miniature, multicolored explosions. Green peas had not only followed their designated stakes, but also branched outward, attempting to strangle their neighbors in their enthusiasm.

"Oh." Clare, grinning, pressed a hand to her chest. "It's beautiful."

It should have been impossible. In that moment, she didn't care. The overhead lights were on, bathing the scene in a warm glow. The plants were lush, welcoming, vibrant. It felt like home.

Dorran moved forward to explore between the garden beds. Without human intervention, the plants had grown as they pleased, turning into something that looked more like a jungle than a garden. Clare ran her fingertips across a crop of spinach as she looked over the riot of green. They had more than enough to keep her and Dorran fed. It wasn't as sophisticated as Johann's garden in the research institute and didn't have any crops to mill into bread or turn into tofu, but it was earthy and rich and fresh, and Clare loved it.

Dorran turned back to her. His earlier stress had evaporated. He grinned as he lifted a twirling tendril to show her a pumpkin flower.

"It will need some work," he said, laughing. "I don't think there will be any way to get the tomatoes onto their trellises without snapping the branches, but—"

"It lived. It *thrived*."

"That it did." He returned to her and kissed her deeply. "I think we will be just fine, my darling."

Clare rested her forehead against Dorran's chest. The organic smell of the garden had expunged the lingering scent of hollows. The room was warm, the lights were bright, and she felt safe. She would be happy to live there, she thought.

Sounds came from the floor above them. Heavy footsteps thumped along a hallway, a staggering gait that seemed to lurch drunkenly. It only lasted a second, then fell silent.

Dorran kept his arms around Clare, but he had tensed at the sound. He dropped his head to rest it on top of Clare's, then inhaled deeply, seeming to brace himself.

"We have to secure the house," he said.

CHAPTER 24

"WE SHOULD CHOOSE ONE priority room," Dorran said. Clare led the way out of the garden, and he locked the door behind them. "Somewhere with food, running water, and warmth."

"The upstairs bedroom?"

"That's what I was thinking. As long as the hollows left it untouched, at least. We'll go there first, see if we can secure it, then consider our next move." His glance was tense. "Stay behind me. If we're confronted—"

"Retreat instead of engage." She pressed him into a brief hug. "I remember."

"I need you to be safe above all else."

"You know I will be."

He matched her smile. "Sorry. I worry."

"Yeah. I do as well."

They turned toward the hallway. The upstairs rooms were

silent. Clare didn't trust the quiet, though. The stench in the house was too strong and fresh for how little confrontation they had encountered.

She took up the candleholder in one hand and the crowbar in her other, and shadowed Dorran as he led her back into the foyer. A wooden support beam to Clare's left creaked and she swung toward it, but Dorran didn't flinch. He'd lived in the house long enough to know which noises came from the building's age and which were foreign.

They entered the foyer from the statue's back. Light came through the snow-caked windows to shine between gaps in the bones and hair lashings. Dorran only spared the statue a glance before skirting around it to reach the stairs.

Dust had coated most surfaces in their absence. When Clare had first arrived at Winterbourne, the building had been nearly pristine, having recently been tended by dozens of maids. They had left their duties behind along with their humanity, though. The dark wood railings had seen their shine dampened, and the gilded frames around the paintings were coated with a thin layer of gray, much like snow had coated the building.

They reached the top of the second flight of stairs. Clare had made this journey often enough to remember it. Ahead, partway along the dim hall, was their bedroom. If she continued onward, the passageway branched into four, each terminating in a window overlooking the field surrounding Winterbourne. She and Dorran stood at the top of the stairs just long enough to listen for noise, then began moving forward.

A sigh echoed from behind them. Clare turned, and the candle flickered from the sudden motion. She stretched it ahead of herself, willing it to pierce through the shadows clustering around the passageway's innumerable side tables and display cases. She could have sworn Winterbourne hadn't been this dark when she and Dorran had left it.

They closed the curtains, she realized. At the end of the hallways were windows, but the thick cloth shades had been drawn down to block them.

She wondered how much they had used the building in her and Dorran's absence. Maybe they had treated it like their own castle, sleeping in the beds, crawling through the rooms, staring out of the windows once night fell. Maybe the hallways had been full of them right up until the bus's engine cut through the cold air. The building was perfect for them: dark, enclosed, cold.

Dorran held the hatchet at his side, the pose deceptively relaxed. Clare could feel the energy in his muscles, carefully contained, poised to move at the slightest provocation. His other hand grazed Clare's shoulder, not quite holding her, but ready to pull her away from some unseen threat.

Behind him, in the hallway that led to their room, movement caught Clare's eye. One of the panels in the wall slid out. An arm moved through it, long, thin as a stick, tipped with clawlike fingers.

She barely had time to draw breath. The hollow lunged out of the opening with incredible speed. Its movements were silent except for the muffled click of its bones grinding against each other. An elongated head stretched further as the jaw opened, aiming at Dorran's back.

Clare lunged, breaking out from under his hand and pushing him aside as she put her crowbar between the hollow's maw and Dorran.

The teeth clashed around the metal with a noise that made Clare flinch. She shoved back, pushing the monster away. It released the crowbar, and Clare angled the point at the monster's head. She thrust forward. Pain shot into her hands and along her arms as she used brute force to break through its skull. The hollow stood for a second, hanging off the end of the crowbar, one eye bulging and the other sunk into its skull. Then it dropped, its weight dragging the crowbar down until the angle let it slide off with a sluicing noise.

The candle threatened to die, then stabilized. Clare looked behind herself. Dorran stood a pace away, panting, his hatchet bloodied. A dead hollow lay at his feet. Behind it, a second compartment in the hall had opened, just a few paces behind where Clare had stood.

They cornered us. An ambush. The noise we heard was designed to lure us up here.

Clare met Dorran's eyes and saw the same realization flash through his. Then his gaze shifted and he yelled, "Behind you!"

She could hear the clatter of teeth coming from her back, but she couldn't look toward it. A second hollow crept out of the doorway behind Dorran, followed closely by a third.

We can't stay here. We're pinned from both sides. Continue to the room? Or retreat? Both directions were filled with the creatures. The bedroom was closest, but there was no certainty that it hadn't been tampered with. Clare made a snap decision. "Follow!"

She charged along the hallway, toward their bedroom. Three hollows blocked her way, one still wearing the scraps of its maid uniform. Clare swung at the closest one, slamming the metal into its skull, the bones along her arm reverberating from the impact. Dorran closed in behind her, slashing with fierce precision, decapitating the remaining two monsters. Still more poured out of the concealed hallway, but they were already past it, racing for the door.

"Keys," Dorran barked.

Clare dropped the crowbar as he tossed the key ring to her. The candle guttered as wax spilled off it, but the flame held. Dorran faced the oncoming swarm, feet planted, center of gravity low, teeth bared. Clare bent over the door, fighting to fit the right key into the hole. The first hollow's head tumbled past her legs. The two creatures behind it balked, backtracking from the blade, slowing the swarm.

The lock clicked open. Clare yelled Dorran's name as she darted inside. He backed through the opening, weapon held at the ready, and Clare slammed the door behind him. Fingernails scraped across the wood as Clare put her shoulder against it and fumbled for the lock. Metal clicked as it turned, sealing them inside, and she stepped back, panting.

Dorran turned in a slow circle, examining their environment. "All right?" he asked.

"Fine. You?"

He gave a short nod, then held out his hand for the candle. She passed it over. He moved through the room, searching every gap large enough to hide a human: the closets, the bathroom, the space under the bed, and behind the thick red curtains flanking tall, narrow windows.

Clare pressed her palm into her forehead. The bedroom was exactly how she remembered it. A little dustier and a little darker, but the blankets were still strewn around the cold fireplace she and Dorran had spent their nights in front of. Her travel case—one of two cases she had brought from her home when the stillness first began—sat open in the corner, still holding an assortment of spare clothes and food.

She chuckled. The memories were strangely powerful. She had felt a lot in that room. The fear and shock as she realized the outside world no longer existed. The hope of hearing voices on the radio. The sharp pang of new love as she realized what Dorran meant to her.

He returned from the bathroom, posture relaxed despite the incessant scrabbling at the door. "We are safe."

No matter what else the hollows were capable of, it seemed the locks had kept them out of the room during the past month. They had already scoured every inch of it in search of secret passageways and knew there were none. Clare rubbed at the back of her neck, an unsteady smile growing. "Any regrets about leaving the Evandale bunker now?"

He chuckled and placed the candle on the fireplace's

mantelpiece. "Dreaming about Winterbourne and actually standing in it are two very different experiences, aren't they?"

"Sure are." She tilted her head back, examining the ornate edging bordering the maddening wallpaper and the way every single fixture and piece of furniture made it clear that they had cost a small fortune. The room had always intimidated her, as though it had resented her presence there. As though she wasn't worthy. Now, it stank of hollows and the dust had dulled some of its luster. It was starting to feel desolate. Like a wealthy heiress who had chased off all of her friends and was spending her last years alone.

Some of Clare's emotions must have appeared on her face. Dorran's hand grazed over her neck, his voice soft. "Do *you* regret it? It is not too late to return to Evandale—"

"No," she said, putting warmth into her words. "Don't worry. No regrets here. This is our home, and it feels *right* to be back here, fighting our own fight. Though…you might get a different answer tomorrow, when I'm missing hot showers and air conditioning."

He laughed and ran his hands through her hair. "You are a good woman."

Clare leaned into his touch. Then her eyes peeked open to look at the door. The scrabbling noise had fallen silent. "They're gone. Normally they don't give up if they can still hear you."

"Not unless they're being controlled."

The tenseness in his voice was unmistakable. Clare pressed closer. "We still know so little about them. The maids might be operating under their last instructions—to stay hidden unless they have a chance to attack. It might just be blind, witless obedience at this point."

"Hmm."

Clare frowned. Another, less pleasant thought occurred. "There were a lot of them, though."

"I noticed that as well."

"How many maids did your mother have?"

"Twenty."

Clare shook her head. "We killed at least half of them more than a month ago. They've got to be recruiting new members from the forest."

"New members that follow the same instructions."

"Wouldn't have thought hollows would be much for peer pressure, huh?"

The shutters were pulling over Dorran's face, hiding any sign of emotion. Clare tugged on his hand before he had a chance to lock himself away completely. "That's a problem for a later day. Come on. It's freezing in here; let's get a fire started."

They had left the fireplace well stocked with wood and kindling. Clare worked on starting the flames while Dorran fetched basins of water from the bathroom for them to wash up. They opened some of the old cans from the travel case in the corner, heating up soup and eating straight out of the pot.

An hour later, Clare sat on the fireside blankets while Dorran knelt behind her. He ran a comb through her damp hair, working out the tangles and cleaning it as well as he could without running water. He was silent, and Clare could feel his mind ticking over, feeling around an impossible puzzle with futile stubbornness. *Is Madeline still alive?*

Clare pulled him back to an easier, more urgent question. "What do we do now that we have our room secured?"

His hands fell still for a second, then resumed. "The house is compromised. Before we left, we could move through it freely while the hollows hid in the secret passageways. But they seem to have grown bold. Perhaps from hunger."

"So the first step is to reclaim our territory."

"That is what I think. We need to ensure we can move between our room and the garden at will. We'll seal the hidden doorways first, then scout the house until we are certain we are alone in it."

Clare chewed on her lip. "We have food here to last us for a day or two, and water, but we'll need to go back to the bus soon. The rest of our supplies are still there. Your family didn't have any other fencing masks, did they?"

"No. But I'm sure we can improvise something. We will want the radio as well."

Clare nodded. Evandale Research Institute's leader, Unathi, had implied it might take some time before they were ready to trial the cure but that she would broadcast a warning in advance of deployment. Clare couldn't guess how long it might take the team to ensure the code was safe for humans, but it would help to be ready for it, whenever it was.

"We'll need some way to move through the building," Clare said. "The furnace will need stocking, and we'll need to visit the garden daily."

His fingertips grazed along the back of her head, and she shivered. "That can all wait until tomorrow. You are tired, and the night is black. At least now, here, we are safe."

The windows set into the wall looked out over the fields and the forest ringing the estate. A hollow screamed in the distance, the note rising into a painful screech before breaking. The echoes lingered, seemingly trapped in the frozen air.

CHAPTER 25

CLARE WOKE SLOWLY. THE fire had burned down to embers, but it was still too early to see much outside of the golden glow. A face stared out at her from behind the fire. Beth's face. She grinned, her eyes as lifeless as her smile.

Fear pulsed through Clare, but in a second, it was gone. She blinked and saw she was only looking at the fireplace's back wall, where the bumps and shadows in the stone had formed a pattern that resembled a face.

She felt behind herself for Dorran. He'd fallen asleep with her by the fire, his chest against her back, his arm over her waist in the familiar hug. Her back was cold now, though. Her hand only touched air and empty blankets.

Clare rolled over to face the room. With the fire near dead and their candle extinguished, she had to squint through the moonlight drifting past the windows' gauzy curtains. It ghosted across the furniture and ran up the walls in irregular streaks. The shadows were so deep it took her a moment to find Dorran. He stood facing the door, arms at his side, head tilted as though listening to something that came through the gap between the top of the door and its frame.

"Dorran?" She crawled out of bed, reaching for him.

His glance was brief. "Go back to sleep."

Clare didn't like the way he was whispering. She got her feet under herself and crossed the room, moving as quietly as she could. As she neared the door, she stopped to listen. Wind whistled through gaps in the stone, a mournful, tuneless song. A door somewhere in the distance creaked, then creaked again. It had been left open, Clare thought; its hinges complained as the breeze tugged on it incessantly. She couldn't hear anything else.

Dorran didn't move as she stepped up to his side. His skin looked colorless in the bluish light. His lips were set, his eyes unblinking. Uneasy prickles ran across Clare's arms. She kept her voice to a whisper, just like Dorran had. "What's wrong?"

He gave his head a small shake, his eyes not moving.

Clare rested her hand against his arm. She was shivering from the cold, and Dorran's skin didn't feel any warmer. *How long has he been standing here?*

The wind howled. In the distance, the unsecured door groaned again and again, moving like a pair of lungs struggling to breathe. The house unnerved Clare at night. There was never enough light, and there were too many empty rooms. Dorran should have been familiar with the building, though. The creaks and rattles shouldn't have bothered him. Even hearing a hollow shouldn't have been enough to make him leave their bed.

She hated how dark it was. She hated how silent and tense Dorran had become. She slipped away from him, back to the fire, and began stacking fresh kindling onto the embers. Dorran still didn't speak, but his head turned slightly as he watched her.

"Come over here." Clare held out her hand. "Sit with me."

He didn't respond, half his attention on Clare, half on the door.

"You'll freeze to death." She struggled to force a smile. "It's nice and cozy here."

Finally, he moved, approaching Clare and sinking down at her side. His motions were stiff and halting, as though he had to think every movement through before performing it. Clare waited until he was settled, then pulled the blankets around both of their shoulders to protect them from the chill while the fire regained its heat.

"I thought I heard her," Dorran said at last.

Clare found his hands and pressed them. They were like ice. "Was it real, do you think? Or just a dream?"

"I...don't know." His eyes closed. "I was asleep when I first heard it. But then...it continued after I got up. Coming from just outside the door."

Clare pictured her last memory of Madeline: rebar impaled through her skull, her eyes blank, her face twitching before she pitched backward. She shouldn't have survived that. *But maybe she did. Maybe she lived just long enough for the thanites to start repairing her. We never found the body.*

"What did she say?" Clare asked.

Dorran shook his head.

She scooted closer to him, her voice gentle but coaxing. "We're in this together. It's important that I know. Please tell me."

"She said…she was going to hurt me for leaving. That…" His voice caught, and a shudder ran through him. "That she would skin you."

"Lovely woman." Clare leaned her head against Dorran's chest. "So eloquent, so classy."

A thin, choked laugh escaped Dorran. He sounded like he was in pain. Clare wrapped her arms around him as she waited for him to stop shaking.

"What will we do?"

The question was rhetorical, but Clare answered it anyway. "Guess I'd better impale her again."

This time, the laughter sounded closer to something real. His hand found hers where she rested it on his chest and stroked it gently. "You'll stay close to me, won't you, Clare?"

"Of course I will."

"I can endure almost anything. But I cannot endure losing you."

"You won't have to." She tilted her head up to meet his gaze. His eyes were so dark and so full of fear, it hurt her to see them. "Do you want to leave?"

He looked toward the fire, silent. Clare thought she understood.

"You don't want to leave, but you think we might have to."

"Yes."

Clare chewed her lip. They were no longer inexperienced at dealing with hollows. They had even faced two of the intelligent ones; one on the riverboat, and one at Evandale. But this was different. Madeline knew the house like the back of her hand. She had access to all of the secret passageways that Clare and Dorran were still unfamiliar with. And she had her loyal followers: the maids and now denizens from the forest as well.

And, worse, she knew Dorran. She knew how to get under his skin, how to hurt him, how to pick at all of the scabs she had spent her life creating.

If Madeline truly was back, they either had to leave, and fast… or kill her. And Clare wasn't sure they were capable of the latter. Not if her follower count had swelled.

She closed her eyes. It hurt to think of leaving when they had put so much at risk to get back to Winterbourne. But their sanctuary was starting to seem like the greater of two evils.

"It doesn't have to be permanent," Clare said. "We can travel to a town and try to contact other survivors. They might have more effective ways of killing hollows. Something we could use when we come back."

Dorran's fingers continued to trace over hers. She could feel the worry inside of him, eating him up. "We would be leaving the garden."

"We can survive without it. We've done that before." She nodded, using the words to reinforce her determination. "Worst-case scenario, we wait until the Evandale team activates the code. That will kill everything inside Winterbourne without any doubt left."

"It might take months. Are you prepared to survive outside for that long?"

She licked her lips. "We can do that. We'll find a farmhouse somewhere. Make it secure against hollows and looters. We'll be all right."

"Yes," he whispered, and kissed the top of her head. "At least we will be together."

"Do you want to wait until dawn or try to leave now?"

For a moment, the only noise came from the fire and, in the distance, the creaking door. Then Dorran took a breath. "Wisdom says to wait until daylight and the protection it offers. But…"

"But they'll be waiting for that." Clare said.

"It might be better to move quickly, before they expect us to."

"All right." She tried to stop the nausea that wanted to rise through her at the thought. Madeline loved to play mind games, and she would be anticipating their next move. Their best chance of escaping her plans was to take a course she wouldn't expect— and to take it quickly. "Let's go. Right now, before she has a chance to react. We don't need to bring anything. Most of what we own is already in the bus."

We just need to get outside. Two minutes, at the most. She won't be able to form a countermove in two minutes, will she? Once we're in the bus we'll be secure. We'll be out of here. And there's nothing Madeline can do.

He clutched her hand. For a moment, neither of them moved, frozen in that space in front of the fire, listening to the wind and the creaking door and their own heartbeats. Then they were on their feet, grabbing robes and tugging them on over their nightclothes.

"Here," Dorran whispered. He'd found her boots and knelt to help pull them over her feet. While he laced his own shoes, Clare retrieved their scarves and looped Dorran's around his neck. The outside air wasn't as brutal as it had been during the unnatural snows of Clare's first stay at Winterbourne, but it was cold enough to bite.

Then Clare lit a lantern while Dorran found their weapons. They stopped by the door, both breathing heavily. Dorran waited for Clare's nod. Then he turned the handle, and they stepped outside.

CHAPTER 26

THE BEDROOM HAD FELT cold, but it wasn't on par with the chill that permeated the hall. Clare's breath emerged as a pallid cloud as she tried to read the shadows gathered around them.

A tall shape loomed to their left. Clare gripped her crowbar, but the shape was only the door leading to the secret passageways. It hung open, a bitter, musty smell floating out, but nothing moved inside the darkness.

Dorran nodded toward the stairs. Clare lifted her lantern as she matched Dorran's pace. Floorboards creaked under Clare's footsteps, no matter how soft she tried to keep them. The house hadn't been this noisy last time she was here, she was sure. The cold was warping it.

Something twisted stood at the top of the stairs. As the flickering light grew closer, it darted away. Clare could have almost believed it was a retreating shadow, except for the way its eyes had flashed as it turned.

They were at the stairs. Neither of them hesitated as they moved downward, taking the steps two at a time. Speed was vital. They might only have the advantage of surprise for a few seconds. Moonlight lit the lowest steps and the foyer's tiles. Clare focused on it, feeling how close they were to the door, how close they were to *escape*. The retreat might sting, but the bus meant safety, and that was something they couldn't afford to reject.

Her boots created echoes as they hit the tile floor. Dorran craned his head, searching the darkness around them as they crossed the space. Moonlight ran across the hideous effigy. The three skulls stitched together to form the head seemed to be watching them, its arms spread, its presence overwhelming. Something chattered in the distance, then abruptly fell silent. They were at the door. Dorran grasped the heavy bronze handle and pulled. Wood groaned as it rocked inward, and a gust of snow-bearing air flowed around them.

Clare huffed out a quick, tight breath in response to the cold but leaned into it. Only a few shallow steps separated them from the courtyard and the bus. She was halfway down them before she felt Dorran's hesitation.

He'd stopped midstep, his face contracting in shock. Clare followed his gaze toward the bus. At first glance, it had looked no different from when they had left it. The metal front was twisted, the glass cracked, and the wheels muddy. Frost had settled across the bus's side, and someone had scraped away the white to create stark, messy letters: I KNEW YOU WOULD COME HOME.

The painful creaking noise of an open door repeated, and

Clare realized it came from the bus's hood. The metal hatch was open and bobbed in the wind, releasing a piercing whine.

Dark shapes, like rocks, were scattered across the ground in front of the bus. Light snowfall had nearly completely obscured them, but Clare recognized metal: engine parts, disassembled and scattered. Her heart dropped. "Oh."

Dorran took her arm and pulled her closer to himself. They descended the steps and approached the bus. He pushed the metal up from the engine and muttered under his breath. The space was nothing but a tangle of broken wires and disconnected pipes.

"Can you repair it?" Clare asked.

"I...don't know." He used his boot to scuff snow off one of the metal lumps on the ground. "I don't think so. They were thorough."

Clare stepped back from him, squinting through the darkened glass of the bus. There could be an ambush waiting for them. She could barely make out the nearest few seats. Holding the lantern close, she approached the door and pushed on the handle.

The door slid open limply. Clare climbed the step, lantern raised to light the rows of seats.

Worry laced Dorran's voice. "Clare, be careful."

"It's okay. It's empty." The lantern's light caught on the lines of metal and covered glass. The bus's inside smelled wrong, the unmistakable stench of hollows invading the space, but not strongly enough to make Clare retreat. The creatures had been through the inside of the bus, she suspected, pawing over their supplies and tapping at the windows, but they had left. More surprisingly, they hadn't touched any of the clothing or food baskets.

Clare stepped back outside, shivering. Dorran crouched between the discarded parts of the motor, his expression dark. He shook his head at Clare's look. "They punctured holes through them. It will need a new motor."

"Damn it," Clare hissed. She glanced back at the house that rose above them. The curtains in one of the windows swayed, as though something had raced past it, disturbing the heavy fabric.

Dorran crossed to Clare's side. He held the hatchet loosely, but his eyes were constantly moving, roving across the white field surrounding them, the ribbon of dark forest in the distance, and the countless black windows looking over them.

"She left the food intact," Clare said. "I don't understand why. They were inside the bus—it would have been so easy to ruin our food as well."

"No," Dorran said. "She doesn't want to kill us. She wants to keep us."

He faltered on the final word. Clare understood. Madeline didn't want to keep them both; she only wanted her son.

"What do we do?"

Dorran turned to face the forest. The wind whipped at his hair, pulling it away from his face and leaving flecks of snow stuck to the strands. "I don't have any replacement parts in the shed to repair the bus. At least, not the kind to fit this motor. If we need to leave, we will have to walk out of here."

Clare closed her eyes. Her car no longer rested inside the forest. She tried to remember how far the walk would be. Winterbourne was almost exactly in the center of Banksy Forest; there was an hour walk to the road that snaked through the forest and an even longer walk out of the trees.

"That would be…hours."

"Six hours to the edge of the forest," Dorran said. "Farther to find a car."

"And the trees are full of hollows. And we don't have our masks."

We're out of options. We have to stay. Stay…and face Madeline.

Her own thoughts and fear were reflected in Dorran's eyes. He found her hand and pressed it tightly. "Back to the room. Quickly, before they have a chance to intercept us. They won't hurt me, but…"

But I'm fair game.

They turned toward the front door. They'd barely taken a step when Dorran yanked her back so suddenly that she nearly slipped on the icy ground. She clutched at him to keep her balance, the lantern swaying dangerously, then looked around his shoulder.

The curtains were no longer drawn over Winterbourne's windows. They were peeled back, and through the dark glass were countless faces; wide, staring eyes; and spindly hands pressed to the panes.

Winterbourne's front door groaned inward, swirling the snow ahead of it in flurries. Hollows bobbed through the shadows inside, jaws opened in muffled hisses. Clare's heart missed a beat. There were so many of them—so many more than she had thought was possible.

"Back," Dorran hissed, tugging on Clare's arm. "Get behind me."

Hollows were creeping out of the front door. The nearest one shivered as it approached them, not from the cold, but from anticipation. Strings of saliva dripped from its jaws.

"Dorran, we can't fight them." She pushed the lantern forward with one hand, hoping the light might work as a disincentive, but the hollows barely flinched.

"Into the bus." Dorran continued to push her back. "Quickly!"

Clare turned to the vehicle and wrenched its door open. Something fastened around her ankle. A skeletal hand protruded from underneath the bus. Clare cried out as it pulled on her, stealing her balance. The lantern tumbled out of her grasp and extinguished in the snow.

More hands reached out of the dark space beneath the vehicle. Snapping jaws, ragged breaths, eager chattering. The hands gripped her leg, pulling her under to join them in the darkness. She kicked and felt her heel connect with something solid, but they wouldn't stop. Her hips disappeared, then her waist. She grabbed the bus's edge, hands planted against the metal in a desperate attempt to keep herself from sliding further.

"No!" Dorran dropped to his knees beside her and hooked his arms around her. He leaned back, trying to pull her out. Teeth pierced the skin just above her boot. Clare clenched her teeth to muffle the scream that ripped through her throat.

She kicked again, thrashing, panicked. The hands slipped on her blood-slicked skin. Dorran threw his weight back, dragging her out from the undercarriage. As her feet reappeared, red-tinged fingers scrambled after her, blindly feeling through the bloodied snow.

A hollow landed on Dorran's back, biting into his shoulder. He gasped and twisted away from it. A scrap of his coat tore loose in its teeth. More eyes appeared behind it, the countless denizens of Winterbourne descending from the open door to encircle them.

Dorran leaned to the side, his arms still around Clare, and hauled her into the bus. She hit the driver's seat with a gasp, the air forced out of her, sharp pains running across her shoulder and back. She rolled to her knees. Dorran was still outside the bus, and he had almost disappeared underneath a swarm of hollows.

No. They're not supposed to hurt him.

They were in the thrall of a frenzy. The smell of Clare's blood had overridden their instructions and filled them with nothing but blind hunger.

She'd lost her weapon and her light. She looked over her shoulder, toward the steering wheel. *The horn. It doesn't need the engine to work.*

She scrambled up the seat. When she tried to put weight on her injured foot, it collapsed from under her. She clung to the seat to hold her balance, then slammed her palm into the center of the wheel.

The horn was near deafening. The creatures ringing the bus

pulled back like a wave. The effect lasted for no more than a second before their faces contorted into fury and they began to surge forward again.

But that second was all Dorran needed. He leaped into the bus and wrenched the door closed. Fists hit the other side of the glass, the monsters hissing and howling. Dorran engaged the lock. The door rattled with each pounding fist but held closed.

Clare sank back to the ground, panting. Dorran crawled to her. His hands reached for her leg, hovering over the bloodied skin without touching. "Oh, Clare. No."

"I'm okay." She was faintly aware that shock was setting in. Her whole leg throbbed like it had been dropped into a fire, but it wasn't as bad as it had been a moment before.

"Shh. Hold on. This will be all right." He stayed just long enough to run his hand across her cheek, brushing wet hair away from her sweaty face, then turned to dig through their supplies.

A scream rattled their enclosure. Four of the hollows poised on the windshield above her. They slammed their fists into the glass, fingernails digging at the cracks, dark blood oozing from their battered fingers.

Dorran returned to her side, the first aid kit open. His hands shook as he sorted through the supplies.

"Dorran." Clare pointed toward the glass.

He barely spared them a glance. "That's okay. Try not to move, my darling." He found a syringe of a clotting substance that could be used to stem the flow. Clare flinched as he pulled the saturated boot off her leg. The hollows continued to beat on the glass above her, smearing blood and grease across the pane, and she flinched at the unrelenting drumming noise. Fingernails dug around the door. Teeth chewed at the plywood fastened over the windows. They were clawing at every angle, ravenous to get in.

"Shh," Dorran whispered as he pressed the syringe into her. The sting was barely worse than the burning throb. Clare leaned her head back against the seat. Her heart felt like it was running too fast, fast enough to kill her, and when she looked at the bus's floor, it was a wash of her red blood.

"Dorran, we can't stay here. They'll get in."

"Don't worry about that. I'll take care of everything."

His voice shook, though, almost as badly as his hands. He used the full syringe to stop the bleeding. Clare tried not to look at the scores in her leg. But when she turned away, her eyes landed on the staring faces above her.

"Everything will be all right." He took a clean cotton pad and pressed it to the gash, then wound bandages around it to hold it in place.

She caught sight of the rip in his jacket. "Are you okay?"

"I'm fine. They weren't trying to hurt me. They were trying to hold me down."

He dug a packet of painkillers out of the kit and handed her two, then stood and approached the window. Shutters had been installed above it and Dorran wrenched them down, blocking out the light and the chattering, mad creatures beyond.

As darkness rushed around them, Clare finally felt as though she was able to breathe again.

"Clare."

She could barely see him, but she could feel Dorran at her side again. She reached out, found his face, and traced her fingers across the planes of his beautiful features. "Hey. I'm sorry."

"Don't be." He turned his head far enough to kiss her fingers. "I'm going to move you. Is that all right?"

She nodded before she remembered he probably couldn't see her. "Yeah."

His arms scooped under her, then lifted her off the ground. The noises continued, scrabbling, clawing, panting breaths interspersed with furious chatters. But it was easier to ignore them when Clare couldn't see them.

Dorran carried her along the length of the bus. He moved carefully, holding Clare tightly against his chest and walking at an angle to make sure he didn't bump her against any seats. He moved her to the back row, where blankets and pillows had been used to construct a bed.

Clare clutched at his shirt, afraid he was going to step out of reach, but he settled onto the edge of the bed. He pulled blankets over her, being careful around her leg, then found her hands and held them.

Feet pattered over the metal above them and dug at the edges of the plywood. There was so little light that Clare couldn't see anything except the ghost of the driver's seat at the other end of the bus.

"What are we going to do?" Clare asked.

"Wait," he said.

CHAPTER 27

CLARE TRIED TO SLEEP, but it was impossible with the noise surrounding them. As time went by, the throbbing in her leg returned. She lay as still as she could, chewing her lip until it was raw to stop herself from fidgeting. Dorran was like a statue at her side. His only movement came from his hand, which ran over hers, reassuring her that he was still there.

The hollows would leave if they were quiet enough, Clare knew. It might take time. Beth had said it took two hours for the creatures to abandon her bunker. They just had to keep quiet for a little while longer.

Occasionally, the scratching was interspersed with cracking as a layer of plywood fractured. The hollows weren't able to break through, despite how persistently they tried. They roved across the bus, probing for any sign of weakness. The scrape of nails against metal was unbearable. Her need to move became stronger with each passing moment.

Just a little longer. They'll lose interest soon. Every time the thought passed through her mind, it was quickly followed up with *And then what?*

She'd known hollows were living in Winterbourne, but she'd never expected there to be so many. She should have been more prepared, though. Even without Madeline, Winterbourne was an attractive home for them: darker than the forest and full of the tunnels and crevices they liked.

And the price they paid for their home came in the form of obedience to its mistress.

They weren't perfectly under her control—they had attacked Dorran when the scent of blood put them into a frenzy—but they were operating under Madeline's intelligence, with Madeline's plan in mind.

That led to an awful thought. Maybe they weren't attacking the bus on instinct but under instructions. Which meant they would never give up.

She swallowed around the lump in her throat. *How long have we been here now? Two hours? Three?*

She wanted to ask Dorran, but she couldn't afford to break the silence. Not just yet, not until they were certain it wouldn't work.

That hope grew thinner as minutes ticked by. Dorran continued to stroke her hand, but he seemed distracted. The darkness began to lessen. Gradually, the bluish hue that slipped under the shutters and caught on the driver's seat changed to an orange glow. Clare realized she was able to see the edge of Dorran's face, his strong nose, his eyelashes, and his lips set tight. *Dawn.*

His silhouette turned to look at her. For several minutes the silence was only broken by the incessant scrabbling nails, and then he said, "They're not going to leave."

"No." A horrible resignation filled Clare. She blinked furiously, trying to keep the growing dread in check. "Help me up?"

"Of course. Here."

He wrapped his arms around her and helped lift her. Clare flinched as she lowered her leg to the floor. She shuffled around to rest her back against the wall and sighed, grateful to finally move tired muscles.

The fingernails continued to pick at the window behind her, inches from her shoulder.

"I suppose this removes all doubt," Dorran said, settling at her side. "My mother still rules over Winterbourne."

Clare remembered the words written on the outside of the bus. *I knew you would come home.* "We were surprised by how healthy the garden was. I bet Madeline kept it going. Making her subjects water it and add fuel to the fire each day."

He glanced at her. "Because she hoped I would return. And she knew I would need food—human food—if I was going to live here."

"Yeah."

"I am sorry, Clare. I never should have asked to come back."

"We didn't think she was still alive. If she wasn't, this would have gone down very differently." Clare adjusted herself, grimacing as the foot moved. "We'd be facing maybe a couple dozen hollows. Mindless ones that could be frightened off and outsmarted. If Madeline hadn't been here, this would have been perfect for us."

His smile was bitter. "I should have turned us around as soon as I saw the bone statue of her. I was so complacent—"

"*We*," Clare corrected. "We made that decision together. I know you want it all for yourself, but you're going to have to share the blame, okay?"

"Ha." His shoulders shook, but he was smiling. Guilt had been one of his mother's favorite weapons, and for all of his progress in the outside world, Winterbourne was trying to drag him back into his old self-loathing mentality. Clare was powerless over a lot of what Madeline did to them, but that, at least, was one thing she could fight.

They sat, shoulders touching, watching the sliver of light coming from under the shutters as it brightened.

What do we do now? In a bus that doesn't run, surrounded by monsters, what are our options?

"We have food, at least," Dorran said, nodding to the baskets above them. "We were lucky not to move all of it inside last night. I'll get you some breakfast."

"I'll help."

"No." He pushed her back down as she tried to stand. "Rest your leg."

"It's not so bad." The dull throb refused to abate, and a bloom of red had developed on the bandages. Clare was frightened of what her leg would do if she tried to stand on it, but she needed to make it work. Their odds were so poor already, she couldn't afford to be a liability.

"No," he insisted, his voice gentle. "Not just yet. Please."

Clare reluctantly sank back. Dorran made two bowls of food. The bus had no way to heat the water without its engine, so the meal was dry and unappetizing. Clare forced it down, though. They needed all of the energy they could get.

The noise just wouldn't abate. It was wearing Clare down, shattering her resilience a fragment at a time. She wondered if that was their intention—not to get into the bus, but to stop the occupants from resting or thinking. Clare longed for just a moment of silence. She put her empty bowl aside and pressed her hands over her ears. It didn't stop it.

Dorran watched her, sadness etched over his features. Clare tried to smile for him, but the expression came through crooked. He didn't return it.

"I'm so sorry," he said.

"This isn't your fault." She shook her head, hands still in place to muffle the creatures.

"We have the radio," Dorran said, his eyes brightening. "It won't stop the noise completely, but it will be a distraction. Would that help?"

"Yes, please!" The radio would attract additional hollow ones, but it wasn't like that could make their situation any worse than it already was. Her only regret was that it didn't have the ability to transmit.

Dorran found the light-gray box near the front of the bus and carried it back to her. It turned on with a flick of the switch. Static played.

Before leaving Evandale, Unathi had given them the frequency to listen to for updates. Clare was desperate to hear from them. Even if they had no news, just hearing one of her friends' voices would have been a welcome relief. Dorran switched to it and they waited expectantly, but the channel was silent.

Don't read too much into it. They wouldn't broadcast continuously. Not unless they had significant news.

She couldn't stop her heart from sinking, though. Dorran began turning the dial, hunting through stations. They pressed close to the radio, fighting to find any human sounds inside the white noise. There was nothing—not even Ezra's station, the radio channel that had played one second of noise at a time as a way to conceal directions to his location. His generator must have died. The hollows gathered around the building had probably already dispersed.

Dorran searched the band twice with no results. Clare tried not to let her disappointment show as he turned the radio off.

"I am so sorry," he said.

"Not your fault," she repeated. *There has to be some way to get out. We can't stay in the bus much longer. But if we step outside, we're as good as dead.*

Her mind flitted around the problem, teasing it at every angle. If the hollows had been sent to stop them from thinking, it was working. She was exhausted. The thin sliver of light escaping from under the shutters was moving with slow, ponderous precision as the sun rose.

They have to stop eventually. Their hands will wear out. They'll need to sleep. Won't they?

Beth had said she didn't need rest. That had to be true for the rest of the hollows as well. Clare closed her eyes. She became aware of the bus rocking in tiny increments under the ceaseless hands. Her leg throbbed in time with it. She wanted to scream.

There has to be something we can do. An angle I've overlooked. Some way to get past them, stop them.

Her conscience waxed and waned, and she wouldn't have even known she'd slept except that the sun's direction changed in abrupt shifts. Its angles had become long when Dorran stood and paced along the bus toward the door. He stood facing it, staring toward Winterbourne even though the covers blocked it from sight. In the dimness, it took her a moment to make out his expression. There was wildness in it. Something desperate, something furious. Darkness around his eyes told Clare he hadn't rested.

"I want to try something reckless," he said. "Do you trust me?"

"Yes," she answered without hesitation.

CHAPTER 28

A CRACKED, DESPERATE SMILE grew. "You shouldn't. We might
not survive this."

She returned his smile. "Honestly, I don't think survival is my
top priority anymore. I'll do anything if it gets us out of this bus."

"Yes, it will certainly do that." He tilted his head. "Can you
walk?"

She stood. Her leg screamed. She closed her eyes, breathing
deeply through her nose, and waited for the pain to subside. It
held her weight. She took a limping step. "Yeah. I'll be all right."

Dorran was at her side. His hands ran across her face, a soft
caress, then he kissed her. "Please forgive me."

She shivered. "What for?"

"You deserved better than this."

"I wouldn't be anywhere else. I love you."

"And I love you, my darling Clare. More than you could guess."

He held her, and for that moment, it was almost possible to forget the clawing sounds surrounding them. Dorran, her rock, the best thing in her life, rested his lips on the top of her head, breathing in the scent of her hair, his hands shaking as they ran over her shoulders. Then he stepped back, and there was a steady resolution in his eyes. "Let's get out of here."

Dorran moved through the bus in long paces, pushing supplies into a backpack, which he dropped by the door. "We have the radio, the first aid kit, and the remaining food. Is there anything else in the bus that you want to keep? Because this is our last chance to get it."

Clare turned her eyes over the space. The bus had carried them well, despite the abuse it had been put through. "Nothing we can't live without. What can I do?"

"Stay at my side. I never want you out of arm's reach, no matter what. You can lean on me as much as you need. But we will likely have to move fast. Are you ready?"

"Yes."

Dorran reached above her to pull down the last carton of fuel they had bought from West Hope. Clare drew a breath. Realizing what his plan was sent chills through her, but she didn't try to argue; Dorran was right—it might be their only chance to get out.

He unscrewed the cap and tipped the canister. Fuel splashed across the bed and the rear seats. The gas filled Clare's nose, drowning out the stench of the hollows, and stung her eyes. She backed up, moving toward the front of the bus, and Dorran followed, resealing the jug with half of the fuel still inside.

Clare opened the storage hatch near the driver's seat and found a matchbox. She passed it to Dorran. He nudged Clare so she would be behind him, close to the door, then gave her a grim smile. "I love you, my dearest Clare."

Terrible anticipation quivered inside, but her voice stayed strong. "Light it up."

He flicked the match across the abrasive strip. It hissed, bright, fed by the gasses. Dorran extended his arm and flicked his wrist, tossing the match toward the back seats.

The area ignited before the match even landed. A rolling wave of fire burst toward them. Dorran wrapped his arms around Clare and leaned over her, shielding her, as the sudden warmth stung her skin.

The first rush of heat was gone within seconds. Clare squinted her eyes open. The rear half of the bus crackled with flames so large that she could feel their warmth radiating across her. Already, smoke began to fill the cramped space.

Dorran crouched to unscrew the fuel carton again. He took a cotton shirt and wrapped it around the end of a piece of rebar, tying it into place, to form a makeshift torch. He then doused the fabric in fuel before resealing the carton, still a third full.

"Stay close," he said. His eyes looked feverishly bright with the flames reflecting off them. Clare nodded. Smoke stung her throat and her eyes, and the air tasted too thin. Dorran extended the torch toward the inferno and lit it. Flames rushed up from the cotton, scorching the bus's roof.

Dorran gave her a short nod. Clare unlocked the door and

shoved it open in a single motion. Smoke poured past them as fresh air rushed in, and the flames redoubled their strength. Hollows had clustered around the door, prepared to scramble on board. Dorran snarled and thrust the torch at them. The nearest hollow wailed as the flame hit its face, singeing the flesh.

The multitude of creatures backed away, leaving a small patch of clear ground outside the bus. Glass cracked somewhere within the inferno. The roar was deafening.

Dorran stepped out of the bus, torch extended toward the monsters, bag of supplies slung over one arm. Clare followed, leaning on his shoulder to take pressure off her injured foot. The fire was already spilling out of the windows, scorching the plywood and sending a pillar of black toward the sky.

"Back," Dorran snarled, swiping the torch at the closest creatures.

They barely paid him any attention. They stared at the flaming bus, mouths agape in voiceless screams, bones rippling under their skin as they backed away.

"Up the stairs quickly," Dorran whispered to Clare. He threw the backpack over his shoulder, lifted the can of fuel in one hand, and carried the torch in the other.

Every step sent agony surging up Clare's leg. She tried to lengthen her paces, but it was as though she'd lost control over her ankle. It didn't want to land properly, always threatening to twist, to drop her to the ground. Dorran felt her falter and stopped, tilting his body to offer her his shoulder. Clare grabbed for it, grateful, and he pulled against her weight to help hold her up.

The ring of hollows broke as Clare and Dorran moved through it. They were at the steps. Clare looked down and saw she left a red imprint in the snow with every step. She tried to move faster and staggered. Dorran waited for her to tighten her hold on him, then pulled her up with himself. The doorway loomed open ahead of them. Behind, the hollows skittered, racing with frantic energy, their howls rising into the cooling night air.

An explosion rocked them. The heat rushed around Clare like a shock wave, and her bones felt as though they were rattling. She gasped, breathless, tumbling forward onto the top step. Dorran dropped the fuel can and hooked his arm under her.

"Please, Clare, please, we have to keep moving."

He spoke softly, but the urgency in his voice was unmistakable. Clare put her leg back under herself and almost screamed. She clenched her teeth until her jaw ached. Dorran lifted her back up, then retrieved the fuel canister as they stepped inside Winterbourne.

She sent one final glance behind them, through the doorway. The bus burned, the entire structure engulfed in flames that rose twenty feet into the sky. The metal was warping, the plywood peeling off the windows, the wheels melting. The red flames blended into the sky, and, for a moment, it looked as though the whole world was burning.

Then Clare faced the foyer again. It was a polar opposite of the fiery outside world. Cold. Barren. It was winter, resentment, bitterness. Faces appeared in doorways, multi-jointed limbs slinking across the marble floor and creeping down the stairs.

Dorran lifted the canister of fuel in one hand and the torch in his other. When he spoke, his voice boomed, carrying into the deepest parts of the house. "Winterbourne will burn just as easily!"

The torch sent embers floating toward the floor as the cotton shirt charred. Dorran pointed it toward the hollows on the stairs. His voice didn't waver. "Touch her, and I will set flame to this cursed building. Hurt her, and everything you cherish will be burned to the ground. We can be consumed by the fire together. There is enough wood in Winterbourne for a merry blaze."

Clare's heart raced. She held on to Dorran's arm, trying to stay upright. The hollows didn't react to Dorran's words. They continued to creep closer, their naked bodies and hairless heads shining in his light.

Then a sharp chatter pierced the building. It was loud enough to make Clare flinch. Dorran shuddered under her hand. The hollows dropped their heads, eyes blinking rapidly as though in fear of a blow. Then, as one, they began creeping backward into the darkness.

That was her. Madeline.

Dorran's expression was tight, pained. He'd heard his mother's voice in the bestial scream. "We have to move quickly, before she can change her mind."

Clare nodded. The stairs were daunting. The second floor looked impossibly high above them, and her leg was a tangle of searing pain.

Dorran tucked the fuel under the arm that still held the torch and slid his other arm under Clare's shoulders. He pulled her up, carrying most of her weight, as they moved toward the stairs. Clare closed her eyes for the climb, relying on Dorran to keep her moving. The pain was spreading through her body, threatening to pull her consciousness away. She focused on their goal. They were so close to safety. It didn't matter how little strength she had once she was in the room; she just had to hold on for then.

They reached the third floor. Clare opened her eyes again. Hollows lined the hallway. They crouched like living gargoyles in the gloom that clung across the walls, staring at the two humans. Clare took a sharp breath, afraid of moving closer when they were both so vulnerable, but Dorran pulled her forward. They passed between the first flanking of hollows, and the monsters hissed at them.

"Keep going," Dorran urged, breathless.

The torch was fading, the scorched remains of the shirt withering as the fuel ran out. Clare focused on the door ahead of them. Three of the monsters clustered around it, and they drew back as Clare and Dorran stepped closer.

She moved as quickly as she could, dragging the injured leg. Her vision swam, her lungs gasping futilely as though the air had been stripped of oxygen.

One of the hollows lunged forward, jaws snapping just shy of Clare's arm. Dorran barked at it, thrusting the torch toward its face, and it lurched away. The other hollows set up a screaming clamor and Clare grit her teeth against the noise.

They were at the door. The torch was dead. Dorran dropped

it as he pulled the keys out. Hands touched Clare's back. She flinched. The hollows had pressed in horribly tight, almost suffocating, their clammy, blistered fingers running over her body.

The door's lock clicked. It swung open. Dorran moved Clare through and slammed the door on the prying fingers. The lock clicked shut. Clare felt her grip on Dorran's arm weakening, and a stuttered, relieved chuckle escaped her before she slid to the floor.

CHAPTER 29

DORRAN CAUGHT HER. HE threw the can of fuel aside, then one hand went around the back of Clare's head to keep it stable. She dragged in a shuddering breath, trying to fight the dizziness and sickness that threatened, and smiled. "We did it."

"We did." He smiled back, but the expression faded as he looked down at her leg. His eyes darkened as he carefully touched the bandages. They were soaked in red. "Oh, Clare. Hold on."

He lifted her and moved her onto the bed. Clare grimaced as her leg turned, but she was just grateful to get her weight off of it. The dizziness was fading, and she pushed herself up onto her elbows as Dorran dropped the backpack beside them and hunted through it. "I can't believe that worked," she said.

"Lie down." He lightly pressed her shoulder, his attention still fixed on her leg, but Clare didn't budge. As he began unwrapping the soaked bandages, he said, "It was a risky gamble. We were lucky that my mother values her home as much as she does."

Clare flinched as the wet bandages peeled off her leg. Dorran muttered unhappily, then pulled out the box of painkillers.

"This must have hurt you badly. I am so sorry."

"It was worth it to get out of the bus." It might have been the exhaustion distorting her emotions, but Clare couldn't stop grinning.

"Ha." Dorran rose and disappeared into the bathroom. When he returned, he had a glass of water for her.

Clare swallowed the tablets. The cold water felt good on her smoke-scratched throat. "Madeline must *really* love this house."

Dorran laid out his equipment—clean towels, surgical needle and thread, water, and fresh bandages—before speaking. "It's a chess game. My mother is not reckless. She can sit with an unpleasant situation for weeks or even months if it means she ultimately gets what she wants. If she were more given to being ruled by emotions, we likely wouldn't have made it past the foyer. But she still thinks she can turn this into the outcome she most desires."

"She wants you to stay here willingly," Clare said.

His glance was quick and full of anxiety. "Yes. I threatened to take everything she sought—the house and my own life. She is allowing you to live to appease me for now, but it will not be a permanent concession."

"No, of course it wouldn't be." Clare bit the inside of her cheek as the needle dipped into her torn skin. She looked toward the ceiling, seeking patterns in the paint to distract herself.

"She has made a conservative move," Dorran said. "She is prepared to bide her time. It might take days, weeks, or even months for her countermove, but I am certain it will come, and it will be dealt when we are most vulnerable to it."

He knows her so well. That's from a lifetime of dealing with her mind games, trying to guess her motives and having to protect himself against her schemes.

"I'm sorry your family sucks," Clare said.

Dorran looked up, surprised, then began chuckling. "I'm sorry you had to become involved in it."

"Eh. I won't lie; it would be nice to get along with my mother-in-law, but at least you let me stab her, so that's a consolation."

Dorran sat back on his heels, shaking with laughter. It took a moment for him to subside. "Oh, I am glad you are with me. You can make anything bearable."

"Do you have a plan for a countermove, or are we playing it by ear?"

"I have an idea." He lowered his voice. "It will require patience and prolonging this stalemate for as long as possible."

"Ah," Clare smiled. "Until Becca activates the code."

"Exactly. It is the only possible way out that I can see. We cannot attack Madeline; even if we knew where to find her, she would be too well guarded. We cannot leave Winterbourne now that the bus is gone. So, we will stay sheltered and keep you protected. We will let her own patience be her downfall."

Clare glanced at the suitcase in the corner. "What about food? We only have enough there for another couple of days."

"She will not harm me; she wants to keep me alive. I will visit the garden and the furnace room. You will need to stay here."

Clare grimaced. "I don't like that. What if you're wrong? What if she *does* try to hurt you? If we go together, I can watch your back—"

"And you would be vulnerable. If you accompany me through the house, there are too many ways we could lose control of the situation. If I took my eyes off you for even a second..." He shook his head. "Stay here. We will keep the door locked. She will not make a move to get at you until she is certain she will succeed. We need to buy as much time as possible."

"Okay." Clare blew a breath through pursed lips. Already, the dark-blue wallpaper and gold edging was beginning to feel claustrophobic. She hated the thought of Dorran moving through the house alone on the mere assumption that he had immunity, but they had precious few choices. "Okay, but you still have to be as safe as possible. Carry weapons everywhere you go. And maybe some way to call for me if you need help. A whistle or—"

"I will be safe. I promise. My mother is a patient woman, and she believes she has us trapped. Our advantage is that she does not understand the nature of the thanites and has no control over the Evandale Research Institute."

Clare understood why he was speaking so quietly. "And, as long as she doesn't know, she won't realize her time is limited."

"Exactly." He finished tying the bandages around her leg, and rinsed his hands in the basin of water. "We simply need to wait... and hope Becca is fast at her job."

Dorran stayed close to Clare that night. A storm moved across the region near midnight, and they huddled close to the fire as snow and gale-force winds lashed the windows.

Their wood supplies were growing low. Dorran threw the final log on the fire, then he dusted his hands on his knees and stood. "I'll fetch more."

Clare's heart flipped. She grabbed his hand, keeping him beside her. "Not yet. At least wait until it's light out."

His soft smile was almost enough to assuage her fears. "I am not afraid. The creatures will be under instructions not to harm me, and they won't dare disobey. Waiting for sunlight won't make a difference."

Trust him. Clare's instincts were screaming at her, but she clamped down on her objections. She stood, though, her aching leg held off the ground and one hand braced on the closest wingback chair as she watched Dorran don a thicker coat, light a candle, and slide the hatchet into his belt.

"I will leave the keys with you to prevent any risk of them being stolen. Madeline may try to lure you out, but you must not open the door unless you hear my voice. Promise me that."

"I promise." Clare dragged him into a quick, tight hug. "And you promise that you'll be careful. If you start to feel unsafe, come back immediately."

"Agreed." He kissed her, lingering, then drew back as he placed the key ring on the table near the fireplace. He took up the candlestick and the fire poker, then crossed to the door. Clare ignored the sparks of pain sizzling up her leg as she limped after him, unwilling to let him out of arm's reach. He turned the door's lock and eased it open.

The space outside the door was empty, but as Clare leaned into the hallway, she saw flashes of eyes near the stairwell. Dorran saw them too. He smiled at Clare as he closed the door behind himself.

Clare didn't immediately turn the lock. She couldn't shake the fear that they had misread the situation, that the hollows lurking throughout the building weren't as subdued as they had imagined, and the idea of locking Dorran out of their sanctuary when he was about to be attacked filled her with sick dread. But his footsteps faded down the hallway, then she heard the stairs creak in the distance, and Clare finally turned the lock.

Please, come back quickly.

She shuddered and drew her coat more tightly around herself. The fireplace was warmer, but it put her too far away from the door, especially with her foot hobbling her. Instead, she drew up one of the ornate wooden chairs to sit in front of the entrance, ready to open the lock in less than a second if Dorran needed it.

Minutes ticked by, burning her insides like slowly seeping lava. The house complained under the freezing wind. In the distance came the pained squeak from the bus's hood. As irrational as it was, she felt guilty for what had happened to the bus. It was her last gift from Beth. It had served them loyally for weeks, surviving incessant abuse and never giving up on them. Even its fiery death had protected them, buying them the seconds of distraction they needed to get into the foyer. She wished they could have saved it.

A door slammed on the second floor. Clare wondered if that might be where Madeline was. Since the building had been abandoned for so long, the matriarch might have moved out of the tunnels and back into the main part of the house. Clare hated the idea of the deformed woman stalking through the rooms.

Will she try to talk to Dorran? Clare clenched her hands, glowering at the door with all of the loathing she felt toward the older woman. Madeline had manipulated Dorran for years, emotionally and physically tormenting him, and Clare didn't put it past her to try to whittle down her child's will now. If Madeline did show herself, Clare hoped Dorran would be smart enough to come back to their room. He didn't have to face his mother alone any longer.

The clock's ticks counted down the passing minutes. The anxious, angry fire in Clare's stomach cooled into thick fear. The journey to the basement and its stores of firewood wasn't short, but it still shouldn't have taken Dorran this long.

Madeline confronted him. Or he's become trapped. Or the hollows attacked after all, and he can't get back here. He's hurt and he can't even call for help—

Footsteps approached along the hallway. Clare drew a sharp breath and rose. She reached toward the lock but didn't turn it, waiting for Dorran to call.

He knocked: four sharp raps that made the wood under Clare's fingertips tremble.

She bit her lip, the anxious prickles spreading across her shoulder blades and making them itch. "Dorran, is that you?"

He knocked again, more urgently this time.

It's not him, part of her mind said. The other half retorted, *But what if it is?*

He could have been hurt. She imagined him in the hallway, leaning against the door, shaking and voiceless. His throat ripped away, his mouth torn up, trying to call to her but unable to.

Her hand moved to the lock. Touched the cold metal. She itched to turn it, and it took effort to hold her fingers still.

"Dorran, I need to know it's you."

She thought she could hear him breathing. It was thick and wet, not the sound of a healthy throat, not the sound of the Dorran she loved. Her fingers twitched. She forced them still. Her voice cracked. "Speak to me."

"*Help…me…*"

Clare stepped back from the door. She was shaking, nauseated, her world feeling like it was tipping over. She forced herself back into the seat and clasped her hands in her lap so she wouldn't be tempted to reach toward the door's lock again.

The voice wasn't Dorran's. It played like a broken record, a memory of human words, spoken without feeling or awareness.

Four more knocks shook the door. Then the voice came again, reedy and unnatural, playing on a loop. "Help…me…help… me…help…me…help…me…"

Clare closed her eyes and bowed her head, fighting the urge to cry.

The clock above the fireplace continued to count down the seconds. Dorran had been gone for nearly half an hour.

CHAPTER 30

THE VOICE OUTSIDE THE door grew louder with each echo. "*Help… me…help…me…*"

The words were punctuated by the fist, beating in a steady tempo, hard enough to make the frame around the door tremble. Then, all at once, it was joined by a dozen other fists. They not only beat the door, but pounded along the length of the wall. Clare clenched her hands together. They were slippery with cold perspiration.

Then, abruptly, the fists fell silent. The voice croaked one final rendition of its song: "Help…me." Then it faded away. The hallway was silent.

Clare turned her burning eyes toward the ceiling. She struggled to remain silent, afraid that any noise might bring the creatures back. The charred hood of the bus creaked as the wind tugged at it. The fire popped behind her. The gale continued to dig at

Winterbourne's loose shingles and claw its way through gaps in the stone. It was gradually transitioning into a blizzard.

The house's noises were suddenly interrupted by approaching footsteps. Clare reflexively recoiled from the noise, but it was different from the sounds from before. Faster, heavier, more regular. Knuckles rapped against the door in a soft, quick tempo. And then Dorran called, "Hello, Clare. It's me."

She leaped out of her seat, flinching as she put weight on her leg, and turned the lock. Dorran pushed the door open with his back and stepped into the room. He carried a stack of firewood under his arm, and a rough cotton bag over his shoulder. He shoved the door closed behind himself, and his smile faded as he saw her.

"You're ghost white. Did something happen?"

Words choked in her throat. The relief of seeing Dorran safe blended with the anxiety until it was overwhelming. She grit her teeth and shook her head.

Dorran dropped his burdens on the floor. His hands roved across her face and neck, and he hissed between his teeth. "You're freezing. My darling, I'm so sorry. I know I was away for a long time—too long. I should have returned sooner."

"Yep," she managed.

He scooped her up, lifting her feet from the ground easily, and carried her to the fire. Clare was too emotionally fatigued to argue against it. He settled them into the seat, one arm around her back to hold her. "What happened?"

She told him about the hollows that had tried to mimic him. He scowled at the flames, jaw working.

"I knew she would try to manipulate us, but I hadn't expected it to begin so soon. I am sorry. It should have been a shorter trip. I should have guessed they were trying to distract me."

Clare searched his dark eyes. "What? What did they do?"

"After I refueled the garden's furnace and gathered wood for our own fire, I stopped to check on the garden. The tap had been turned on, flooding the floor."

"Why?"

"That's what I wondered." Dorran shook his head. "The beds are raised, so it wasn't as though they could kill the garden. I turned the tap off and checked around the plants to ensure no other damage had been done. As far as I can tell, they are intact. But it raised another concern."

Clare's mouth dried. "How did they get into the garden?"

"Exactly. My first fear was that they might have some secondary set of keys. I was preparing to run back to you when I realized the true answer: the garden has a secret compartment leading to the concealed tunnels."

"Seriously?" Clare blinked, shocked. Before leaving Winterbourne to search for Beth, they had attempted to map the passageways and their concealed doors. But somehow, neither of them had considered searching the garden's walls. "We've been so careful to lock the door…and all this time they had a back entrance?"

"I was just as disturbed. They don't seem to intend to damage our food source, but I don't appreciate the idea of them in there, regardless. I found the door in the back wall, behind a row of shelves. It had been left open a crack. I nailed it shut."

"Good."

"That is the reason I took so long: finding the supplies to secure the door and searching for any others. I didn't even consider that they might have intended for me to be distracted. Regardless, I should have checked in with you. It was not fair to make you worry so much." He kissed her forehead. "I won't leave you again tonight, my dear."

"You'd better not," she grumbled.

"Ah. I forgot. I brought a peace offering." Dorran squeezed her shoulder as he left her side. He returned with the armful of wood and the cloth bag, which he placed at Clare's feet. "Lettuce. Tomatoes. Snow peas. Even a cucumber…which is admittedly on the small side, but those are the sweetest."

"Oh!" Clare felt a smile grow as she sorted through the bag. "We can have a salad."

"Exactly. Our first rewards from the garden. There is not much to celebrate in our current situation, but this is something."

The salad was as basic as Clare had ever eaten. They had no dressing, no tangy or crunchy elements, not even salt for the tomatoes. But it had been weeks since Clare last tasted fresh produce, and that made it one of the most delicious things she had ever eaten.

She and Dorran shared the meal out of the same bowl, nestled together with their shoulders bumping. The leaves were warm from the garden's lights and sap beaded at where the stem had been cut, but it was crisp and juicy, and Clare felt a small thrill to remember she had been the one to sow the lettuce seeds.

"The plants are thriving," Dorran said, spearing a cherry tomato. "There are others ready to be picked, more than we could eat in one meal. And the slower plants are gradually maturing. We will have more variety soon."

"I want to see it again." Clare didn't realize how true that statement was until she spoke it. The garden had always been the best part of Winterbourne: her refuge, a place of life and safety. As happy as she was to eat the dividends, she wanted to walk among the plants again.

Dorran brushed her hair behind her ears, his voice sad. "I know. This won't be forever. We just need to wait."

I'll try.

While Dorran washed up the bowl and cutlery, Clare limped to the window. The blizzard forced endless flecks of white against the glass, its chill drifting into the room and stealing their warmth. She leaned close, breath misting, squinting to see through the frost plastered to the panes. In the distance, the forest was barely visible, a seemingly endless tangle of old trees. Something moved across the white yard near their burned-out bus. She frowned, pressing so close to the window that her exhalation fogged it.

Hollows paced through the snow like grim, mindless sentinels. Their fingers and toes must have been breaking with frostbite, the thanites rebuilding the cells in chaotic patterns, but they didn't seem to feel it. Their bulging, watering eyes stared up at Clare's window. She pulled the curtains closed to block the hostile gazes.

Clare was too wired to sleep for the rest of the night. While Dorran napped in front of the fire, she flitted about the room.

She placed the radio on the windowsill and turned it on, its volume low enough that the static wouldn't be disturbing but just loud enough that she would hear if Evandale activated their channel. Then she unloaded the backpack from the bus, laying their hoarded goods on the dresser.

Between the supplies from the bus and her own suitcase, they had forty-five cans, an assortment of fish, beans, and vegetables. In addition, there were some packets of dry food—pasta, rice, and even a box of pancake mix.

Enough for a week or two. Clare ran her hand over the back of her neck. Dorran stirred by the fire, his eyebrows pulling together as some dream turned sour. Clare approached and knelt to run her fingers through his hair. He relaxed. *We'll have to rely on the garden heavily, and only use the canned food as a last resort. Before, we had the bus to search for more supplies. Now, everything we need to survive has to come from Winterbourne.*

She shivered and added a fresh log to the fire before pulling her knees up under her chin. Winterbourne had always felt bereft to her, as though it were dying without any souls moving through it. Now, in the depths of night, she couldn't believe how *alive* it felt. Feet moved through the passageways. Most of the time, she could barely hear them. But occasionally, the creatures loped through the halls outside their room, running their fingers across the wallpaper, the maddening clicking and chattering reverberating. In the distance, doors whispered open and closed. Winterbourne had never felt so full of life, and Clare hated it.

She slept in broken patches. The storm had quietened to gentle snowfall by the time dawn broke. Clare returned to the window to watch the golden light spear across the sky. Hollows continued to circle below, relentless, their eyes trained on the windows. The bus had almost vanished under a blanket of white, the earlier ferocity of its blaze erased as completely as nature could manage.

"Good morning," Dorran said.

She turned a smile on him. "Hey there. Didn't realize you were awake."

He stretched in front of the fire, arms reaching overhead and back arching as he shook off the stupor of sleep. "Have you been up long?"

"A while." She glanced back out toward the pacing monsters. "It's hard to sleep when the house is so noisy."

"Hmm." He stood and crossed to her. His arms wrapped around her, hugging her against his chest. "I'll need to leave again, to revisit the garden."

She'd known it was coming, but she still dreaded it. She scowled at the blinding-white snow outside the window.

"I'll return quickly this time," he promised. "If I suspect they're trying to delay me, I'll come back for you immediately."

It wasn't much of a comfort, but they didn't have any choice. Clare pressed her eyes closed. "Be safe out there."

"I will." He stepped back and Clare shivered against the sudden rush of cold. "Be patient. Wait for my voice before opening the door."

CHAPTER 31

LIKE THE DAY BEFORE, Clare remained a sentry at the door. She sat facing the immense wooden slab, the metal key ring clasped in her hands. The door dwarfed her, larger and thicker than any bedroom door had a right to be. Everything in Winterbourne seemed to have been designed that way. To impress. To intimidate.

She kept one eye on the clock. The ceaseless noises in the house continued to hum around her: the scraping, unstable footsteps; the scratching fingers running across kilometers of wallpaper; the whispering chatters so unrelenting that she thought she might never be free from them.

How long will I be trapped here? Her eyes roved across the maddeningly patterned wall. The room was decadent enough to be called luxurious, but Clare had never sought luxury. She preferred cozy comfort. And her prison had very little of that.

Thunder crackled in the distance. Clare hoped the storm

wouldn't pass over Winterbourne. She was exhausted by the charged air, the noise, the frenzy.

It seemed like such an obvious choice to return to Winterbourne when we were at the research institute. I imagined it would be like before we left. Working beside Dorran to seal the hidden passageways, and running between the garden and the kitchens. I thought I could turn this place into our home. It was so stupid. Stupid, stupid.

Footsteps approached. Clare recognized them as Dorran's before he even reached the door. She approached, one hand held over the lock, as she waited for his voice.

"It's me," he called, and Clare pulled the door open.

Dorran stepped in, the cloth bag full of vegetables slung over his shoulder. His hair was wet and flecked white with melting snow.

"You went outside," Clare said, shocked.

"I did." He locked the door behind himself, placed the bag on the ground, and ruffled the moisture out of his hair. "I had an idea while I was in the garden. Do you remember what I said about my mother and how she would be treating this as though it were a chess match? She will be expecting us to have a plan. If we stay in our room and don't appear to be trying anything, she will grow anxious and may play her hand early."

"Oh." Clare nodded, her mind churning. "That makes sense. What did you do?"

"Not much. I didn't want to leave you for long. I went outside and pretended to assess the wall. Then I found the sled from the foyer and dragged it to the space below our window." He flashed

her a smile. "That will give her something to wonder about…
and to sabotage."

"Was it nice outside?"

"It was cold." He began lifting vegetables out of the bag. "I
am already looking forward to spring. You will like it. Everything
becomes so vibrant—even the forest."

"Ha. Just as long as I'm allowed outside by then." Clare had
meant it as a joke, but her laughter was too strained.

Dorran's hands stilled, and he dropped a tomato back into the
bag. Clare didn't like the way he watched her, as though he was
picking his words carefully, afraid of the response. "I know this is
not easy for you. But, please—"

"Be patient! I know. *I know!* I won't leave the room. Stop
worrying."

Clare turned aside, hating the way her voice cracked. She
felt like her insides were under pressure, boiling, as angry words
searched for an outlet. She folded her arms across her chest as she
tried to get her emotions back under control.

"Clare…"

"Forget it. I'm tired right now, that's all. Give me some space."

Dorran stood by the fire, his back straight, his cheeks a shade
paler than normal. The shutters had been drawn over his expression. He wouldn't meet her gaze but bowed his head in a formal
nod as he said, "Please excuse me."

He crossed to the door in quick strides and, before Clare could
say anything, slipped through it. His fading footsteps echoed in
time with Clare's thumping heart.

At least one of us can leave whenever they want.

Clare pressed a hand to her mouth. She crossed to the table carrying the radio and slammed her fist against the surface. As her frustration and the anxiety converged, the radio's quiet static hissed, its erratic tempo feeling as frantic as she did. She bit onto a groan, cutting it off before it could escape.

Get yourself together. This is hardly suffering.

She took a breath, leaned over the table, then straightened her back as she fought with her racing heart.

Dorran is the one shouldering all of the risk…and all of the work. Be kind to him. Heaven knows there's precious little else you can do right now.

She turned to look at the door. The anger faded like a coal dropped into chilled water. Dorran was uncomfortable with volatile moods; he'd learned to fear them after a lifetime around his mother. Clare had tripped his natural defenses and it had driven him away, out into the house, the situation that was the most dangerous to him.

For a wild second, she imagined running after Dorran. He moved through the house so easily, it seemed insane that she couldn't take even twenty steps in it. Clare struggled with the impulse before sinking into the seat facing the door. The risk was too great.

Her hands shook. Her mind felt scattered, and she struggled to pull it back together. A pit of guilt grew in her stomach.

She owed Dorran everything. He was doing his best to keep her safe; he was tired, pushed beyond his comfort, hounded by stress and uncertainty. And Clare, the one person he was supposed to be able to rely on above everything else, had turned on him.

Clare swiped her hand across her eyes, which were growing wet. She prayed Dorran would keep his cool. That he wouldn't take any risks or do anything dangerous.

How long until he comes back?

He didn't seem to feel the danger as acutely as Clare did, not unless he was doing a good job of hiding it. He could easily spend the rest of the day away from her. There was an excess of space in Winterbourne and plenty of rooms with their own locking doors.

For that matter, he could decide to spend the night in a different room. It was possible he wouldn't return for days.

Clare doubled over, feeling queasy. But almost as fast as the fear hit, it dissipated. *Dorran wouldn't do that.*

She knew him too well. He hadn't left her when she'd turned cold on him after stopping at Marnie's house. He hadn't left her when the phantoms in Winterbourne had caused her to doubt her own mind. He hadn't left when Beth tried to push him out of their group. He would be back before the day was over.

I don't ever want him to dread returning here. This should be the one place he feels safest. She would be better. Warmer. She still had a lot to be grateful for, she knew. The captivity was grating on her, but she still had a much, much better life compared to many others.

Three knocks rang from the door. "Clare, it's me."

She blinked, shocked. She'd been certain Dorran would

return, but she still hadn't expected it to be so soon. She crossed to the door as quickly as her leg would allow.

Dorran waited outside, a crate balanced under one arm. He met her eyes, and for a moment, they stood wordless, silently trying to read each other.

Then Dorran jostled the box, half of a smile lifting his lips. "May I come in? I brought a peace offering."

"Of course you can." Clare grabbed his jacket's lapel and pulled him inside, locking the door behind them. The words came so quickly that they nearly choked her. "I'm so sorry. There was no reason to snap at you like that. Please forget what I said. I didn't mean it."

"No, you did, and you're entitled to. You're trapped in this room with nothing to do except think." He raised a hand to indicate their surroundings. "There is no enjoyment here, nothing distracting or entertaining, nothing pleasant."

Clare shrugged. "It's warm and comfortable and safe. It beats the alternative."

"That is not enough. And I was remiss not to realize it earlier." He placed the crate on one of the fireside chairs and began pulling the contents out. First was a stack of five cloth-bound books. "You already know how outdated our library is, but its contents are at your disposal. If you want a book on a particular topic, tell me, and I will do my best to find it for you."

A lump had developed in Clare's throat, forcing her to nod wordlessly as she took the books. Two names she recognized as Regency-era writers; she had never heard of the other three.

Dorran reached deeper into the box. To Clare's shock, he had managed to fit a ceramic pot into it, filled with dark soil and with a young tomato plant sprouting from the earth.

"You miss the garden," he said, setting the pot onto the desk beside the radio. "I know how you love it. This is a poor substitute, but it will give a little life and brightness to the room."

Filled with wonder, Clare traced her fingertips across its young leaves. Dorran must have transplanted it from the garden. Despite its small size, it was vibrant and filled with life, something that she'd been missing more than she'd realized.

"One more gift." He lifted the final item out of the box. A bottle of red wine, its label dusty, rolled in his hand, and his lips quirked into a smile. "Normally I would not recommend alcohol to cope with an unpleasant situation, but, well, these are abnormal circumstances. The garden has been tended to for today, so I propose we both get drunk."

"Stop being so good." Clare pressed her palms into her eyes, shaking with laughter and tears. "I feel guilty enough as it is."

He placed the bottle aside, then his hand found her face. Clare shivered at his touch. "You have gone from being trapped in one situation to another for weeks now. Trapped in this house, in the research institute, in the bus, and finally, in this room. And you have no control over it. *Choice* is something we often don't value until we lose it. And I'm sorry that your choice has been taken away from you."

He would know that all too well. A life spent controlled by his mother, forced to abide her whims to protect his nieces and nephews, had left Dorran starved of freedom for years. It meant he could put Clare's emotions into words far more clearly than she could.

"I wish I could give you your choice back," he whispered. "But until then, I can try to make your situation a little more bearable. Heaven knows I would not like to trade places with you."

Clare hugged him as tightly as she could. Her emotions felt too thick, like they were drowning her. "Let's put on the kettle. You could probably do with something warm to drink."

"Tea sounds wonderful."

"And I wouldn't say no to that wine either."

Dorran laughed, kissing the top of her head.

CHAPTER 32

"WHAT ABOUT SNOW PEAS?" Clare asked.

Dorran lounged beside her, legs extended toward the fire, a nearly empty cup of wine clasped in his hands. He pressed the back of his hand to his mouth as he laughed. "It will be horrible."

"How do we know that, though?" Clare leaned against his shoulder. A buzz from the wine ran through her, making her feel warm, cozy, and a little dizzy. "I never believed chili would taste good in chocolate until I tried it. Maybe it just takes an entrepreneurial soul to discover a new, magical form of food."

He spoke through stifled laughter. "You can try."

"All right!" Clare rifled through the bag of vegetables until she found a snow pea, then stabbed it onto the end of a fork.

She and Dorran had begun eating dinner cold—a salad, like the day before—until Dorran suggested cooking some of the tomatoes over the fire. That had led them on a path of experimenting with different charred vegetables. Some were unsurprising; neither of them could stomach the cooked lettuce, and they agreed the baby spinach needed some butter and salt. They were pleasantly surprised by how nice the radishes were.

Clare held the snow pea over the fire, then yelped as the green skin scorched black faster than she'd anticipated. She pulled it out, blowing on it until she thought it would be cool enough, then tore half off for Dorran and placed the other half in her mouth.

"Oh," Clare said, frowning as she chewed. "It's weird, but maybe it's not so bad?"

"I think that's the wine talking." Dorran looked beautifully happy as he grinned at her. "It is truly awful, my darling."

"That's because you didn't get enough of the char. Just wait, I'll cook another one for you."

Dorran hooked his arms around her waist, dragging her away from the vegetable bag. "No, no, you won't ruin any more. It is an affront to nature, and I wish for no part in it."

Clare ended up in his lap, laughing uncontrollably. Dorran joined in, nuzzling around her neck, his chuckles rumbling through them as he began to kiss her throat.

She knew she had been unhappy earlier that day, but at that moment, Clare couldn't remember why. She leaned into Dorran's kisses, shivering, and ran her hands through his hair. As he murmured in response to her touch, she thought she would be perfectly happy if they never moved from that room.

"You smell like nature," he said between kisses. "No wonder

you love the garden so much. You smell like…lavender, and old forests, and warm air that has traveled across fields."

"I should get you drunk more often. You turn poetic."

"Ha. And you turn pink."

"Oh no." Clare pressed her hands to her cheeks to hide them, but that only made Dorran laugh again before descending for more kisses. Then he abruptly stopped, raising his head, his expression darkening. Clare felt her stomach drop. "What is it?"

He lifted a finger to his lips. Clare held her breath as she listened.

Someone was speaking. The voice came from a long way away, distorted by distance, barely audible above the fire and whistling screams of the wind.

Dorran carefully reached for the nearby fire poker. Then something clicked in Clare's mind, and she grabbed Dorran's arm. "It's the radio!"

He drew a sharp breath. Clare clambered to her feet and crossed to the table, hope rushing through her. A voice, faintly distorted, had replaced the ever-present static. Clare wound the volume up until the voice was clear. "Unathi," she breathed as she and Dorran bent over the radio.

"—be prepared. Ensure all wounds are treated appropriately and avoid unsafe situations. I repeat, the chemical keeping the hollow ones alive will be destroyed at noon in three days' time. If successful, all hollows will be eliminated. The destruction of this chemical may impact your health and reduce your ability to recover from injuries. We encourage you to be prepared. Ensure all wounds are treated appropriately and avoid unsafe situations. Spread the word."

She's keeping it simple. Instead of trying to explain what the thanites are and how they work, she's calling it a chemical. That's smart. Less confusion, less room for people to doubt her.

The static held for a moment, then Unathi's voice returned, this time losing its formality. "Clare. Dorran. I don't know if you're listening, but we're doing well. Niall is beginning to walk again. He'll probably have scars, but…well. This is almost over. We hope you're healthy. We hope you're in a safe place."

Another pause, then her voice resumed its earlier coolness. "This is an important announcement from an anonymous group of scientists working to eliminate the hollow ones. Please share with any communities you can. Any situational updates will be broadcast each hour on the hour. Otherwise, this announcement will repeat on a loop. The chemical keeping the hollow ones alive will be destroyed at noon in three days' time—"

Clare met Dorran's gaze, hope and excitement exploding through her. His grin matched hers, and his eyes shone. They grabbed each other, laughing and crying in the same breath.

"Three days!" Dorran said. "Three days and it will be over."

"Three days," Clare echoed. She had been desperate to hear the announcement, but until that moment, the cynical part of her had begun to fear that it would never come.

Dorran picked her up and twirled her, and Clare shrieked with laughter as she clung to him.

"Three days," they said in unison, and Clare grabbed his collar and pulled him into a kiss.

His lips were good. His hands were good, too, tangling in her hair. She felt him melt against her, all warmth and love, and as Unathi's voice repeated the recorded message in the background, Clare arched her back to taste more of Dorran.

A door slammed above them. They broke apart, breathless, and Clare's euphoria died. She shared an alarmed look with Dorran, then lunged for the radio and turned the dial to mute Unathi's voice.

They held still for a moment, listening to the house. Wood creaked. Hollows continued to move around the halls, feet scraping, nails digging. The windows rattled as the wind snagged at them. There were no other noises.

"Do you think she heard?" Clare whispered.

Dorran opened his mouth, then closed it again, still staring at the ceiling.

I shouldn't have had the radio so loud. What if she did hear? What if she knows her time is limited?

Dorran believed Madeline would bide her time…but only if she believed time was on her side. She was the kind of woman who would want to win, even if death was imminent. Clare shuddered and clung to Dorran. He hugged her back, and she could feel how shallow his breathing was. He was worried too.

Three days. That's all we need to get through.

When she'd first heard Unathi's announcement, it had felt like almost no time. Now, it seemed like an eternity.

"We will take additional precautions," Dorran said. "I will ensure I'm never away from the room for more than five minutes, even if I have to make multiple trips. And we can barricade the door more securely."

Clare shook her head. "You have to stay here. We can survive off the canned food for three days."

"My darling, I can't. The temperature is dropping. The garden will die if I don't keep the furnace running."

Clare shook her head again. "Let Madeline worry about it. She kept it alive while we were away from Winterbourne."

"I do not think she will tolerate it now that we are back. It would put her in a subservient role. And—"

"And there's nothing she'd hate more." Clare released a slow breath through clenched teeth.

Dorran turned his gaze from the door to the windows. When he spoke, he seemed to be fighting to keep his voice even. "It will be all right. We can come up with a way to distract her. Perhaps we can pretend we plan to walk to the nearest town in four days' time and have her concentrate her energy on foiling that."

Clare felt sick. She wanted to believe Dorran, but she could hear beyond the confidence in his voice. He wasn't certain distractions would work. Madeline was smart. She was not the kind of woman who took things at face value or relied on a single plan.

But they had no alternatives. Dorran was right; he needed to continue visiting the garden. Even just one day of cold could kill the plants, and without transport away from Winterbourne, they couldn't risk losing their only ongoing source of food.

Relenting felt like sacrificing something valuable, but Clare swallowed, her throat aching, and said, "All right."

CHAPTER 33

CLARE NAPPED THROUGH THAT afternoon, catching up on missing sleep from the night before. Her dreams were scattered and anxious. Dorran had promised not to leave while she was asleep, but every time she woke, Clare still had to search for him before her heart fell back to a healthier rate. He was never far away, either relaxing beside her, or reading a book on the nearest chair, or staring toward the door, his eyes sharp and jaw tense.

The last time she woke, she caught Dorran looking at her. He smiled, but Clare could see how forced it was. He had heard something outside.

She sat up, her back aching and her head foggy from sleep. Dorran moved to put the kettle over the fire, brushing a hand over her head as he passed her.

"Everything okay?" Clare asked.

"Of course." He smiled again, but it still lacked the natural ease Clare had grown to love. He laid out their two mugs on the hearth while the water heated, and Clare pulled her knees up under her chin.

"What's it like out there, when you go to the garden and the library? Do the hollows avoid you, or do you see them?"

Dorran faced the fire, and although he was clearly trying to keep his expression neutral, the flames highlighted the tenseness in it. "I see them sometimes."

"How often?" When he didn't immediately answer, Clare shuffled closer to him and rested one hand on his arm. He still wouldn't look at her. "I'd rather know."

"They line the hallways," Dorran admitted. "Every corner, and beside every door. They watch me, but they never try to touch me."

Clare shuddered. She imagined walking through the hallways; the wallpaper and furniture were near invisible in the gloom, with the hollows, so still that they could be statues, flanking him on either side, their bulging eyes catching in the scarce traces of light.

"Are you ever afraid Madeline will lose control of them and they'll attack you from behind?"

A thin laugh escaped. "Oh yes. I do my best not to think about it. I don't like walking past them, though. After killing so many of the beasts, it seems unnatural to cohabitate with them."

Clare licked her lips and broached her next question carefully. "Have you seen Madeline?"

"No." The kettle began to bubble, so Dorran pulled it off the flame and poured the steaming liquid into their mugs.

Clare watched him as he used a single tea bag to flavor both of their drinks. She waited, sensing that Dorran was keeping something from her. After a moment, he sighed.

"I hear her sometimes. Not just when I'm moving through the house but in our room, as well."

"What does she say?"

"Horrible things. Violent things." He threw the tea bag into the fire, then passed Clare her mug with shaking hands. "I do my best not to listen to her."

"It won't be long now." Clare leaned back, her toes digging between the rug's threads. "The code must be ready. Unathi wouldn't announce it otherwise. I just wish she would unleash it. This could be all over by now. I wouldn't have to worry about you."

Dorran stroked her hair back from her head. "She must have wanted to give people warning. If losing your thanites feels anything like what I experienced, it could be devastating if you were driving or in any other precarious sort of situation."

"Hmm." Clare pressed her lips together. "She probably thought three days would be reasonable. Maybe even on the short side, since it's so hard for news to spread now. But it feels like an eternity when you're trying to survive."

"Things were simpler in the institute. They hadn't truly experienced the new world and didn't know what it was like. Days blended together too easily."

"I wish we had some way to contact them. Or a way to contact anyone."

"I do as well."

Clare wondered if Dorran was thinking along the same lines as her, toward what they would do if the code worked. No one except John from West Hope knew they were at Winterbourne, and no one was likely to stumble on it. Even with the hollow ones gone, they were still essentially stranded. *We'll figure it out. We've come this far; we can see it to the end.*

It was better than imagining the alternative: a world where the code failed and killed them all.

Two more nights. She shivered. It was so close.

Dorran drained his cup of tea and exhaled. "It's time to visit the garden."

The familiar anxiety squirmed its way through Clare's stomach, turning her cold. "Already? Can't you put it off for another hour?"

"I would very much like to, but I shouldn't delay. This will be the last time."

She drew a sharp breath. "Really?"

"Yes. I will overload the furnace with fuel, like we did on the day we left to search for Beth. The heat should hold until Wednesday evening. I will bring back as much food as I can, and we will stay here until the code has been activated. Does that sound like a good plan?"

"Yes, please, yes." She grabbed his arm, squeezing it. "And come back quickly. It doesn't even matter if we don't have enough vegetables; we can use some of the cans."

"I will. I promise." He kissed her, and smiled as he drew back. "Twenty minutes. And then I will be all yours, and the next time we leave this room, we leave together."

They were some of the sweetest words Clare had ever heard. She let Dorran slip his hand out of hers and followed him to the door.

He gave her one final, fond look on the threshold. "Can I bring you anything else from the house? More books? Wine?"

"No. This is going to sound cheesy, but as long as you're here, I have everything I need."

His smile broadened. "I love you."

"I love you too."

Then he stepped through the door, closing it with a click behind him. Clare turned the lock and clutched the keys in both hands, nerves and hope thrumming through her. It didn't matter how often Dorran left; the fear was never any easier to handle. *We're on the edge of a new world. Three more days…*

Clare left the keys on the seat by the door and crossed to the fire. It was growing low, so she stacked more wood on it, then filled the kettle and hung it on its hook. Dorran would have a fresh drink as soon as he returned. It would help warm fingers that had been chilled by the frosty air that saturated the rest of the house.

A door slammed above Clare. She stared at the ceiling as the floorboards creaked. Something heavy moved through the attic. She tried to picture the kind of hollow that would make that noise, scrunched up her nose, and turned away.

The room no longer felt like a prison now that they were so close to the end. Clare pulled on her boots and then went to the ceramic pot on the bureau. She thought the tomato plant had grown even in the time she'd had it. She would keep it with her once the house was theirs again. It could stay in their room, something green and beautiful to look at each morning.

The radio rested beside the pots. A pang of loneliness ran through Clare, and she turned the radio on and raised the volume just enough that she could make out Unathi's voice, but without letting it grow loud enough that anyone outside the door would hear. She'd already memorized the looped message. Her smile faded as unfamiliar words were broadcast to her.

"Update...the deadline has changed..." Unathi took a sharp breath. "The code will be activated at sundown today. Please prepare yourself. Find a secure location. Ensure all wounds are treated. The code will be activated today."

There was a click as the recording ended, then the original message resumed. Clare's mouth was dry. She hung close to the radio, clutching it with both hands, waiting while the original, memorized announcement played itself out. Once it finished, there was another click, then Unathi's voice became harried again as the two recordings played in a loop. "Update...the deadline has changed..."

Why would they have moved the deadline closer? Unathi sounds stressed. But why? I'd think they were being harassed by survivors looking for supplies, but she never broadcast the shelter's location.

Wait... Clare closed her eyes. The radio transmissions would have attracted the hollows, just like Ezra's transmissions resulted in a pile of the monsters around his tower. Some of them, the smart ones, might have even heard and understood the announcement. The research center was probably under assault as hollows tried to break into it and destroy the one thing that was guaranteed to kill them.

She chewed on her thumb as she paced the length of the room. The station couldn't have been breached; otherwise, Unathi would have enacted the code out of desperation. The fact that it hadn't been unleashed meant their situation wasn't dire. Yet.

Please, don't leave it too late. Don't wait until they have broken your systems or clawed through the doors.

An idea hit her, and she paced faster. The two messages looped automatically. Clare didn't know how long they had been running. Maybe the station *had* been breached. Maybe everyone was dead. Maybe the code would never be coming, and all that was left of her friends was a recording that would play endlessly, always promising *Today...today...today...*

"No." Clare kicked at a chair as she passed it. She didn't want to think about that. She would know, one way or another, by the end of the day.

Dorran, where are you?

It would be easier if she had Dorran with her. He had a calming effect, his steady presence and logic settling the storms in her mind. She looked at the clock. He had been gone for twenty minutes. The kettle above the fire had nearly bubbled dry.

Clare wrapped a cloth around her hand and removed the pot

from the flames. She poured fresh water into it, then, moving as patiently as she could, she returned it to the fire.

Twenty minutes, Dorran. Time to be back.

She approached the door in slow, measured steps. Her breathing was even, her movements cautious, both belying the painful thumping of her heart.

I don't need books. I don't need wine. I don't even need food right now. I just need you.

Footsteps still moved around her, roving through the passageways, but they had lost their scraping, slouching cadence. Now, they beat faster, almost eagerly, the teeth chattering as they raced through the house.

No. It's your imagination. You're growing paranoid. This is fine. It's only been twenty-two minutes. Dorran will be back any second; just wait.

She wrapped her arms around herself and strode to the window. Snow drifted past the glass. She tweaked the curtains back just far enough to see the field outside.

The hollows that had been pacing around the building had come to a halt. A dozen of them stood, staggered in the snow, as motionless as statues as they stared up at her.

Something's happening.

The taste in her mouth turned sour as fear ran through her. She dropped the curtain, her chest so tight she thought she might hyperventilate.

They're doing something. The hollows have stopped being passive. They're doing something, and Dorran is out there.

She was back at the door in five long paces. Her fingertips pressed against the wood as she tried to still her mind long enough to think.

Dorran had been gone for twenty-five minutes. He had promised twenty. He knew how important the deadline was to her; he wouldn't leave her waiting. Not willingly.

You can't leave the room. That was the one thing we agreed on. You have to stay here.

But Dorran had thought he was safe in Winterbourne. Clare had struggled to believe it as readily, but she had trusted him. Now, that trust was crumbling.

He's strong. He's smart. If he's in trouble, he can either get himself out, or the trouble is so bad that there's very little I could do to help.

She knew it was true, but that made it no easier to stand at the door. She and Dorran had always faced their challenges together. Clare was prepared to hurt; she was prepared to struggle; she was even prepared to die. The only thing she couldn't conceive was being left alone in the new world. If Dorran died, she wanted to die at his side, doing everything she could to protect him.

He wants you to stay in the room.

Her fingers dropped to the lock. Her eyelashes were wet, her lip aching from where she bit it. Dorran had been gone for nearly half an hour. A lot could happen in half an hour.

And then she heard it, rising out of the house's deepest levels, echoing as it bounced between countless layers of wallpaper. Dorran screamed.

CHAPTER 34

CLARE MOVED ON INSTINCT, one hand turning the lock as the other shoved on the door.

Dorran's scream, raw and pained, cut out abruptly. He had tried to muffle it. He hadn't wanted Clare to hear.

Liquid fire pumped through her veins. It scorched every atom of her body, filling her with frantic energy. Her feet flew, carrying her toward the stairs. Faintly, she was aware that she didn't have a weapon. Going back for the fire poker would waste seconds she didn't have. She would figure it out when she reached Dorran.

Faintly glinting eyes stared out at her from the shadows. The hallway was lined with hollows. Clare barely spared them a glance. She didn't have time to fight them. They didn't try to stop her.

She reached the stairs, grabbed the railing, and swung herself around. The foyer was almost pitch-black. The windows had been shuttered; if Dorran had lit candles on his way to the garden, they had been extinguished. Clare took the stairs three at a time, risking a twisted ankle with each step, breath catching in her throat as she raced to find Dorran. Pain pulsed through the cuts in her leg, but she pushed it to the back of her mind. She hit the foyer's tiles and kept moving.

Something immense loomed out of the darkness. Clare skidded as she tried to avoid its clutching hands. It wasn't moving, though; it was only the statue constructed from bones, Madeline's replica, arms outstretched. Clare ducked under them.

Dorran, where are you? To her right were the house's living areas: the dining room, the library, the ballroom, the drawing rooms. They had scarcely been used since the stillness.

Straight ahead and down a hallway were the doors leading to the house's staff areas: the kitchens, the garden, the furnace room, and the cellar.

Clare's heart pulsed unevenly. She dreaded visiting those lower levels. They were the farthest from safety, the most inhospitable, and the darkest. But that was where she was most likely to find Dorran.

Creatures watched her as she moved along the hallway. They pressed their backs to the walls, maws open, eyes swiveling without blinking as they followed her progress.

She passed the kitchens. Clare didn't expect to find him there, but she still had to be sure. She pushed the doors open, shivering as the freezing air rolled around her. The counters, ovens, and utensils were all shrouded in darkness, untouched for weeks.

Clare was prepared to leave when she glimpsed the knife block near the door. It would be better than nothing. She grasped the largest handle, pulling out a long metal blade. She held the knife at her side as she followed the passageway to its end, where it let into the stone chamber.

The garden's lights flowed out through the door's small window. The glow landed across something made of cloth lying on the stone floor. Clare approached it, her heart in her throat. It was the bag that Dorran had used to gather produce. Vegetables had fallen from it, tomatoes and cucumbers scattering across the dusty floor. To her right was the door to the furnace room. Clare glanced at it but didn't approach. Madeline wouldn't have taken Dorran there. The furnace room was where she had lost to him the last time they had crossed paths. She would want this new confrontation to happen on her own terms. Somewhere dark. Somewhere quiet.

Clare's eyes drifted toward the stone archway to her left. It led to the cellar, and anxious prickles crawled across Clare's back. She hated that room more than any other in Winterbourne. Of course that was where Madeline would choose. Dorran had said it himself: *She will wait until we are at our most vulnerable.*

She fought to strike a match and light one of the candles on the table by the wall. Every wasted second pulled on her, fraying her, and filling her with horror about what it might be costing. But there was no light in the cellar, and Clare knew stepping into it blind would be suicide.

The candle caught, its flame tiny and struggling in the cold air but slowly growing as the wax warmed. Clare lifted its holder and turned toward the wine cellar. The opening stretched like a screaming mouth, black and toothless, threatening to drag her inside. She forced her legs to move faster than they wanted to. The house was cold to begin with, but the chill rolling out of the cellar was intense. Clare grit her teeth as she passed the threshold and began to climb the worn stone steps that led to the lowest level.

Please, Dorran, please be all right. I'm coming.

The stones were damp. Clare's foot slipped on one. The flame guttered and the knife clanged as she threw out her hand to stabilize herself against the stones. Clare took a gulping breath, then righted herself, her limbs shaking. It seemed impossible to keep moving. She forced herself to regardless.

Her steps echoed horribly. Clare tried to listen through them, to hear the telltale gasps of breath or the crunch of feet on grime that would tell her the wine cellar was occupied. She couldn't hear anything. She extended her arm as far as she dared, trying to force the candlelight to penetrate the gloom beneath. A dozen tiny reflections twinkled out at her, and at first Clare thought she was seeing eyes. Then she took another step and saw they were only the wine bottles, stacked upon the racks filling the space.

It felt reckless to speak, but Clare didn't think she had much to lose. The hollows knew she was there; she was making too much noise for her arrival to be a surprise. So she licked dry lips and hazarded, "Dorran?"

The cold air moved around her in eddies. The echoes lasted

longer than she thought they should. A soft, dripping noise came from the room's back corner.

Was I wrong? Maybe he's not here. But where else could he be?

Then her light caught on the edge of a stone slab protruding from the wall. She recognized it: the concealed doorway that opened into the maze of secret passageways running through the building. She and Dorran had nailed it shut before leaving Winterbourne, but evidently, the house's mistress had wanted access to it. And it wasn't an accident that it had been left open. It was an invitation.

Clare adjusted her grip on the knife and stepped through. A ragged path ran away from her, leading deeper into the building, the walls high and oppressive, the darkness so complete that it seemed to be trying to smother her candlelight.

But she knew she had chosen correctly. Beneath the sound of panic running through her veins, she could hear other noises. Rasping, chattering breaths. The shuffle of countless bodies rubbing together.

Clare lifted her head. Above her, hollows clung to the passageway's ceiling. Their awful, spindly fingers and toes locked to any roughness in the rocks, the greasy remnants of hair hanging near enough to Clare's head that the stench made her gag, their teeth bared in silent snarls. Clare froze, shudders running along her spine, shoulders hunching as she tried to sink away from the creatures. She kept moving.

The passageway led her downward two or three steps at a time. Her nose and ears stung from the cold. The path turned so often that she lost her sense of direction. The whole way, the creatures lurked above her, watching, ravenous, drops of saliva hitting the stone floor before her feet.

Then the walls disappeared up ahead, and Clare knew where she was. She was stepping into the chamber she had been dragged to on her first encounter with Madeline. The cathedral-like room, hewn out of bedrock, that the matriarch seemed to favor as her court. She pushed forward, racing her own terror, afraid of what she would find in the room but unable to survive not knowing. As she moved faster, the candle's glow spread over more of the stone floor, catching on the rows of eyes filling the space, running up the jagged walls—

And there was Dorran. He appeared at the edge of her dome of light, kneeling, his hands behind his back. A wash of blood ran across his right cheek. Clare's heart skipped. "Dorran!"

He lifted his head, teeth clenched and eyes wide. "No, Clare, no—!"

Motion rushed toward her. Clare slashed at it and felt cool blood splash across her forearm as she severed digits. Another creature was already at her back. She twisted, driving her knife into its throat. The flame guttered, then died.

Blind, Clare found herself fighting against an enemy that could see in the dark. She turned to her hearing, relying on the sounds of scabbed feet scraping across the floor and gurgling, gasping breaths.

Overgrown nails slashed at her arm, sending hot pain through it. Clare stabbed toward the creature, but the knife only touched air. She stepped back and gasped as something brushed her shoulder. It was only the wall. Clare pressed her back to it, eyes wide and blind as she stared into the abyss, knife held ahead of herself.

Then a voice croaked from near the back of the cavern. "Bring her, my darlings."

Clammy hands fastened over Clare's arms and legs. She lashed out and felt her blade connect with flesh. She pulled the knife free and prepared to strike again, but something grasped the blade and tugged. Clare's grip was slick with blood, and the handle slid between her fingers. The knife clattered over stone as it was cast aside.

Clare swung her fists instead. She hit two of the creatures and reeled her arm back for a third before bony fingers looped around it. They were pulling her in all directions, grabbing at her clothes, squeezing at her skin, their rancid smell surrounding her, the rush of hissing breaths deafening. Her feet were pulled out from under her. Clare thrashed but couldn't break free. She was being dragged, scraped over rough stone, countless monsters pressing in at all sides. Then they slammed her down onto something hard and cold. Clare gasped as stones bit into her back. Metal touched her hands, then, with a harsh *click*, she was chained. Clare pulled on the manacles. They were bolted in place.

The presences around her vanished. Clare sucked in a breath. She was clammy all over, shaking, her stomach on the edge of revolt. She wanted to call to Dorran. She dreaded what retaliation it might bring.

For a moment, the cavern was near perfectly silent. Then the rasping voice spoke again. "Let us give our guests some light, my darlings."

Flames hissed. Torches dotted around the cavern burst to life. Hollows screeched at the sudden intrusion of flame and withdrew further into the shadows, until only their eyes and dripping teeth were visible.

Clare was on the dais in the room's center. Heavy steel manacles pinned her hands at one end. She twisted them, trying to find any leeway to work her hands free, but the metal was tight enough to pinch.

Now that the cavern was lit, she could see Dorran no more than twenty feet away. He must have put up a good fight. His shirt was torn and the blood on his face wasn't the only red on him. His hands had been fastened behind his back with a set of shackles similar to what Clare wore, their chain looped around the pillar his back was pressed against.

His face was sheet white and dusty. His lips were pressed tightly together, silent, but his eyes followed Clare's movements with a fierce urgency.

Madeline stood over him. One of her hands rested on top of his head, tangling in his hair, a mockery of a mother's loving caress.

CHAPTER 35

BILE ROSE IN THE back of Clare's throat. Madeline had changed since their last confrontation. She stood at least eight feet tall, lifted up on nearly a dozen clawlike legs. Their sharp tips clicked on the stone when she moved. They poked out of the shreds of her old dress, a decadent design of black and red silk, one of her last reminders of her former life.

She still bore the fire poker Clare had stabbed into her. It entered through her open mouth, angled up to pierce into the skull and extend from the back of her head, through her hair. The metal bar had run straight through her brain, but even that hadn't been enough to kill her.

The thanites had worked furiously to repair her, but the results were sickening. Flesh had filled her mouth, surrounding the metal as it tried to fuse with it. Large growths protruded from each side of her skull, lumpy and bony, each bearing two swollen, skin-covered circles and a lopsided mouth.

Clare pictured the statue in the foyer and how three skulls had been used to represent the head. That had not been an artistic choice, she realized. Madeline appeared to be growing additional faces on either side of the original.

Clare's gaze ran down the woman's body. Red gashes marred her flesh, appearing on her throat, arms, and what was visible of her torso. Clare's first thought was that she'd been injured, but the gashes seemed too clean and straight for that. Then the skin around them quivered. Madeline drew a breath to speak. As the two new mouths on either side of her defunct original opened, so did the gashes across her body, revealing rows of teeth embedded in her flesh.

"I told you she would come if you screamed."

One of her clawlike legs reached out and tapped Dorran's arm. He flinched, jaw clenched, sweat beading over his forehead. The skin Madeline had touched was an angry red, Clare saw. *She burned him. That's how she made him cry out.*

Horror was replaced by a rush of fury. Clare pulled on her shackles, jarring her shoulder as she tried to wrench free. Heat filled her stomach and turned the edges of her vision black.

Madeline's hand ran through Dorran's hair, ruffling it, then forced his head down before she stepped away.

"You made a mistake to think I would not hurt you. I admit, I have been overly lenient in the past. A mother's love knows no bounds, and in too many cases, it stilled my hand when harsher punishments were deserved. And look what it has done for you. You are *weak*. Foolish. Spoiled."

Madeline took a deep breath, her back lengthening with a horrible crackling noise. All of the imitation mouths across her body fluttered, attempting to draw breath as well.

"I am afraid we will have to work harder to correct your ill-suited tendencies. I doubt you will enjoy it, but things that are good for you are rarely enjoyable."

A flash of movement caught Clare's attention. Something small fell from the ceiling and hit the ground near Dorran. The cavern was still too dim for Clare to see it clearly, but it looked like a shard of rock. She glanced up. The ceiling was covered with the creatures, their bodies moving lithely as they crept over the stone.

Madeline's claws were carrying her closer to Clare. She laced her hands ahead of herself, the fingers triple jointed but somehow still elegant.

Finally, Dorran spoke. The words were raspy, pained. "Don't touch her."

Madeline began to circle the dais. Clare tried to pull away, to keep her distance from the woman, but the manacles kept her fixed. One of Madeline's long hands reached out and caressed over Clare's back. She shuddered.

"You received a message," Madeline said, looking at Dorran over Clare's body. Her heavy-lidded, red eyes watched him impassively. "Someone claims to be capable of killing my darlings. You will put a stop to it."

Dorran's lips pressed in a hard line. Madeline lifted her eyebrows, then reached out and pinched Clare's forearm between her nails.

"Don't!" Dorran snarled. He pulled at his chains. "I don't have any control over it. There is nothing I can do to stop it."

"That is a lie," Madeline said, and pinched Clare harder. She gasped, fighting the urge to writhe. "That woman used your names. She knows you. She will listen to you, if you contact her."

Madeline released Clare, and she slumped, breathing heavily. The second message, half-forgotten in the panic of losing Dorran, resurfaced. *The deadline has been moved to today. Madeline doesn't know that. Madeline thinks she still has time.*

"Just…just go along with it," Clare called. She met Dorran's eyes, trying to share what she knew without words. *If we can get through this, if we can just survive for a few hours—*

Dorran's whole body shook. His eyes flicked from Clare to his mother, and when he spoke, the words were carefully measured. "I have no way to contact them. No radio, and no phone."

Madeline exhaled deeply, her eyes closing for a moment as though she needed to collect her patience. Her fingertips pressed together in a steeple, and when she opened her eyes, her voice was sweet, as though she were speaking to a child. "You are giving me excuses. Did I ask for excuses?"

"Just give him time," Clare said, again shooting Dorran a meaningful look. *Time, Dorran. That's all we need. Buy us some time.*

"Yes—" Dorran's words were halting. "I will figure it out. I…I will find a way…"

"How?" Madeline asked. "Give me details."

His mouth opened, but he didn't speak. He was struggling,

Clare knew; caught between fear of his mother and fear of what consequences a single wrong move could create, he was gripped by panic, barely conscious of anything except a fight-or-flight response and unable to follow either impulse.

Madeline's hand landed on Clare's head, forcing it down onto the stone. "And this is why we brought your friend here. *Motivation.*"

The chains clattered as Dorran pulled on them, muscles straining underneath his torn shirt, desperation flashing in his eyes. "Do anything to me, but if you harm her, I swear I will never give you what you want."

"Hmm." Madeline's hand released its pressure, but didn't leave Clare's head. It stroked through her hair, the too-long nails snagging at tangles. "I know you are fond of her. That is your weakness manifesting as attachment to someone who indulges your vices. Once, I wanted the opportunity to kill her. But not any longer. You care for her too much. She will be far more valuable alive."

"Don't touch her," Dorran repeated, a vicious edge entering his voice.

"She will be your motivation to behave." Madeline's fingers continued to run through Clare's hair. "She will stay here, with me. If you do as you are told, you will be rewarded. You will be allowed an hour to sit with her each day. You may even bring her additional food if you exceed expectations. But when you disappoint me, she will bear the punishment."

"No." Sweat ran down Dorran's face, creating tracks through the dust. He was shivering, and not from the cold.

"We will skin her," Madeline said, and every mouth on her body smiled. "A strip for each failure. It will not kill her. No, I will be careful to keep her alive. But her skin will come off a piece at a time if you do not behave."

Dorran shook his head. His eyes had lost their humanity; all that lived inside them was the terror of a cornered animal. Clare clenched her teeth, trying to suppress her own shivers. Madeline knew Dorran too well. She knew how to find his weaknesses, how to hurt him, how to break him.

"Now, tell me." Madeline's voice was soft and sweet, a mother's coo. "What will you do to contact your friend from the radio?"

"I need time. I'll do it, just give me time—"

"You disappoint me." Madeline's fingernails dug into Clare's skin.

"*No*," Dorran screamed, lunging forward, the chains sounding out as they were pulled taut. "*No*—"

Clare bit her tongue, turning her head to face the stone. She was powerless to escape Madeline as the nails cut into her skin. But she could stay silent, endure it without noise. She could at least spare Dorran having to hear her scream.

"No!" he yelled again, the word cracking. Underneath the cry was another sound. Metal breaking. Then the scrape of chains dragging over stone. The pressure from Madeline's hand disappeared.

Clare sucked a thin breath into air-starved lungs and lifted her head. Dorran was no longer chained to the pillar. He moved toward them with furious speed. Madeline had just enough time to raise her hands before he hit her torso, forcing her away from Clare.

Madeline's insectile legs jerked as she fell backward. The hollows around them screamed, darting over each other, heads thrown back, ravenous but fearful of angering their mistress.

Dorran tumbled off of Madeline. Her three faces twisted as she stabbed her legs at him, but Dorran rolled out of reach. The legs stabbed into the floor instead, cutting chips out of the stone.

She's actually trying to kill him. Clare fought against her bindings, twisting her wrist inside the metal until a sheen of blood covered it. They wouldn't loosen.

Dorran crouched, ready to charge his mother again. She rose up onto her multitude of feet, towering over him, arms open as she welcomed the attack. The many mouths across her body fluttered with wild laughter.

He can't kill her. She's too strong. She'll shred him.

A shimmer of movement caught Clare's eye. A plastic container, knocked over by one of the scrambling monsters, fell into the torches' light.

The fuel container. How? She'd last seen it in their room. Dorran must have taken it at some point to refuel the generator, she realized. He would have had it on him when he was attacked, and the hollows brought it when they dragged him down to Madeline's lair. Clare didn't know if it still had fuel in it, but it was the one thing that could give them a chance.

"Dorran!" Clare rose as high as the manacles would let her. "Over there!"

He followed the direction of her nod, and his eyes lit up as he saw the container.

Madeline struck again. Dorran leaped to the side, and the sharp claws scraped across his shoulder. He didn't stop moving, though, but raced past the dais to reach the fuel. Madeline's mouths quivered as her voice boomed. "Catch him!"

The hollows swarmed Dorran. Clare sucked in a sharp breath as he, and the fuel container, disappeared under a pile of gray limbs. He needed a distraction. Even just a second's worth. Clare screamed, making the note as loud and piercing as she could.

Dozens of hollow heads swiveled to stare at her. Open jaws worked. Then Dorran lurched out of their pile, heaving the fuel container upward so its liquid would splash through the open top.

He'd aimed for the nearest torch. Fire billowed up from the trail of fuel and filled the cavern with dancing reds and golds. Clare finally got a sense of the scope of the hollow infestation. There had to be hundreds of them: clinging to the walls, scuttling across the ceiling, a grisly tangle of excess limbs and overgrown skin. Still more stared through doorways in the stone walls. They all faced the fire, eyes unblinking, maws twisted in miserable howls.

"Catch him!" Madeline screamed.

Dorran lowered the container's opening toward the flames licking across the ground. An explosion of heat burst up as the fuel inside caught alight. Dorran turned back to the horde, teeth bared in a snarl as he wielded his new weapon.

Every swing of the container sent liquid fire flowing from the spout. He hurled streams of it at the nearest creatures. They backed away, howling, fingers clawing at their melting skin. As they staggered into their companions, they spread the fire like a disease. The hollows were shrieking, scrambling over each other, desperately seeking the exits as they made their escapes.

And Dorran kept advancing. The trail of fire spread black smoke behind him, the shadows blending into his hair until he looked like something mythical emerging from the underground. His eyes were on Clare. Then they turned upward and hardened, and Clare knew, even before she looked, that he was staring at Madeline.

The matriarch was approaching Clare. Her multiple faces twitched with mingled disgust and rage.

"Get away from her." Dorran's voice rose above the hissing, crackling fire and the many-voiced screams of the hollow.

One of Madeline's feet stabbed into the stone platform near Clare's head. The matriarch rose up onto it, enormous, hands flexing into fists at her side.

She was ignoring Clare, wholly focused on her son. Clare couldn't contain a grim smile. She held her chained hands above her head as she rolled onto her back. The underside of Madeline's abdomen was immediately above her; it was a roiling mess of the sharp, insect-like claws crosscutting as they burst out from the remains of her dress. Clare pulled her knees up to her chest and kicked upward, driving her boots into that nest of appendages, pain sparking through her injured leg.

Madeline's gasp, raw and ragged through her newly formed throats, was one of the most satisfying things Clare had ever heard. She'd stolen the matriarch's balance and tilted the angle of her legs to the side, rolling Madeline forward to meet her son.

Dorran was ready. He raised the fuel container, spraying the last of the flaming liquid onto Madeline. Clare flinched as fiery drops rained around her. Madeline howled. She buckled, the legs twitching in discordant directions, as she clawed at the flames spreading across her torso and face, stumbling backward as she fell to the floor.

The cavern was a maze of flames. The last of the hollows chattered as they clawed their way into the tunnels to escape the heat and smoke. The toxic smell of burned fuel was rapidly thickening; Clare pressed her face into her arm as she coughed.

All of the anger fled from Dorran's expression. It was replaced with stark, gray horror as he staggered to her. His hands ran across her hair, then to her hands, stained with her own drying blood. "I am so sorry. My darling. Oh, I am sorry."

"Hey," she said, smiling despite how badly she shook. "You okay?"

His hands hovered over Clare's arm where Madeline had torn the skin. It wasn't bad; the cut was no larger than an inch, and not deep. They had both had worse. But Dorran stared at it with so much pain in his expression that it seemed as though the guilt was crushing him.

He's in shock. This must be like a living nightmare for him. She wanted to ask him to check his mother, to make sure she was truly dead this time, but she wasn't certain he could handle it. Clare swallowed and pushed some levity into her voice, hoping it would knock him out of the panic that was consuming him. "No more family reunions, okay? They don't work out for either of us."

His eyes were uncomprehending.

Clare felt a cold trickle of fear move into her chest. Dorran stood at her side, but he felt like a stranger. There was almost nothing of the man she loved left in his expression. *What if Madeline got her wish? What if she finally broke him?*

"Hey," she tried again, softening her voice even further. "Everything's okay. I love you."

"I love you," he echoed, the words emotionless. Then he blinked, and his eyes began to shine with unshed tears, and his hands clutched for hers as feeling returned to his voice. "I love you…Clare…I'm so sorry…Clare—"

He was back. Clare grinned, trying not to cry herself. The manacled hands were numb from lack of blood flow, but she still held him in return. "We're okay, Dorran. I'm not hurt. You did great."

"Oh," he said, and his head dropped against hers as his arms wrapped around her. He was close enough that Clare could kiss his neck, so she did. He tasted like dust and smoke.

"Hey," she whispered, not wanting to rush him, but aware that they were horribly vulnerable. The fire was gradually dying as it exhausted its fuel. Smoke was filling the chamber, sapping the oxygen and making it harder to see. Breathing was becoming painful. It was keeping the other hollows away, but not for much longer. And she needed to be certain that Madeline was dead. Because, if she was, the other hollows would no longer be heeding the matriarch's instructions. And they were *hungry*. "D'you think we can find a way to get me out of these?"

"Yes. Hold on."

Dorran bent over the manacles, exploring their welds and the chains, searching for weakness.

Clare turned her head aside as she coughed. Something twitched through the smoke in her peripheral vision. She barely had enough air in her lungs to call, "Dorran! Behind!"

Madeline lurched toward them. Blackened skin cracked as her arms reached out, her legs jerking erratically as the nerves misfired. Her face was barely recognizable. The skin was charred and traced through with rivers of red. The original mouth, the one that had grown flesh around the rebar, pulsed in time with her heartbeat. Her eyes had turned gray as they cooked. She was blind, but she had still heard their voices. And she was coming for them.

Dorran twisted to face his mother as her blackened fingers gripped either side of his head. The pulsing mouth, still bearing the rebar, loomed above him. He was pinned between Madeline and the dais, and Madeline raised four of her insect legs, their tips aimed at him.

He seemed frozen. Madeline's fingertips crumbled as she dug them into the sides of his head. The pulsing mouth was growing closer and closer, as though she hoped to eat him or impale him on the same rebar that had forever deformed her face.

Clare yelled. "Dorran!"

He flinched, then responded, reaching up to grasp the rebar. The legs stabbed down, aiming to impale Dorran, but hit the stone platform instead as he twisted the metal bar. The blind eyes rolled up. Her hands spasmed and her legs thrashed. The pulsing mouth gushed a clot of black, rotting blood. Dorran kept pushing. The skin around her neck cracked. Madeline could no longer support her own body weight. Her legs fell out from under her, and the force wrenched her head back. Burned flesh separated. Dorran gasped and dropped the rebar, still speared through his mother's decapitated head.

The insect legs continued to twitch for a full minute after Madeline fell. Slowly, they coiled inward, curling up like a dead spider. Dorran stared down at her until the last shivers subsided, then he shakily bent to pick something off her body. He staggered back to Clare, his eyes wide and wild. A necklace was clasped in his soot-coated hand and suspended from it was a silver key.

Dorran fit the key into Clare's manacles. It was old and tarnished and scraped in the lock. The metal clicked as it unlocked.

Clare pulled her hands free and massaged where the metal had bitten into her skin. Dorran still looked ashen. He stayed close to her, one hand on her arm, as he stared at his mother's body. He needed time to process what had happened, to come to terms with it, maybe even to grieve. But time was something they didn't have. Clare took his hand, rubbing it, trying to draw his attention. "We need to get back to the room. This is almost over. Unathi made another announcement while you were gone. They're activating the code today, at sundown."

"Ah." He blinked and shook his head, as though trying to clear it. "Sundown. Back to the room. You'll be safe there—"

Something screamed in the passageways behind them. The flames had almost completely burned out, leaving just smoke and the odor of fuel in its place. Clare searched, but the torches weren't bright enough to show any movement around the room's periphery. The creatures would be out there, though. And they would be closing in. She pulled on Dorran's hand. "We have to go."

CHAPTER 36

CLARE DROPPED HER LEGS over the side of the dais. She couldn't see far, but she could feel the hollows moving closer. She tried to orient herself, to remember the way out, but there were at least a dozen crevices in the walls and she couldn't recall which direction she'd come from.

"Dorran."

He'd been staring at the corpse behind the dais, but at Clare's voice he blinked and focusing back on her. "Yes?"

"Do you remember which way I came from?"

"Ah. That way."

He indicated toward one of the nearer walls. They set off, each step long as they crossed the uneven stone floor.

There had to be a faster way back to their room, but it would involve traveling through the concealed passageways, and the circuit was still too unfamiliar to risk trying it. The route out through the wine cellar would be slower, but at least they wouldn't become lost.

"Clare, careful."

Something moved along the shadowed walls ahead. Multiple bodies scuttled like cockroaches, teeth gnashing.

A flash of color stood out among the stone. Clare recognized the knife she'd brought with her, the one the hollows had knocked out of her hand, and beside it, a small red cylinder. She quickly scooped them both up, frowning at the red tube. "A flare. But I didn't bring one. Dorran, did—?"

A vicious noise rose from the passageway ahead. Clare wiped the knife clean on her shirt, ensuring she wouldn't lose her grip on it again. Dorran moved closer to her and swept one arm out, placing himself in front of her. The sounds floating from the hallway set Clare's teeth on edge. Full of violence and fury, they rose until they seemed to be shaking the walls around them. The hollows slinking around the edge of the cavern disappeared into the tunnel, moving toward the sounds.

It's like wildcats fighting. Or a madman's screams.

Clare's mouth was dry. She held the knife tightly, prepared to fight whatever was going to appear in the opening. Nothing did. Instead, the noise broke off, its echoes taking longer to fade.

"What was that?" Clare asked.

Dorran's breathing was shallow. He could only shake his head.

The sounds had come from the path they needed to take. Clare didn't want to move toward it. But they had no alternatives—not unless they wanted to be trapped in the hellish passageways for hours, lost among a sea of hollows. She clenched her teeth, then lit the flare.

For a moment, the hissing flame masked any other noise. Clare extended the light, painting red across the rough walls as she stepped forward. Dorran moved like a ghost at her side, his hand just barely resting on her arm to tell her he was still with her. She was grateful. She didn't think she could endure being separated from him again that day.

More of the passageway was revealed in gradual shimmers. It was disconcertingly still. Clare kept looking for the source of the screams, waiting for movement ahead, but it looked no different from the passageway she had followed an hour before. Water pooled on the floor, shimmering red in her light. Scratches ran along the walls where claws had cut into them, but Clare suspected the marks had been made weeks before by the denizens that called the tunnels home.

Then her shoe landed in something she had assumed was water, and Clare's heart lurched. The liquid didn't move quite like water was supposed to. It was thicker, rippling lazily out from the impact. Clare stepped back and scraped her shoe over the ground. It left a smear.

The water had looked red. She had assumed it was tinted by the flare, but it didn't need any light to color it. She had stepped into blood.

"Clare." Dorran nodded to the side.

At first glance, the shape seemed to be a broken rock kicked into the corner. Clare extended the flare toward it. Two empty eye sockets stared back at her. The gray skin was pinched too tight over the bones, the jaws hanging open in an imitation of a scream. The hollow was already dead.

The hellish noise came again. It was distant, farther along the passageway they needed to take. Dorran's hand tightened over her arm, and she thought she could feel his pulse beating as quickly as hers did.

"The hollows are fighting," she whispered.

"They must have been denied meals for a long time. Perhaps now…now that Madeline is dead…they are seeking food wherever they can find it."

Clare gave a stiff nod. Everything she knew about hollows told her they didn't see their companions as prey and only resorted to consuming one another when they were trapped in a restrictive enclosure—such as a car or a small room—or when they were already dead. Before Clare and Dorran had left Winterbourne, Madeline had been sacrificing members of her party to satisfy the surviving hollows' appetites. Clare assumed the habit had continued, perhaps in greater numbers once the creatures from the forest had been brought inside.

It made no sense for hollows to be fighting among themselves, especially when there was human prey within the mansion. But very little of Winterbourne's situation was natural. Now that Madeline no longer controlled the creatures, Clare couldn't guess what they might resort to.

Get somewhere safe. Quickly.

She pushed forward, hastening her steps. Her shoes landed

in another pool of blood. She tried not to look at it as they kept moving. Vicious screams rang through the building as hollows fought. They were louder than Clare had ever heard them before: ferocious, wild, terrifying. Every fiber of her being focused on the only thing that mattered—getting behind a door that locked, where they could wait out the remaining hours until sundown.

The flare was dying. Clare thought they were close to the door to the cellar. She shook the flare, trying to get some more life into it, but it hissed a final time and fizzled out.

No. She hit it against her palm, but the glow was gone. There was no natural light in the subterranean levels. It made no difference whether she kept her eyes open or closed them. Already, she was starting to forget what the hallway looked like. She reached out but only touched air.

Dorran's fingers ran down her arm until he found her hand. "I think I know the way," he whispered.

His hand tugged, and Clare followed it. Her eyes were wide but blind. Her mind conjured up images: a swarm of hollows slinking through the hallway ahead, open jaws aiming for them. The smell was everywhere. Clare told herself she would be able to hear if hollows were approaching, but her breathing and faltering footsteps seemed deafening.

She tried not to think about what would happen if the monsters came across them in the darkness. There would be no way to fight. No way to defend themselves. No way to run…

The atmosphere seemed to change. The air was a fraction cleaner, and the scent of smoke was replaced by dust. Dorran led them to the right, and Clare thought that meant they had entered the wine cellar. Her suspicions were confirmed as a bottle clinked, and Dorran adjusted their direction.

Clare's hand was clammy. She wanted to pull it out of Dorran's and wipe it clean, but his grip was like steel. *For good reason. If we were to be separated now…*

Her shoulder grazed one of the walls. She flinched, squeezing her eyes closed reflexively. Then the hand in hers abruptly pushed back, halting her steps.

Did he hear something? Feel something?

Clare had a split-second image of an unseen hollow biting into Dorran's face. She prepared to drag him backward. Then Dorran's voice floated out of the darkness near her ear. "The stairs are ahead. Move carefully."

He led her upward. Clare reached one arm out as she blindly shuffled forward. Her boots hit the lowest stair, and she stepped up, misjudged its width, and nearly lost her balance. Dorran dragged her back, bracing her, until she had a flat surface under her feet again.

Her breathing shallow, she tested the stair's width, bumping her feet into its back before trusting her weight to it. The climb was agonizingly slow, but they had to be cautious. The stairs had no railing, and a fall from that height would crack their heads open like eggs.

Something hissed behind them. Dread ran through Clare. One of the hollows had followed them out of the hidden passage-ways and into the wine cellar. She tried to guess how far behind it was, but the question was nearly immaterial. The hollows weren't hindered by the darkness. It would only take seconds for it to catch up to them.

Dorran heard it, too, and tugged on her. They began to move faster, racing up the stairs. The coldness stung Clare's cheeks and the exertion ached deep in her leg. She was starting to lose her orientation. Even though she could feel the ground beneath her feet, she had lost her sense of which direction was up.

She misstepped, her toes sliding off the edge of the stone, and keeled forward. Dorran gasped and pulled on her hand to keep her up, but she still hit the stairs. The knife clattered as it fell from her grip. Her outstretched palm lost a layer of skin, but she barely felt it. Every fiber of her being was focused on getting to the top of the stairs, away from the creature below them.

She had a strange sensation—the feeling of something passing her without touching her. It was so fast and so faint that she wasn't sure she could trust her judgment. She scrambled upright, her heart thundering.

A scream shook the air ahead of them. Clare flinched, bracing for claws across her shoulders or teeth sinking into her throat, but nothing came. The screams gurgled, descending into something like incoherent ravings. A wet, tearing sound caused the wails to abruptly break off. Something heavy hit the floor. Claws scrabbled on stone.

There are two of them. And they're fighting, instead of coming after us. That makes no sense.

She didn't have enough of her mind left to wonder about it.

In the distance, she thought she saw light. It was only a whisper, but one patch of the blackness that stretched across her vision seemed slightly less dark.

"The stairs end," Dorran said.

Even with the warning, Clare still tried to step up and felt her world rock as her foot plunged through emptiness. She put out her hand, found the wall, and righted herself.

"The garden," she whispered. *We don't need to get to the room. We only need to get somewhere secure. Somewhere with a lock.*

Her shoulder brushed the immense archway leading into the cellar. To her right was the passageway taking them back to the main sections of the house. The fleeting traces of light came from there, refractions from the foyer's windows.

The garden would be to her left, but as Clare turned toward it, uneasiness ran through her like shivers. Normally, light came through the window in the door. It was a small and muted glow, but it had always acted as a beacon toward the room. Now, though, there was nothing but darkness ahead.

Dorran didn't try to move. Clare held her breath, knowing he must be listening. She strained to hear but didn't detect any signs of life ahead.

She said, "The lights should be on at this time of day, shouldn't they?"

"It is possible the generator ran dry…"

Clare felt the wariness in him. She knew him too well to believe he would forget to refuel the generator.

She hated moving through the darkness, not knowing what

horrors might surround them. The sooner they found a safe place, the better, and their room was two floors above them.

"Dorran." She didn't want to hound him, but chewing noises rose from the cellar's stairwell, and she didn't want to think about what would happen once the surviving hollow finished its feast.

He made a quiet noise of dissatisfaction, then stepped forward. He had a better sense of the space than Clare did and moved with confidence. The dark felt like it was burning Clare's eyes, so she closed them and followed in Dorran's wake, trusting him not to lead her into any obstacles. Then, abruptly, he came to a halt, pushing her back. She waited as stress burned her insides. When Dorran spoke, he sounded like he was having trouble breathing.

"The door is open."

"The garden door?" Clare frowned. "How—"

"Don't move." He let go of her. Clare pressed her lips together, hand still outstretched, waiting. His coat rustled, and she knew he must be feeling through his pockets.

He hissed his frustration. "The garden's key is gone. They must have taken it when they caught me."

Clare twisted to face the wine cellar's entryway. She couldn't see it, but she could picture it, the cavernous archway leading directly into the worst parts of the house...and inviting its denizens out. "We can still shelter in the garden. We'll lock it from the inside, and even if they have the key, they won't know how to use it."

"Unless there is another intelligent one," he murmured.

Clare hadn't considered it before. Cold sweat stuck her shirt to her back. It seemed too cruel to think that Madeline wasn't the only mindful monster that called Winterbourne home. She licked dry lips. "We need the key ring."

"Did you bring it with you?"

"No." She cursed herself. "I left it in our room."

"Then we will go there."

She wanted to argue, to tell him that it was too dangerous to think about moving through the house, but screams interrupted her thoughts. The noises came from the opposite direction than they had before, rising from the stairwell that led into the furnace room.

Dorran pressed her shoulder, then took her hand again. He led her toward the chamber's third entrance, the one leading back into the main part of the house.

Something had opened the garden's door and presumably destroyed its lights. Clare silently prayed it hadn't killed the plants, as well. That would be Madeline's style, though. Clare could imagine her leaving instructions with her minions to destroy her child's chance of survival in the event that Madeline died.

There was no time to dwell on the possibilities. Dorran, familiar with the passageways, increased his speed, and Clare had to jog to keep up to his long paces. She marveled at his ability to run into what might be certain death. The edge of an archway grazed her shoulder, and Clare knew they were moving out of the servants' areas.

Dorran's outstretched arm hit a door, and it burst open with a bang. Finally, Clare could see. She sucked in a breath in appreciation of the sunset leaking through Winterbourne's half-boarded windows, but the air caught in her throat. Something moved ahead.

CHAPTER 37

"WHAT—" DORRAN STARTED, THEN pressed his mouth shut.

A hollow lay on the floor. It lifted its head, jaw quivering with a muted hiss. Gangly arms reached forward and began to drag its body toward them. There were no legs.

The monster's body ended at its waist. A clump of intestines spread behind it, painting a trail of red across the tiles like a repulsive paintbrush.

Clare's mind went blank. The sight was too horrible and too perplexing to take in properly. She couldn't imagine what was capable of severing a hollow in half. Normally hollows focused on biting into the nearest flesh, rather than inflicting widespread damage.

Behind it, Madeline's effigy had been destroyed. The bones and ropes of hair were strewn across the marble floor, torn apart as though in a fury.

The hollow lifted itself as high as it could, hands slapping on the floor as it eagerly crawled toward them. Dorran finally moved and pushed Clare toward the stairs. They circled the foyer in a wide arc, avoiding the creature that unerringly rotated to face them.

A chorus of chattering voices rose from all directions. The light was bad enough that Clare could barely make out the stair rails, but she still ran. One monster appeared behind them, clambering along the walls, its head bulging like a deformed bulb. Clare didn't allow herself to stare. She just ran, snatching at Dorran's sleeve to keep him close, breaths shallow and raw, her whole body aching.

They skidded as they reached the third-floor landing, and Clare barely grazed the wall as they raced for their room. The chattering calls suddenly broke into screams, awful and unending, so loud that they seemed to rattle the paintings on the walls. Clare wanted to look back, but every wasted second could be the one that mattered the most. Their room was directly ahead. She'd left the door open when she went in search of Dorran; firelight glowed through the opening. Something snagged at her shoulder, fingernails grazing through fabric, then disappeared again.

Then they were through the door, and Dorran slammed it behind them. Clare snatched the key ring off the floor where she'd dropped it. They turned the door's lock and stepped back as the scratch of fingernails roved around the door's edges.

We did it. Clare doubled over, breathless and shaking. *Madeline is dead. We're safe. It's so close to being over.*

She reached out to Dorran. "Are you all right?"

"Ha." He tucked her in against himself, holding her. He smelled like smoke and dust and hollows, but Clare didn't care. His hands trembled as he let her go. "We should search the room."

"Yeah." Clare blinked to clear her eyes. They still couldn't let their guard down. The door had been left open. As she stepped back from Dorran, she began to see signs that the room hadn't been left untouched.

The meddling was in small doses and, in some cases, almost undetectable. But Clare's anxiety was high, and as she looked around the space, the sense of wrongness only intensified. The curtains were all closed. She was sure at least one had been open when she had left the room. The blankets by the fire looked more rumpled than she remembered. She pictured a hollow picking through them, crawling among her bed, and felt sick.

Dorran went straight to the fire poker. He indicated for Clare to stay in the room's corner, where she would be sheltered, but she narrowed her eyes, picked up the shovel from beside the fireplace, and shadowed him.

The search only took a few moments as they scoped out the normal hiding places: behind the curtains, the closet, under the bed, and in the bathroom.

Dorran's breath hissed between his teeth as their search ended at the bathroom's second door, which opened into the adjacent bedroom. The cabinet they had used to block it was gone. Dorran turned the lock, reengaging it, and pushed a chair under the handle to hold it in place. "She made sure she would have a back door into our room if we managed to escape her."

"Figures. She liked to cover all her bases, didn't she?"

"She did." Dorran stared at the door for a moment, then abruptly swiveled and returned to the bedroom. "Oh, Clare." He took her head in his hands and, for a moment, simply stared down at her. There was a strange, frightened sense of wonder in his eyes, as though he couldn't believe she was really there. Then he tilted forward to rest his forehead against hers, his skin warm and damp, his breath ghosting over her, his eyelashes close enough to brush against her cheeks.

Clare leaned up, rising onto her toes to graze her lips across his. It was more of a taste than a kiss. He shivered at the touch.

"You left your room." There wasn't any reproach in his words, just the same dull sense of shock.

Clare's fingers clenched on his shirt, bunching the fabric between them. "She was hurting you."

"I could take it." He shook his head a fraction, just enough for his too-long hair to tickle her ear. "I can take anything, if only you are safe."

"Maybe you could have taken it, but I couldn't." She smiled against the bittersweet relief and pain. "What about you? Are you...okay?"

"Of course." He returned the fire poker to its holder, then stared at the low flames. They seemed to entrance him as the lights played over glazed eyes.

Clare took his hand. The fingers felt cold. "It's okay to feel bad. Today...was not good."

"No," he replied, agreeing.

Clare licked her lips, trying to pick her words carefully. "I know sometimes you don't like to talk about bad things right away. And that's fine. But I'm here to listen when you're ready."

He smiled a broken-looking smile at her. "I don't know how I feel. I…"

"It's all right."

His fingers slid out of hers as he pulled away. "I killed my own mother. I watched as the most important person in my life was tortured. I thought I was about to lose everything."

Clare waited as he worked through his thoughts. It took him a moment. Then he turned back to her, and his smile looked slightly more genuine. "What's that phrase you used? *Today was not good.*"

"It sure wasn't." Clare chuckled as she ran her hand over his arm. He flinched, and Clare immediately pulled back.

"I forgot, you're hurt—"

"It will be fine."

"No, it won't." She began tugging at his shirt collar, trying to see the burns. "It must be painful. Unathi's message—they're implementing the code today. I hope. You'll lose half of your thanites and might have other things compromised too. We need to get this cleaned and dressed."

He neatly stepped back from her hands, tugging the shirt back into place. "Then I will take care of it."

He's done this before. He doesn't like being seen when he's in pain. He tries to hide away until it's over because vulnerability was always punished.

For a second, she saw cracks in his outer layer. There was the man she loved: competent, intelligent, powerful, tender toward her, and yet tough enough to endure any attack. Through the gaps, she caught the echoes of a child, frightened and alone, starving for love but terrified to ask for it. It made her heart ache. She gripped his hand and refused to let go when he tried to withdraw again.

"I'm taking care of you." She kept her voice gentle, coaxing. "I won't hurt you, I promise."

He tried to laugh, not quite fighting her but still resisting. "You don't need to do that. Why don't you wait by the fire? I will clean up in the bathroom and join you in a few minutes."

"You should know by now that I love you too much to let that happen." She pulled him toward the chairs, and finally, he relented.

She went through the familiar routine of boiling water and finding the first aid kit. Dorran sat with his back against one of the couches with his shirt hung off one shoulder, so Clare could work on the burns. They looked deep and had started to blister. She felt sick at the thought of how much they must have been hurting him.

"You don't have to be so careful," Dorran said. A faint smile hung around his lips, even though his eyes were tight.

Clare was rubbing antiseptic cream across the burns and lifted her head just enough to frown at him before returning to the job. She moved slowly and carefully, doing her best not to damage the skin any further.

As she worked, her mind returned to the escape from the underground cavern and how they had passed so close to hollows and still escaped. It didn't make any sense for the hollows to ignore the two vulnerable humans and fight each other.

Maybe they didn't. Maybe there was only one rogue hollow.

The screams had only ever come from one location at a time. It had been ahead of them in the cavern, moving through the hallway that led to the wine cellar, killing multiple other hollows. Then, it had attacked the monster on the stairs behind them. Then, again, it attacked something coming from the furnace room—which meant it had passed right by Clare and Dorran as they stood in front of the garden.

A hollow that craves hollow flesh. She had never heard of anything like it before, but then, there were a lot of things in the new world that were unexpected. Her knowledge of the monsters was based on what she had seen with her own eyes and what Beth had told her, along with a mix of advice and rumors circulated by other survivors. She was sure there would be many aberrations— like the immense monstrosity that had blocked the tunnel—that she simply hadn't heard of yet.

Whatever had killed the other hollows, it was probably the only reason she and Dorran had made it out of the tunnels. She didn't know whether to be grateful for its presence or repulsed. Clare briefly wondered if it would look like other hollows, bones and skin overgrown, or whether it was something entirely different.

Whatever it is—whatever happened back there—we'll deal with it tomorrow. After this is all over. After the hollows are gone.

Clare screwed the cap on the antiseptic cream, then found rolls of white bandages and began unspooling them. "Unathi said the code would be activated at sundown. But it sounded like Evandale was under siege."

"Their bunker is fortified," Dorran said. "I am certain they will be safe. We will stay here, where we're safe, until the code goes live. Though I lost our food outside the garden…"

Clare grinned. "Good thing we have the cans. We'll treat ourselves tonight. It's not every day the world is saved, after all."

"Ha. True."

Clare adjusted Dorran's arm so she could weave the bandages over his shoulder. "Do you think we'll know when the code goes live? Or will we just have to open the door and see if anything comes at us?"

"I suppose it depends on how much Becca altered it, and if she was able to remove the negative side effects. I imagine we will feel it, though."

When Dorran was exposed to the code designed to detonate the thanites, it had crippled him. Except for a blood transfusion to return some of the nanobots to his system, he would have died.

The Evandale scientists' plan to protect against those negative side effects involved destroying only *half* of the thanites. The idea was that the damage would be great enough to kill the hollows, who had significantly more of the machines inside them, while leaving enough healing nanobots in the humans' systems to repair the damage. Clare prayed the plan would work. The alternative was too awful to consider.

The incessant scrabbling had fallen silent, Clare realized. The hollows must have grown tired of trying to break through the door. She pressed her lips together. Somehow, the silence was worse than the sound. Like having a cockroach in the room, but not being able to find it. Clare pushed a pin into the bandages, fastening them closed. "All right, that's—"

Dorran's fingers rose up, touching her lips, asking for silence. His eyes had darkened. She followed his gaze toward the fire.

Something was moving on the other side of the wall. The noises were subtle enough that Clare wouldn't have caught them on her own.

Is something in the bedroom next to us? No—the sounds are too close. Like they're coming from inside *the walls.* She frowned. *Does one of the secret passageways run through there? We never heard anything in it before.*

Clare silently placed the unused supplies back into the medical kit and shut its lid. Based on how the noises ran together, Clare guessed there was more than one creature traversing the passageway. She hated knowing they were so close, but she tried not to let the sounds play on her nerves. She and Dorran had been through the room repeatedly, testing every wall and every fixture as they searched for hidden compartments. There were none. As long as they stayed where they were, the hollows couldn't reach them.

Still, she didn't like how unsettled Dorran looked. He kept still, eyes fixed on the wall at the point where it met the ceiling. The sounds were slowly working their way down. Almost as though…

Clare's eyes dropped to the fire. It had been allowed to dwindle into coals. Specks of soot fell onto them. Her heart skipped a beat. "They're coming down the chimney."

Dorran moved before she could finish speaking. He crossed the room in two quick paces, snatching up the carton of kindling.

How? A clump of soot fell, billowing black smoke over the grate. Clare scrambled back from it as it rolled across their bed. *The hollows hate heat. They hate light. They fear fire above everything else.*

Dorran was back beside her, forcing handfuls of sticks into the fireplace. "The novels I brought you—tear the pages out. Quickly."

"Ah." They needed to make the fire bigger. Hotter. She snatched up the novels and tore out wads of paper, scrunching them up into loose balls. She dropped them directly onto the smoldering coals, trying not to flinch as heat scorched her forearms. Then she rocked back as Dorran took her place, dumping more kindling onto the flame.

The coals were hot, and the response was faster than she'd even hoped. Flames rocked upward, quickly growing as they consumed the dry paper and caught onto the kindling, filling the stone enclosure with heat and light, funneling up to the outside world. Dorran emptied the kindling basket into it, then stepped back.

Hollows screeched. The noise was distorted by the chimney and bounced around and echoed until it was deafening. Clare pressed her hands over her ears. Dorran flinched back as something scraped against the stone, growing closer. A scream rose in volume, then a body landed in the flames, blackened but still alive, its scarred limbs writhing and its jaw flexing even as its eyes bubbled and liquefied in its skull.

Dorran pushed Clare back, then picked up the fire poker. A single blow pierced the skull, and the screams choked off. Black smoke rose from the body as flesh charred, and both Clare and Dorran gagged. She had never smelled anything so repulsive before; the musk the hollows all bore intensified and mixed with the sickening tang of burning flesh. Smoke began to fill the room, making Clare's throat itch even when she covered her nose and mouth with her sleeve.

The scratching noises in the chimney continued, frenzied, but they were growing fainter as the creatures fled back to the roof.

I've watched hollows become trapped behind a simple car door. They aren't smart, and yet they figured out which chimney to climb down to reach us and even persisted despite their fear of fire. Clare blinked as the toxic smoke scorched her eyes. *Are they still being controlled? Or was this just dumb luck?*

Dorran convulsed against the overwhelming smell. He leaned close to the fire, using the poker to pull the blackened corpse free from the flames to stop the cooking process. It tumbled onto the hearth, sending clumps of ash rolling onto what had once been their bed.

No, it can't be luck. And I don't believe it's a second intelligent hollow either. This is Madeline's legacy. She left instructions for what was to happen if she died.

Even clear from the flames, the body continued to smoke, its toxic smell making Clare wish they could escape the room and slam the door behind them. They couldn't, though. Not enough hollows would have been able to fit down the chimney to be a serious threat. They would have been sent in an effort to flush Clare and Dorran out of the room.

Or maybe something more. Madeline was clever. She liked to use distractions.

Clare turned, her throat aching. A cold wind grazed across her back. When she and Dorran had returned to the room, the contents had been tampered with—including the curtains being pulled over the windows. The same windows that relied on a single, internal latch to stay closed. And they had to stay closed, because hollows could climb stone walls.

Three sets of lamp-like eyes glowed in the flames as monsters spilled through the open window. Jaws widened, grinning through the haze of smoke and darkness.

CHAPTER 38

"NO!" CLARE DARTED FORWARD, arm outstretched, desperate to shut and lock the window before any more of the monsters came through. The nearest hollow lunged at her, teeth snapping for her hand, only to be knocked aside by Dorran's fire poker.

Clare took the second of reprieve to grab the shovel. It was small and light, designed for removing soot from the fire, but it would work in a pinch. She pushed forward again, ducking around Dorran's arm and knocking a hollow back as she tried to reach the window.

As long as we can close it, as long as we can stop the flood, we can handle whatever is inside.

The scrabbling coming from the chimney had been a perfect disguise for the noises outside their window. Dozens of the creatures jostled to get in, their distended limbs slapping on the windowsill as they crawled through the narrow opening in ones and twos.

"Clare!" Dorran barked. "Get back!"

"The *window*," she insisted, using the shovel's edge to stab through a creature's throat.

"There are too many!"

Clare wanted to scream. Dorran was right. Already, her path was blocked by eleven of the twisted bodies, barely held at bay by her shovel, filling up that half of the room, creeping onto the bed, beginning to climb onto the closet and up the wallpaper. Every second, another joined the throng. They poured through the window like water, and as their numbers swelled, their eagerness grew, the snapping teeth and grasping hands slinking ever closer.

We're out of options. Surrounded in here, surrounded outside.

Dorran pushed Clare back, putting himself between her and the hollows. Her mind spun, searching for an escape, and her eyes lit on the door near the fireplace. "The bathroom," she hissed. "We can lock ourselves inside."

"Yes. Go."

Clare turned for the door. The tiled bathroom had no windows. It would be cold and void of supplies except for water, but it would be secure. She wrenched the door open and was confronted by a blast of chilled air.

Something moved in the fireplace. Clare swiveled just in time to see one of the monsters creeping over the coals. The flames had subsided as the fuel burned off, but even so, the monster's limbs were bubbling from the heat. The outer layer of skin dripped off its arm as it reached toward Clare.

She took a shaky breath and sidestepped through the bathroom doorway. "Dorran!"

He was still facing the hollows, trying to keep the mass at bay. One of the approaching creatures snagged his sleeve.

Clare moved forward, shovel raised to stab through the gray arm, but her path was blocked. The burning, smoking hollow from the chimney staggered between her and Dorran. Its neck was too long, its eyes sunken deep into its skull, its mouth incapable of closing. Clare swung at the head, and the shovel made an unnervingly wet noise. It stuck to the bubbling skin, and when she tried to pull it away, strips of flesh and hair came with it.

Clare's stomach felt cold, like it did when she needed to be sick. Her ears rang. She took a step back, and that was all the opening the hollows needed. They swarmed toward her, some coming from the fireplace, their skin smoking, others spilling around Dorran. They pressed toward Clare, a mass so thick and hungry, she knew her shovel would not survive the fight. She thrust it out ahead of herself like a shield, and a set of crooked teeth fastened around the metal.

She could barely see Dorran. He had his back pressed to the wall near the window, teeth set in a grimace as he struggled to keep the bodies off of himself. The gap between them was widening as Clare was forced back an inch at a time. It was deliberate, she thought; Madeline had wanted them separated in their last moments.

Clare tried to wrench the shovel free. A gnashing mouth forced her to stumble backward, through the bathroom door, isolating her further. The bathroom offered nothing but soaps, immovable fixtures…and the second door.

The connected bedroom. Get out through it, then circle around through the hallway to get back to Dorran.

She still had the key ring in her jacket pocket. She hated letting Dorran out of her sight for even a second, but she was now divided from him by a small sea of the creatures. Going through the hallway would at least give her a better chance of reaching him.

The nearest hollow still had its teeth clamped around the shovel. Clare released it and leaped back. She wrenched the chair out from under the door and threw it at the creatures chasing her. Its leg became jammed between the sink and bathtub, sticking it in place, and forcing the hollows to struggle over and around it.

She didn't stop to watch. She turned the lock and the handle, shoving into the door with her shoulder at the same time and barreling into the second bedroom. It was a near-perfect mirror to their room, with the same furniture and fireplace. Only the walls were different: red wallpaper instead of blue. The room had belonged to Dorran before the stillness. He still kept many of his old clothes in the closet, but scarcely little else of his identity existed in the room. Probably, Clare knew, because his mother had forbidden it.

Clare didn't try to shut the bathroom door behind herself. She wanted to lure as many of the creatures into the second bedroom as possible—get them away from Dorran. She put her head down and ran for the door that let back into the hallway.

The door opened with a bang, bouncing off the wallpaper and leaving a dent, and Clare slammed it closed behind her. Bodies hit the other side, guttural chattering fueled by growing frustration.

The door to the main bedroom was no more than fifteen paces away. Clare ran for it, her breathing strained. A shape loomed out of the gloom, its narrow shoulders hunched, its head scraping the ceiling. Gangly arms reached almost to the floor as it staggered, bowlegged, toward Clare.

Of course they're guarding the hallway. She wouldn't want us escaping.

The bedroom was close. Clare pulled the key ring out of her pocket as she lengthened her paces, racing the monster to reach the door. She was going to make it. The shambling behemoth was too slow and unsteady. She could get through the door in time, grab one of the weapons, and reach Dorran—

A horrific sense of dread washed through her, sending prickles sizzling across her skin. The gangly hollow wasn't the only sentry in the hallway. The ceiling was *moving*. Hollows writhed across it, so thick that she could barely see the plaster. Their lidless eyes followed her every movement. One by one, they began letting go, dropping to the hallway, plunging toward Clare.

There was no chance to reach the door any longer, no time to fight with the lock. She put her head down, no longer breathing, simply focused on *moving*.

The behemoth's long arms swiped at her but missed. Clare aimed for the gap between its knees and passed through, her shoulders grazing its clammy flesh. Something snagged at her foot, making her stumble, but she regained her balance and kept moving.

Clare was barely thinking. She knew she had to find a new weapon and fight her way back to Dorran, but had no concept of how she might achieve that. Each step carried her farther from the door and closer to the stairs. Eyes appeared near the railing, catching the muted light. Clare tried to count how many there might be and her odds of getting past them: too many and not good.

Hollows were coming up behind her. The passageway ahead bulged with bodies. Clare stumbled to a halt, surrounded on all sides, her ears filled with their ravenous howls.

Suddenly, a new noise boomed around Clare. A familiar voice chanted. "Ten minutes. Find a safe location. Ten minutes."

Unathi. The radio.

Dorran must have reached it. He'd turned the volume up. That was smart; the shock of the noise might buy him a few seconds. Maybe he could do what Clare hadn't and be safe inside the bathroom. She prayed he wouldn't come looking for her. He wouldn't get through the wall of creatures.

Ten minutes. I just need ten minutes. Got to find a room, take shelter—

Something hit her from behind. Her hip slammed into the railing. She felt herself toppling and grabbed at the nearest object: the hollow, a large one, pockets of fat billowing its body like countless tumors. It pressed forward, and Clare had no time to even gasp as her feet left the floor. She was tumbling, her arms tangled around the hollow, the hollow's arms tangled around her, as they dropped toward the ground two floors below.

The hollow hit the tiles first. Clare landed on top of it, and her world exploded into pain. She groaned and drew a strained breath as feeling came back into her limbs. The monster's jellylike body had cushioned her—she was certain it was the only reason she was still alive—but it hadn't been a perfect protection. Her neck ached from the way it had been twisted. Her throat stung from where the monster's teeth had cut her—not from a bite, but simply from the impact forcing them into her. Her whole right side smarted like it had been slapped, and her leg flared with pain every time she tried to move it.

But she was alive. And considering how high Winterbourne's ceilings were, that was a small miracle.

The hollow beneath her was still moving. The back of its head had broken open like an egg, spilling fluids and blood across the tiles, but the eyes rolled and the teeth opened and closed in a spasmodic loop. Clare shifted to the side, falling off the body, cringing as every small movement jarred her. The hollow twitched two more times, final firings of a brain that was more outside the head than in, then it fell back, limp.

Dorran…where is Dorran?

She tilted her head to look up at the stairs. Just that small motion sent waves of dizziness through her and caused rivers of black to bleed in from the edges of her vision. She clamped her mouth shut to silence a moan. The creatures on the stairs were looking down at her, flashes of light sparking across their count-less eyes.

Get up. You have to fight.

She tried to pull her feet underneath herself. She felt boneless, uncoordinated. A hollow stood on the lowest step of the stairs, its head tipping to the side as it watched her with curious eyes. It took a step forward.

They were cautious. One of their companions lay dead on the tiles, and to their primitive minds, that was enough of a threat to make them wary. But that wouldn't last long. Nothing ever did in the face of their hunger.

Get up!

She tried again. Pain rushed along her left side, severe enough to make her think she'd fractured bones. Her feet slipped out at an angle. The hollow took another step forward. Bony nubs protruded from its skull, the skin stretched taut over them like canvas pulled too tight. It crept on all fours, using its hands as extra feet, and as its jaw widened, a string of saliva glistening toward the tiles.

Fight! You have to fight!

She couldn't hear anything from the floors above except for the low, quiet chatters. No sounds from Dorran. That frightened her even more than the body creeping toward her. She couldn't stand, so she took the only other choice available and crawled backward.

A heavy hand, its cracked nails grown too long, landed on her shoulder.

CHAPTER 39

THE HAND PUSHED HER down, and Clare gasped as her back hit the floor. She had no strength left to resist. A hollow loomed over her. It had lost part of its throat and its nose. The open flesh was rotting, spreading black veins across its features and clouding its bloodshot eyes. The jawbones clicked as they opened.

No. Please. Not like this. We were so close.

The creature's head moved down, angled toward her throat. Clare thrust her hands up, pressing into the cold flesh, jabbing her thumbs into its eyes and nose, trying to hold it off, but it didn't even seem to notice. The teeth fastened over her throat and squeezed.

Clare convulsed. The teeth pulled off her throat, grazing hot lines across the skin. She clamped her hand over the site and felt liquid. Hollow saliva mingling with her own blood. Not enough blood to kill her, though. It had only grazed the skin; her throat was still intact.

The hollow's head hovered above hers, its bloodshot eyes staring down at her. The teeth flexed, tongue running over them to lap up any traces of blood. But it had stopped.

Why? How am I not dead yet?

It was holding its own head, Clare saw, one hand on either side of its skull. She blinked. *No. That can't be right.* Its hands were still on her shoulders. The cracked nails dug into her, trying to drag her up to its maw.

Something *else* was pulling on its head, dragging it away from her, holding the gnawing teeth at bay. Those hands came from behind it. The fingers tightened on the skull, and gray flesh bulged around them. One eye turned out sideways from the pressure. Clare guessed what was about to happen a second before it did but wasn't fast enough to turn away.

The head was yanked back. The force was immense, greater than a human's muscles could handle, and a series of horrible cracking noises preceded a glut of blood and spinal fluid as the head tore free from the body.

Clare had enough presence to close her eyes and mouth as the gore sprayed across her. She felt the body slump next to hers, the stump between its shoulders leaking over the tiles.

She crawled back, limbs shaking, dizziness rocking her. She swiped a hand across her eyes to clear the blood away.

A figure stood where the hollow had been a moment before. It held the decapitated head in one fist. At first glance, Clare thought it was wearing red gloves up to its shoulders, then realized she was looking at blood painted across the limbs. Spines protruded from its back, eight inches long. A halo of thinning gold hair surrounded its face.

Clare's throat burned. Her mouth opened, and a name left her before she was even conscious of it: "Beth."

As soon as she said it, she knew it was true. Her sister's back was straight and her neck long, although there was more monster than human about her. Her cheekbones, always pronounced, were growing sharper. Patches of her scalp were visible through the vanishing golden hair. She'd lost weight since she and Clare had parted, and her graying skin lay thin over bones. She stood naked except for the blood sprayed across her body.

Beth moved, suddenly, her expression growing harsh as she raised the decapitated head. She hurled it toward Clare with supernatural force. Clare ducked to avoid the projectile. She hadn't needed to. It wasn't aimed at her but made a heavy smacking noise as it hit the monster creeping up behind her.

Beth loped forward. She was graceful. Animalistic. Her whole body worked in perfect synchrony as she passed Clare, stabbing one hand toward the hollow. The blow was harsh enough to puncture through the creature's ribs. It began to scream, blood and froth mixing with rage and spilling out of its mouth. Beth shook the hollow and, in one sharp movement, broke its spine and dropped it to the floor.

It was her. The thing that was attacking hollows. She cleared the tunnels for us to escape the cavern. She kept us safe when we were climbing the cellar stairs. She's been killing any of the creatures that got in our way, because they don't recognize her as human, because they don't try to fight her.

And even before that... Clare blinked and saw the fuel container, the one she'd thought should still be in their room, tumbling into the torchlight. She saw the flare that had appeared right when they needed it. She saw the chains that had been binding Dorran breaking, something that called for unnatural strength. *It was her all along.*

Beth straightened again, standing over her latest kill, and stared down at Clare. There was no familiarity in her eyes. No love.

How long has she been here? We told her where to find Winterbourne before we split from her. She could have been here for weeks, waiting for us. Slowly losing her mind. Slowly forgetting why she even came.

Tears dropped over Clare's lower lids. She reached a hand out toward her sister. Beth quirked her head to one side. She hesitated, then extended her own hand. Her fingertips grazed over Clare's, smearing traces of red onto her. The touch was small and brief. But for that second, Clare thought she saw the remnants of her sister in the sunken eyes.

"Be...safe." Beth's voice rasped. She withdrew her hand, stepping back from Clare, and in one fluid motion turned toward the hollows that had been creeping closer.

They were surrounded. There were eyes in every direction, all fixed on Clare, oblivious to the woman who stood between them.

Beth dropped into a crouch and sprang. A body smashed into the floor, a shocked scream rising before Beth's heel stomped on the back of its skull, crushing and silencing it.

The voice floated from the radio, loud enough to crackle through all of the rooms. Even distorted by the static, even muffled by layers of stone walls, Clare could hear the fear wavering in Unathi's careful pronunciation. "Two minutes. Take shelter. Two minutes."

The hollows were coming for her. Clare crawled back, trying to avoid the bodies that littered the floor. The creatures slipped over the blood, ungainly arms and legs scrambling for purchase. Beth moved with furious precision, striking them back, knocking them down. Her fists broke through bones and her teeth tore flesh. A wildness filled her face, and Clare could no longer recognize her sister.

Clare's back hit the staircase's paneled wall. A small side table was near her. Clare's legs ached, not wanting to lift her, but she hauled herself onto her knees. The side table held few objects, but her eyes landed on a wooden clock the size of her head.

Beth's attention was broken. She seemed to have forgotten Clare's presence, and instead lashed out at anything that moved, tackling indiscriminately.

A bony hand fastened around Clare's ankle and tugged. She swung the clock, feeling it fracture as it impacted the creature's head. The hand refused to release her. Clare scrambled, fingers clutching at the broken wood and gears. Teeth fixed around her injured leg, squeezing, cutting through her pants as it sought out the blood-soaked bandages. Beth was at the other side of the room, writhing in a delighted frenzy as she tore into her peers.

The tinny voice from the radio came again, aiming for

authority but quivering, breathless. "One minute. May God have mercy on us all."

Clare tightened her hand around one of the wood fragments. It came to a sharpened point, a makeshift stake. She drove it into the hollow's face, aiming for the eyes but missing. She pierced near its ear instead. It was close enough; the hollow's jaws released her as it bucked. Another was already at her shoulder, and Clare didn't even have time to breathe as she brought the fractured wood around and gouged it into the monster's neck.

The radio abruptly clicked off, its static falling silent. It was replaced by a new noise. Bellows. Screams. They rose from the horizon, exploding out of the forest like birds taking flight. Swelling closer. Clare shrunk away from it, her instincts reacting even when her mind had gone blank. It was coming, unstoppable, like a tsunami. The end.

It passed from the forest into Winterbourne. A chain reaction rippled through the hollows as the thanites passed on their message of destruction. It started with the creatures closest to the door and moved inward. The hollows stiffened, backs arching and bulging eyes turned toward the ceiling. Their jaws opened as involuntary screams exploded out of them.

Beth wasn't spared. Shock and pain registered on her features. Clare saw everything in those precious seconds: the way her back quivered as though an electric current ran through her. Her eyes rolled. Her head jerked toward Clare. They made eye contact. Beth's lips opened: a plea for relief, an apology, or words of blame, Clare couldn't tell.

The spines on her back burst like balloons filled with jelly that had been squeezed too hard. Blood ran from the sites, mingling with what had already covered her. Her skin turned blotchy gray and white. She crumpled like a puppet that had had its cords cut. Clare had just enough time to see her sister hit the floor, then she clenched her eyes closed as the code caught up to her.

The sensation was unlike anything she had felt before. It was as though a million threads ran through her body, and all at once, someone took hold of them and tugged. She was being pulled, but in what direction, she didn't know. It was agony. Her skin, her muscles, and her bones all burning. In the span of a second, the heat was overtaken by cold. She couldn't breathe. She tumbled, sliding down the wall, barely conscious of the screams and thumps of falling bodies around her.

The noise ended in a matter of minutes, the howls growing fainter in waves as the code flowed past Winterbourne, until Clare couldn't hear it any longer.

Her eyes were blurred. She blinked, trying to clear them, trying to shake the ringing out of her ears. She felt as though she had been hit by a train.

Around her, bodies lay in heaps. Some faced the ceiling, eyes dead and mouths slack. Others had fallen with their arms stretched out, as though they hoped to crawl away from their destruction. A gray pus-like ooze ran from their orifices and any open wounds on their bodies. It mixed with the blood in awful patterns.

Clare couldn't prevent her eyes from moving to the one body

that was familiar. Beth, no longer bearing spines, lay facing away. One arm had been thrown backward, and Clare had the awful idea that Beth had been reaching toward her in those last seconds. She tried to lift her own hand, to reach toward her sister in return, but the muscles wouldn't obey. Everything was painful, even breathing.

Footsteps approached from behind. They moved slowly, heavily, each one accompanied by the creak of the stairs' floorboards. Clare forced herself to move and tilted her head back to rest it against the wall. She could see Dorran at the edge of her vision, pausing at the base of the stairs, one hand braced on the railing. He shook as he scanned the scene. It took Clare a second to realize he must be looking for her. She was so covered in blood that she was almost unrecognizable among the massacre.

"Hey," she croaked. It hurt to talk.

The fear in his eyes gave way to relief. He moved toward her, his steps not as stable as normal, but filled with purpose. Clare blinked furiously, trying to see him more clearly. He was splattered with blood as well. But he was standing. He'd held the hollows off.

"Are you okay?" He dropped to his knees beside her. Hands ran across her cheeks, then roved lower, searching over her body, seeming to find every place that ached.

Clare flinched as he tried to pull the fabric away from the bite on her leg. "I'll be fine. You?"

"Nothing I can't handle." His smile was shaky. "Oh, my darling."

Something shone in his eyes, an emotion Clare couldn't properly read. "Yeah?"

"It's over."

She smiled, then coughed and tasted blood on her lips. She felt herself slipping toward blackness but still didn't let her smile fade as she echoed him. "It's over."

CHAPTER 40

CLARE WOKE LAYING ON something soft and warm. Her mind was fogged, memories and dreams blending into something unrecognizable. She forced her eyes open. The world was desaturated and dark, and she couldn't see much except an indistinct figure moving toward her. The voice was familiar, though, and spoke in soft, warm tones. "Hey there."

The mattress bowed as weight settled onto it. Clare rubbed her palm across her eyelids, flinching at the raw skin and bruises on one of the knuckles. When she opened her eyes again, she could see Dorran more clearly. He was clean again, wearing a fresh burgundy knit top and with his hair combed back from his face. She could see hints of bandages across him: one wrapped around his hand, one on his neck where it peeked out from the collar, and a bandage covering a mark near his temple.

He looked better than he had in a long time. His posture was relaxed, but there was something else different about him. He'd lost the quiet desperation that had taken up residence in his eyes. They were filled with warmth now, calm and confident as they smiled down at her.

She grinned back. "Sorry. Fell asleep."

"You needed it." His fingers traced over her forehead, brushing strands of hair out of the way. He almost sounded like he was purring. "Rest awhile longer. I'll bring you some food."

The pressure left the mattress as Dorran stood. She watched him as long as she could, until he'd left the room. He pulled the door nearly shut but left the latch free. Clare felt a split second of panic at the sight. She had to consciously unclench her hands.

We can leave doors open now. Nothing will be coming in.

The offer to rest was tempting. She felt like she'd been tied down with bags of sand, and each movement was a herculean task. It would be all too easy to close her eyes and fall back under.

Nope. Time to get up, lazy. You've slept enough.

She grumbled to herself, then put in the effort to sit up. Muscles screamed. A hundred cuts scattered across her body burst into fire. Clare clenched her teeth.

She'd thought she'd grown tougher in the silent world, more able to push through pain. In retrospect, she realized, adrenaline was probably owed a lot of thanks. The thanites too. They had stopped the hollows from feeling most pain, so it made sense that they would dull the aches in a regular person too.

That's a shame. I liked thinking about myself as a tough, no-compromise woman. Turns out I'm still a wuss.

She chuckled to herself, but the laughter faded quickly. Everything was still too recent. Too raw. Making jokes felt somehow sacrilegious.

How long was I out?

Clare squinted toward the windows and frowned. They were in the wrong side of the room. It took her a second to realize why. Dorran had put her in the mirror bedroom, the one that joined the shared bathroom. That made sense. The original bedroom would need a deep clean after what had happened to it.

It was night. The room was lit by the fire and a candle left on the bedside table. She couldn't have been out for more than a few hours, Clare thought, but Dorran had been efficient. He'd cleaned the worst of the grime off of her and bandaged her cuts. Her clothes were gone, except for her underwear. She touched her hair and guessed he must have tried to clean it for her too. It wasn't revolting, but she was still looking forward to a proper bath.

The door creaked as Dorran nudged it open with his shoulder. He carried a soup bowl in one hand and a towel and spoon in the other. As he closed the door, Clare shuffled to sit up properly.

"No, don't try to get up." Dorran placed the soup on the bedside table and fetched the pillows from the bed's other side. He plumped them behind Clare's back, giving her support, then resumed his place on the bed's edge, sitting at an angle so he could face her. The towel was draped over her lap, the soup bowl set on it, and then Dorran dipped the spoon into it and brought it up to Clare's lips. She tilted forward to drink. She tasted parsley, celery, and what might have been eggplant. It was good. He had a knack for bringing out the best in plain ingredients.

"I can feed myself," Clare said once her throat was wet enough to let her talk.

"Of course you can," he said, the contented note still in his voice as he dipped the spoon into the soup and brought it back up for her.

She laughed, realizing the exercise was as much a comfort for him as it was for her, and drank.

"Much of this comes from our garden," Dorran said, and moved his thumb to catch a drip running over Clare's lip. "The plants were left intact, thank mercy. I only needed to repair the wires for the lighting where they had been chewed through."

"The hollows chewed the wires?"

"One did. And was cooked for its efforts. It must have been part of their attempts to escape the light. They couldn't get to the bulbs; otherwise, they likely would have smashed those directly. We were lucky."

"We sure were." Clare frowned, taking another mouthful of soup. "What's it like out there?"

"Ha." He took a deep breath, his chest swelling, then let it out in a rush. "Except for the garden, I would be inclined to call this place a lost cause and torch it all."

"That bad?"

He shrugged lightly. "I'm making progress in pieces. There are many priorities, though, so I am not as fast as I would like. I have begun removing bodies and burning them in the furnace.

But the dead hollows are everywhere, and…they *ooze*. It will take some scrubbing."

Clare's memory snapped back to Beth, and a sharp hit of grief washed through her. She closed her eyes, breathing through her nose, trying to bring herself back to the present. She had been forced to accept Beth's death weeks ago, before they had ever arrived back at Winterbourne. "I'm amazed you've had a chance to do anything. How long have I been out? Four, five hours?"

Dorran laughed. "I am not quite that efficient, though I appreciate that you think I am capable of it. The code was activated a little over a day ago. Don't worry, I spent my share of time asleep as well."

Clare lifted her eyebrows. "I slept through the day?"

"The code hit you badly." He lifted the spoon again, nudging it against her lower lip until she drank from it. "Not to mention the blood loss. And there was swelling on the side of your head. You may have a concussion."

"Huh." *That explains the headache.* Clare rested her hand on Dorran's forearm, searching his features. "What about you? How are you coping?"

"Much better than the first time. I didn't have as many thanites as you, just what I received through the transfusions. I felt sick for a couple of hours, but that was all."

"What about after we were separated? You were trapped in the room with the hollows. How badly were you hurt?"

"A couple of scratches, that is all."

She searched his face for any sign he was hiding serious

injuries, a habit she couldn't get him to shake. But there was no sign that he wasn't telling the truth. She sighed.

"I had my back to the wall." Dorran lifted the spoon again. "I was able to keep them from overwhelming me, but I was pinned, and the exertion wasn't sustainable. Ten more minutes and they would have won. We were very lucky."

"Very," Clare said. She saw Beth in her mind's eye: that final, sad glance, the way her sister had crumpled. Her throat suddenly felt too tight, and she shook her head as Dorran offered her more soup. "I think I'm full. Thank you, though."

His expression grew somber. One hand stroked over her cheek, a wordless comfort. She leaned into his caress. *Did he find her body? Did he even recognize her? She barely looked like herself.* Clare exhaled and forced herself to smile. "I'm all right. It's just…a shock that it's all over. We're finally free. And that's good."

"It is," he murmured. The thumb lingered on her chin, and his voice fell into a whisper. "Do you feel well enough for a short walk?"

"Yeah. Yeah, it would be good to move about a bit, now that I can." She managed a laugh. "I was waiting for freedom for so long, so I'll enjoy this."

He kissed her lightly, then took her hands and helped her out of bed. Clare staggered. Her legs took a moment to remember how to walk, but Dorran held her until she was steady. Then he took an oversize robe off the back of a chair and helped thread her arms through the sleeves. He knelt and carefully slid socks over her feet.

"I can go without socks." Clare laughed as he put slippers over them. "I don't need coddling."

"Hmm." His fingertips traced over her leg as he stood. "Perhaps. But it is cold out, and I am never taking another risk as far as you are concerned. Not for the remainder of eternity."

"Oh no, we might have a differing opinion on that."

He matched her grin as he kissed her again, then took her hand and drew her toward the door.

He hadn't been exaggerating about the cold. Even with the robe, Clare shivered as she stepped through the door. It was so cold that she expected to see frost growing across the stones.

"Another storm set in after the code was activated," Dorran said. He kept a firm hold on her hand, rubbing his fingers over hers. "The snow is deep. At least, this time, we have enough supplies inside Winterbourne that we will have no fear of going hungry."

"And we'll have plenty of cleaning to keep us busy."

Dorran had opened many of the curtains, and Clare could see signs of the massacre. The nightmarish, gray ooze stained the carpet in patches, showing where each hollow had fallen. In some areas, there was blood where a skirmish had occurred. The bodies were gone from the upstairs hallway, but the smell lingered, overwhelming. Clare breathed through her mouth to fight the rising nausea.

"Not far now," Dorran said.

"Where are we going?"

He smiled, but there was a trace of sadness in it. "I had not planned to show you until later. But...I think you need it now."

"Dorran?"

They stopped in front of a door. It was several rooms down from Clare's own, and when Dorran turned the handle, she saw it opened into a bedroom almost identical to hers, only with green-and-gold wallpaper and green curtains.

The fire was lit. Clare blinked at it, trying to understand the logic of maintaining a fire in a room they weren't using.

"Nothing is certain yet, but..." All of a sudden, Dorran seemed anxious. One hand hovered over her shoulder, as though he was preparing to pull her back.

A body lay in the bed. Resting chest-down, her back had been crisscrossed in thick layers of bandages. Blooms of red had soaked through the fabric wherever the spines had once cut through. Her head was facing toward the windows, away from Clare, but a halo of thin, shoulder-length gold hair spread behind her, limp on the pillow.

Clare felt as though her world was slipping away. She rocked back, and Dorran caught her and steadied her. She looked up at him, not ready to believe, half-afraid that she had misunderstood, that it was somehow a cruel joke, that she was looking at her sister's corpse on the bed. But Dorran was smiling, even if hesitantly. Clare looked back at the body. Beth's back rose a fraction as she breathed.

"I..." Dorran licked his lips. "I cannot make any promises. The damage is extreme. By all rights she should not be alive."

Clare stepped closer, and Dorran followed, the steadying hand still in place. She didn't think she was going to cry, but then a tear slipped over her lower lid and disappeared into the plush green carpet. She grazed her fingers over Beth's hair. Dorran had tried to wash it, but the gold strands were still stained red. The color would take a long while to come out, Clare knew.

"You saved her," she whispered.

"I did my best. But even if she lives, there was a lot of damage to her spine. And…and even then…there may not be much of *Beth* left." His hands squeezed her shoulders gently. "Do you understand?"

She nodded, past the point of speaking. She rested her hand on Beth's shoulder, one of the little parts of her back left unbandaged. The skin was warm. Human.

He saved her. Clare tried to stop herself from crying, but more tears came. *Out of everyone, he had the most reason to resent her, to fear her. She almost killed him. He could have ignored her in the foyer. Simple neglect would have ended her, and I never would have known. But…he saved her.*

The bandages had been tied with care. Even the way he'd washed her hair showed a level of compassion that Clare doubted many people could have brought themselves to.

She still couldn't speak, so instead she turned and hugged him as tightly as she could. Warmth enveloped her as his arms cocooned her, and they held each other for a long while.

CHAPTER 41

DORRAN PREPARED A WARM bath for Clare, then helped wash her hair and rebandage the cuts. Then he wanted Clare to sleep more.

She thought she'd slept plenty and wanted to do her part in cleaning the house. It turned into an argument that ended with Dorran physically picking her up, cradling her to his chest, and carrying her back to her room. Clare, laughing hysterically, slapped his shoulder. "Put me down. I want to clean!"

"No, you want to sleep." He adjusted his hold on her, barely smothering his own chuckles. "I promise, you really do."

"You fiend." She ducked as he used his foot to knock the door open. "What sort of brute forces a woman away from her mop?"

"Absolutely unforgivable," Dorran agreed as he placed her onto the bed. "Now, would you like something to drink?"

As they sipped black tea, sitting cross-legged on the bed together, they came to a compromise. Clare would work in the garden, an environment Dorran deemed safe and comfortable enough, while Dorran continued to dispose of the bodies.

"I'm cautious about putting too many through the furnace at once." He swirled his drink thoughtfully. "They release an awful black smoke."

Clare pulled a face. "Like the one that came down the chimney."

"Exactly. But it's probably still the best way to dispose of them, isn't it?"

"Hmm. I don't like the idea of burying them."

"No, neither do I. There is no way to know what they might do to the soil. If they were just dead humans, I would expect them to decay naturally, but…"

"Yeah. The hollows were a long way from natural." Clare rolled her shoulders as she glanced out the window. The storm continued, beating flecks of white against the glass, its chill threatening to invade their haven.

"And I would not enjoy finding any of their bones washed up after a storm," Dorran added. "So, the furnace it is."

"Other people must be facing the same dilemma. There must be a thousand hollows for every surviving human. Or more." Clare bit her lip. "Now that they're dead, people will be reclaiming their homes…returning to towns that were overrun just yesterday… How are they going to adjust?"

"In gradual stages, I imagine. A home at a time."

"Hmm."

"We will not be trapped here forever. Do not fear that fate."

Clare gave him a thin-lipped smile. Dorran had a knack for guessing her thoughts. She'd been thinking about how cut off they were: no transport out of Winterbourne and no way to contact anyone outside.

"It might mean waiting until spring and then walking until we find habitation," Dorran said. "A walk like that would likely take a few days. But if the weather is stable enough, it would be possible."

"Thank you." She reached across the narrow gap between them and squeezed his hand. "Until then, we have plenty to keep us busy here, don't we? Returning the house to a livable state."

"Perhaps it will eventually feel like a home."

"I'd like that."

Once their tea was finished, Dorran bundled Clare in too many layers and escorted her downstairs. It was her first time seeing the foyer since the code's activation, and she tried not to grimace. Dorran had removed enough corpses to create a path to the kitchens and garden, but the floor was still covered with dried blood and the gray substance, which had started to flake as it dehydrated. He'd removed the scraps of his mother's effigy at least.

"All right?" Dorran asked, watching Clare closely.

"Yeah. Fine." She did her best to ignore the way the floor crunched under her shoes. "But…let me help you with this. It'll do us both good if we clean it up faster."

The gentle pressure on her back didn't relent as it moved her toward the rear of the house. "I think the garden will do you a greater good."

He was right. Stepping into the hothouse felt like having a weight lifted from her shoulders. Under Dorran's care, the plants had thrived. They continued to spill out of their beds and tangle over each other in unruly, beautiful snarls.

Dorran stayed just long enough to settle her, then kissed the top of her head. "Call if you need me."

Bent over the plants, coaxing strangling tendrils loose from their victims and refastening them to their designated poles, Clare felt transported back to her earliest days at Winterbourne. She remembered working in the dark earth beside Dorran, barely daring to let herself trust him as they built toward their survival. It only made his absence more acute.

He was never far away, though. Footsteps moved from the foyer, through the chamber outside the garden, and down the stairs to the furnace room in unerring loops. Sometimes, as he passed, Clare would approach the frosted window and peek through. She could see Dorran's blurred outline as he passed, dragging a heavy sack. He nodded when he saw her.

Once Clare was happy that the garden was on a good track, she left it and retraced the familiar path to the foyer. She stopped in the archway, admiring the transformation.

With the bodies gone, the patterns of gray and muted, discolored red looked almost like a deliberate, if chaotic design. The front doors were open, letting gusts of icy air roll through. Clare tightened her jacket around herself as she approached them. "Dorran?"

"Clare. Are you all right?" He appeared outside the doors, and

Clare couldn't hide a smile at the sight. White flecks scattered through his dark hair and stuck to his eyelashes. He was flushed and breathless, a cloud of mist rising from his lips with every breath.

"I'm good. I finished with the garden and wanted to see what I could do here."

"Ah." He stepped inside the foyer and indicated through the door. Snow had banked up against Winterbourne's entrance. He'd been using a shovel to dig a channel through it, one that sloped down, toward the front yard. "I've been thinking about the best way to clean the floors. It will take days if we try to use buckets and mops. I thought, instead, to hose it down and sweep it outside."

"Oh! I like that. It's a bit less gross."

"It's not so much removing the problem as simply relocating it." He shrugged. "The slurry will remain outside the door, frozen, until the snow melts. Though, if we are lucky, it will be washed away then."

"Well, that's a problem for tomorrow." Clare laughed. "Where should I start?"

He grazed his thumb across her chin. "Maybe you should rest, instead."

"Nope. I feel fantastic." That was mostly the truth. The aches and soreness were still present, but Clare was feeling more like herself than she had in a very long time. "Come on, I let you win that last argument. This one's mine."

"Very well." He was laughing. "Let's make a start."

They found two pairs of boots in the kitchen, then Clare pulled her skirt up, tying it above her knees so it wouldn't be dirtied. Dorran connected a hose to the kitchen tap and ran it into the foyer, washing down the floor. Then, using two pairs of hard-bristled brooms, they swept the fouled water toward the door and into the channel leading outside. It froze not far past, creating what would probably be a deadly flat of ice for anyone who stepped outside, but Clare and Dorran had no intention of leaving Winterbourne in the near future.

By the time they swept the third batch of soapy water outside, the floor actually looked the way it was supposed to. The walls would still need washing, and the water probably hadn't been good for the wood paneling, but Clare was pleased by the progress.

"Good enough," Dorran said, putting the broom aside. "I'm ready for lunch. How about you?"

"Lunch sounds great."

They harvested vegetables from the garden before making their way to the kitchens. The ingredients weren't varied; it would take a few more weeks before any of the root vegetables began cropping. Clare didn't mind, though. She'd survived on far worse.

While Clare watched over the cooking soup, Dorran excused himself and disappeared upstairs. Clare knew where he was headed: to check on Beth. She would have liked to accompany him, but she could guess why he was going alone. Dorran was prepared to lose Beth. Whenever they talked about her, an anxious note entered his voice as he cautioned Clare that they might not see a good outcome. He believed her life hung in the balance and that she might slip away at any moment. He didn't want Clare to be present for the discovery that Beth was gone.

But Clare wasn't afraid. She couldn't even explain it to herself, but a strange confidence had formed inside of her. She'd already gone through the loss of her sister, not just once, but multiple times. Now, when she thought of Beth, the only thing she felt was hope. That might have been misguided optimism. But no matter how many times Dorran cautioned her, it didn't dampen.

Dorran returned half an hour later. At Clare's raised eyebrows, he smiled sadly. "Still asleep. I changed her bandages."

Clare ladled soup out for the pair of them. "I can keep an eye on her this afternoon if you want to sleep. I don't want her to be alone if she wakes."

"I thought of that. I set up a bell on the bedside table, attached to a string in her hand. If she stirs, she has a way to call us."

Dorran slept that afternoon, exhausted from the day's work and having watched over both Clare and Beth the previous night. Clare lay beside him, watching his eyelashes twitch over his cheekbones as he dreamed. He rolled over, his arm coiling around Clare and holding her near, the way he usually did when he slept. She smiled and nuzzled closer, grateful for what they had, grateful for how much brighter their future was.

A steady routine formed over the following days. Dorran and Clare spent much of their time cleaning the house. They moved through the most-used rooms first, clearing out bodies and doing what they could to scrub stains out of carpet. The chilled house helped preserve the bodies, but even so, a slow decay began. Some days, they would open the windows and endure the burning ice just to get some fresh air through the rooms.

Through the work, they allowed themselves frequent breaks. There was no deadline they were rushing to meet, no disasters they were trying to stave off, and they indulged in the chance to spend time together.

Every few hours Dorran and Clare checked on Beth. They kept her bandages clean, adjusted her as much as possible to prevent bed sores, and dripped water into her parched mouth. With no medical equipment, there was no safe way to feed her. Once, Dorran tried to gently broach the idea that Beth might never wake. Clare didn't believe that. And, five days after the code was activated, Beth's bell finally rang.

CHAPTER 42

"SUN." CLARE LAUGHED, PRESSING close to the window, admiring the way the light caught on the bare branches of the shrubs flanking the driveway. It was twenty days since what she'd begun to think of as the end of the stillness. After weeks of blanketing snowstorms, they had endured two days of heavy rain. It had melted the snow and flooded the region for days.

Now, finally, the water had subsided. The gray clouds had cleared, and the sun, weakened by winter but still resilient, had appeared.

"It's still cold out, so I don't imagine we'll last long, but…" Dorran shrugged, smiling. "Shall we have lunch outside?"

He looked good, dressed in a thick sweater and fur-lined jacket. She'd given him a haircut. Dorran had told her to cut it however she liked, but Clare had become so fond of his long hair that she couldn't bear to remove much of it. Now, he looked a lot like he had when she'd first met him.

Clare, for her own part, wore a mix of her old clothes and ones claimed from Winterbourne's closets. It created an odd blend that she quite liked: jeans and silk dresses, classic floral patterns and modern stripes.

They pushed Winterbourne's front doors open, then Clare and Dorran ferried out supplies for a makeshift picnic. They wouldn't be sitting on the ground—the stones were too cold, and Clare still hadn't forgotten the vile slurry they had washed over the front steps—but on chairs, with an end table covered in cooked vegetables and a few treats from the long-life supplies. They tried not to dip into the cans as a rule, but that day was a celebration. The sun was back.

With their setting arranged on the courtyard outside Winterbourne, Clare wrapped a thick scarf around her neck and picked up the stack of blankets. Dorran appeared on the stairs, moving slowly. His hand was under Beth's arm, guiding her and supporting her.

Clare caught up to them at the base of the stairs and took Beth's other side. Her steps were halting, shuffled, like a woman of ninety instead of thirty. She looked like a memory of herself. Her skin had sunken, her hair had fallen out, and her lips were always cracked. She didn't speak, but simple instructions were obeyed; Clare could ask her to hold out her arms to put on a jacket and she would. That meant she could still understand what was happening, at least to some degree. She ate, but reluctantly.

The most disconcerting change was her lack of emotion. She didn't seem to feel happiness, frustration, or even boredom. She spent most of her day in her room, lying down and staring at the opposite wall, only moving when Clare or Dorran made her.

But Clare thought she could see tiny improvements each day. The places where the spines had cut through her skin had finally sealed over. She could still walk. That was a victory.

Clare supposed that was one benefit of her higher exposure to the thanites: she had more left over after the code. They were still working to heal her.

The sunlight was shockingly bright compared to the rest of Winterbourne, and Clare squinted as she stepped through the door. Beth flinched as the light touched her skin. Clare and Dorran stopped, still holding on to Beth's arms to keep her steady. They waited, watching to see how she responded and whether she tried to pull back into the darkness.

Beth blinked slowly, as though dazed, then began to shuffle forward again. They helped her into one of the chairs spaced around the table, and Clare draped the blankets over her shoulders and lap before taking her own seat.

It was the first chance any of them had had to step outside since the storm. A haze of dissipating mist drifted across the field. Their burned-out bus, coated in snow and developing rivers of flaking rust, was starting to look like an artistic sculpture. Behind it, the massive pine trees cut a ragged line across the horizon.

Dorran poured tea for them while Clare served their food. The air was sharp on her skin but tasted fresh and clear.

Clare held a bowl out for Beth, but she wasn't looking at the food. Instead, her watery eyes had fixed on the sharp blue horizon and the green line of trees. It wasn't unusual for her to stare into the distance, but this time felt different. She was watching the sky with more focus than normal. A bird appeared—a rare sight in a world where most living creatures had been eaten. It circled above the trees in two slow loops before diving back down. Beth's eyes tracked it. Then she took a shaky breath and spoke for the first time since she'd woken. "Pretty."

From then on, Beth's recovery progressed in leaps. She began pacing the house, restless. Clare found herself searching through the halls before each mealtime to find where Beth had wandered that day. Often, she would be stopped at a window, swaying as she stared into the outside world. She still rarely spoke, but she was showing more interest in her environment.

The daily maintenance of Winterbourne kept Clare and Dorran more than busy. The garden was their priority, and to keep the garden heated, they needed to run the furnace beneath it constantly. The stock of firewood stored in the furnace room dwindled faster than Clare had expected. In response, Dorran left every morning, an ax braced over his shoulder and the sled trailed behind him, to carve up fallen trees from the forest. He would return several hours later with chilled fingers and pink-tinted skin. Clare made sure she was waiting for him each time, with a mug of coffee and a warm embrace on standby.

One night, five weeks after the stillness ended, Clare woke to the sound of creaking wood. It was dark out, and she and Dorran were nestled together on the bed. Sheets tangled around her legs, and Dorran's arm was heavy across her waist as Clare rolled over.

The weather remained patchy, and the clouds were too thick to allow much moonlight through, but Clare thought the bedroom door was open. She squinted, trying to read the shadows through the maddening wallpaper, then her heart missed a beat as something moved inside the darkness.

Monstrous, round eyes flashed. Clare clutched at Dorran's hand. He stirred, half-asleep, murmuring an indistinct question, and she gripped his hand tighter.

The situation was familiar. When she'd first arrived at Winterbourne, before she'd heard of the stillness or the thanites, she'd seen disfigured creatures standing over her, watching her while she slept. She'd thought she was going mad.

It's happening again. We're not alone. I was so foolish. I should never have lowered my guard. They're still here, still alive—

The head tilted, eyes flickering, and lips pulled away from ragged teeth. Clare's heart missed another beat, then came back online, pounding with shock and relief. "Oh. You scared me."

Beth stared down at her, her mouth formed into a grimacing smile. She was always slightly more strange at night—one of the echoes from the hollow nature. She didn't sleep much but kept active during the night hours, moving through the mansion with long, loping strides.

Clare pressed her palm into her eyes, rubbing sleep out of them as she waited for her heart to slow. "How're you doing, Beth? Are you thirsty?"

She liked to talk with her sister the same way they always had, even though Beth never replied. There was something comforting about it, and she hoped it would help remind Beth of her old life too.

Beth's head tilted to the side. Her smile didn't falter, but her throat bobbed as she spoke. "Good…bye. Good…bye."

"Goodbye?" Clare propped herself up on her elbows. Dorran stretched at her side, only half-awake. "You mean good night?"

"Good…bye. Good…bye. Love…you. Good…bye." Beth abruptly turned, her unblinking eyes and wide grin disappearing as she paced along the hallway.

"Clare?" Dorran's warm hand rubbed across her side. "What was that about?"

"I think she just wanted to talk." Clare shuffled back under the blankets, her brain already trying to drag her back into sleep, a dozy smile forming. "She's getting better. Did you hear? She said she loves me."

"Mm. I heard."

Clare nuzzled back at his side, felt his warm breath ruffle her hair, and sank back into the security of his arms. Conscious thought was already beginning to flit away when her brain made a connection and her eyes snapped open.

No—she wasn't actually… She didn't mean… Was she?

Clare threw the blankets off and dropped her legs over the side of the bed. Dorran, shaken out of sleep for a second time, mumbled as he sat up, squinting at her. "Clare?"

"I think she was *actually* saying goodbye." All tiredness fled. Clare yanked her boots on with shaking hands. "I—I think she's trying to—"

A muffled booming noise sounded from deep in the house as a door slammed. Clare could barely breathe. She snatched her robe off the back of the nearby chair and raced for the door.

Beth had been growing increasingly restless over the previous days. She'd been staring through the windows at the forest with eager eyes. Clare had assumed it was an instinctual thing, that she was hypnotized by the birds and rabbits among the trees, like a housebound cat.

But Beth wasn't a cat. Despite what the thanites had done to her, she was still a person, capable of forming plans and carrying them out. Clare prayed she was wrong, that she was overreacting, but as she ran for the stairs, she realized Beth had been wearing boots and a jacket as she stood in the bedroom doorway.

No. No. She can't leave. It's not safe out there. It's too cold. There's no food. I can't lose her again—

Clare hit the foyer at an angle that jarred her leg. She didn't slow down, though, but dragged her robe's lapels tighter around herself as she crossed to the front door.

Its hinges groaned as she dragged it open. Cold air assaulted her. Snow lay across the ground in patches, thin enough that flecks of raw earth were still visible underneath. Boot prints marred it. Clare stumbled onto the steps leading into the court-yard, squinting against the moon-dappled field.

Something was moving away from Winterbourne, weaving lithely as it loped toward the distant trees. Clare's voice caught, and she pulled in a ragged breath as she began running after her sister. "Beth! Beth, wait!"

The figure stopped just long enough to send Clare a piercing look, then Beth kept on her course. She had a significant lead and was already halfway to the forest's edge.

"Beth!" Clare slipped on the frozen earth as she lengthened her strides, but refused to slow. The icy air stung her face and hands. Her loose hair fluttered behind her, snatched up by a fierce wind.

Beth's lead was increasing. As fast as Clare could run, she was no match for her sister. She would be at the forest's edge before Clare could catch up, and once she was among the trees, she would be lost forever.

"Beth! No!"

Clare was winded. Her limbs, pulled from sleep just minutes before, were heavy. Her lungs burned, and each time Clare breathed out, a plume of mist billowed away from her. Beth was at the forest. Clare staggered to a halt, gasping, her face stinging as tears coursed down it. "No. Beth. Please."

Beth turned toward her a final time, poised between two of the massive pines. Her back was straight, her head held high. She pressed a bony hand against her chest, over her heart, and then extended it toward Clare.

"I love you, too," Clare whispered. The words were snatched away by the wind, but she thought Beth still sensed them. Beth turned to the trees, beautiful and wild, her muscles rippling. In the space of a heartbeat, she was gone.

Clare squeezed her lips together, fighting to hold a moan inside. She wrapped her arms across her torso and buckled over, loss searing her insides.

Candlelight spread across the ground ahead of her. Then a hand, hesitant and gentle, touched her back. Dorran was beside her, his own robe put on as haphazardly as Clare's, his hair tousled in the brisk wind, a lantern held to light their steps.

"She left," Clare managed, not quite believing it.

Deep sadness was reflected in Dorran's eyes. He held his arms toward her and Clare accepted the hug, burying her face into his shirt.

"I think…" Dorran hesitated, his hands running over her back. "I don't think she wanted to leave you. But she *needed* to."

Wasn't I enough for her? Was she lonely? Did she think she was a burden? She wasn't; she never would have been.

Dorran's chin rested on top of Clare's head. He spoke softly. "Once, while we were on the road, you told me how you had moved out of your sister's house. You loved her. She loved you. And it hurt the both of you to be separated. But…you *needed* to be separate."

Clare drew a shaking breath. She lifted her head just enough to see the forest's edge in the distance. "Because as long as I lived with Beth, I would never be able to grow."

"I think she wants to grow now," Dorran murmured.

She opened her mouth to argue, then closed it again. Objections swirled through her head, deafening. *It's dangerous out there. What if she's hurt? What if I never see her again?*

Those were the same fears Beth had been plagued by when Clare bought her own house.

This is different. This isn't like buying a house in a different suburb. This is real.

And Beth was strong—stronger, perhaps, than Clare or Dorran. She had survived the stillness, had fought against the new nature being forced upon her, and half-mindless, had still returned to protect Clare when she needed it.

Now, Beth believed her greatest chance at a full life came from throwing herself into the wilderness. She would struggle, but she would also grow.

Clare didn't like it. But she didn't have to. She just had to trust in Beth.

She held on to Dorran's arm as the two of them turned back to Winterbourne, leaving the forest behind.

CHAPTER 43

DAYS PASSED, AND SOMETIMES Clare and Dorran were kept so busy that they barely had time to speak to each other, let alone relax together.

Dorran, as always, never complained, but she could tell something was weighing on him. When he finally opened up to her, it was with a quiet voice, late at night, when they were so surrounded by darkness that she could barely see his features. "I am worried."

It was five weeks after the stillness's end. They lay in their bed of blankets beside the fire. Clare was nestled against Dorran, her head on his shoulder, one of his arms wrapped around her back. His fingers played across her skin in small, intricate patterns.

She'd been half-asleep. That might have been deliberate, she realized. Dorran wanted to talk to her but hadn't been able to work up the courage until he thought she wouldn't hear.

She ran her hand under his shirt and rested it there, against his warm skin, so he could feel her presence. "What about?"

The silence lasted for a long time. She could feel Dorran swallow, her fingers rising and falling with each breath. Then he said, "This isn't the life I wanted you to have."

"We're alive. We're safe. That's plenty for me."

It was something Clare had been telling herself ever since the stillness ended. On days when her muscles were sore from work, or when she wanted to sigh at the sight of more zucchini and tomatoes for lunch, or when she missed being able to walk any distance without the cold consuming her. She had everything she'd been desperate for during the stillness: a house she could live in. Dorran was with her. They didn't have to fear starvation, and there were no longer hands scrabbling at the doors or windows.

His head tilted toward her. Firelight caught on his hair and the edge of his face, and although she couldn't see his expression, she could hear the slow, seeping anxiety in his voice. "You need more than the garden can give. Protein and fats. More nutrition and less work."

Keeping Winterbourne running had been easier in the first few weeks after the stillness, when relief outweighed almost everything else. But as more time passed, Clare began to think about the future. And what had once been everything she had hoped for suddenly didn't seem to be enough.

Dorran swallowed again. "You are lonely as well."

"I have you."

"But you need more than just one person."

"No." She buried her face against him. "You're my family. As long as I have you…"

She trailed off, not sure how to finish that sentence. This time, the silence lasted until it ached at Clare's bones.

She had been trying as hard as she could not to think about what they were lacking. She hadn't wanted to be ungrateful. Now, she realized, that had been a mistake. It had put the burden of their future entirely on Dorran's shoulders and left him responsible for solving it. He didn't like to talk about his fears. He had probably been stewing on this for weeks, afraid to say anything and unable to share his worries about what the future likely held.

As Clare finally let herself go down that path, she could see how bleak their choices really were. They had to reestablish contact with the outside world somehow. If they didn't, they faced a lifetime in Winterbourne, slowly running out of every resource, malnourished, never again hearing another human's voice.

This is the fear Dorran has been living with. He didn't need her to blindly trust him. He needed her help. Clare bit her lip. "Is there anything in the shed that could be used for transport?"

"I am afraid not. I looked, but there are not even enough parts for a partial motor." His fingers continued to move in slow patterns. "I could walk out of the forest. I would try to either find someone who can help or find a car that still runs and bring it back here."

Clare closed her eyes. Even if he could find a car that ran, fuel would be worth more than gold in this post-stillness world. And any easily available fuel supplies would likely have already been looted.

"I would have wanted us to leave together." Dorran's voice was so quiet that she could barely hear it through the wind whipping about the house. "That was always our promise. That we would stay together."

"Yes."

"But that would mean sacrificing the garden, which is a risk I am struggling to commit to."

"Beth might come back too. I'd want to make sure someone was here, just in case."

"Which means you would need to stay here while I look for transport. If the journey went well, I might be gone for as little as a week. But...I worry then too. What if something happened to me?"

She would stay at Winterbourne, but she couldn't keep up with the work of two people. Once the furnace room ran out of wood, she wouldn't be strong enough to chop and transport enough logs out of the forest to keep it running. The garden would die with no heat. She would either starve or die of hypothermia. It was a bleak future.

And there were so many ways an excursion outside could go wrong. They didn't know what state the world had turned into. Humanity could be trying to piece itself back together...or it could have devolved into a dog-eat-dog world, where bands of survivors would kill any vulnerable soul they crossed.

Even if the humans Dorran encountered weren't hostile, there were a dozen other ways he could be lost. A broken ankle would be a death sentence. If the temperature dropped drastically, he could die of exposure. If he couldn't find water. And it was a long walk from the forest to any sort of habitation.

Clare couldn't stand it any longer. She rolled away from Dorran, her pulse pounding, feeling sick. She stood and crossed to the window. The moon's light caught on the snow flurries, turning them into something ethereal. She blinked, furious, fear gripping her more tightly than it had since the stillness's end.

Dorran followed her. His arms wrapped around her, warm, solid, shielding her against the chilled night air.

"I am sorry," he whispered as he kissed the top of her head. "I did not mean to frighten you."

She wanted to say *Promise you will never leave* but swallowed the words. If they stayed in Winterbourne, they were condemning themselves to a poor, and likely short, life. It was an impossible, maddening scenario.

"What will we do?"

She hadn't meant to ask that question—if Dorran had an answer for it, he would have told her already—but it slipped out before she could stop it.

He rested his chin on the top of her head, his sigh ruffling her hair. "We will keep thinking, my darling. We will find a way out."

They stayed by the window until Clare's shivers were bad enough that she let Dorran coax her back to bed. He held her tightly that night. Clare couldn't sleep for a long time, and even though Dorran didn't speak again, she thought he might still be awake too.

I can't let him go alone. We can't both leave. And we can't spend the rest of our lives in Winterbourne. It is an impossible choice.

Clare's sleep was broken. Her nightmares had been better since the stillness's end, but they returned with a vengeance that night. She saw herself back on the bus, clinging to the seats as the vehicle rocked dangerously. They were going wildly fast, racing through a forest, the trees creating a blur as they passed on either side.

She called to Dorran, who was driving, asking him to slow down, trying to tell him that it wasn't safe. He turned around in his seat to smile at her, and she saw the blood running over his chin as his life dripped out of him.

Clare jolted awake, breathing heavily. The sky was on the earliest edge of brightening—not yet light enough to see clearly, but no longer the deep black of night. There was at least another hour before she and Dorran needed to rise.

The dream had been vivid, even down to the purr of the bus's engine. Clare reached for Dorran to reassure herself. She didn't need to go far; he was still at her side, one arm halfway draped across her, head tilted back as he slept. Clare pressed her hand against his chest. She could feel his heartbeat through his shirt.

There was another noise disturbing the early morning: a slow rumble, the same noise that had come through into her dream. Clare's pulse pumped, a punch of shock ripping through the tiredness.

She was really hearing an engine.

CHAPTER 44

"DORRAN!"

Clare grabbed his shoulder, urgently shaking him awake. He startled and rolled over, a reflexive movement that shielded Clare. "What is it? What's wrong?"

"Listen." Dorran's face was barely inches from her, and she could see his wide eyes in the faint light. She gave him a second to hear the rumble, then said, "That's an engine."

He took a sharp breath, his eyebrows rising. "Yes. Yes, quickly."

The bedsheets and quilts scattered as Dorran cast them aside. He grasped his robe and pulled it on as he crossed to the door in two steps. Clare was close behind, struggling into her boots, her own robe dragging in one hand as Dorran slammed the bedroom door open.

An engine. Someone found us. The hope coalesced in Clare's throat as a painful lump. She ran alongside Dorran, the robe streaming behind her as they traversed the mansion. Cold air bit at her skin, sucking her breath out of her in thin gasps, but there was no room for hesitation.

They had no way to guess how long the visitors might stay. They could have been searching for a specific location or hunting for animals. Confronted by what looked like an abandoned house, they could very well turn around and return to the forest. And if they left, they would take Clare and Dorran's chance of escape with them.

Dorran bounded down the stairs three at a time. His feet were bare, but that didn't seem to slow him as he skidded into the foyer. He threw a look over his shoulder, checking Clare was still with him, as he reached for the door.

She was only a few steps behind him. The door ground open, straining over the ice that had attempted to freeze it shut. The snowfall that day was nearly a foot deep, and fresh flakes drifted through the air, obscuring the view. Clare could make out a familiar black mark ahead: their scorched bus, half-buried under the snow. Beyond that, she thought she saw another shape. Something large. Something that could have been a van.

Spare boots stood by the door, and Dorran breathlessly pulled a pair on while Clare wrapped the robe around herself. Then he took her hand. A kaleidoscope of emotions played through his eyes. She felt all of them echoed inside of herself, confusing and overwhelming.

Rescue. A threat. Humans. Strangers.

Her nerves hummed, filling her with a sudden fear of moving

forward. They didn't know what the strangers wanted. She imagined herself and Dorran being gunned down as they descended the steps. Beth's words played through her mind: *There aren't many kind people left in this world.*

They could lock the doors, hide, defend their fortress. It would be safer. But grasping for safety wasn't how they would build a future. The only way they could survive in this world was if they learned to trust.

She trusted Dorran.

Dorran had trusted Beth, even after what she had done to him.

Now, they would have to trust their lives to the strangers in the van.

Dorran's hand tightened over hers. They stepped out together, their boots sinking deep into the snow. They took the stairs cautiously, fighting for purchase in the treacherous snow. The van became clearer with every step. It was an old model but recently painted black. Windows had been boarded over, much like their own bus. That meant it had been in use during the stillness.

Survivors. They can be unreliable. This time, it was Ezra's voice in her head. *It would be a gamble of whether they would help me, or whether they would shoot me dead, loot the place, and run.*

Her mouth was dry. Her hold on Dorran's hand must have been painful, but he didn't try to stop her. They reached the courtyard, where shrubs formed mounds in the snow. The burned-out bus lay like a skeleton on their yard. They passed it, moving closer to the van, its details growing clearer with each step. She didn't recognize it. The front windows were tinted. Clare couldn't see inside.

Please, be kind.

Then the door slammed open. A figure appeared in the opening, a slightly too-small sweater straining over his muscles, his beard catching snowflakes as they drifted past. His expression was near wild: bulging eyes, lips pulled back from his teeth. It would have frightened Clare if the face hadn't been so familiar.

"You're alive!" Johann bellowed. He slapped the side of the van, then leaped out, his legs sinking into the snow. "Damn it, I knew you'd be okay!"

The Evandale scientist began jogging toward them, arms swinging furiously as he waded through the snow. Clare gasped in delight, Dorran's shocked laughter in her ear, then the pair of them were racing forward to meet Johann. He grabbed them with an arm each and pulled them into a bear hug. Scratchy beard scraped over Clare's forehead, and her nose was filled with the smell of his leather jacket and floral shampoo.

For a moment, Clare couldn't hear anything except their shocked, delighted laughter and Johann's repeated, "Hey, hey, you're all right!" Then he released them, grinning, his face turning pink from the exertion and the cold.

"You found us!" Dorran beamed, one hand on Johann's shoulder. "How?"

"Ha! You were pretty secretive about where you were going." Johann winked. "But I stopped by a place called West Hope a few days back and shared a bottle of scotch with this old fellow who lived there. We got talking and figured out we had a mutual acquaintance in the form of yourselves, and sometime around two in the morning he *might* have let slip where to find you. But he made me swear not to tell on him. I guess neither of us are any good with secrets."

Clare shook her head, wondering. "That was a lucky encounter."

"Well, truth be told, I *was* looking for you. Unofficially. Have been for a couple of weeks now." Johann tilted his head back to admire Winterbourne. "Didn't expect your home to be this bloody big. What, are you rich or something?"

"Ah." Dorran shrugged, faintly embarrassed. "I...suppose I was. Not that it matters much now."

"No, I guess not, not now." Johann brushed his hand through his beard, clearing snow from it. "No one uses money now, since there was so much lying around to be looted. Hey, do you mind if we come in? The cold's killing me."

"Of course." Dorran placed a hand on Johann's shoulder, guiding him toward the house. "Did you say...*we*?"

"Oh, yeah, Becca came with me." Johann waved to the van. "C'mon! We're going in!"

Clare squinted through the snow. A small face peeked out of the van, gray hair whipped about by the wind, mittens held over her red nose. She gingerly climbed out of the vehicle, shutting the door behind herself, then jogged through the snow to reach them.

"Hello, hello," Becca squeaked. She was clearly suffering in the cold. Clare put an arm around her shoulder, and the four of them ascended the stairs to Winterbourne.

"How are the others?" Clare asked, stomping her shoes in Winterbourne's entrance to clear the snow off them.

Johann rolled his shoulders, stretching. "Pretty good. Niall's healing. It's slower now that we destroyed so many of the thanites, but he's walking. Somewhat. Unathi has been making contact with survivor groups around us. We've been careful not to share the location of our bunker, but that's become less of a worry now that the hollows are gone. There's more food, more places to shelter, more of everything."

"What happened on the day you activated the code?" Clare asked. "What made you move the timeline sooner?"

Becca shuddered. "Those hollows heard our radio broadcast. Or, at least, some of the smart ones did. And they realized what it meant for them. Within the span of an hour, we had thousands of them swarming over our compound—so many that we couldn't see anything through the cameras except for a blanket of skin."

"The bunker's meant to be impervious to attacks, as long as we don't unlock the doors," Johann said. "But we still didn't want to put it to the test for too long. Plus, we could hear them screaming, even two floors underground. It made it hard to sleep. Or think. Or do much of anything, really."

Clare shook her head, thinking of the days of work it had taken to scrub the living areas of Winterbourne. "That must have left you with a mess to clean up."

"It sure did," Johann said. "Miserable things were piled up

against the door, and we had to dig our way out through the bodies. Cleanup is keeping us all busy. I had to wheedle at Unathi for days to be allowed to look for you. Before you left, you promised you'd come visit once the stillness was over. We waited for weeks, but you never came. And the whole time, we were hearing more and more horror stories from people we met. It was starting to freak me out. What if I'd sent you to your death? Eventually, I got permission from Unathi to drive around and see what I could find."

"I'm glad you did," Dorran said. "We lost our bus. We've been trapped here."

"I saw. When I pulled up, I honestly thought you might have gone up in flames inside it. I was trying to get up the courage to step out and check when you appeared."

They led their guests up the stairs, Becca still shivering under Clare's arm. Both of their friends were staring about the ornate building with the same sense of self-conscious awe Clare had felt when she'd first arrived at it. Even Johann's voice had taken on a subdued tone.

"Bartering has become common now that cash holds no value. And Niall's doctoring skills are in high demand, as you could guess. We jokingly call him the golden goose. We got that van and fuel in exchange for medical treatment for a small settlement. Fuel is running out, which made it pretty valuable."

They had reached their bedroom. Dorran ushered the party inside, shutting the door behind them, and Clare took a deep breath as the warmth washed over her.

Dorran knelt beside the fire, rebuilding the coals, before setting a pot of water over it for drinks. Clare brought out a spare quilt for the still-shivering Becca. "Does Niall travel to wherever he's needed, or do people come into the ship?"

"He traveled at first." Johann settled into one of the chairs, with Becca next to him. "Now, he's set up a makeshift hospital in an old church hall. He has assistants—people who know first aid or want to learn. He's been working like crazy, just trying to do what he can, even when people don't have anything to trade. Luckily, the thanites help. Chronic conditions like diabetes and arthritis are essentially gone. Most of Niall's work is advising on malnourishment and deficiencies, and stitching cuts."

"That's good news." Clare sat and pulled her legs up under herself. "Becca's idea to leave a portion of the thanites intact has probably saved a lot more lives too." *Like ours.* Her fingers traced over the bandages on her wrist. If not for the thanites, she likely would have succumbed to infection long before.

Becca smiled at the compliment. "We intend to wipe out the remaining thanites in stages. Niall thinks it's dangerous to leave any inside the body permanently, but we can afford to take it slow at this point. Another fifty percent in a few weeks, and fifty percent more a month or two after that. There are so few hollows left that they're not a serious danger."

The pot clanged as Dorran bumped it. Clare blinked at her friends. "There...are still hollows?"

"A few." Johann shrugged, apologetic. "Not all of them went down when the code was activated. Possibly for the same reasons some humans survived when the thanites were originally released. They lived in places the code couldn't reach."

Dorran's expression had darkened. He poured their hot water into mugs, then passed them out.

Clare felt vaguely sick. She'd imagined the code would have annihilated the monsters. That she would never have to fear them again. To know they were still out there, that she still shared her world with them, felt like a bitter slap.

"Sorry," Becca whispered. "There aren't many. They don't outnumber humans anymore. And the ones that are left seem to hide. We saw some on our drive here, but they ran away when the van got close."

"Oh, wow, did we see some stuff." Johann stretched, one hand rubbing at the back of his neck. "Unofficially, I was looking for you two. But officially, I'm supposed to be reestablishing contact between groups of survivors. We've been zigzagging between safe havens and known survivor groups, passing out directions to our town for anyone who wants to see a doctor or who is looking for a new home. For groups that are settled where they are, we leave a two-way radio to stay in touch with us. It's slow work, but progress."

When night set in, Clare and Dorran harvested vegetables from the garden for their guests. Johann and Becca had their own stores of food and brought in pasta, stock, and dried spices. Clare hadn't ever imagined it was possible to miss seasoning as much as she had, but it made a world of difference in their food.

They chatted as they ate. Clare listened as Dorran told the story of what had happened since their return to Winterbourne.

It was heavily tied in to his past, something he had been trying to escape, but he seemed more willing to talk than he had to anyone other than Clare.

Johann listened to the tale of Dorran's mother and what had become of her, nodding, then simply said, "What a mess." Dorran laughed.

In return, Johann told them about his own journey across the country and the people he had encountered. He told stories of farmsteads that had become involved in multiday standoffs against the hollows, their homes fortified, the owners standing on roofs and using rocks, sticks, and boiling water to deflect the siege of monsters. He talked about a farmer who, on his own with nothing but a gun and a stack of ammo, had defended his fifty head of cattle from the horde.

"He did it because he loved his cows," Johann said. "But now, those fifty animals are almost priceless. They're probably some of the last cows left in the country."

He told them about a woman who had survived with her cat on an island in the middle of a river. She had built shelter out of debris that floated by and lived on the fish she caught.

"Hollows kept trying to get to her, but the water moved so fast that they would be swept away before they could make it to the island. She's back into her home now and still has her cat, which is a small miracle. Ah...that reminds me. There was this miserable old ginger cat at West Hope. It bit me when I tried to pet it. John said it would be significant to you, though. Something about, uh, a nest...?"

"Mother Gum's Nest," Becca supplied.

Clare's head shot up. She remembered the ginger cat, blinking at them as Mother Gum served them poisoned tea. "What did they tell you?"

"Yeah, apparently one of the council members burned the whole place down. Set fire to the forest around it, too, which caused smog through the area for weeks. She seemed pretty pleased about it, even though John was grumpy the whole time she told the story. Apparently, they rescued the cat from there, along with a whole group of kids who couldn't talk. The cat lives in the council room now, even though it hates everyone."

"Good," Clare said. Johann didn't seem to know the whole history of the compound, and she didn't feel ready to tell him, but she shared a private smile with Dorran. "That's probably the best outcome it could have."

As the shadows grew longer, Becca curled up in her chair, looking sleepy but content. Clare covered her with a blanket.

"We should probably work out what we're going to do," Johann said at last, stretching his legs out toward the fire. "I'd be awfully grateful if you let us sleep here tonight. Even the floor will be a million times more comfortable than those van seats."

"We can do better than the floor," Dorran said. "I'll get a bedroom set up for both of you."

"That'd be nice. I miss real beds, and it'll be good to have more time to talk tomorrow. But we can't stay forever. Unathi has us on a strict deadline, and we'll need to be back home within five days. The dictator."

Becca chuckled. "You say she's a dictator, but do you know what I think? She's more like a mother hen. She can't stand letting us out into the world for too long. She wants us back where she can watch over us and make sure we're safe."

"Eh, well, that dictatorial mother hen said I wouldn't even have the responsibility of tying my own shoelaces if I didn't get back by the deadline. So...we'll need to be moving on tomorrow." He squinted at Clare and Dorran. "What do you think? You can come back with us, if you want. There's room in the van, and now that the ship's gardens have established, you're more than welcome to live there. Or we could drive you somewhere else if you wanted. There are plenty of new settlements forming. Or if you wanted to stay here, we have a whole stack of two-way radios in the van, and we can leave you with one. That way you won't be cut off any longer, and you can ask for people to visit and whatnot."

Clare swallowed and looked up at Dorran to gauge his reaction. They had gone from having no options to having every option. It was bordering on overwhelming.

"You don't have to decide right away." Johann scratched his beard, smiling contentedly. "But the way I see it, humanity owes you one. We never would have gotten the code if it weren't for you two. Whatever you need, whatever you want, we'll make it happen."

CHAPTER 45

THE STORE SMELLED OF many good things. Grains filled tubs along one wall. Soaps and yarn left their distinct scents along the hand-crafted wooden shelves. Bulbs of drying garlic and herbs hung from string along the ceiling, and homemade candles caught the light near the window.

Clare loved the store. She and Dorran spent a part of each day in it, restocking it and handling trades. Dorran leaned over the large wooden counter, one hand braced on the table and the other running a pen down columns of a logbook as he tallied entries. The light caught his features in just the right way, running across his strong bone structure. Bent over like that, he was the perfect height for Clare to steal a kiss on the way past, so she did.

Dorran's surprise turned to laughter, and he caught at her jacket as she tried to skip past, pulled her back, and took a kiss of his own.

Johann's visit had left them with a difficult choice. The Evandale bunker had always presented a temptingly luxurious future: air-conditioned rooms, clean linens, a garden designed around science and with machines to lessen the workload. But Clare wasn't sure it would be right for them. Sequestered away underground, sheltered from the harshest parts of the world but taking up a space that might be needed by someone more vulnerable—she would be comfortable, but she needed more.

And then she had considered Winterbourne. Won through a hard-fought battle, it was a hostile home, but a home nonetheless. Its thick walls, well water, and internal garden made it an invaluable stronghold—but not one she wanted to spend the rest of her life in. She had never felt truly welcome at the ancestral estate.

She and Dorran had talked late into the night. Their final agreement had been that they could not abandon what they had built at Winterbourne...but that it would be a temporary home. Johann had left them with a two-way radio and a promise that he would return.

When he came back three weeks later, he brought new occupants for Winterbourne. A family, feeling displaced in the world, seeking security above all else. Winterbourne had not been an ideal home for Clare or Dorran, but it was for other people.

Five months after the end of the stillness, Winterbourne was known as a popular communal home. It housed more than sixty individuals. Once the snow melted, the ground around it had been converted into gardens, including fruit trees and livestock brought by the new occupants.

Madeline would be turning in her grave if she knew how many muddy boots stomped through the doorway or how many shrieking, laughing children ran along the halls. Clare hoped they could visit it soon. She thought she would like the ancient building a lot more now that it was filled with life.

She and Dorran had traveled for a while. There had been an emotional visit with the staff at Evandale, then they had spent several days in West Hope, which still functioned as a meeting point for separated families. Finally, they had settled in New Climate, a frontier town.

Clare liked the location a lot. The village only held six hundred homes and was nestled in a valley circled by mountains. The weather was pleasant through most of the year, and the town was only a two-hour bike ride from several other outposts, including Evandale, where Niall's hospital flourished.

The new world was vastly different from the old one. Real estate was free. Clare and Dorran had walked through the town until they found a house they wanted, then claimed it by painting the new universal sign for "occupied" on the front door.

Those signs were appearing everywhere, helping travelers navigate the world. *Occupied, building contains no more resources, dangerous environment, meeting point.* Anyone searching for food or shelter could walk along a street and know which buildings to try first by the marks on the door.

Clare loved their new home. At first, it had been hard to forget that it had belonged to someone else just months before. But with each new piece of furniture they moved in and each new day spent there, it felt a little more like her own. She had a reading nook near a window that overlooked the front garden. The bedroom had a fireplace, and some nights she and Dorran fell asleep in front of it, a habit that had stayed with them from Winterbourne.

Dorran and Clare had only been living in New Climate for a few weeks before they were inducted into the committee overseeing the town. Dorran thrived in the role. He helped decide which utilities were most needed and how the store was run, and he was a mediator in disputes. He had earned a reputation for having a fair hand and a good mind for solving problems.

As part of their roles, he and Clare spent time in the central store—a trading post of sorts where visitors could exchange supplies. Each town ran slightly differently, but New Climate had adopted a system very similar to West Hope's. They had a set of guidelines for each item's value depending on its supply and demand. Any visitors who didn't have anything to trade could pay with labor. There were always projects that needed an extra set of hands: wells to be dug, defensive walls to be built, and greenhouses to be constructed. Anyone who wasn't able to handle the labor-intensive tasks could help in the communal gardens. Three hours of hard work could be exchanged for a meal and a place to sleep that night. It was a simple system, and one that was as fair as they could make it.

Every occupied house in New Climate had its own garden, but the town also had a communal plot of farmland that was designed to be harvested on an as-needed basis. Everyone helped out in it, so if their own crops failed, they would not go hungry.

They also had a growing trust of livestock. During the months they had dominated the world, hollows ate anything that moved. There were not many surviving animals. A woman had arrived at New Climate with five hens and a rooster, which was a huge boon. The eggs weren't being eaten yet. The council had helped devise a plan where the chicks would be raised and slowly gifted to different families in the community. Once they had enough, they would trade a small flock of the young chickens to a neighboring town in return for several cows. The goal was that, eventually, each home would have its own supply of eggs.

Clare stacked bottles of oil on a wall. Someone had brought in a drum of it that morning—a trade that had earned them a can of the increasingly rare gasoline. These days, most people rode bikes for transport, but fuel was still valuable for various machines. Clare had spent the last hour dividing the oil into more manageable bottles for the rest of the town. It was food grade and would make cooking easier.

Now that most traditional jobs were obsolete, many people had turned to a nomadic lifestyle. They traveled vast distances, collecting valuables from homes and abandoned businesses they passed, then trading them at any towns they stopped at. It was a lucrative way to live, if not entirely safe. There were still stories of hollows being spotted along remote roads, even though the thanites had been almost entirely eradicated.

Communication was still patchy. Every settlement had its own notice board erected somewhere prominent. New Climate's was in the town square, not far from the shop. On one side was memorials: flowers both real and fake, ribbons, pictures, and messages to lost loved ones. It was a kaleidoscope of color. The other side was much more utilitarian but no less precious: the names of people who had passed through the town, plus instructions for how to contact them. Those names, arranged alphabetically, were a way for separated families and friends to find each other. Hope was slow to die, and its flames were fanned by the stories of families being reunited against all odds.

The bell above the door jingled as the afternoon manager came to relieve them. Clare pushed the final bottles of oil onto the shelf as she heard Dorran call out, "Hey, Owen, how are you today?"

"Doing great, thanks," the familiar voice replied.

Clare stood, grinning, and wiped her hands down on a dish towel as she approached the counter. "How are the girls?"

Owen's close-cut bronze beard bristled as he smiled at her. He was starting to look healthier now that he was putting on weight again. A delicate necklace was barely visible under the collar of his shirt, but Clare knew what it carried: the gold wedding band. "They have a playdate with the neighbor's children, so they're happy. And you remember Elena, down the road? Her golden retriever just had puppies. I'm trying to calculate how many of my limbs I'd have to sell to get one for the girls."

Clare laughed. "Well, tell Elena we'll throw in fifty extra credits to sweeten the deal. That's okay, right, Dorran?"

"Of course." He nodded, seeming pleased.

"Oh, no, don't." Owen held up his hands, looking apologetic. "I swear, you don't owe me anything. You can stop trying to help."

Dorran closed the logbook as a deep, warm chuckle rumbled through him. "You assisted my wife when she needed it most. The least I can do in return is help you get a puppy for your daughters."

"Honestly—"

"No time for arguments." Dorran took Clare's hand as they moved toward the store's exit. "We're already gone. If you want to object to our blatant bias, you can lodge an official complaint with the council, which I will happily dismiss tonight."

"Ha." Owen shook his head as they left him to watch over the store. "All right. Have a good afternoon, you two."

The afternoon was clear, and even though the sun was still dampened, they had more days with comfortable weather than not. Clare tilted her head back and basked in the sun as they meandered toward the town center. "What's on the cards for the rest of the day?"

"Hmm. You and I have a council meeting tonight. I heard a visitor arrived who used to work for a hydroelectricity company before the stillness. He's talking about taking a team to one of the larger rivers, to see whether it might be possible to put in a dam. It would be a large project. Something that could supply power to most of the town."

Clare's eyebrows rose. "That would be helpful."

New Climate had a range of small-scale energy efforts, including two windmills, but they only generated a modest amount of energy and only on windy days. A more reliable source of power could create huge changes in the town. Homes already had the wiring to make use of it. Clare still occasionally flicked the switches out of habit when she entered a room. She had always hoped to see the day when the lights would respond, but it had felt like a lifetime away. Now, suddenly, it seemed much closer.

"We're rebuilding," she whispered. Around her, the town was filled with life. Familiar faces moved between houses, carrying home-baked breads and the first jars of preserve of the season as gifts for their neighbors. The countless mementos fluttered on the notice board behind them, a patchwork of faces that would never be forgotten. Their gains were small, baby steps in every way, but steps forward nonetheless.

"Yes." Dorran kissed the top of her head. "I used to fear the future, but now...I look at it and I see hope."

Clare's throat was tight. Smog still filled the sky, but the sun fought through it, stronger than it had been for a while. There were very few dull days. But every day seemed better than the last.

Her eyes landed on a figure standing on the cobblestone path leading into town. A constant flow of travelers moved through New Climate. It wasn't unusual to see unfamiliar faces, but something about this one caught Clare's attention. The woman clutched a backpack in her arms. She was thin, frighteningly so, but her blue eyes were bright and alert. Scars formed a web across her skin, which she'd tried to cover up with a long skirt and scarf, despite the mild weather.

She was familiar and a stranger all at once. Gossamer-like hair floated around her head; it was still short but slowly growing back. The blue eyes lit on Clare and her lips parted.

"Beth," Clare managed.

Her sister's scar-mapped face twisted. She was trying to smile as tears filled her eyes. This was a new Beth entirely: not the over-cautious, micromanaging woman Clare had grown up with, and not the aggressive, ferocious presence from the bus. She looked apprehensive and made no move to come closer.

Clare's heart was in her throat. She ran down the stone path-way, closing the distance between them, arms outstretched.

Beth pressed her eyes closed, fingers turning white as she gripped the backpack, as clearly rehearsed words fell out of her. "I want to apologize for what I did. I don't expect forgiveness because I understand how—"

Clare collided with her, pulling Beth into a hug that left them both breathless. She pressed her cheek to Beth's, gratitude thrum-ming through her. "You have no idea how badly I hoped you would find us."

"I—I didn't know if I should…after everything." Beth swal-lowed and carefully extracted herself from Clare's arms, even though she seemed reluctant to. "I've known where you were for a while. But wasn't sure I would be welcomed."

"Of course you are." Dorran's warm voice came from just behind Clare. He was beaming. "I hope you like casserole because that's what I'm making for dinner tonight."

Beth's shaky smile cracked further. "I'm sorry. Oh, I am so, so incredibly sorry—"

"The world ended once when the stillness changed every-thing." Dorran placed one hand on the small of Clare's back, his dark hair flicking in the wind. "I feel as though it ended again on the day the cure was deployed. It's a new world now, with new rules, new communities, and new lives. I believe that justifies a fresh start for all of us."

"I'd like that." Beth dropped her backpack. Her arms reached out, and Clare pulled both her and Dorran into a hug. "I'd like that a lot."

Their arms felt good around her shoulders. Beth was crying and laughing at once. Clare could feel Dorran's happiness, a thick, tangible sense radiating out of him. She couldn't stop smiling. And she couldn't stop thinking of what Dorran had said earlier, a seed of truth that had taken root inside of her.

I look at the future and I see hope.

ABOUT THE AUTHOR

Darcy Coates is the *USA Today* bestselling author of *Hunted*, *The Haunting of Ashburn House*, *Craven Manor*, and more than a dozen other horror and suspense titles.

She lives on the Central Coast of Australia with her family, cats, and a garden full of herbs and vegetables.

Darcy loves forests, especially old-growth forests where the trees dwarf anyone who steps between them. Wherever she lives, she tries to have a mountain range close by.